KT-559-398

Squishy McFluff

The Invisible Cat!

000000900072

For my muses, Ava and Ruby,
and for the real Great Grandad Bill,
to celebrate his 100th birthday
on February 13th, 2014 xxx

First published in 2014
by Faber and Faber Limited
Bloomsbury House
74–77 Great Russell Street
London WC1B 3DA

Designed by Faber and Faber
Printed in China

All rights reserved
Text © Pip Jones, 2014
Illustrations © Ella Okstad, 2014
The right of Pip Jones and Ella Okstad to be identified as author
and illustrator of this work respectively has been asserted in
accordance with Section 77 of the
Copyright, Designs and Patents Act 1988

This book is sold subject to the condition that it shall not,
by way of trade or otherwise, be lent, resold, hired out or
otherwise circulated without the publisher's prior consent
in any form of binding or cover other than that in which
it is published and without a similar condition including this
condition being imposed on the subsequent purchaser
A CIP record for this book is available from the British Library

978–0571–30250–5

FSC
www.fsc.org
MIX
Paper from
responsible sources
FSC® C008047

2 4 6 8 10 9 7 5 3 1

Squishy McFluff

The Invisible Cat!

by *Pip Jones*

Illustrated by *Ella Okstad*

ff

FABER & FABER

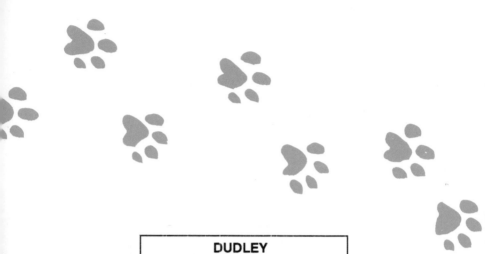

DUDLEY PUBLIC LIBRARIES	
000000900072	
£5.99	JF
13-Mar-2014	PETERS

Can you see him? My kitten?

Close your eyes tight.

His fur is so soft

and all silvery white.

Imagine him quick!

Have you imagined enough?

Oh, good! You can see him!

It's Squishy McFluff!

1

As Ava played out

in the garden one day,

When the air was all foggy,

the sky rather grey,

Something appeared

(or rather, did not)

From among the wet leaves

in the vegetable plot.

The marvellous creature

was fluffy and tiny,

As cute as a button,

with eyes big and shiny,

A tail that swished proudly,

first this way, then that.

A fabulous, friendly,

invisible cat!

EASTWOOD

ROBERT TANITCH

791.43028 TAN
158535

FOR PETER AND ELIZABETH CORNISH

First published in hardcover, in 1995 by Studio Vista
This edition first published in Great Britain in 2005 by Cassell
Illustrated, a division of Octopus Publishing Group Ltd
2-4 Heron Quays, London E14 4JP

Copyright © Robert Tanitch 1995, 2005

The moral right of Robert Tanitch to be identified
as author of this work has been asserted by him in
accordance with the Copyright, Designs and Patents
Act 1988.

All rights reserved.

ISBN 1 84103 424 0
EAN 9781844034246

No part of this publication may be reproduced or
transmitted in any form or by any means, electronic or
mechanical, including photocopying, recording or any
information storage or retrieval system, without prior
permission in writing from the publishers.

A CIP catalogue record for this book is available from the
British Library

Printed in China

Frontispiece: Clint Eastwood in *High Plains Drifter*

Acknowledgements

The author would like to begin by thanking Barry Holmes,
his editor.

The author and publishers express their appreciation to the
Kobal Collection and the following companies for their
assistance and/or permission in relation to the following
photographs:

The Kobal Collection, frontispiece, pp. 6, 9, 10, 18, 20, 24,
25,26,29,30-1,32-3,34,35,38-9,40-1,42-3,45,46,47,
48-9,51,52,53,56,57,58,59,60-1,62,66,70-1,72,73,
74,75,76-7,79,82,83,84-5,87,89,92,94,95,96,97,98,
100,101,102-3,107,108,109,111,112-13,114,115,116,
117,118,120-1,122,124,130,131,132,133,134-5,136,
140,141,142,145,146,147,149,150-1,152,153,154-5,
156,157,163,164,170,171,173,174,175,178,179,180-1,
182, 184, 185, 189, 191, 192, 194, 198; BFI Stills, Posters and
Designs, pp. 12, 15, 21, 22-3, 81, 138-9, 143, 165; Columbia
Tristar, pp. 182, 184; Columbia Warners, pp. 92, 94, 111; Getty
Images, pp. 202, 203; MGM, pp. 51, 52, 53, 65, 66, 67;
Paramount Pictures, pp. 56, 62, 118, 120-1, 122; RGA, pp. 188,
190, 193, 197, 199, 201; Technicolour, pp. 54-5; United Artists,
pp. 45, 46, 95, 96, 97; Universal Pictures, pp. 2, 9, 20, 26, 47,
48-9, 50, 57, 58, 59,60-1,70-1,72,73,74,75,83,84,85,87,
89,98,100; Warner Bros, pp. 10, 76-7, 79, 101, 102-3, 104,
105, 108,109,115,116,124,126-7,130,131,132,133,134-
5,136,137,140,147,149,150-1,152,153,154-5,158-9,160,
163,166,169,170,171,173,174,175,176-7,178,179,180-1,
185, 186-7; Warner Bros/Malpaso, pp. 141, 142, 145, 146,156,
157, 162, 164, 166, 169.

The author would like to add a personal note of thanks to
Gabrielle Mander of Cassell Illustrated, Ron Callow, Christine
Lloyd Lyons and her staff at the Kobal Collection and to
everybody at the BFI reference library and stills department.

Also by Robert Tanitch

A Pictorial Companion to Shakespeare's Plays

Ralph Richardson, A Tribute

Olivier

Leonard Rossiter

Ashcroft

Gielgud

Dirk Bogarde

Guinness

Sean Connery

John Mills

Brando

The Unknown James Dean

Oscar Wilde on Stage and Screen

Blockbusters!

Contents

Introduction

Clint Eastwood, one of the great film stars and icons of the twentieth century, has been at the top of his profession for over 30 years. This book is a pictorial record of his career from the 1950s to the present day.

Clint Eastwood, actor, director and producer, has always had an instinct for what the public wants and he has achieved popularity across a wide range of genres: Western, detective, thriller and comedy. Though, initially and regularly, accused of being wooden, technically weak and having only one expression, he quickly established himself with the cinemagoing public. The critics, seemingly immune to his personality, humour and sex appeal, tended to underestimate him, both as an actor and as a director, and they did so precisely because he was so successful.

Eastwood, tall, lean and laconic, an actor of strong physical presence and loose-limbed grace, has been likened to a gazelle in jeans and cowboy boots. Totally confident in his masculinity and totally without vanity, he has always been able to mock his macho image; indeed, so often has he taken his image apart that it has seemed at times as if he wanted actively to erode it altogether.

He is famous for having created two charismatic cult heroes, The Man With No Name and Dirty Harry, two superguns, ultra cool, solitary, single-minded characters, deceptively lethargic, with hidden reserves beneath their stoical exterior.

Eastwood knows his limitations as an actor and within those limitations he has climbed mountains, scaled a fortress, escaped from prison, driven a bus through a hail of bullets, driven a steam train into a saloon bar, flown over the Arctic in a supersonic fighter and been chased by a dinky car all over San Francisco.

In his films, he has run a travelling Wild West Show, served in Korea, Vietnam and Grenada, gone AWOL to rob a bank behind enemy lines and watched the President of the United States having rough sex.

His roles have found him auditioning for the Grand Ole Opry at Nashville, falling in love with a country and western singer, having an affair with a murderess, making friends with an orang-utan, photographing bridges, flying in space, saving a man from execution at the twelfth hour, receiving a heart transplant, developing a taste for bondage, being picked up by a gay in Madison Square Gardens and talking to the trees (but they didn't listen to him). He has also been lynched, raped, castrated and come back from the dead on more than one occasion . . .

Clint Eastwood was born in San Francisco on 31 May 1930 and educated at Oakland Technical High School and Los Angeles City College. Before he became an actor he did a number of jobs, including lumberjack, steel-furnace stoker, gas-station attendant and swimming instructor, the latter while he was in the army from 1950 to 1954.

His film career, which began in 1955 with bit parts in a number of instantly forgettable films, took off four years later when he landed the second lead in a new television Western series, *Rawhide*, which proved so popular that it lasted until 1966. (It has been revived constantly ever since.) The Italian director Sergio Leone saw him in episode 91 *(The Incident of the Black Sheep)* and, having failed to get an American star with a bigger name, offered him the leading role in *A Fistful of Dollars (Per un pugno di dollari,* 1964), which was so phenomenally successful in Italy (outgrossing *My Fair Lady* and *Mary Poppins*) that they went on to make two sequels, *For a Few Dollars More (Per qualche dollari in più,* 1965) and *The Good, the Bad and the Ugly (Il buono, il brutto, il cattivo,* 1966).

Audiences expecting such old-fashioned things as romanticism, morality, honour and loyalty (the traditional ingredients of a Hollywood Western) were in for a violent awakening. The critics hated it. 'Everyone susceptible to the illusion that shooting and killing with fancy flourishes are fun can indulge his bloodlust to the fullest,' wrote the *New York Times.* The public loved it. The Man With No Name became a cult figure on a par with James Bond and Eastwood's career was completely transformed. Vittorio de Sica declared he was the new Gary Cooper and cast him in the fifth episode of *The Witches (Le Streghe,* 1966), an indifferent portmanteau vehicle for his wife, Silvana Mangano, which has rarely been seen outside Italy.

His first starring role in an American Western was in *Hang 'Em High* (1968), which explored the pros and cons of capital punishment. It was not long before he was being hailed as John Wayne's heir, though his anti-heroes were as far removed from Wayne's screen persona as can be imagined. *Coogan's Bluff* (1968), a sharp, off-beat thriller, which followed, began a long and profitable association with Don Siegel. Coogan established Eastwood as the maverick in action and can now be seen, with hindsight, as a dummy run for *Dirty Harry.*

Brian Hutton directed him and Richard Burton in Alastair MacLean's *Where Eagles Dare* (1968), an incredibly silly World War II adventure, which was dismissed as

Clint Eastwood in *Two Mules for Sister Sara*

'dreadful piffle', 'corny cliffhanger', 'unashamed hokum', 'turgid tosh', 'two-fisted idiocy', 'a mindless bloodbath', and went on to become 1969's biggest earner.

He played the juvenile lead in Alan Jay Lerner and Frederick Loewe's *Paint Your Wagon* (1969), opposite Lee Marvin, the first and last time he would appear in a musical, though not the last time he would sing on screen. So appalled was he by the waste of money on location that he decided to form his own production company, Malpaso (named after a creek near his home in the Carmel area), which gave him the opportunity to produce, direct and star in his own productions in a more economical manner.

He starred with Shirley MacLaine in *Two Mules for Sister Sara* (1969), an enjoyable, tongue-in-cheek, comedy-romantic adventure, which he has described as 'African Queen Goes West'. *Kelly's Heroes* (1970), a large-scale spoof of wartime heroics, a blockbusting mixture of mordant humour, crude slapstick and loud explosives, proved equally popular. 'Men,' said Brian Hutton, its director, 'like to see Eastwood in action. Women like to see him in anything.'

Don Siegel always believed *The Beguiled* (1970) to be his best film. Unfortunately, the producers, keen to get Eastwood's fans to see it, made the error of giving what was essentially an art-house movie a commercial release, with the result that the movie flopped at the box office. His regular audience didn't like the idea of him being castrated and poisoned and stayed away in large numbers. Eastwood has been quoted as saying that *Beguiled* would probably have been more successful if he hadn't been in it.

Sixteen years before *Fatal Attraction*, there was a first-rate adult thriller called *Play Misty for Me* (1971), which marked his debut as a director and was also notable for a brilliant and frightening portrait of sexual paranoia by Jessica Walter.

Dirty Harry (1971), which made him a superstar, remains one of his most popular films. Ironically, he was not the first choice: Frank Sinatra and Paul Newman, bigger names at the box office, were preferred. Though there were many who found the violence horrific and gratuitous, the violence was an integral part, making a serious comment on law and order. Harry stood for vigilante justice. His actions were condoned by his audience, who identified with him, rather than his critics, who accused Harry of being vicious, sexist, racist, fascist and the film of being an attack on liberal values and propaganda for para-legal police powers. The police liked what they saw and invited Clint Eastwood to speak at one of their gatherings.

Clint Eastwood in
The Outlaw Josey Wales

John Sturges (who had directed *Bad Day at Black Rock* and *The Magnificent Seven* so successfully) failed to make *Joe Kidd* (1972) work and it remained a dull, rambling Western. Vastly superior was *High Plains Drifter* (1972), a ghostly Western, which he directed himself, after he had sacked the original director, Philip Kaufman, who had written the screenplay. He was excellent as an archangel of death and retribution. *High Plains Drifter,* stylish and stylized, was one of the best Westerns of the 1970s, though few would have been able to guess this from reading the reviews at the time. Eastwood then went on to direct William Holden in *Breezy* (1973), a love story, in which he did not appear.

The critics were not so wild about Harry and *Magnum Force* (1973), many of them feeling that it didn't have either the style or the narrative energy of the original. On the other hand, *Thunderbolt and Lightfoot* (1974), a modern-day crime story, written and directed by Michael Cimino making his directorial debut at 31, was a perceptive comedy. Cimino had sent the script to Eastwood saying he could have it, but only if he were allowed to direct it.

The Eiger Sanction (1975), a badly scripted mountain spy thriller, variously described as 'time-passing rubbish', 'appalling tripe' and 'a good film to sleep to', was also (to quote one of the script's many mechanical lines) 'too shabby to be called cheap'. The actors played a secondary role to the Alps. However, with the release of The *Outlaw Josey Wales* (1976), it was obvious, even to his detractors, that Eastwood was a major talent both as a director and as an actor. This sombre story of vengeance and reconciliation, a personal favourite of his, was one of the best films of the 1970s.

The Enforcer (1976, not to be confused with the 1951 Humphrey Bogart movie of the same name) was advertised as the dirtiest Harry of them all. It was, in fact, the poorest of the three, routine stuff, a pale carbon copy of the original. In *The Gauntlet* (1977) he played a disillusioned, disreputable cop, well past his sell-by date. The only thing wrong with the casting was that he never actually looked like the loser he was meant to be playing; he still looked like Dirty Harry.

Every Which Way But Loose (1978) was mindless violence masquerading as macho fun and a big disappointment to everybody, except the general public, who turned up in large numbers to see it. Such was its success that two years later there was a revamp, *Any Which Way You Can* (1980), even more juvenile, and it, too, proved hugely popular.

Clint Eastwood in
The Enforcer

Don Siegel had a simple and gripping story to tell in *Escape from Alcatraz* (1979) and he told it in a straightforward, methodical, low-key manner, midway between the Warner Brothers prison dramas of the 1930s and Robert Bresson's *Un Condamné à mort s'est échappé* of the 1950s. Eastwood, understated yet eloquent, gave one of his most powerful performances.

Bronco Billy (1980), a modest, nostalgic movie with a light and engaging touch, felt like a wacky 1930s screwball comedy. Eastwood played a kiddywink cowboy, living in a dream world. The critics were disarmed; the film was a commercial failure. *Honkytonk Man* (1982), gentle, likeable and bittersweet, also received high praise, but it didn't do well at the box office, either. Eastwood may have liked playing losers, but his fans didn't like seeing him playing losers and they certainly didn't want to witness him having a death scene second only to Marguerite Gautier. Eastwood would say later that it was films like *Bronco Billy* and *Honkytonk Man* that gave him the confidence to make *Unforgiven.*

Firefox (1982), a lethargic, tacky, Cold War spy thriller, was so bad that it produced loud laughter at the press show and all the way to the bank. *Sudden Impact* (1983), the fourth Dirty Harry film, was excellently scripted and tightly directed; though, once again, the brutality, the right-wing moralizing and the vigilante justice were not to everybody's liking.

He played a cop with a taste for rough sex, morally corrupted by his job, in *Tightrope* (1984), another first-class adult thriller, one of his best films, popular with fans and critics alike, admired for its candour and bravery, even if there were objections to what were perceived to be its voyeurism and misogyny.

City Heat (1984), a pastiche 1930s gumshoe movie, in which he joined forces with Burt Reynolds, got a luke-warm response, the critics generally finding it a tedious romp and rejecting it as 'botched, superannuated *Butch Cassidy and the Sundance Kid*'.

Eastwood, reared on Westerns and having a particular liking for William Wellman's *The Ox-Bow Incident,* Howard Hawks's *Red River* and the films of Anthony Mann, has always thought the genre not only good entertainment but a good way to put over a message. In 1985, with *Pale Rider*, he made a conscious effort to revive the Western (which had fallen out of favour), feeling it was the right moment to explore its classic mythology and spirit.

Clint Eastwood in
Unforgiven

There were those who thought *Heartbreak Ridge* (1986) the most gung-ho movie since John Wayne's *Sands of Iwo Jima.* 'Welcome to Camp Cliché!' said the wits; but Eastwood's performance as a truculent, disillusioned, old combat veteran, at odds in the modern world, was one of his most impressive characterizations.

Eastwood had been a jazz aficionado from an early age. *Bird* (1988), an unsentimental yet humane account of saxophonist Charlie Parker's harrowing life, was a labour of love, making no concessions whatsoever to the box office. Despite having a superb soundtrack and being one of the best films ever made about jazz, *Bird* did not prove popular with either black or white audiences. Black cinemagoers, in particular, criticized it for not addressing itself to racism and the pressure of being black in a white world.

In 1987, he slipped out of the polls for the first time (having been ranked among the top 10 box-office stars for 17 years, an amazing record) and he stayed out with the release of two mediocre thrillers, *The Dead Pool* (1988) and *Pink Cadillac* (1989). Much more worth while, yet no more successful at the box office, was the ecologically timely *White Hunter, Black Heart* (1990), though it was never meant to be an anti-hunting statement. Peter Viertel's screenplay (based on director John Huston's fixation to shoot an elephant) was highly literate; rarely has Eastwood had to speak so many lines. Both the film and his performance were underrated.

In the hope of reaching a younger market, he teamed up with Charlie Sheen (who had just had a big hit with *Young Guns*) to make *The Rookie* (1990), which was no more successful than *The Dead Pool* and *Pink Cadillac* had been. 'Back on the trash track,' said the *Mail on Sunday*. 'Astonishingly inadequate piece of piffle,' said *Time Out*. 'Pretty dire slice of video fodder,' said the *Daily Telegraph*.

He made a stunning comeback in 1992. *Unforgiven* (not to be confused with the 1960 John Huston film of the same name) shattered box-office records and went on to win four Academy awards, including best picture, best director, best supporting actor (Gene Hackman) and best editing (Joel Cox). All that was missing was the award for best actor; Eastwood lost out to Al Pacino in *Scent of a Woman*. The movie made a strong statement condemning violence by describing it in graphic and brutal detail. Some saw the film as an apologia (strongly denied) for the violence in the earlier movies. Eastwood has said that if *Unforgiven* were to prove to be his final Western, then it would be the perfect Western for him.

In the Line of Fire (1993), directed by Wolfgang Petersen (whose submarine saga, *Das Boot*, Eastwood had much admired) was an exciting and well-written political thriller and a first-rate vehicle for him and John Malkovich. He then, generously, played a supporting role to Kevin Costner in *A Perfect World* (1993).

He was cast against type as a romantic hero in *The Bridges of Madison County* (1995), a low-key tearjerker, which worked far better than anybody who had read the book expected. *Absolute Power* (1997), a political murder thriller, was hokum. *Midnight in the Garden of Good and Evil* (1997) was good for Savannah's tourist industry. *True Crime* (1999) was an implausible anti-capital punishment drama and *Space Cowboys* (2000) was geriatric nonsense which had to rely on the self-depreciative charm and hammy acting of 'four old farts.' *Blood Work* (2002) was badly in need of a transfusion.

Just when some people were beginning to feel he should concentrate on acting and not directing, he was back on form in a big way, directing Sean Penn, Tim Robbins and Kevin Bacon in *Mystic River* (2003), a character-driven story of crime and retribution. He went on to consolidate his position with *Million Dollar Baby* (2004), one of cinema's best boxing films, which won him Oscars for best film and best director. His latest film is *Flags of our Fathers*, the story of the six servicemen who raised the flag after the World War II Battle of Iwo Jima.

Few people in the film business have made so great an impact and for so long as Clint Eastwood. The pages which follow are a record of and a tribute to his magnetism as an actor, his professionalism as a director and his business acumen as a producer. He works with the same repertory of people again and again. His movies are famous for coming in on time and under budget. Now in his mid-seventies, he continues to maintain a shrewd balancing act between the movies he makes for commercial reasons and the movies he makes for himself. It is not always as easy to separate the two as might be thought.

The 1950s

FRANCIS IN THE NAVY

Directed by Arthur Lubin 1955

Francis was a talking mule and *Francis in the Navy* was the sixth in the series of his adventures. Donald O'Connor played two roles – bumbling idiot and war hero – and didn't get to sing or dance in either. Clint Eastwood played one of the sailors.

The jawing of a jackass is one of nature's most unlovely sounds and *Francis in the Navy* proves it.

Oscar Godbout, *New York Times*

Donald O'Connor,
Clint Eastwood and
Francis Genks in
Francis in the Navy

THE FIRST TRAVELING SALESLADY

Directed by Arthur Lubin   1956

An emancipated saleslady (Ginger Rogers), who
had gone bankrupt selling corsets, decided to
head west in 1897 and sell barbed wire to the
Texans instead. She was accompanied by her
partner, an ex-chorus girl (stage comedienne
Carol Channing), who got to growl an indifferent song, 'A corset can do a lot for a lady
because it helps to show what a lady's got'.

Clint Eastwood headed the featured players,
cast as a very shy and very handsome rough
rider, a US cavalry of one, who met the ex-
chorus girl while he was manning a recruiting
desk in a hotel foyer. 'Do you like girls?' she
asked. 'Yes, mam, I do.' A handful of scenes
followed. Eastwood, who was a bit young to be
playing her suitor, proposed off-screen. *The
First Traveling Saleslady* should have been a
full-scale musical.

**Clint Eastwood is very attractive as Carol
Channing's beau.**

Hollywood Reporter

Clint Eastwood and Carol
Channing in *The First
Traveling Saleslady*

AMBUSH AT CIMARRON PASS

Directed by Jodie Copelan 1957

Clint Eastwood has been quoted as describing this low-budget Western as 'the lousiest Western ever made'. He was cast as a member of a gang who ambushed a group of ex-Confederate soldiers. Unwilling to accept the South's defeat in the American Civil War, he was all in favour of killing them. In between fighting the Apaches, he found time to have a fight with the sergeant (Scott Brady) over the heroine (Margia Dean).

Fine portrayals also come from Margia Dean, Frank Gestle, Clint Eastwood and Dirk London.

Variety

Scott Brady and Clint Eastwood in *Ambush at Cimarron Pass*

RAWHIDE

1959-1966

Clint Eastwood in
Rawhide

Margaret O'Brien, Mercedes McCambridge,
Victor McLaglen, Cesar Romero, Neville Brand,
Peter Lorre, Agnes Moorehead, Woody Strode,
E.G. Marshall, Mary Astor, John Cassevetes,
Zachary Scott, Brian Aherne, Barbara
Stanwyck, James Coburn, Walter Pidgeon, John
Ireland, Claude Rains, Walter Slezak, Frankie
Avalon, Mickey Rooney, Warren Oates, Lee Van
Cleef, Dean Martin, Rip Torn and Charles
Bronson. Frankie Laine, who sang the theme
song, also made a guest appearance.

Eastwood would later invite one of the
directors, Ted Post, to direct him in *Hang 'Em
High* and *Magnum Force.*

I would rate veteran actor Eric Fleming and ex-
lumberjack Clint Eastwood, the men in charge of
driving the herds, the only two Western stars
outside of *Wagon Train* apparently able to act and
move the muscles of their faces at the same time.

James Thomas, *Daily Express*

Move 'em on, head 'em up, head 'em up, move
'em on. *Rawhide,* the whip-cracking story of a
long (very long) cattledrive from San Antonio,
Texas, to Sedalia, Kansas; kept rollin', rollin',
rollin' for 217 episodes to become one of the
most popular television Western series ever.
The scripts, praised for their authenticity, were
loosely based on the diary of a real-life cattle
drover who lived in the 1860s.

Clint Eastwood, one of the few regulars to
remain with the show for its entire run, played
the young and impetuous second-in-command,
ramrod Rowdy Yates, until 1965 when Rowdy
became the trail boss and he took over the
leading role from Eric Fleming.

The series employed any number of guest
stars, including Dan Duryea, Brian Donlevy,

They were fun years and they were frustrating, too
. . . I was pigeon-holed as an actor. It was pretty
restrictive, but I sure learned a lot.

Clint Eastwood

Clint Eastwood in
Rawhide

The 1960s

Clint Eastwood in *Two
Mules for Sister Sara*

A FISTFUL OF DOLLARS

Directed by Sergio Leone   1964
Italian title: *Per un pugno di dollari*

You ask most people what they were about and they can't tell you, but they can tell you the look.

Clint Eastwood

The story of *A Fistful of Dollars,* a low-budget spaghetti Western, was borrowed from one of Clint Eastwood's favourite movies, Akira Kurosawa's *Yojimbo,* the Samurai classic, starring the great Japanese actor Toshiro Mifune. The result was that the film was not released in the US for three years due to copyright problems.

An anonymous Stranger arrived in a small Mexican town. It was the sort of place where you only got respect by killing other men. The body count was high and the coffin-maker was kept busy. The Stranger was tall (6' 4"), lean, good-looking, enigmatic and he wore a poncho. (The poncho immediately became all the rage with Italian young men.) His hat was pulled down over his eyes. He smoked thin black cigars; the half-smoked cheroot in the corner of his mouth was his trademark. Cool, intelligent, soft-spoken, polite, steely, he stared hard and kept his eyes skint. He was quick on the draw and he had a laconic sense of humour. He would open a door. 'Hello!' he would say and shoot five men dead.

The Man With No Name (actually his name was Joe) was a new type of hero, cold-blooded and unscrupulous, a symbolic figure, who displayed no emotion and was immune to the cries of children and women. Honour and morality were not part of his baggage. He looked mean. He was mean. He had barely arrived in the town before he was ordering three coffins.

The story was banal melodrama. Two rival families were locked in a bitter feud. Joe hired himself out to both, playing them off against each other. He was so badly beaten up at one point that it became absurd he could carry on. The violence was graphic, the dialogue stilted and the dubbing atrocious. The production was shot in Spain. ('Pity it wasn't buried there,' said *Time* magazine.)

The cowboys were laughing sadists, much given to torture, vicious beatings, whippings, kickings, stringing up old men and hammy acting. There were so many close-ups of their faces, it was like flicking through an actors' directory. Eastwood got his effects by remaining impassive. Some people, including the Italian producers, thought he wasn't acting.

The final showdown in the empty square was classic Hollywood Western, with the hero taking on all the bad guys single-handed. Eastwood was given a dramatic entrance, silhouetted against a smoking building which had just been dynamited, his entrance directly lifted from *Yojimbo.* As he advanced, the leading villain (Gian Maria Volonté) shot him down not once, not twice, not thrice, not four but five times and each time Joe got up and kept advancing. The man was indestructible. (Well, actually, he was wearing armour plating.)

Sergio Leone's approach to the Western may have been tongue-in-cheek, but his use of the wide screen, with its unusual camera angles, and the enormous close-ups of faces, eyes, guns, boots and spurs, had tremendous visual flair. Ennio Morricone's distinctive, twanging score was very much part of the film's success.

José Calvo and Clint Eastwood in *A Fistful of Dollars*

The calculated sadism of the film would be offensive were it not for the neutralizing laughter aroused by the ludicrousness of the whole exercise.

Philip French, *Observer*

The most unnecessarily violent film I can remember. If this is parody, it needs to be a good deal lighter on the trigger.

Felix Barker, *Evening News*

The only thing that could possibly explain why such a film made a killing at the Italian and UK box offices is the amount of killing that goes on in it.

Alexander Walker, *Evening Standard*

Eastwood as the stranger makes full use of his one expression.

Hollis Alpert, *Saturday Review*

Sergio Leone has a certain gift for striking compositions. But the overall effect is hardly such as to set the Thames on fire, whatever it did to the Tiber.

John Russell Taylor, *The Times*

He is a morbid, amusing, campy fraud.

Bosley Crowther, *New York Times*

Has all the psychological depth of Bugs Bunny.

Ian Christie, *Daily Express*

José Calvo and
Clint Eastwood in
A Fistful of Dollars

FOR A FEW DOLLARS MORE

Directed by Sergio Leone   1965
Italian title: *Per qualche dollari in più*

Where life had no value, death, sometimes, had
its price. That is why bounty killers appeared.

Legend

A horseman advanced. Off-screen a man
hummed and loaded his rifle. The advancing
horseman was shot dead. The horse bolted. The
credit titles began, accompanied by the
whistling, jolly gunfire and male choir first
heard during the credits for *A Fistful of Dollars*.

There were two bounty hunters. The first
was Colonel Douglas Mortimer (Lee Van Cleef),
a former Confederate officer, who looked evil
but wasn't. He was out only to avenge the rape
and suicide of his sister and the murder of her
young husband. The second hunter was a cold,
amoral gangster (Clint Eastwood), a sharp-eyed
opportunist, solely in it for the money.
Mortimer, more mature, classier, recognized in
the younger man his younger, reckless self.
There was a jokey encounter early on when the
two men, showing off, gave a display of their
shooting skills, shooting each other's hats.

Eastwood had a good first entrance in the
pouring rain. First the poncho, then the cigar,
then the hat and only finally the bearded face.
The Man With No Name (formerly Joe, now
Manco) had youth and cheek, delivering
dynamite to prison with a smile, his appearance at the barred window heralded by the
smoke of his cigar. 'He's nothing but a wild,
vicious animal,' said a nervous hotel manager.
'He's tall, isn't he?' gushed the bosomy recep-
tionist, thrilled to hear he didn't wear long
johns. (The film didn't confirm whether this
was true or not.) Eastwood, once again, wisely,
left 'the acting' to the Italians, who went in for
big, operatic performances.

Clint Eastwood in *For a
Few Dollars More*

33

Lee Van Cleef, Clint
Eastwood and Gian Maria
Volonté in *For a Few
Dollars More*

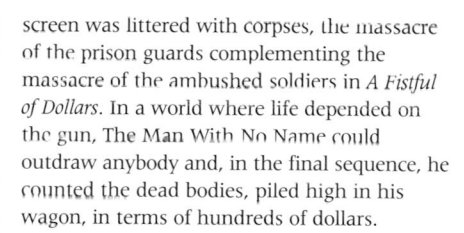

Clint Eastwood and
Gian Maria Volonté in
For a Few Dollars More

screen was littered with corpses, the massacre
of the prison guards complementing the
massacre of the ambushed soldiers in *A Fistful
of Dollars*. In a world where life depended on
the gun, The Man With No Name could
outdraw anybody and, in the final sequence, he
counted the dead bodies, piled high in his
wagon, in terms of hundreds of dollars.

The film veers to what you would call the
pornography of violence.

Alexander Walker, *Evening Standard*

It is the meat of sadistic morons.

Felix Barker, *Evening News*

Enough gratuitous violence to satisfy a
concentration commandant.

Ian Christie, *Daily Express*

The story concerned a robbery of a bank. The
bounty hunters joined forces to kill the robbers
and to take the loot for themselves. The villain
was Indio, a deranged drug addict and
murderer, who enjoyed torturing his victims
and addressing his gang from the pulpit of a
ruined church. Ennio Morricone's music scored
his hysteria and gave him a haunting tune to
soothe his jangled nerves, which was played
every time he opened a locket watch he had
stolen from Mortimer's sister. Indio was played
by Gian Maria Volonté, perfect casting for a
villain in a Jacobean melodrama. Klaus Kinski
appeared as one of his twitching henchmen, a
hunchback on whose hunch Van Cleef, so
memorably, struck a match.

Sergio Leone, never subtle, plunged
cinemagoers into a raucous bloodbath. The

Sergio Leone keeps the style somewhere just short of
burlesque.

Patrick Gibbs, *Daily Telegraph*

For those who like an elemental Western with
galvanic gestures, a twanging score full of Jew's
harps and choral chanting, and a lofty disdain for
sense and authenticity, the film will be ideal.

Time

The two American stars (Clint Eastwood and Lee
Van Cleef) are used more for their looks than as
actors.

David Robinson, *Financial Times*

THE GOOD, THE BAD AND THE UGLY

Directed by Sergio Leone   1966
Italian title: *Il buono, il brutto, il cattivo*

I don't want to be remembered as a philosopher, unlike so many of my celluloid brothers. I want to be remembered as an entertainer – or forget me.

Sergio Leone

The Good was Blondy, played by Clint Eastwood, the Bad was Angel Eyes, played by Lee Van Cleef, and the Ugly was Tuco, played by Eli Wallach. Jokers said the title referred to the camerawork, the acting and the violence. The title, admittedly, was ironic. All three men were bad, keen to lay their hands on a Confederate cashbox hidden in a cemetery. It was ages before anybody spoke and when they did, it was the usual awful dubbing.

Eastwood had a long-delayed first entrance. He was his familiar, anonymous, casually assured self, bemused by what was going on around him. He smiled. He squinted. (Eastwood would say later that if he ever lost his squint, 'his career would go down the tubes'.) He never raised his voice. He could recognize a man by his gunfire: 'Every gun makes its own tune.' If anybody wanted to find him, they just followed a trail of cigar butts.

Blondy had formed a partnership with Tuco, a Mexican bandit. The idea was that he would capture Tuco, hand him over to the law, collect the bounty, wait until the noose was round Tuco's neck and then, just as he was about to be hung, he would shoot the rope and they would make their escape on Blondy's horse. They would then go on to the next town and repeat the process, splitting the reward. One day Blondy thought it was no longer worth his while and he left Tuco to die in the desert. Tuco was not amused.

Tuco was a greasy, cunning, greedy, treacherous, lying rat who had committed such a catalogue of crimes that it was funny just to listen to the sheriff reading them out: murder, robbery, extortion, rape, arson, perjury, pimping, kidnapping . . . You name it, he'd done it. Wallach, a wonderfully comic villain, had all the best scenes: robbing a gunsmith; pleading with Blondy not to die ('Please don't die, I'm your friend'); pleading with a dying Confederate soldier to reveal the location of the grave; and sitting in his bath, calmly killing his would-be assassin with a gun hidden under the soap suds and offering some good, if belated, advice: 'When you have to shoot, shoot, don't talk.'

Tuco had one serious scene with his brother, whom he accused of cowardice and deserting their parents. For a man who didn't want to die of poverty in Mexico, there were, evidently, only two options. He could become either a bandit or a priest. His brother had chosen to become a priest.

There was a good old-fashioned scene, well edited, when Blondy was in his hotel bedroom and the noise of the soldiers marching by in the street drowned the sound of three assassins climbing the staircase. There was an electrifying moment when the soldiers came to a halt and Blondy was suddenly aware of the men on the landing outside his door.

The story was set during the American Civil War and the screenplay had as many climaxes as a Victorian novel awaiting serialization. Just as Tuco was about to kill Blondy, a bomb destroyed the hotel. Just as Tuco was about to kill Blondy for the second time, a driverless coach, full of dead and dying Confederate

Eli Wallach and Clint Eastwood in *The Good, the Bad and the Ugly*

Eli Wallach and Clint
Eastwood in *The Good,
the Bad and the Ugly*

soldiers, arrived (an extraordinarily eerie
moment, this). Just as they were making their
getaway, they mistook Confederate soldiers for
Yankees and were arrested; the mistake was
understandable, as the dust of the desert had
turned the soldiers' dark blue tunics light blue.

The Civil War gave the story its bitterness
and cynicism; it also gave it its dignity and
tragedy. The battlefield had an epic sweep, the
trenches recalling the trenches of World War I.
Though there were some schoolboy heroics,
with Blondy and Tuco blowing up a bridge, the
war was there essentially to register the
appalling waste of life.

The scenes in the POW camp were a grim
replay of the war crimes at the notorious camp
at Andersonville. Angel Eyes was cast as a
sadistic torturer and murderer, the agony of the
soldiers underlined by Ennio Morricone's
shrieking score. The prison band was forced to
play to drown the screams, and the tune they
played was especially haunting. It was a
sequence to recall the band that had been
forced to play during World War II in the Nazi
concentration camp as the Jews were marched
off to the gas chambers.

The Good, the Bad and the Ugly was filmed
in a variety of magnificent outdoor settings.
A familiar Western scene – a shoot-out in a
deserted town – was given a new lease of death
by taking place while the town was being
bombed and its streets and alleys were filled
with smoke. The sequence was wittily acted
and wittily scored.

Towards the end of the film Blondy gave his
coat to a dying soldier, a good action totally out
of character and there only, so it seemed, in
order for Eastwood to put on his poncho and

Lee Van Cleef, Eli Wallach
and Clint Eastwood
in *The Good, the Bad and
the Ugly*

become The Man With No Name for a memorable and breathtaking climax, a three-cornered shoot-out in a ring at the very centre of a massive cemetery for the war dead. The measure of a man in a Western has always been his ability to shoot faster than the other fellow, but the question here was who did you shoot first? Leone built up the pressure in his characteristic manner by endless delays with bold close-ups of faces, eyes and hands moving to triggers. Morricone quoted the locket-watch tune he had used in *For a Few Dollars More*.

There were those who thought Blondy a cardboard comic-strip hero, but there was nothing either cardboard or comic strip about Eastwood's cool and understated performance.

A curious amalgam of the visually striking, the dramatically feeble and the offensively sadistic.

Variety

Presumably the savagery is another sign of the times.

Dilys Powell, *Sunday Times*

Deaths are numerous, violent and lingered on – and the Western itself is one of the victims.

David Wilson, *Guardian*

Those Italian Westerns with Clint Eastwood chewing his cheroot and acting with as much expression as a man with neuralgia are really the bitter end.

Dick Richards, *Daily Mirror*

Must be the most expensive, pious and repellent movie in the history of its peculiar genre.

Renata Adler, *New York Times*

41

THE WITCHES

Directed by Vittorio de Sica   1966
Italian title: *Le Streghe*

Le Streghe was divided into five episodes.
Eastwood appeared in the last, *Una sera come
le altre (A Night Like Any Other)*, which
described the fantasies of a housewife (Silvana
Mangano), who was bored with her husband
(Clint Eastwood), who was too tired to do
anything but sleep when he came home from
work.

The piece gives Mr Eastwood nothing much to do
but look patient.

Vincent Canby, *New York Times*

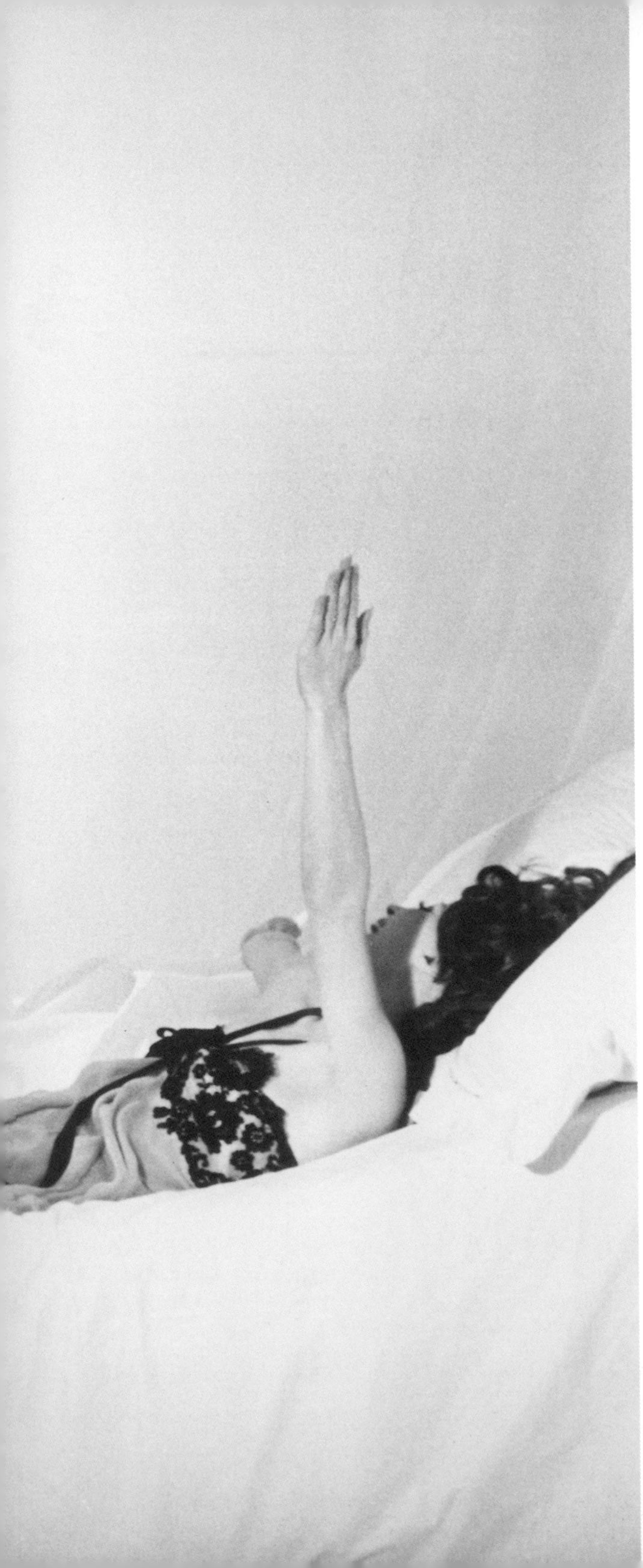

Clint Eastwood and
Silvana Mangano in
The Witches

HANG 'EM HIGH

Directed by Ted Post   1968

Jed Cooper, an ex-lawman, was driving a herd of cattle. The next minute he was being lassoed, dragged through a river, strung up and the credit titles hadn't even begun. He was accused of being a rustler and a murderer. Despite pleading his innocence he was lynched and left for dead. A passing marshal saved his life. *Hang 'Em High* was never as good again.

The hanging left a nasty scar and not just on Jed's neck. Invited by Judge Fenton to become his deputy, he accepted the badge, but only so that he could exact his revenge. He spent the rest of the movie tracking down his lynchers.

The central event was a public hanging, turned into a holiday by the town and given the full carnival atmosphere, with families coming from miles around, bringing the children. A young preacher led the assembled crowd in community hymn singing, while the camera lingered over the black hoods, the adjusted nooses, the sandbags, the trapdoors and the hands ready to trigger the final drop. The gallows were an exact replica of the original gallows built to hang 12 men simultaneously, scaled down to six-men size. Dominic Frontière's score, heavy and melodramatic, provided a brass percussion chime replica of the sound of a scaffold being tripped. Some critics found the detail too morbid. 'Strictly for ghouls!' was the *Daily Mirror* headline.

Jed (a far more heroic character than The Man With No Name, even if he was liable to stub out his cigar in a cowboy's beer) disapproved of the mass hangings, arguing that the men might just as well have been lynched. The judge contended that there was a difference between being lynched and being judged and if he didn't know the difference he had better hand in his badge. It was interesting that Jed should argue for mercy while he was vigorously pursuing his personal vendetta. Clint Eastwood, acting with flinty certitude, dealt with the ambiguity by simply ignoring it.

Judge Fenton was based on the real-life hanging Judge Parker, the only representative of US law in the Oklahoma Territory in 1873. 'I'm the law,' he said. 'All the law.' Fenton, who had to cover 70,000 miles with nine marshals and only one courthouse, wanted the territory to become a state and he knew that so long as the lawlessness continued, it wouldn't. His jails overflowed.

Fenton had a genuine affection for his protégé and, after one successful sortie, had rewarded him with a freebie in the local brothel. His behaviour in his own courtroom, however, made many people feel it was he who should be locked up. Pat Hingle found it difficult to reconcile the two sides of the judge's character: the folksiness on the one hand and the mercilessness on the other.

A romantic interest was dragged in. There was a widow (Inger Stevens) who was looking for the men who had killed her husband and raped her. It was she who nursed Jed back to health after he had been shot. They shared a sentimental picnic during which she allowed him just two kisses. A storm came up. Jed collapsed and they took shelter in a log-cabin conveniently nearby, where she gave him a good rub before lying next to him to keep him warm. The camera, tactfully, stayed outside the cabin all night.

There was also a second woman, a jolly prostitute (Arlene Golonka). Rather than watch

Clint Eastwood in
Hang 'Em High

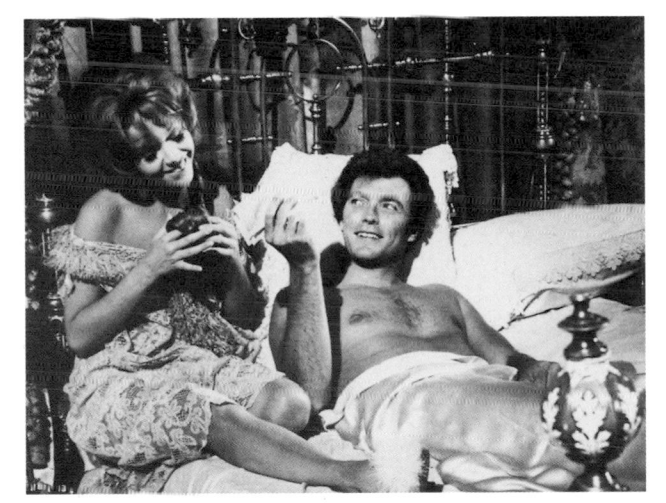

Arlene Golonka and
Clint Eastwood in
Hang 'Em High

the hangings, Jed got drunk and dragged her off for a quickie, during the singing of 'Rock of Ages', which was so quick, it was all over before the crowd had finished singing the last verse.

Ed Begley was cast as the wealthy ranch owner who had headed the unauthorized posse. Essentially a decent fellow, he realized too late that, if you hanged an innocent man by mistake, you should make certain that you finished off the job. Begley had a good scene right at the end when he was all alone in his house, a frightened old man, his two henchmen having just been killed. Running out of ammunition, he shut the door. By the time Jed had climbed the stairs, walked down the landing, tried a few doors and found the right room, he had had time to hang himself.

The director, Ted Post, had worked with

Eastwood on the *Rawhide* series. *Hang 'Em High* was his feature debut and it felt like an efficient television movie without the commercial breaks.

Eastwood has made his first talking picture.

Ian Christie, *Daily Express*

Hang 'Em High comes across as a poor American-made imitation of a poor Italian-made imitation of an American Western . . . Eastwood projects a likable image, but the part is only a shade more developed over his Sergio Leone Italoators. Some change of pace is sorely needed, lest he become typed.

Variety

It must be said that, as an actor, Clint Eastwood has perfected the sound of silence, which is quite impressive at times.

Margaret Hinxman, *Sunday Telegraph*

Films grow steadily more violent, and will continue to do so unless we apply the obvious remedy. Stay away.

Felix Barker, *Evening News*

Most unfortunate of all, Mr Eastwood, with his glum sincerity, isn't much of an actor.

Howard Thompson, *New York Times*

COOGAN'S BLUFF

Directed by Don Siegel   1968

He insists on being an anti-hero. I've never worked with an actor who was less conscious of his good image.

Don Siegel

Coogan's Bluff, well-made, fast-moving, was that rare thing, an urban Western, probably the first Western to be set in modern New York. An Arizonian deputy sheriff was put among the metropolitan policemen. The contrast between their more sophisticated approach and his frontier-style policing offered opportunities for dry humour at his expense and also at the expense of the big city and its liberal attitudes.

Deputy Sheriff Coogan (Clint Eastwood), a loner, tough and stubborn, was an instinctive hunter and his character was established in the opening sequence in the Arizona desert when he arrested a renegade Indian (Rudy Diaz) he had been tracking for three days and tied him up on the porch of the house of a local whore, while he had a bath and sex. The Indian was treated as if he were an animal, no different from any other blood sport. Compassion and humanity were low on Coogan's list of priorities; the last time he had shown pity for a criminal he had ended up with a six-inch blade in his gut.

He was sent to New York to extradite a prisoner, a murderer. Outside his territory, the sheriff cut a comic figure in his brown suit, stetson, bootlace tie and boots with the pointed toes. Tall, tanned and incredibly good-looking, he was so like everybody's idea of a cowboy that everybody instantly presumed he was from Texas and fair game. Cab drivers, hotel clerks and prostitutes tried to take him for a ride. One whore, whose advances he turned down,

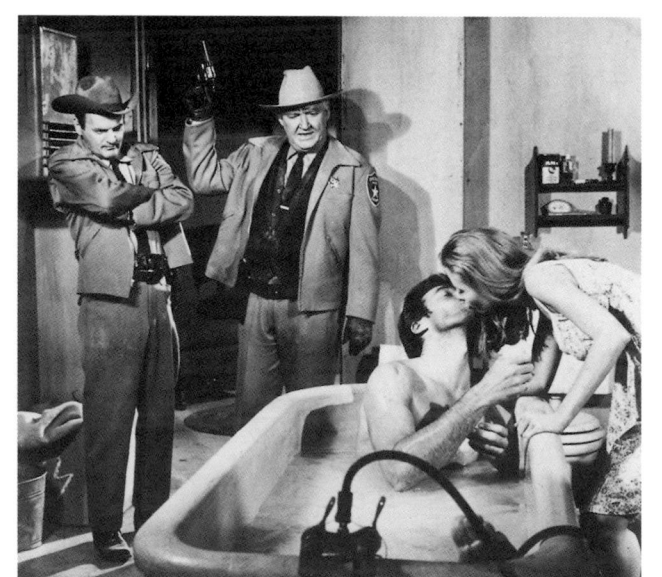

Tom Tully, Clint Eastwood and Melodie Johnson in *Coogan's Bluff*

thought she could steal his wallet and when she found she couldn't, she was so mad, all she could do was scream, 'Texas faggot!'

The murderer, James Ringerman (Don Stroud), was in a prison hospital, recovering from an LSD trip. Coogan, accustomed to direct action, took matters into his own hands, cutting through the red tape, ignoring District Office. Having bluffed a doctor into handing Ringerman over, he was then zapped into unconsciousness at the airport. The prisoner escaped and he was taken off the case. Feeling that his reputation was on the line, he simply disregarded the order. (A man's gotta do what he's gotta do.)

Clint Eastwood in
Coogan's Bluff

Lee J. Cobb, wearing a hat to hide his baldness, was cast as a tired, cynical, disenchanted detective who, hamstrung by his bosses, had to do everything by the book. 'This isn't the OK Corral,' he reminded Coogan in one of their many confrontations, exasperated by his arrogance.

Don Siegel captured the underworld in action in a poolroom when Coogan, taking on nine men wielding cues, suffered a terrible beating, the sort of martyrdom cinemagoers had come to expect from Marlon Brando in his films. A psychedelic experience which followed in an overcrowded discotheque (125 extras plus 400 genuine hippies) was overlong, but it allowed Coogan to have a characteristic, laconic exchange: 'I don't like violence,' he admitted, parodying the traditional, American tough guy. 'You drop that blade or you won't believe what happens next, even when it's happened.' The man, naturally, dropped his knife.

The climax took place in the cloisters and grounds of Fort Tryon Park, an urban parkland, with Coogan chasing after Ringerman. The sequence complemented the opening, the camera looking down on the action, through the trees, almost as if the sheriff were hunting prey back in Arizona. The chase, on motorcycles, along paths and up and down steps, ended with Coogan forcing Ringerman to collide with him. 'I'm making a citizen's arrest!' he yelled, hurling the thug at the detective's feet, the detective having arrived, as regular filmgoers would expect, only when it was all over.

Eastwood managed to remain likeable even when the sheriff's behaviour to prisoners and

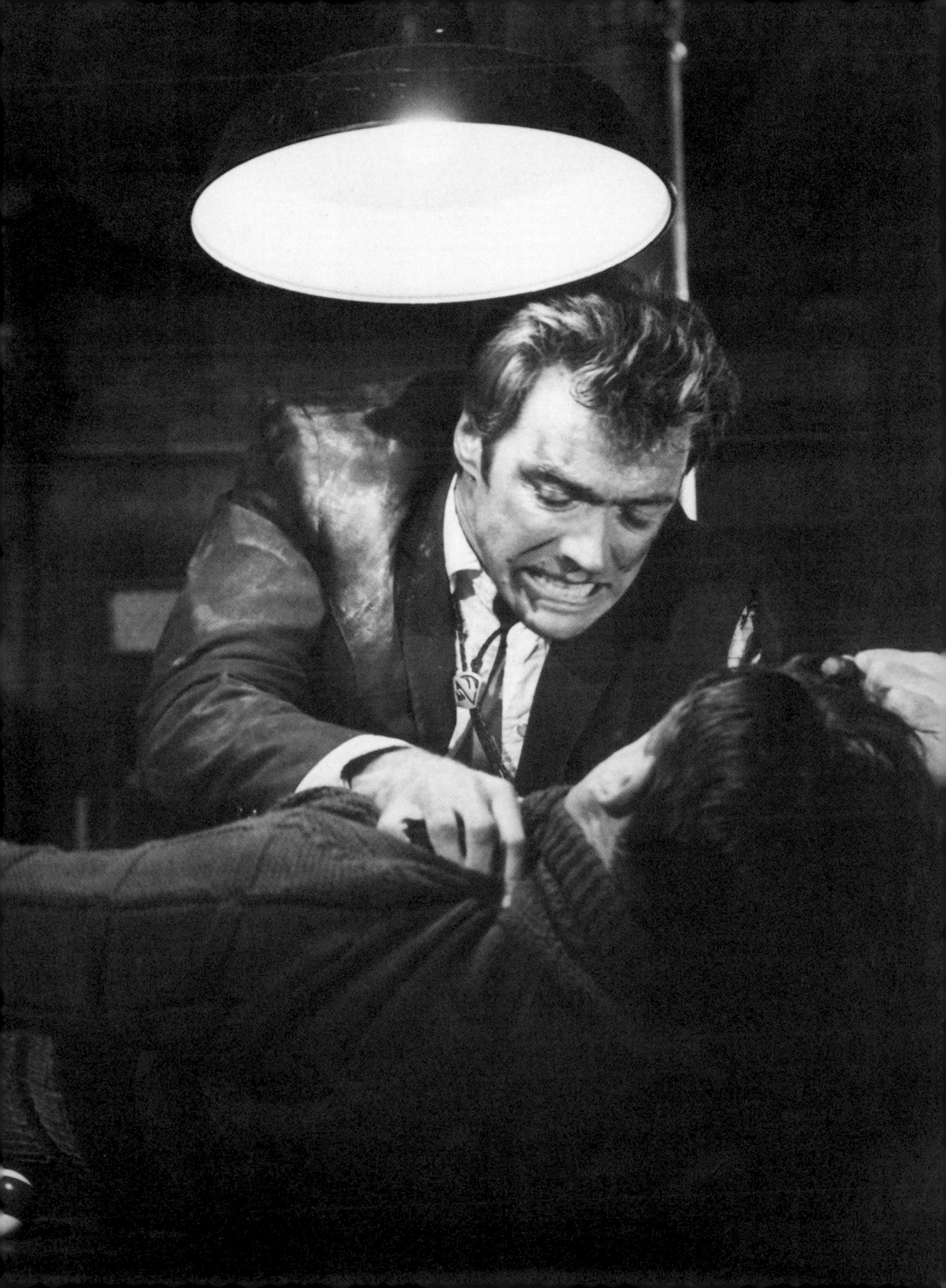

Clint Eastwood in
Coogan's Bluff

women was despicable. However, what gave
the role an extra significance was his regret for
the passing of rural America. There was a key
scene when he was looking at a panoramic
view of New York, trying to picture the way it
had been before people had come along and
fouled it up.

Susan Clark was cast as a softly spoken
probation officer who humanized him. The
foreplay was nicely judged by Eastwood, who
acted with gentle, sexy humour. Don Stroud
and Rudy Diaz had obviously been cast as the
fugitives because they had the same sort of
features. Ringerman's hippie girlfriend (Tisha
Sterling) was a ding-dong bore. A much more
interesting character was Ringerman's nutty
mother. Betty Field had only one scene and she
made the most of it.

And suddenly Mr Eastwood, released from the
crudity of the Italian imitations, moves with the
cool, deliberate elegance of the real thing. At last he
looks like the true Western hero.

Dick Richards. *Daily Mirror*

Eastwood, who hitherto displayed nothing more
than a capacity for iron-jawed belligerency in a
series of Italian-made Westerns, performs with a
measure of real feeling in the role that fits him as
comfortably as his tooled leather boots.

Time

Some may find the Eastwood character Fascist
beyond redemption, or at least beyond
identification, but in an American context, he is all
too believable, the cool, emotionless, slightly
sadistic man of the sixties.

Richard Raud, *Guardian*

WHERE EAGLES DARE

Directed by Brian G. Hutton   1968

*Richard Burton and I killed so many Nazis in
two hours, it made me wonder why the war
took so long.*

Clint Eastwood, quoted by Maureen Dowd,
New York Times

Alistair MacLean's *Where Eagles Dare*, built on
the same lines as his *The Guns of Navarone*,
was an action-packed espionage thriller, a
ripping yarn, full of death-defying feats and no
characterization whatsoever.

Major John Smith (Richard Burton) was given
the mission of rescuing an imprisoned
American general from the impregnable and
inaccessible Schloss Adler - the Castle of the
Eagle - mountain headquarters of the German
Secret Service and Gestapo in south Germany
during World War II. His team included an
American, Lieutenant Morris Schaffer (Clint
Eastwood), a woman (Mary Ure) and four
others. It wasn't exactly a perfect team. Three
out of the seven turned out to be traitors. 'The
whole operation looks impossible,' moaned
Michael Hordern, back in London, in his role
of Naval Intelligence officer. 'The Germans
have totally penetrated M16.' (The dialogue was
not the film's strong point.) A game of double
bluff was played by double agents doubling all
over the place; even the American general they
were meant to be rescuing turned out to be an
ex-actor (Robert Beatty) impersonating the
general.

'You shouldn't go on these insane missions;
you're getting too old,' observed the woman
team member to Smith. 'See you in the
woodshed,' he replied. Evidently, they'd been
on missions together before. Much publicity
was made of Burton letting down his hair and

Ingrid Pitt, Clint
Eastwood, Mary Ure
and Richard Burton in
Where Eagles Dare

taking a holiday from his more serious work. It
was reported that he had made the film to
please his children. 'Why do you always get
killed?' they had asked. 'Why don't you do a
picture in which you do the killing?'

There was certainly a lot of cold-blooded
shooting and the production went with a bang.
Castle, buildings, bridges, trees, trucks, cars,
motorbikes, airports were all blown up. It was a
big-budget movie and no expense was spared.
By the end of the picture there wasn't a
German left alive. In fact, the Germans were
there just so Smith and Schaffer could mow
them down.

The storyline was so wildly improbable and
so ridiculously complicated that even those
participating didn't know what was going on.

Richard Burton and
Clint Eastwood in
Where Eagles Dare

Clint Eastwood in
Where Eagles Dare

A bit of old-fashioned, schoolboy excitement was provided by a desperate fight in, round and on top of a moving cable car, but for the most part the action was devoid of drama, wit and tension. The legendary stuntman Yakima Canutt (who had organized the chariot race in *Ben Hur*) was responsible for the technically impressive final sequence, which had plenty of pace, but the feats and odds were so preposterous, they ceased to be hair-raising.

Lieutenant Schaffer of the American Rangers was a professional killer. Like everybody else in the cast, he played a supporting role to the bullets and dynamite explosions. Eastwood trudged through snow, scaled castle walls and blasted anything and everything with his machine-gun. 'Hello!' he would say before he shot or knifed somebody. 'Hello!' was a

running gag. (He had said 'Hello!' in *A Fistful of Dollars*, too.) There wasn't much acting to be done. Eastwood took second billing and let Burton do all the talking.

The German officers were played by Anton Diffring, Ferdy Mayne and Derren Nesbitt. Diffring rarely played anything else but German officers. Mayne sported a monocle and Nesbitt played a nasty ginger-haired Gestapo. Patrick Wymark was a campy, treacherous Brit. He made his exit from a plane while it was flying over the Alps. As he stood in the open doorway, it looked for a moment as if he was about to say, 'I'm going outside and may be gone for some time.'

Eagles was a sophisticated, illogical film, a very complicated story. I'm still not sure we quite figured out the plot.

Brian C. Hutton

But it's the action that counts - and on this level *Where Eagles Dare* is an undeniable success.

Clive Hirshhorn, *Sunday Express*

No end of fun for stony-hearted boys.

Dilys Powell, *Sunday Times*

It reaches such heights of absurdity, it is hootingly funny. Do not resist it. Yield, uncritically, and it is really quite enjoyable!

Madeleine Harmsworth, *Daily Mirror*

Clint is in the great line of Spencer Tracy and James Stewart and Bob Mitchum. They have a kind of dynamic lethargy. They appear to do nothing and they do everything.

Richard Burton, quoted by Jean Vallely, *Esquire*

PAINT YOUR WAGON

Directed by Joshua Logan   1969

Paramount had hoped to repeat the success of *The Sound of Music* and *My Fair Lady*, instead *Paint Your Wagon*, overblown, interminable and uncinematic, proved a costly failure, going way over budget.

Alan Jay Lerner and Frederick Loewe's musical Western had had a modest run on Broadway in 1951, but by the time it reached the screen in 1969 it was barely recognizable. It had a new book by Paddy Chayefsky and new music by André Previn, neither of which was distinguished.

The story was set during the Californian Gold Rush of the 1840s and traced the growth of a mining town, No Name City, from shanty town to boomtown. Its Sodom and Gomarrah-like destruction was the film's best and funniest sequence; its collapse caused, however, not by lust and corruption but by greedy prospectors tunnelling underneath it.

The highlight of the original Broadway show had been the choreography of Agnes de Mille. The movie had no choreography by either Agnes de Mille or anybody else for that matter, Joshua Logan left the chorus just standing and sitting around in a series of static tableaux during the songs, while the extras (behaving like a lot of extras) ran around, jumped about and waved their arms. What the movie desperately needed was the wit and energy Stanley Donen and Michael Kidd had brought to *Seven Brides for Seven Brothers*. Only the arrival of the whores ('There's a Coach Comin' in') gave the show a momentary lift. The best number remained the rousing opener, 'Paint Your Wagon', sung in a number of languages.

Lee Marvin and Clint Eastwood were chosen for their clout at the box office rather than their singing voices. Marvin, an untrained baritone, growled his way through 'Wand'rin' Star'. It was his most underplayed moment and the song, in Great Britain, went straight to the top of the charts. The only lead actor who was really able to sing was Harve Presnell (playing the gambler, Rotten Luck Willie) and he belted out 'They Call the Wind Maria' in the pouring rain.

The two leading characters were prospectors: the wild 49-year-old Ben Rumson and his young 'Pardner', who looked after him when he was drunk and melancholy. Marvin, always larger-than-life, worked hard for his laughs, recycling the Oscar-winning performance he had given in *Cat Ballou*. Top-hatted, white-haired, white-whiskered, sad-eyed, he looked comical in his red long johns and spent much of his time falling flat on his face.

The sentimental friendship was put to the test when Ben, in a drunken stupor, bought himself a wife off a Mormon (who had two wives), paying $800 for her in open auction. He invited 'Pardner' to share her with him. She, being a Mormon, had no difficulty in accepting a *ménage à trois*. 'I'm willing,' she said. 'I think it's a humane, practical, beautiful solution. I was married to a man who had two wives. Why can't I have two husbands?' They became a happily married triple. The producers, failing to get Julie Andrews after her enormous success in *The Sound of Music*, cast Jean Seberg, who had a Mormon-like steeliness, but she, too, was no singer.

Since Ben's wife was the only woman among 400 men in a 90-mile radius, the all-male community immediately voted in favour of prostitution and kidnapped six French whores.

Clint Eastwood, Jean
Seberg and Lee Marvin
in *Paint Your Wagon*

As Ben explained to a fresh-faced, churchgoing
youth (Tom Ligon), if you didn't have a woman
you could go blind. Fortunately, the youth had
a natural talent for dissipation and was soon
drinking, gambling, smoking and whoring with
the best of them.

'Pardner', clean in mind and body, the
decentest man Ben had ever known, neither
drank nor gambled; he talked to the trees. He
also sang 'I Still See Elisa', which was rather
odd, since it had been Ben's song when *Paint
Your Wagon* played in the theatre. An old
man's remembrance about his wife was turned
into a young man's fantasy about a girl he had
never even seen. Eastwood's best number was
'Gold Fever' (one of the new songs), which at
least made an effort to say something about
what he and the town had become.

Eastwood, who built his reputation by speaking very
little in a string of Italian-made Westerns, sings
pleasantly enough but takes apart his reputation by
speaking often and badly, as if the scriptgirl had
neglected to give him each succeeding line.

Joseph Morgenstern, *Newsweek*

Compared with Marvin's agonized histrionics and
the wild overplaying of most of the rest of the cast,
Clint Eastwood preserves a certain uncomfortable
dignity.

Penelope Mortimer, *Observer*

The stars have singing voices that would be assets to
any bathroom.

Alexander Walker, *Evening Standard*

No music to my ears.

Arthur Knight, *Saturday Review* headline

TWO MULES FOR SISTER SARA

Directed by Don Siegel   1969

*I won't reveal what Shirley MacLaine's real
occupation is, but she's not the kind of girl you
would be likely to take home to your mother's
for tea.*

Ian Christie, *Daily Express*

Two Mules for Sister Sara had a good story by
Budd Boetticher, cult director of many classic
B-movie Westerns in the late 1950s, and a
witty, intelligent and funny screenplay by
Albert Maltz. The action was set in French-
occupied Mexico in 1865, during the Mexican
revolution, at the time of Juárez and
Maximilian. Clint Eastwood was cast as Hogan,
a disillusioned veteran of the American Civil
War, who earned his living as a mercenary,
working for the Mexicans, hoping to make
enough cash to open the best gambling saloon
in San Francisco.

The action opened in long shot. Don Siegel
explained later that the owl, big fish jack
rabbit, wild cat, rattlesnake and tarantula that
Hogan passed during the credit titles were all
emblems of aspects of his character. Lean,
tough, unshaven, Hogan was a laconic gunman,
a hard-bitten, dry-humoured loner, with nerves
of steel and an endless supply of cheroots.

The film proper began with Hogan rescuing a
semi-naked woman from three drunks who
were trying to rape her. It was a big surprise
when the woman put on her clothes and she
turned out to be a nun. Not that this stopped
Hogan flirting with her: 'I sure wish you
weren't a nun . . . Maybe a nun ought not to be
so good-looking . . . I sure would have liked to
have met up with you before you took to them
clothes and them vows.' But, randy though he
was, he was a good boy and behaved himself.

There were many clues early on that Sister
Sara was not a nun: she smoked a cigar, she
swigged whiskey, she extracted a cork from a
bottle with her teeth and her behaviour and
language were rarely nun-like. 'Sober up, you
dirty bastard, or I'll kill you!' she yelled,
socking him on the jaw. It might have been
better for the story if the clues had been more
subtle and delayed until at least that moment
when a dying French officer, to whom she was
giving the last rites, recognized her and sat up
on his deathbed, screaming, '*C'est toi!* You
filthy bitch!' Sara dismissed it as delirium. If
Boetticher had had his way, nobody would
have known she was a prostitute until the end
of the picture.

It would have been better, too, if Sara had
made suckers of cinemagoers as well as Hogan,
though it is very doubtful that regular cinema-

Shirley MacLaine and
Clint Eastwood in *Two
Mules for Sister Sara*

goers would ever have believed in Shirley MacLaine as a nun. MacLaine had made a career out of playing whores with hearts of gold in such films as *Some Came Running, Irma La Douce* and *Sweet Charity*. The role had, originally, been intended for Elizabeth Taylor. It is doubtful that many people would have believed in Taylor as a nun, either.

Sara, as became the most popular whore in the best whorehouse in Chihuahua, was a tough cookie, capable of frightening off the Yaqui Indians merely by brandishing her cross in their faces and dazzling them with its shiny surface. She was also capable of clambering up the trestle of a bridge, high over a gorge, to plant dynamite to blow up a supply train, and this despite having just said she had no head for heights. Siegel's favourite scene was the one where she removed an arrow protruding from Hogan's left shoulder after he had been wounded by the Yaquis. She had to cut a shaft in the arrow, fill it with gunpowder and then, when he ignited the powder, she had to knock the arrow right through his body with a sharp crack. If she didn't hit straight, the arrow would break inside him.

Sara wasn't just a sexual animal; she was also a political animal, helping the Juáristas (the Mexican guerillas) in their revolution against the French. Unlike Hogan, she was not in it just for the money. When he discovered she was a whore (being the last person to do so, having, strangely, not noticed her eyebrows and mascara), he was initially furious, but, quickly making up for lost time, he barged into her bathroom. 'Come back later,' she said. 'I want to be all dressed up for you.' 'Who in the hell wants to see you dressed?' he asked, getting

into the bath with her, fully clothed. 'The least you can do is take off your hat,' she said. 'Haven't got time for that,' he replied, taking the cigar out of her mouth and sinking into the soap suds.

Siegel handled the comedy and the violence with equal skill. The climax, a raid on a French garrison, was carried out with characteristic vigour, realism and excitement. Tautly photographed, there were vivid scenes of destruction and death, including some horrific close-ups. The Juáristas were mown down by machine-gun bullets. The French were cut down by machetes. The staccato montage looked as if it had been lifted from the murals of Diego Rivera. Eastwood, meanwhile, nonchalantly lobbed dynamite, while smoking his cheroot.

Don Siegel directs Clint Eastwood in *Two Mules for Sister Sara*

Clint Eastwood in *Two Mules for Sister Sara*

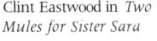
Clint Eastwood in *Two Mules for Sister Sara*

The final scene had Sara and Hogan riding off to San Francisco with numerous hatboxes. She was dressed in gaudy scarlet, every inch the tart. Clearly, she was going to be an invaluable asset in his saloon. Just in case cinemagoers still had not appreciated the pun in the title, the shot made it clear that Hogan, her stubborn and reluctant aide, whom she had manipulated, cajoled and bullied throughout the picture, was the second mule.

Ennio Morricone's score maintained the tension and, as always, used church music with irony and wit. The Mexican locations, with their sweeping panoramas and brutal countryside, were superbly photographed by Gabriel Figueroa.

Clint Eastwood is the cowboy and Shirley MacLaine is the nun. Things might have been more entertaining if the roles had been reversed.

Derek Malcolm, *Guardian*

Two Mules for Sister Sara is a solidly entertaining film that provides Clint Eastwood with his best, most substantial role to date; in it he is far better than he has ever been. In director Don Siegel, Eastwood has found what John Wayne found in John Ford and Gary Cooper found in Frank Capra.

Los Angeles Herald-Examiner

Eastwood looks grizzled, stares into the sun and sneers, but anything more demanding seems beyond his grasp.

Time

Clint Eastwood smoulders his way through a panierful of cigars.

C. Miller, *Listener*

The 1970s

Clint Eastwood in
Escape from Alcatraz

KELLY'S HEROES

Directed by Brian G. Hutton   1970

We hope the laughs will come as thick as the bullets. The violence is de-personalized in the pop style of a comic book.

Brian G. Hutton

Kelly's Heroes came out the same year as *M*A*S*H* and *Catch-22* and treated World War II in the same flippant, ribald and cynical manner. Fourteen thousand bars of gold worth $16 million were in a bank 30 miles behind enemy lines, just waiting to be picked up. Twenty-seven GIs went absent without leave during their rest and recreation period. They set out to rob a bank and damn near won a war instead. If they'd got to be killed, they argued, they might just as well be killed risking their lives for themselves. Originally, there were going to be 30 GIs, but three characters were deliberately cut from the script so nobody would be able to tag the film 'The Dirty Thirty'. On set, the movie was known as 'The Clean Dozen'.

Kelly's heroes were not heroes; they were lechers, black marketeers, thieves and cowards. When they questioned prisoners, they weren't interested in military information; they wanted only to find out where the girls, hotels and restaurants were. 'You've got to think of us as tourists,' said the interrogating sergeant. The officers hadn't a clue what was going on. The army was run by men like Private Kelly, a former lieutenant who had been busted as a scapegoat for somebody else's error. Kelly was played by Clint Eastwood, cool, reliable, resourceful. There was never any doubt that he was the man in charge.

The action was very noisy. Everybody shouted. Everybody went way over the top.

Eastwood didn't. He left the 'acting' to Telly Savalas, Don Rickles, Carroll O'Connor and Donald Sutherland. He was the straight man; they were the comedians. Savalas was the bald, fatherly sergeant. Rickles was the enterprising, hustling, ever-complaining quartermaster. O'Connor was the bombastic, farcical general who dished out medals to the looters and was mistaken by the French for General de Gaulle.

The actor who ran away with all the reviews was Donald Sutherland, playing Oddball, a drugged-up-to-the-eyeballs, bearded hippie, totally freaked-out and given to saying things like, 'Don't hit me with the negatives so early in the morning.' What this pot-puffing, half-asleep, 1970s' dropout was doing in 1945 post D-Day France was anybody's guess.

Oddball was involved in the production's most unforgettable sequence, when his tank blasted its way through a railway goods yard to the sound of Hank Williams singing 'Sunshine', playing from its loudspeaker. (Twenty years later Francis Ford Coppola's helicopters in *Apocalypse Now* would go on a bombing raid with their loudspeakers blaring Wagner.) 'Sunshine' was a pleasant tune for cinemagoers to listen to while they were watching the enemy being massacred and buildings being blown up. Music was used satirically throughout; the ever-popular 'Burning Bridges', sung by The Mike Curb Congregation during the credit titles, was reprised twice.

Kelly's Heroes was an excuse for unlimited violence and mass killings. As he had proved in *Where Eagles Dare*, Brian Hutton was very adept at deploying vast numbers and he stage-managed the carnage and destruction with considerable flair. The film was shot in

Yugoslavia, the Yugoslavian government having allowed MGM not only to use their army but also to destroy the petite seventeenth-century town of Vizinada on the Istrian peninsula.

There was something obscene about the way the camera could watch any number of Germans being killed for the public's so-called entertainment, yet the moment two Americans were shot the soundtrack immediately went all plaintive and audiences were asked to take their deaths seriously. By the end of the picture there was hardly a German left alive, yet only three Americans had been killed and one wounded.

A confrontation between three American GIs and a German tank in a deserted street was a parody of every Western showdown. There were close-ups of the men's faces, close-ups of their rifles, close-ups of their hands on holsters and close-ups of their feet marching down the street to a twanging guitar parodying Ennio Morricone's score for the *Dollars* trilogy. The tank guarded the bank. The Americans negotiated a deal with the tank commander. If he blew a hole in the door, he could share in the spoils. The Americans' argument was simple: 'Look, Max, you and us, we're just soldiers, right? We don't know what this war is all about. All we do is fight and die. For what? We don't get anything out of it.' Max blew down the door.

Donald Sutherland, Clint Eastwood and Telly Savalas in *Kelly's Heroes*

65

Clint Eastwood in
Kelly's Heroes

On the screen Clint Eastwood is a man who knows where he's going. He knows what he's after and he knows how to get it. In an age of uncertainty in the arts, politics and everything else, people enjoy watching a man like this in action. They don't want to see the anguish of a Brando or a James Dean any more. They want to escape into something more positive.

Brian Hutton

Eastwood's performance remains in his traditional low-key groove, thereby creating an adrenalin vacuum filled to the brim by the screen-dominating presence of Savalas and Sutherland.

Variety

Clint Eastwood, who is not generally a funny man, plays with a quiet, thin-lipped determination of such withdrawn ferocity - as if he was a kind of

Clint Eastwood in
Kelly's Heroes

Gary Cooper whose essence had not just preceded but utterly superseded his existence - that you would expect his goal to be murder rather than money.

Roger Greenspun, *New York Times*

Eastwood manages not to change expressions once during the 146 minutes of this nonsense.

Judith Crist, *New York Magazine*

The film could have been one of the best war movies ever. And it should have been; it had the best script, a good cast, a subtle anti-war message. But somehow everything got lost. The picture got bogged down shooting in Yugoslavia and it just ended up as the story of a bunch of American screw-offs in World War II.

Clint Eastwood

THE BEGUILED

Directed by Don Siegel   1970

The Beguiled, a superb, stagey melodrama, was given the full-blown Southern baroque treatment by Don Siegel. The time was towards the end of the American Civil War, which was economically established during the credit titles by a black and white montage of Matthew Brady photographs. As the credit titles finished, colour seeped into the frame.

The setting was an elegant, dilapidated, colonial mansion in a desolate Louisiana wasteland. The mansion was a seminary for young ladies, where the two teachers and their six charges lived in daily fear of being raped by both armies. They took a wounded Union soldier, with a broken leg, into the school and nursed him back to health.

Since there was no other man in the house, Corporal John McBurney (called McB), a sexual philanderer and opportunist, seized the moment. Clint Eastwood, at first bedridden and in his nightshirt and then hobbling about on crutches, was a manly, handsome, sexy rooster among gullible hens. He had plenty of seductive Yankee charm and gallantry. He was also a liar, pretending to be a pacifist and a Quaker when he was neither, his statements instantly belied by flashbacks on the screen.

'I am nobody's slave,' he declared; but he was, his captivity symbolized by a black crow with a broken wing, tied up on the porch. The women kept him prisoner and he offered them his services, partly to serve himself and partly because he didn't want them to hand him over. Siegel's taut direction maintained the tension throughout as to whether they would betray him or not.

The frustrated women, eavesdropping on each other, quickly made fools of themselves.

Mae Mercer, Jo Ann Harris, Geraldine Page, Clint Eastwood and Pamelyn Ferdin in *The Beguiled*

McB confessed he wasn't keen to have his head on the chopping block but, unable to deny his sexual urges, he abused his hospitality, flirted with them all, playing them off each other, and paid an exceptionally heavy price.

Geraldine Page was excellent as the strong minded headmistress, Miss Martha, who had made love with her brother and who also given half the chance, looked as if she might make love with her 22-year-old assistant, Miss Edwina, a former pupil. 'If this war goes on much longer,' she observed, 'I shall forget I was a woman.' Initially, she had intended to hand McB over, it being treason not to do so, but she changed her mind and invited him to stay. ('The place needs a man,' she argued.) She fantasized in front of a *pietà* by Van der Weyden, dreaming she and Edwina were in bed with McB and that McB was Christ and they were taking him down from the cross.

Elizabeth Hartman was affecting as Miss Edwina, a timid, Pre-Raphaelite virgin. McB said she was a sleeping beauty waiting in a castle for a prince to wake her with a kiss and so, when she found McB in bed with 17-year-old Carol, she threw him downstairs, breaking his leg. 'You lying bastard! You filthy lecher! I hope you're dead!'

Miss Martha (who had been expecting him to come to her room) exacted a terrible revenge. There was a memorably gruesome scene when, in order to save him from gangrene (so she said), she cut off his leg below the knee with a saw. He looked like a crucified figure, tied down on the dining table, and the sound of the saw was horrific.

'You dirty bitch!' he raged when he woke up and discovered what she had done. 'Just

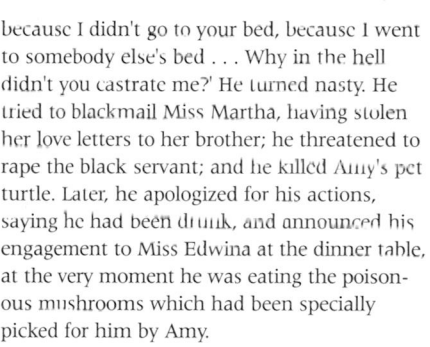

Mae Mercer, Geraldine
Page and Clint Eastwood
in *The Beguiled*

because I didn't go to your bed, because I went
to somebody else's bed . . . Why in the hell
didn't you castrate me?' He turned nasty. He
tried to blackmail Miss Martha, having stolen
her love letters to her brother; he threatened to
rape the black servant; and he killed Amy's pet
turtle. Later, he apologized for his actions,
saying he had been drunk, and announced his
engagement to Miss Edwina at the dinner table,
at the very moment he was eating the poison-
ous mushrooms which had been specially
picked for him by Amy.

The actresses gave highly strung
performances, in keeping with the theatrics, yet
at the same time kept themselves tightly reined
in, never descending to crude melodrama.
Pamelyn Ferdin was 12-year-old Amy ('old
enough for kisses,' said McB), who idolized
him and believed he loved her. Jo Ann Harris
was Carol, hussy and blackmailer, who
encouraged McB's advances ('I bet there's not a
soft spot on you'). Mae Mercer was the servant,
who had been raped by Miss Edwina's brother.
Of all the characters, she came across as the
most modern, the only anachronism.

The Beguiled had a marvellous feeling for
period and place. The darkened corridors, the
rich furniture and the shuttered rooms
provided an ideal setting for the claustrophobia
and hysteria. Bruce Surtees's atmospheric
camerawork was exceptionally fine. The
production had a strange dream-like quality,
the action regularly punctuated by flashbacks
of reveries and hallucinations. There was a
particularly haunting moment, which managed
to be both realistic and eerie, when a
Confederate wagon full of wounded and dying
Yankees passed by the plantation.

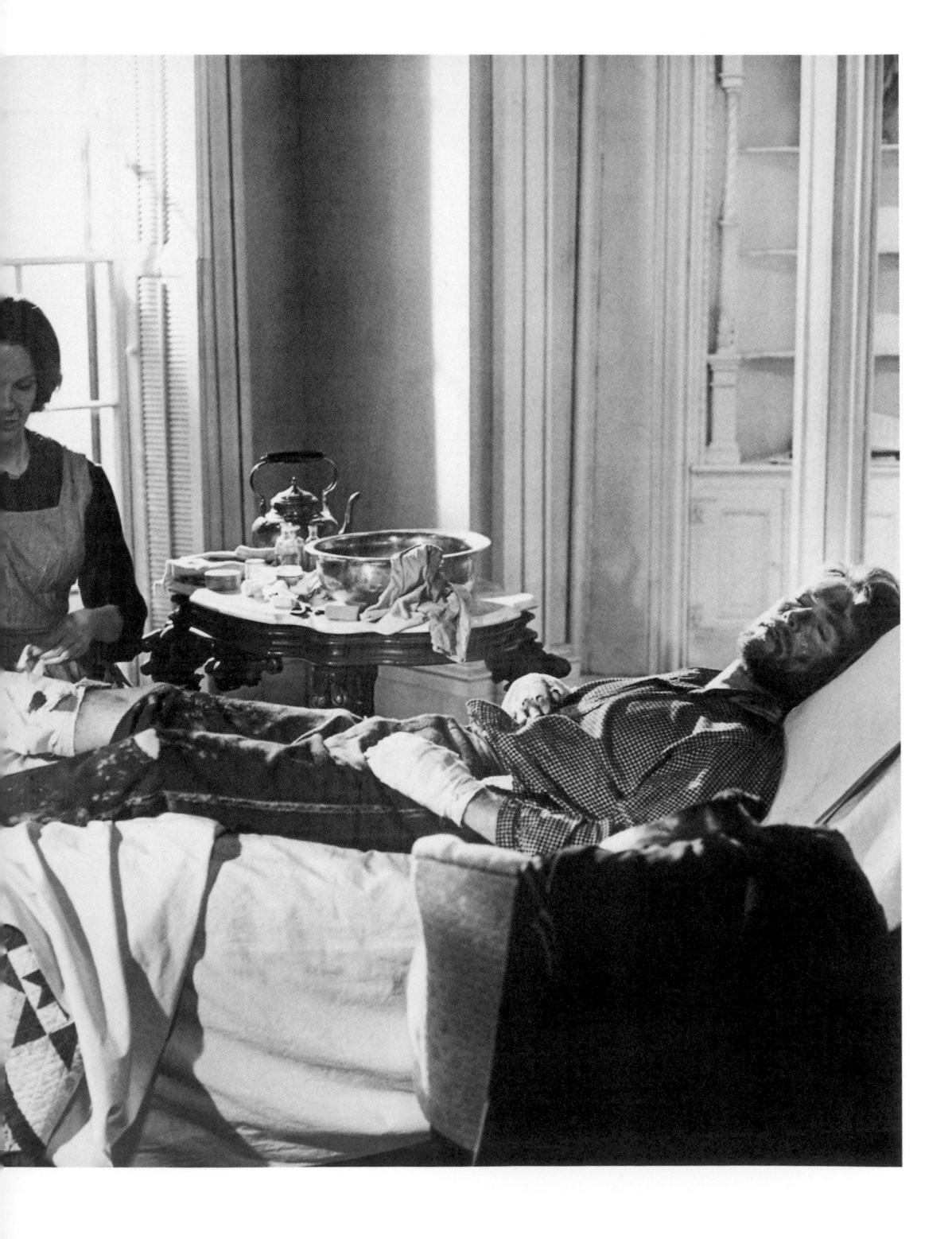

At the end of the film, with McB's death, the colour seeped out of the frame, in the same way that it had seeped in.

Don Siegel directs this ironic, lethal story with a nice feeling for the grisly.

Dilys Powell, *Sunday Times*

Eastwood, working with Siegel for the third time, exudes cool, threatening sexuality.

Time

He seems only to exist that the sexual repressions of the women who surround him can find their ultimate expression. In consequence the movie takes on a misogynistic tone which a stronger actor would have countered. Eastwood's McBurney is strictly one-dimensional.

Andrew Tudor, *New Society*

The whole thing is managed with great address, well-paced, with atmospheres and undertones vividly and economically suggested, and a balance held adroitly between horror and *grand guignol* scepticism.

David Robinson, *Financial Times*

The family that likes to vomit together can do it at the movies . . . A must for sadists and woman-haters.

Judith Crist, *New York Magazine*

Elizabeth Hartman and
Clint Eastwood in
The Beguiled

PLAY MISTY FOR ME

Directed by Clint Eastwood 1971

Play Misty For Me, an updated *film noir*, paid homage to the psychological thrillers of the 1940s and borrowed freely from Alfred Hitchcock, Roman Polanski and Claude Chabrol.

The camera flew in to Carmel and the Monterey peninsula. Clint Eastwood was cast as Dave Garver, a popular, late-night Californian disc jockey on a local radio station who offered 'a little verse, a little talk and five hours of music to be very, very nice to each other by'. One of his regular fans, who kept asking him to play Errol Garner's 'Misty', picked him up at a bar (where Don Siegel, making his acting debut, was the bartender).

At first Evelyn was merely an embarrassing nuisance who refused to be rejected after a one-night stand. 'There are no strings,' she agreed, 'but I never said anything about not coming back for seconds.' The story became every man's nightmare. Dave found he had a neurotic and persistent sexual blackmailer on his hands, pathologically possessive, impossibly demanding. 'Why are you pretending you don't love me?' she screamed. 'We don't even know each other!' he retorted.

The suicidal intensity was carefully charted, Jessica Walter, eager and edgy, sweet and savage, sexy and predatory, acted with frightening believability, redefining a woman scorned, There were plenty of fireworks, sudden, unnerving bursts of temper and incredible rudeness towards strangers, neighbours and, on one memorable occasion, towards a woman producer who was having a business lunch with Dave.

Eastwood played a surprisingly passive victim. Why didn't he go to the police? (Had he

Clint Eastwood and Jessica Walter in *Play Misty For Me*

done so, there would, of course, have been no film.) Dave may have looked a nice guy, but he was essentially dishonest, a not very bright womanizer, thoughtless, selfish, sleeping around, quick to take advantage and not wanting any emotional involvement. The strength of Eastwood's performance was its honesty; he did not hide what Dave was.

The mood of terror was sustained throughout. Evelyn became a homicidal maniac, wielding scissors and carving knives, destroying his home and attempting to murder his housekeeper and his girlfriend. Particularly effective was the scene when he was asleep, having a nightmare that Evelyn was in his bedroom with a knife, only to find that he was awake, that he wasn't having a nightmare and it was for real.

Clint Eastwood and
Jessica Walter in
Play Misty For Me

Clint Eastwood and
Don Siegel in
Play Misty For Me

wounds, he managed to summon up enough strength for the final *coup de grâce*, a punch to the jaw which sent her reeling over the balcony and on to the cliffs below. The climax, depending upon your point of view, was either parody of the genre or sheer banality.

Brad Whitney of Carmel got a credit for Eastwood's wardrobe and at times it did seem that he was modelling clothes and underwear for them.

Clint Eastwood's *Play Misty For Me* is a doubly encouraging directorial debut, successful both as a controlled and original psychological thriller and as a stylish *homage* to Eastwood's cinematic mentor, Don Siegel.

Nigel Andrews, *Monthly Film Bulletin*

Eastwood displays a vigorous talent for sequences of violence and tension. He has obviously seen *Psycho* and *Repulsion* more than once, but these are excellent texts and he has learned his lesson passing well.

Jay Cocks, *Time*

A performance even more understated than usual. He doesn't rise to such parts but allows himself to lapse into them.

Andrew Tudor, *New Society*

The film is grotesque, narcissistic (Eastwood in his underpants), but without sparkle. The actor being transparency itself, it was difficult for him to have a presence. A real zombie.

M. G., *Cinéma*

There was a long lyrical sequence in the forest with his former long-time lover, who had abandoned him because of his promiscuity. They kissed, they bathed, they made love, There was even a red sunset. It all looked like an advertisement for the song 'The First Time Ever I Saw Your Face,' sung by Roberta Flack, which went straight into the charts. The lovemaking gave way to the Monterey Jazz Festival, to which Eastwood took a documentary rather than a dramatic approach. These two intervals, deliberate respites from the violence, went on far too long.

The end degenerated into melodrama, the camera constantly cutting from Evelyn slashing away at a painting to Dave in his car (a cavalry of one) driving to the rescue. Arriving at the house, which was, naturally, plunged in darkness, he bent over the tied-up body of his girlfriend, only to have Evelyn strike his shoulder, his arm, his chest and his leg. Despite his

DIRTY HARRY

Directed by Don Siegel   1971

*It's not about a man who stands for violence,
it's about a man who can't understand society
tolerating violence.*

Clint Eastwood

Dirty Harry, a vicious urban thriller, began with
a shot of a memorial plaque paying tribute to
the police officers of San Francisco who had
given their lives in the line of duty.

Scorpio, a rooftop sniper, was holding the
city to ransom, promising to kill one person
every day unless he was paid $100,000. Girls,
priests and blacks were to be his targets. The
story was based on the crimes of the notorious
real-life Zodiac killer.

Detective Harry Callahan (called Dirty Harry,
because he was willing to do every dirty job
that came along) was given the job of delivering the ransom money. He had to follow a
series of instructions. Scorpio (who wore a belt
with a peace sign, giving much offence in some
quarters) gave Harry the runaround, bouncing
him all over town, from phone booth to phone
booth, allowing him barely any time at all to
get from Point A to Point B and threatening all
the time to kill a girl he had taken hostage. The
girl was, in fact, already raped and dead. Later
there was a gritty, stark documentary shot of
her naked body being lifted out of a manhole.

The destination was the huge cross at Mount
Davidson Park, a good place to get mugged,
picked up by a male prostitute and beaten to a
pulp by a serial killer wearing a mask. An even
better location was the floodlit Kezar Stadium,
where he ran Scorpio to ground. Scorpio
whined, blubbed and pleaded hysterically with
Callahan not to shoot him, insisting on his
rights. There were huge close-ups of his

Andy Robinson
and Clint Eastwood
in *Dirty Harry*

77

frightened face. Callahan was unflinching in his brutality. The last shot was breathtaking, starting with a close-up of him trampling on Scorpio's gaping wound and the camera pulling back and back until the two tiny figures disappeared in the darkness.

Scorpio (a memorable creation by Andy Robinson, son of Edward G.) was not brought to trial because Callahan had denied him medical attention and his legal rights to a counsel. The mayor gave his word that the criminal would not be molested. Harry, who was always much more interested in the rights of the victim than those of the criminal, was bitingly sarcastic ('I'm all broken up about this man's rights') and when Scorpio was released, he continued to harass him. The pursuit became an obsession.

Callahan never bothered to disguise his contempt for his superiors. When he was asked what proof he had that a man he had shot was going to rape a woman, he replied: 'When a naked man is chasing a woman through an alley with a butcher's knife and a hard-on, I figure he isn't out collecting for the Red Cross.' What informed Eastwood's performance was Harry's deep anger, his cold hatred and bitter resentfulness about the sacrifices the public and the cop on the street were expected to make. His fight was as much with the legal and political system that could not protect its citizens properly and stopped him doing his job.

Scorpio hijacked a busload of schoolchildren and threatened to shoot them if he wasn't paid $200,000 and provided with a jet to make his getaway. The major agreed. 'Nothing cute, nothing fancy,' said Callahan's immediate boss,

'just pay the ransom and report back here.' Harry had other ideas. There was a great shot of him waiting on a bridge which ran over the highway. He stood there like some mythical figure out of a Western, ready to leap on top of the bus. (Eastwood did his own stunt.) There followed a manic, gibbering ride, the bus swerving from side to side, as Scorpio tried to throw him off.

The building yard of a quarry company provided the setting for the final chase and shoot-out. Scorpio was cornered and took a little boy hostage, using him as a shield. Harry had a speech he had already used earlier in the film and which has passed into movie folklore: 'I know what you are thinking, punk. You're thinking did he fire six shots or only five. Now to tell you the truth I have forgotten. But being as this is a .44 magnum, the most powerful handgun in the world that will blow your head clean off, you'd have to ask yourself a question. Do I feel lucky? Well, do you, punk?' Scorpio ended up dead in the water. To nail a bastard, you needed a bastard.

Don Siegel, master of narrative, directed at a cracking pace and there was plenty of suspense. Good use was made of San Francisco, its streets, alleys, rooftops, freeways and industrial suburbs. A neon sign (Jesus Saves), lit up at night, dominated the skyline, making a nice, ironic comment. There was an excellent, eerie score by Lalo Schifrin.

The very last shot had Callahan throwing his badge away, just like Gary Cooper had done in *High Noon*. The box office, however, insisted he retrieve it, and he went on to make four more 'Dirty Harry' films: *Magnum Force, The Enforcer, Sudden Impact* and *The Dead Pool*.

Eastwood gives his best performance so far - tense, frill of implicit identification with his character.

Jay Cocks, *Time*

If he had used a better lead than Clint Eastwood, who is really more of a blessing to a lighting cameraman than to a director, he would have made a film to remember.

Christopher Hudson, *Spectator*

With policemen like Clint Eastwood and cowboys like John Wayne civilization has nothing to fear.

Ian Christie, *Daily Express*

His message has the disconcerting tone of someone calling out the vigilantes.

Playboy

Dirty Harry is obviously just a genre movie, but this action genre has always had fascist potential, and it has finally surfaced . . . since crime is caused by deprivation, misery, psychopathology and social injustice, *Dirty Harry* is a deeply immoral movie.

Pauline Kael, *New Yorker*

We were only interested in making the film a successful one, both as entertainment and at the box office. I can't understand why, when a film is made purely for entertainment, it should be criticized on a political basis.

Don Siegel

Clint Eastwood in
Dirty Harry

JOE KIDD

Directed by John Sturges   1972

*A guy sits in the audience; he's 25 and scared
stiff about what he's going to do with his life.
He wants to be that self-sufficient thing he sees
up there on the screen in my pictures. A super-
human character who has all the answers, is
doubly cool, exists on his own without society
or the help of society's police forces.*

Clint Eastwood

The time was the turn of the century, the place
was New Mexico and the subject was ethnic
minority rights and social injustice. The
Mexican Americans were being cheated by
grasping American landowners, who were in
connivance with the legal system to gain
control of their land. Trying to press their
rights in the courtroom of the small town of
Sinola, they were given the runaround by a
prejudiced judge.

Luis Chama (John Saxon), the Mexican
revolutionary leader, gave a public demon-
stration of his anger when he burned the
courtroom records and attempted to kidnap the
judge. He was foiled by Joe Kidd (Clint
Eastwood), who happened to be in the courtroom at the time, having been arrested the
night before for poaching, being disorderly and
avoiding arrest.

Joe, who had killed a deer on a reservation
and threatened to urinate over the courthouse,
preferred to stay in jail for 10 days rather than
pay a $10 fine. Frank Harlan (Robert Duvall),
one of the grasping landowners, paid the fine
and hired Joe to track down Chama. Initially,
dressed like a town dude, Joe looked cute in
his derby and cut a sexy figure. He flirted
openly with Harlan's mistress, even while one
of Harlan's men was looking on, and, strange to

say, the man didn't bother to report the
incident to his boss.

Eastwood, cast in his familiar role of
impassive, fearless gunfighter, acted with his
familiar laconic, laid-back charm and movie-
goers could sit back, safe in the knowledge that
if Joe were captured, he would escape and kill
any number of bad guys single-handed. The
performance was low-key and casual. The
violence was all bottled up, except in the
opening scene when, bruised and hungover, he
threw his coffee over his jailer's face and
bashed him in the face with a saucepan.

Harlan wasn't the sort of man who was going
to waste time arguing his non-existent case in
court. You could tell he was the really bad guy
by the fancy way he dressed and the manner in
which he addressed the Mexicans. 'We can cut
off your ears,' he said to one poor chap. 'We
can cut off something else, too,' added one of
his gang. Harlan had a nasty habit of killing
people in cold blood. However, it was when he
threatened to shoot innocent villagers in
batches of five that Joe, already equivocal in his
loyalties, began to realize he had made a
mistake in working for him and switched sides.

The screenplay was by Elmore Leonard,
author of *Hombre*, one of the best Westerns of
the 1960s. The story was meant to trace Joe's
journey towards moral understanding, but Joe's
motives remained obscure and the transformation of his character never happened,
basically because there was no character to
transform.

Everybody was unscrupulous. Chama was
willing to sacrifice a whole village rather than
give himself up. 'We only win if I stay alive,'
he declared. So it was very unconvincing when

John Saxon, Ron Sable,
Stella Garcia and Clint
Eastwood in *Joe Kidd*

Joe persuaded him to return to Sinola and to allow justice to take its course, especially since Chama had first-hand experience of American justice.

Don Stroud (who had played the murderer in *Coogan's Bluff*) was cast as Lamarr, one of Harlan's gang, and he had a rough time at the hands of Joe, being pushed down the stairs and hit in the face with the butt of a rifle. The only reason he didn't shoot Joe in the back (and he had plenty of opportunities to do so) was because the hero doesn't get killed half-way through a movie. It is the ugly bad guys, like Lamarr, who get killed off.

If the set looked a bit flimsy and ready for demolition, it became clear why this was so when Joe commandeered a steam train and drove through the buffers and into the town, ending up in the saloon. 'Got a prisoner for you!' he yelled. 'Jesus, Joe!' said the bartender, giving him a rifle. The steam train got the best notices.

The final shoot-out took place in the courtroom, where Joe, symbolically sitting in the judge's chair and acting as judge, jury and executioner, shot Harlan down and ordered the weak and compromised sheriff (Gregory Walcott) out of the courtroom. There was a wonderful close-up of Eastwood's searing eyes blazing with anger right across the screen's wide, letter-box frame. 'Is there anything I can do for you, Joe?' asked the sheriff. Joe replied with a very predictable punch to the jaw.

Clint Eastwood in
Joe Kidd

Clint Eastwood is one of the very few new stars who work absolutely in the old way. He is not exactly the most varied of actors; but just as a presence he holds the screen with total conviction: you can safely drape a film around him and be sure it will not crumple to the floor in a shapeless tangle.

John Russell Taylor, *The Times*

The casual authority with which Eastwood wields a shotgun while chucking down sandwiches and beer convinces us that John Wayne's mantle as Avenging Conscience of the Right will not go unclaimed after the Duke's passing.

Michael McKegney, *Village Voice*

The film's sympathies are all in the right liberal place; but it's tiresomely discursive and listless about its story-telling.

David Robinson, *Financial Times*

Clint Eastwood in
Joe Kidd

HIGH PLAINS DRIFTER

Directed by Clint Eastwood   1972

High Plains Drifter *was great fun because I liked the irony of it. I liked the irony of doing a stylized version of what happens if the sheriff in* High Noon *is killed and symbolically comes back as some avenging angel - and I think that's more hip than doing just a straight Western, the straight old conflicts we've all seen.*

Clint Eastwood

For a publicity shot, Eastwood had stood on the set of the town's cemetery, leaning on two gravestones bearing the names of Sergio Leone and Don Siegel, an acknowledgement of his debt to them. Well-written and well-directed, *High Plains Drifter* was a highly imaginative revenge story, one of the best Westerns of the 1970s and probably the first ever supernatural Western. The emphasis was on the archetypal myth rather than believable action. The film's title was a pun.

The setting was Lago, a frontier town in America's south-west in 1870. A lone rider came out of a hazy landscape to a weird and spooky soundtrack. The music stopped and gave way to just the sound of his horse's hooves on the gravel. It was some time before his face was seen. He remained totally impassive until he heard the crack of a whip. Once he had dismounted, the only sound was the clinking of his spurs. The whole sequence, alternating between the Stranger and the townspeople observing him, was a skilful introduction, a leisurely star entrance, beautifully photographed and edited by Bruce Surtees and Ferris Webster respectively.

The Stranger, dirty, unshaven, softly-spoken, wearing a magnificent long coat and a wide-

Previous page:
Clint Eastwood and
Billy Curtis in
High Plains Drifter

brimmed hat, entered the saloon and ordered a beer. 'Sleeping range bums don't usually stop in Lago. Life is a little too quick for them,' he was advised by one of three louts standing at the bar. 'I'm faster than you'll ever live to be,' he murmured and shortly afterwards, to prove his point, he shot the three louts dead. 'What did you say your name was?' asked the barber.

A coarse and volatile whore (Mariana Hill), who called him 'trash' and then, ill advisedly, accused him of not being a man, was dragged off to a stable and given 'a lesson in manners': i.e. she was raped in broad daylight. Nobody came to her rescue; only a dwarf came to gawp. She was so angry she shot him three times while he was taking a bath in a tub and smoking a cigar; he merely disappeared under the water to resurface, still smoking his cigar. He then went to the local hotel and lay down on his bed and dreamt of a terrible whipping. The nightmare (to a spooky accompaniment on the soundtrack) would recur, but the second time round the sequence would be seen through the memory of the dwarf.

The town hired the Stranger as a gunfighter to protect them from three returning troubleshooters who had been in jail for a year. They offered him a free hand and anything he wanted. Taking them at their word, he appointed the dwarf as mayor and sheriff and requisitioned weaponry, drink, food, wood, blankets and the hotel. He bossed, rooked and humiliated them all and soon they were at each other's throats. 'I knew you were cruel, but I didn't know how far you could go,' said the hotelier's wife (Verna Bloom). 'Well, you still don't,' he replied. Finally, he forced them to paint the whole town red, including the

Verna Bloom and
Clint Eastwood in
High Plains Drifter

church, and alter its name to Hell. It couldn't have been worse if the devil himself had ridden into Lago.

The Stranger, having trained them in the art of defence, deserted them at the very moment the troubleshooters were riding into town and he did not return until they had all been rounded up. He then dealt with the trio personally, whipping one to death, hanging another and shooting down the third. The killings were played out against the burning buildings, a flaming, hellish background. 'Who are you?' screamed Geoffrey Lewis in his role of leading troubleshooter.

The Stranger was Jim Duncan, their former sheriff, come back from beyond the grave to settle a private score and take his revenge, not only on his murderers but also on the citizens, who had stood by and let him be killed. The three troubleshooters were the men who had whipped him to death. (This had already been signalled on their first appearance, on their release from prison, when the soundtrack had played a variation on the spooky theme.) Eastwood, impassive, unearthly, totally without pity, was a charismatic spectre in black, a man to make people afraid, yet what was so good about the performance was the dry humour he brought to the role.

The fact that Buddy Van Horn was credited with playing the Marshal was misleading; perhaps deliberately so. Van Horn played the Marshal only in the sense that he was the stuntman who stood in for Eastwood in the scene where he was whipped to death. In the original script, the High Plains Drifter was Jim Duncan's brother; the credit allowed cinemagoers to think he still could be; and, of course,

Mariana Hill and
Clint Eastwood in
High Plains Drifter

if he were the brother, it might help to explain
why the people of Lago did not recognize him.

The supporting characters - the mine owners
(Mitchell Ryan and Jack Ging), the mayor
(Stefan Gierasch), the hotelier (Ted Hartley),
the sheriff (Walter Barnes), the barber (William
O' Connell), the preacher (Robert Donner) –
were all from stock but, within their one-
dimensional terms, they were well-observed
and Ernest Tidyman's cynical screenplay
mocked their 'short supply of guts' and their
farcical ineptitude with firearms. The dwarf
was played by Billy Curtis, who had played the
Lord High Mayor of the Munchkins in *The
Wizard of Oz*.

Eastwood's own performance and his
direction were badly underrated by the critics,
The production, shot in continuity, had a
dream-like quality, the bleak and desolate
countryside ideal for the surreal and allegorical
subject matter. Bruce Surtees's expressive

photography, with its low-key atmospheric
lighting and imaginative angling and framing of
individual shots, was superb.

I suppose you could call it a supernatural Western
except that there is nothing natural about it and it
certainly isn't super.

Ian Christie, *Daily Express*

What emerges is a narcissistic essay in style, in
which characterization and story development are
too often sacrificed to the visual tricks and
mannerisms of Eastwood's camerawork.

Nigel Andrews. *Financial Times*

As a director, Clint Eastwood is not as good as he
seems to think he is. As an actor, he is probably
better than he allows himself to be . . . Rarely are
humble Westerns permitted to drift around on such
a highfalutin plain.

Richard Schickel, *Time*

As a pasta-parable it drowns in its own ketchup . . .
This is the kind of film that relies on the savage
shimmer of its visuals to blind us to its lack of ethic.

Tom Hutchinson, *Sunday Telegraph*

I can see the cineastes hovering over it like vultures
over the body of the West.

Derek Malcolm, *Guardian*

John Wayne didn't like *High Plains Drifter* and let
me know it. He wrote me a letter putting it down,
saying it was not the West. I was trying to get away
from what he and Gary Cooper and others had
done.

Clint Eastwood quoted by Peter Mconnald,
Evening Standard

BREEZY

Directed by Clint Eastwood   1973

Breezy was the name of a 17-year-old vagrant
hippie (Kay Lenz), who was having a romantic
affair with a 50-year-old divorced real estate
salesman (William Holden). The affair was
handled with sensitivity and quiet amusement
by the scriptwriter, Jo Heims. The result was a
matinée mixture of lyrical slush and sharp
mordancy, with a subtle performance by
Holden and an astringent one by Lenz.

It's performed beautifully, laced with a quietly
ironic wit, and quite lovely to look at.

Geoff Andrew, *Time Out*

Unluckily, in the charmless performance and
staging it emerges rather more simply as a middle-
aged man's erotic nymphet daydream.

David Robinson, *The Times*

Fifty-year-old estate agents with a sentimental
streak might enjoy it.

Ian Christie, *Daily Express*

Clint Eastwood and
William Holden on
the set of *Breezy*

MAGNUM FORCE

Directed by Ted Post   1973

Magnum Force began with a famous quote from *Dirty Harry*: 'This is a .44 magnum, the most powerful handgun in the world, and it could blow your head clean off. Do you feel lucky?' Both the line and the gun were aimed directly at the cinemagoer in the cinema. The poster had already made it abundantly clear that Harry Callahan's magnum was his phallus.

Once again the theme was law and order. Two hundred murders had been committed in the city during the previous year. A racketeering trade union leader, who had been indicted for 23 of them and had not been convicted, had murdered a union reformer and got away with it yet again because of a legal technicality. While he was being driven from the courthouse along the highway, he, his attorney, his bodyguard and his driver were all shot at point-blank range by a cop on a motorcycle. Something of a voyeur, the cop then went on to shoot naked gangsters in a swimming-pool and naked drug traffickers in bed, throwing one unlucky girl out of a window. 'Someone is trying to put the courts out of business,' observed Harry's boss. 'So far you've said nothing wrong,' replied Harry.

The cop, in his leather gear, boots and goggles, looked every inch a fascist and, since his face was hidden by the visor of his white crash helmet, every moviegoer who had seen *Dirty Harry* immediately jumped to the conclusion that Callahan was impersonating the cop, killing off all the top criminals in the city and saving the tax payer a lot of money. After all, it was well known that nobody hated hoodlums as much as he did and that he had never seen anything wrong in shooting people, so long as the right people got shot.

Hal Holbrook and Clint Eastwood in *Magnum Force*

Callahan discovered that the cop was actually one of four rookie cops and that there was a whole organization working within the police force (a sort of death squad on the Brazilian model) that was taking the law into its own hands, acting as judge, jury and freelance public executioners. Earlier, before he knew that they were the murderers, he had been impressed with their skill down at the shooting range. When his partner had told him about rumours going round that they were all homosexual, this hadn't worried Harry one bit: 'If the rest of you could shoot like them, I wouldn't care a damn if the whole department were queer!'

The rookies, who had obviously seen *Dirty Harry* and were clearly Callahan's disciples, managed to out-dirty Dirty Harry. The leader of the quartet (David Soul) argued that they were simply ridding society of killers who would be caught and sentenced anyway, if the courts worked properly. 'It's not just a question of whether or not to use violence. There's simply no other way.'

'I'm afraid you have misjudged me,' replied Harry, answering not only them but all his critics and making it unequivocal that he didn't approve of the vigilantes and that he upheld the law. 'I hate the goddamn system, but until someone comes along with some changes that make sense, I'll stick with it.'

Lieutenant Briggs (Hal Holbrook), his superior and a nasty bit of work, was in charge of the vigilantes. He tried to justify their actions by talking about retribution; the police, he said, had to use the same methods as the criminals if they were to win,

Magnum Force ended with *Bullitt*-like car

and motorcycle chases and a facile climax in a deserted shipyard with Callahan and the rookies creeping around the hold of a ship, playing hide-and-seek. Harry was in fine fettle, knocking Briggs out, punching one rookie to death and then driving straight into another. And just when you thought the movie was over, Briggs was back and threatening to prosecute him for killing three cops. 'Who's going to believe you?' he cried, driving off. 'You're a killer, a maniac!' Seconds later his car blew up. 'A man's got to know his limitations,' observed Harry, who had planted the bomb.

In *Dirty Harry*, Callahan had been described as hating Limeys, Micks, Hebes, fat Dagos, Niggers, Hunkies, Chinks, Mexicans. Now, just in case anybody should have got the impression that he was a racist, his new partner was black (Felton Perry) and the girl downstairs (Adele Yoshioka) was Chinese. She asked him what she had to do to go to bed with him. This was a question many female cinemagoers had been asking themselves ever since the 'Dollars' trilogy. The answer was pretty encouraging. 'Try knocking on the door,' he said.

There was a terribly unconvincing sequence on a hijacked plane, when he was disguised as a pilot. It was there for a gratuitous shoot-out and a quick joke. 'This may sound silly, but can you fly?' asked his co-pilot as they drove down the runway. 'No, never had a lesson. 'The incident belonged in another movie. A shoot-out in a shop was more relevant and far more exciting. There was a moment of real tension when a bomb had been delivered to his partner's letter box and he was desperately trying to phone and warn him.

Clint Eastwood in
Magnum Force

93

Clint Eastwood and
David Soul in
Magnum Force

Clint Eastwood re-creates the maverick cop with all
his charismatic if dubious magnetism.

George Melly, *Observer*

The trouble with right-wing films masquerading as
left-wing films attacking right-wing politics is that
they get into such embarrassing knots. How to
convince people that you are against chaps taking
the law into their own hands when your hero can
only survive by doing just that?

Gavin Millar, *Listener*

A cruel and largely humourless film, frenetically
directed by Ted Post, but irresistibly exciting even
when there is hardly a character for whom you give
a damn.

Cecil Wilson, *Daily Mail*

By turning Harry Callahan into a hypocrite, the
makers of *Magnum Force* expose their own
hypocrisy, as well as their lack of understanding of
the Eastwood phenomenon.

Jon Landau, *Rolling Stone*

The violence, as usual, offended a lot of
people. One criminal, making his getaway, had
a metal girder smash through the windscreen of
his car and right into his body. There was also
an unpleasant scene in the back of a taxi cab
when a black pimp (Albert Popwell) got his
orgasm while murdering a double-dealing
prostitute by pouring a can of drain cleaner
down her throat.

As for Eastwood, deadshot and deadpan, he
was his familiar dour, hard-bitten, cynical self.

Clint Eastwood isn't offensive; he isn't an actor, so
one could hardly call him a bad actor. He'd have to
do something before we could consider him bad at it
. . . Eastwood's inexpressiveness travels prepos-
terously well. He's utterly unbelievable in his
movies - inhumanely tranquil, controlled and
assured - and yet he seems to represent something
that isn't so unbelievable.

Pauline Kael, *New Yorker*

THUNDERBOLT AND LIGHTFOOT

Directed by Michael Cimino   1974

The wolf shall dwell with the lamb and the leopard shall lie down with the kid.

Isaiah 11.6

Thunderbolt and Lightfoot, part buddy movie, part chase movie, part bank robbery movie, a story of greed and brutality, began as farce, turned to thriller and ended in tragedy. Michael Cimino's direction was taut and the pace was fast. His screenplay had a genuine freshness, with a real eye for character, situation and detail. The locations in Montana and round Great Falls, photographed by Frank Stanley, were beautiful and provided a wonderful backdrop.

The action got off to an arresting start when a sermon in a small country church was interrupted by a man firing a gun. The preacher beat a hasty retreat across the wheatfield (an Andrew Wyeth landscape), hotly pursued by the wheezing gunman. Shot in the arm, he was saved by a young man who happened to be driving past in a car he had just stolen.

The preacher (Clint Eastwood) was not really a preacher, but a professional safe-breaker in disguise, the notorious Thunderbolt, hunted by his former partner-in-crime, Red Leary, who believed, quite wrongly, that he had pocketed half a million dollars from their last bank raid. The money was, in fact, stashed behind a blackboard in a nineteenth-century one-room schoolhouse.

The amateur car thief (Jeff Bridges) was called Lightfoot, a charming, talkative, self-confident and not very bright 23-year-old drifter, with a big grin and a cliché ready for every occasion. They made a good pair, the camaraderie nicely developed, the age

Jeff Bridges and Clint Eastwood in *Thunderbolt and Lightfoot*

difference and clash of personalities working very much in the script's favour. Bridges, brash and breezy, provided the exuberance. Eastwood, jaded and grainy, provided the restraint. The rapport between the two actors was self-evident.

George Kennedy played the brutal, asthmatic Red Leary. Geoffrey Lewis played Goody, his weak-kidneyed partner who was always getting in the way and seemed never to know what to do in an emergency. 'WHAT DO YOU WANT ME TO DO, RED? ('Kill the son of a bitch!') 'HERE?' ('Yes.') 'NOW?' ('Now.') Lewis and Kennedy made a comic duo, especially when they were driving around, squashed together in a silly ice-cream van; except there was nothing funny about the way Leary kicked Goody out of the car when Goody was shot and left him to die in the road. Leary himself came to a sadistic end, savaged (off-screen) by a guard dog.

Jeff Bridges, George
Kennedy and Clint
Eastwood in *Thunderbolt
and Lightfoot*

There was no consistency of tone and the
appeal of the film lay in the way Cimino mixed
light-hearted humour and freewheeling
violence. The screenplay was often extremely
funny in its small touches, as, for instance, in
an incident when a girl, wearing only her
panties and bra, ran out of a chalet, crying
'Rape!' 'Do you think we should stop here?'
asked a horrified woman, driving up in a car,
'Why not?' asked her husband. Thunderbolt
had just had sex with the girl; or rather, she
had just had sex with him and he hadn't
enjoyed the experience one bit. The leopard
would probably have preferred to have lain
down with the kid; the gay subtext was always
there for those who wanted it.

There was, too, an amusing scene when a
bank manager and his wife were tied up and so
were their daughter and the daughter's boy-
friend, who happened to be in her bed at the
time. The robbers, having put pingpong balls in
their mouths, left the couple as naked as they
had found them and put everything back in
place, only reversing their positions so that the
boy was now underneath the girl.

There were some nice jokes, in passing,
about the use of credit cards and feminists, on
motorbikes, wielding hammers against male
chauvinist motorists. There was also a farcical
cameo performance by Bill McKinney as a
crazy driver, a real nutter, travelling with a
boot full of rabbits so he could let them loose

and shoot them. Cliff Emmich was perfectly cast as a fat security man, whiling away the time reading pornography and seduced by Lightfoot disguised as a flirtatious girl. Bridges in drag remained resolutely masculine and parked his gun in the back of his underpants.

The film ended with Thunderbolt buying Lightfoot his dream car, a white Cadillac. Lightfoot died before he could use it. The unexpected, downbeat finish was highly affecting; all the more so for audiences not having fully appreciated just how severely hurt Lightfoot had been after a vicious beating by Leary. 'We made it,' he said just before he died. 'Do you know something? I felt us accomplished something, a good job. I feel proud of myself, like a hero.' Thunderbolt's loss was palpable.

Eastwood, always an unselfish actor, let Bridges run away with the film and Bridges, easy, relaxed and clearly enjoying himself, was immensely likeable. He got all the notices and was nominated for an Oscar. He had already been nominated for an Oscar at 21 for his performance in *The Last Picture Show*.

Mr Eastwood grows more appealing with every movie.

John Coleman, *New Statesman*

A film that grips the heart without insulting the intellect.

Tom Hutchinson, *Sunday Telegraph*

Eastwood unwinds a little from his customary characterization of a terse, razor-eyed stranger, breaking through to a kind boyish affability . . .

Jay Cocks, *Time*

Eastwood remains Eastwood even when he is showing, in effect, the obverse side of Dirty Harry.

Hugh Herbert, *Guardian*

Clint Eastwood and Jeff Bridges in *Thunderbolt and Lightfoot*

They [the public] prefer the seemingly ordinary fellow who speaks in a voice and idiom they can understand. They identify with him when he merely shrugs his shoulders in disbelief at the inanity that passes across the screen. And they feel for him when he lashes out against it - after society has intruded on his freedom and sense of order. Above all, they admire his street smarts.

Jon Landau, *Rolling Stone*

THE EIGER SANCTION

Directed by Clint Eastwood   1975

The Eiger is a mountain in Switzerland. Sanction was a codename for a killing. The Eiger is grim, observed somebody. So was the film.

Clint Eastwood was cast as an art historian lecturing on art in an American college. He was a former climber who had failed to climb the Eiger twice. ('He could climb all over me,' confessed one of his female students to a girlfriend.) He was also a retired assassin - codename Hemlock - tempted back into service by the promise of $20,000 and a painting by Pissarro. He already had a large and clandestine collection of Impressionists, 21 masterpieces by such artists as El Greco, Matisse and Klee, all bought with the fees from his killings.

Hemlock, without conscience and motivated only by greed and avarice, was liable to throw his assailants out of windows and beat up their bodyguards. He wore dark glasses and was willing to scale drainpipes and even mountains to get his man. He agreed to a sanction if he was given an Internal Revenue statement saying that he was the legal owner of the art collection and without tax liability. 'You drive a hard bargain,' observed Dragon, the head of a spy network, a total albino, who could not stand either light, cold or germs and whose blood needed to be changed every six months. The cartoon-like Dragon, a bulbous, blind freak whose scenes were filmed in a blood-red glow, was just the sort of silly character you would normally expect to find in a James Bond movie.

Hemlock's major target was one of a number of international climbers on the north face of the Eiger. The question was, which one? Dragon didn't know. Hemlock went into

training, limbering up in Mountain Valley, Arizona, a familiar and much-loved location, home of stagecoaches, wagons, Injuns, the US cavalry and John Wayne. 'How old are you? 35?' asked his trainer. 'Give or take,' replied Eastwood with a wry smile, looking as rugged and as weathered as the Eiger. George Kennedy played the trainer, an old buddy, a loud, jovial, hail-fellow-well-met type.

Hemlock practised on the 600-foot needle rock, which the Indians called The Totem, and very phallic it looked, too. There was a staggering helicopter shot to prove that Eastwood and Kennedy had actually been on top of the peak. They were there for five hours while the camera crew got the right shots. 'I defy anyone,' said Clint Eastwood in an interview with Victor David of the *Daily Express*, 'to watch it and not get that lurching feeling that we are in real danger up there. The trick was a hair-raising one to pull off successfully but every time I hear someone say "Wow" I feel happy. However, I don't think I'll be trying anything like it again. The helicopter actually lowered us on to the top, which is criss-crossed with cracks so that you think the whole structure is about to disintegrate.'

One of Hemlock's sanctions was homosexual, Miles (Jack Cassidy), who was so camp that he had a dog called Faggot. Hemlock drove Miles far into the desert and abandoned him without food and water. Faggot decided to ditch his mistress and hitched a lift back in Hemlock's car.

Hemlock, who had quite a reputation as a stud, had sex only twice during the whole course of the film and on both occasions it was with unfortunate results. The first time he was

Clint Eastwood and the professional climbers/ cameramen on top of The Totem in Mountain Valley in *The Eiger Sanction*

Clint Eastwood and
George Kennedy in
The Eiger Sanction

together. The spy story got lost on the mountains. Audiences, who should have been wondering who the killer was, were just watching climbers, played by bad actors. Eastwood's direction was fatally slack and the climbing failed to excite.

The score tried very hard (too hard) to make drama where there was none. The basic trouble was that the whole cinema knew that George Kennedy was playing the villain. The only person who didn't know was Hemlock; and he didn't find out until he was at the end of his tether, hanging over a precipice and the villain was telling him to cut the rope.

Eastwood visibly did his own climbing and there were the occasional dramatic shots of him in crevasses and on the cliff face. The real stars were the genuine climbers and the photographers.

The hazards of the expedition are spectacularly photographed with the north face of the Eiger looking considerably more dramatic than the north face of Eastwood.

Ian Christie, *Daily Express*

Clint Eastwood's direction is only matched by a performance in the leading role that's about as frozen as the Eiger itself.

Derek Malcolm, *Guardian*

robbed by a black air stewardess, who turned out to be a spy. The second time, he was nearly murdered by his topless mountain trainer, who had already put him through it. So much for safe sex.

The Eiger Sanction was really two films: one was about mountain-climbing and the other was about spies, and the two never really came

Most depressing, Eastwood directs in a bland, blunt and boorish fashion.

Richard Combs, *Monthly Film Bulletin*

Fortunately, the Eiger resists even Clint Eastwood as star and director. It is bigger than both of him.

Alexander Walker, *Evening Standard*

THE OUTLAW JOSEY WALES

Directed by Clint Eastwood   1976

Josey Wales was a Missouri farmer, living in the aftermath of the American Civil War, still a time of blood and dying. His wife and child were killed, his house burned to the ground and he himself sabred and left for dead by Union guerillas known as Redlegs. At their grave, the camera framed his grief-stricken face in close-up to look like a medieval painting of Christ collapsing under the weight of the cross he was erecting. Josey, a man of peace, turned avenging angel and joined a band of Confederate irregulars on the rampage, hell-bent on putting things right with summary executions.

The prologue, brilliantly edited by Ferris Webster, gave way to impressionistic credit titles: a fleeting, monochromatic, smoky montage of the war straight out of Matthew Brady. The colour gradually seeped into the frame only when the story proper began, an effect which brought back memories of the opening of *The Beguiled.*

The prologue was immediately followed by another memorable sequence when the renegades, having been promised full amnesty if they surrendered, were massacred at the very moment they were pledging their loyalty to the United States. Josey (who had refused to surrender) rode in to the rescue, firing his pistols, and once he had got hold of the Union machine-gun he killed practically the whole camp. Of the renegades, only he and a wounded boy soldier survived.

From then on Josey was hunted by Union soldiers and bounty hunters alike. There was a $5,000 reward on his head. 'A man's got to do something for a living,' said one bounty hunter. 'Dying ain't much of a living,' replied Josey. (If the film had a message, that was it.) Josey was

Clint Eastwood in *The Outlaw Josey Wales*

not a hard man to track. He left bodies every-where, yet somehow he always managed to escape capture, even when capture looked most certain. His survival was often hard to credit. He spat a lot, too, directing black jetties of tobacco at corpses, dogs, insects and travelling salesmen. The spittle was his trade-mark and signature.

Two men in particular were in pursuit of him, though it could be argued that he was just as much in pursuit of them as they were of him. The first was Terrill (Bill McKinney), a bloodthirsty looter and pillager who had killed his wife and child and was now a Regular Federal Authority. The second was his former friend, Fletcher (John Vernon), who had betrayed the renegades. Fletcher had been tricked, but Josey didn't know that.

Clint Eastwood in *The Outlaw Josey Wales*

There was a good moment of tension when audiences wondered how he was going to escape the horse soldiers crossing on the ferry. The answer was neat and simple: he didn't attempt to shoot them, he simply shot the ferry's rope and let them and their horses drift down the river. William O'Connell was very funny as the nervous ferryman, hedging his bets and singing 'Dixie' and 'The Battle Hymn of the Republic' (the songs of both armies) with equal enthusiasm.

A sentimental relationship developed between Josey and the boy soldier (Sam Bottoms), whose death scene was momentarily interrupted by two hillbilly bounty hunters (Len Lesser and Douglas McGrath). Josey didn't bother to bury them. 'Buzzards got to eat,' he said, 'same as worms.' Later he would use the boy's dead body as a decoy, putting it on a horse and letting it run through the enemy camp while he made his escape during the distraction.

A great part of the movie's success was the casting of Chief Dan George as a wise, old, white-haired Cherokee called Lone Watie. Dressed in top hat and frock coat (in order to look like Abe Lincoln), Watie may have looked comic but he had enormous dignity. He belonged, he explained, to one of the so-called civilized tribes. Indeed, in Washington, the Second Secretary of the Interior had given the tribe medals for looking civilized. 'They call us civilized because we are easy to sneak up on. The white man has been sneaking up on us for years. They told us we wouldn't be happy here. They said we would be happier in the nations. So they took away our land and sent us here. We can't trust the white man. I didn't

Clint Eastwood and
Chief Dan George in
The Outlaw Josey Wales

surrender. They took away my horse and made him surrender.'

When the Cherokees told the Secretary about their land being stolen and their people dying (Watie had lost his wife and two sons on 'The Trail of Tears'), the Secretary exhorted them to endeavour to survive. The Cherokees thought about what he had said for a long time and, when they had thought about it long enough, they declared war on the Union. The dry humour and deadpan irony were perfect and the interplay between Dan George and Eastwood was a pleasure to watch. The witty, humane script was based on the novel *Gone to Texas*, by Forrest Carter who, clear-cut and simplistic in his attitude to the Comanches, portrayed them with solemnity and understanding.

There was a dramatic moment at the frontier town when Josey was recognized by a carpet-bagger (Woodrow Parfrey) selling phoney

medicine for every ailment. 'Well, are you going to pull those pistols and whistle 'Dixie'?' he asked five soldiers and, while they dithered, he shot four of them, leaving the fifth to Lone Watie.

There were two classic Western images of Josey. The first had him standing silhouetted in an open doorway before he dealt with two traders molesting a squaw. The second had him standing on a ridge, silhouetted against the sky, before he rode to the rescue of two Kansas pilgrims who were being attacked by Comancheros. The granny (Paula Trueman) was a doughty, bigoted, cartoon-like old lady. Her daughter (Sondra Locke), who had been stripped naked and nearly raped, was a simple-minded, scrawny girl who, predictably, fell in love with Josey.

They had hardly settled into their new idyllic home before they were being threatened by the Comanches. Josey rode out to meet their

Bill McKinney and
Clint Eastwood in
The Outlaw Josey Wales

chief, Ten Bears (Will Sampson), in order to ward off the attack. 'I say,' he declared in a key line of the script, 'men can live together without butchering each other.' The two men made a blood pact, succeeding where governments had failed.

By treating Josey as a man rather than as a myth, the two women succeeded in turning an avenging angel back into the peace-loving farmer he once had been; but Josey was still an outlaw and he had to move on. As he was leaving the farm, he found Terrill and escort waiting to arrest him. This time it was the pilgrims who came to his rescue. In the final scene he met Fletcher, who affected not to recognize him and told him that he was going to continue his search in Mexico and that when he found Josey Wales, he would tell him that the Civil War was over. 'I guess we all died a little in that damn war,' replied Josey, riding off into the setting sun, a traditional ending, but with one important difference, for he was going back to the farm to begin his life afresh. The story had come full circle.

John Vernon's fine performance as Fletcher had a memorable and much-quoted retort. On being told by the Union commander that 'the spoils of war belonged to the victors', he had replied that there was another well-known saying: 'Don't piss down my neck and tell me it's raining.'

The Outlaw Josey Wales was filmed in a number of breathtaking locations and the changing seasons were stunningly photographed by Bruce Surtees. Jerry Fielding's music was nominated for an Oscar for best original score.

Scratch an Eastwood movie and you'll find a political philosophy three paces to the right of Thomas Jefferson.

Derek Malcolm, *Guardian*

He is not merely part of the landscape. He seems to have grown out of it: a fixture as solid as Monument Valley.

Margaret Hinxman, *Daily Mail*

What is remarkable about the film, however, is the skill with which Eastwood gives this theme a resonantly full orchestration while at the same time silencing any propensities to pretension or sentimentality lurking in the script.

Tom Milne, Monthly *Film Bulletin*

There is nothing in the completion of Wales's full and vicious campaign that justifies all the dramatic headshots and vocal seething - nothing that is except old-fashioned heroics and directorial self-love.

Russell Davies, *Observer*

THE ENFORCER

Directed by James Fargo 1976

Criminals describing themselves as The People's Revolutionary Strike Force were holding San Francisco to ransom. They had enough explosives to blow half the city away and wanted $5 million. They were led by a blue-eyed, ginger-haired, knife-stabbing, gun-blazing psychopath (DeVeren Bookwalter), a dull caricature of a blue-eyed, ginger-haired, knife-stabbing, gun-blazing psychopath.

The Enforcer began with a pre-credit sequence: the murder of two truck drivers. The film proper started with a joke. There was Harry Callahan kicking a man who had just had a heart attack and dragging him out of the restaurant by the scruff of the neck. This seemed a bit rough, even by Harry's normal standards, until it was revealed the man was a professional restaurant pay-dodger who feigned heart attacks. Later, for those who liked that sort of thing, there would be sick jokes during a post-mortem and schoolboy jokes in a massage parlour about customers having a quick lesson in 32 positions of lovemaking with an inflatable doll for $75.

Harry was, as usual, a one-man anti-crime wave, fighting not only criminals but also the police department, bureaucratic blunders, corrupt local government and wet liberals who let crime go unpunished and were willing to pay ransom money when the mayor was kidnapped. Harry, on the other hand, was always ready to meet violence with violence, His ring-wing, chauvinist, sledge-hammer, bulldozing approach to thuggery may not have appealed to everybody, but it undoubtedly continued to strike a cord with audiences, who empathized with one cop's widow. 'It's war, isn't it?' she said at her husband's deathbed.

Clint Eastwood and
Albert Popwell in
The Enforcer

'I guess I never really understood that.'

Callahan had class. He got things done; fuelled by his anger, he never gave up. There was a typical scene when three men were holding hostages in a liquor store. One minute he was spread-eagled on the floor, the next he was driving a car through the shopfront window at them. (As he said, they had asked for a car and he was going to give them one.) The shop, the door, the window, the stock, the shelving, the car and, of course, the hold-up men were a complete write-off. A bill came in to the police department for $14,379. He was reprimanded by his boss for excessive use of force and transferred to personnel division.

Callahan, who treated his new boss, Captain McKay (Bradford Dillman) with exactly the same undisguised contempt he had shown for his previous boss, had a nice line in laconic put-downs: 'Your mouth-wash ain't making it.' McKay, looking after his career and kowtowing to the mayor, pointed out that the minority community had just about had enough with Dirty Harry's dirty methods and he wanted

Tyne Daly and
Clint Eastwood in
The Enforcer

restraint, not a Wild West Show. He was always asking Callahan to hand in his badge and then having to hand it back in an emergency. Harry got on far better with a black militant (Albert Popwell, a stylish actor), who was waiting patiently for the whites to blow each other up.

The mayor (John Crawford), a shallow and devious opportunist, something of a caricature, appointed one of the first full-time women homicide inspectors in America, but only because he thought it would win him votes in the coming election. As a result, Callahan (famed for his misogyny) got lumbered with a woman for a partner. There was an enjoyable moment when he was asked to accept a commendation for something he hadn't done (as part of a photo call for the mayor) and he

told the mayor that the badge was a seven-point suppository and to stick it up his arse.

There was also something endearing about watching Tyne Daly playing cops and robbers, running about, trying to keep up with Harry. She was a good sport and it was not long before she had coaxed some humanity out of him and they were having beers, exchanging *double entendres* and he was paying her pretty compliments. During one of their conversations, she managed to bring up something that most audiences had been meaning to ask for some time but had never dared to ask. 'You're cold, bold Callahan with his great big .44,' she said. 'Every other cop in the city is satisfied with a .38 or .357. What do you have to carry that cannon for? Is it for

penetration?' ('Does everything have to have a sexual connotation for you?' he asked.)

The Enforcer was stronger on comedy than on suspense. There was an over-extended sequence when Callahan was chasing a black suspect down alleys and over rooftops and they both fell through a skylight, landing in a pornographic photographer's studio, which was good for a bit of complimentary nudity. They dashed out into the street and ended up in a church, where the suspect was ultimately caught and knocked out. 'Callahan, I think you are a disgrace to this city!' squalled the priest. The jazz accompaniment, the casting of a comedian as the suspect and the utter lack of urgency made it clear that the chase was not to be taken too seriously, though the man had, in fact, just let off a bomb in a public lavatory.

The climax took place at Alcatraz. The policewoman went the way of all Callahan's partners, taking the bullet while trying to save him. Dying, she found time to apologize: 'Oh, Harry, I messed it up. Don't concern yourself. Kill him!' You could tell how chuffed he was by her death by the way he screamed, 'You fucking fruit!' at the blue-eyed, ginger-haired, knife-stabbing, gun-blazing psychopath and blasted him to smithereens with his enormous bazooka (so much more penetrating than his magnum). Tyne Daly would be reincarnated as Lacey in *Cagney and Lacey*.

As an *homme fatal*, Eastwood is in the Mata Hari class.

Clancy Sigal, *Spectator*

Clint Eastwood in *The Enforcer*

Dirty Harry is as exciting to watch as he would be appalling to encounter.

Alan Brien, *Sunday Times*

The Enforcer is fairish fun - and certainly no threat to liberal democracy.

Richard Schickel, *Time*

How can we liberals be so wet? Why don't we go out and shoot something? A decent film, preferably.

Russell Davies, *Observer*

Its sociological conclusions are glib and too easily aligned with fashionable clichés about violence, but director James Fargo winds it all up to a very tight climatic tension.

Tom Hutchinson, *Sunday Telegraph*

THE GAUNTLET

Directed by Clint Eastwood   1977

The Commissioner of Police in Phoenix was hand in glove with the local Mafia and they had provided him with a hooker. What the Commissioner enjoyed most was to get the hooker to strip, lie on her stomach, open her legs, and then, while he pointed a gun at her backside, he masturbated.

The Mafia boss was arrested. So was Gus Mally (the hooker in question), a key witness for the prosecution in the forthcoming trial, The Commissioner, realizing the whole of Arizona would know that he masturbated unless he could stop Mally getting to the witness stand, dispatched a cop to extradite her from prison in Las Vegas and bring her back to Phoenix. He didn't tell the cop how important she was; nor did he inform him that he intended to get them both killed *en route* from the prison to the airport.

The cop was Ben Shockley, an alcoholic, incompetent and discredited. He wasn't very bright, either, and had no idea what was going on; and even after he had gone to a betting shop and found odds of 50-1 were being quoted that the hooker wouldn't make it to the trial, he still couldn't believe he had been set up and that his own people had betrayed him. He changed his mind, though, when the car he had ordered was blown up and cops were chasing them down the highway, shooting to kill. The Commissioner had picked him precisely because he was a drunken bum, a faded number on a rusty badge, and therefore expendable. Fortunately for him, the hooker was brighter than he was. She said she had a degree. (In hooking?).

Clint Eastwood played the dumb cop. Sondra Locke played the foul-mouthed hooker. The dialogue was racy and the sparring was good fun. She called him a big .45 calibre fruit. He punched her in the face. She kicked him in the balls. You knew they were going to fall in love, get married, settle down and have kids. Occasionally, Eastwood and Locke (who were partners in real life) would share a private joke, which audiences could enjoy: 'You don't even know if I am good in bed!' she said. 'I'll take that on faith,' he replied. Eastwood is on record as saying that he never wanted to play Shakespeare, but, on the evidence of their performances here, they would have been well cast in a reworking of *The Taming of the Shrew*, updated to the nineteenth century, set in America and played as a Western.

There was a sequence where they were on a motorbike, which they had stolen from some hippies, and were being pursued by a low-flying helicopter. The action (well photographed by Rexford Metz) was not as thrilling as it should have been, not least because it was unbelievable that the sniper should have kept missing them. You would not have had to have seen many movies to know that the helicopter was going to end up crashing into either the mountain or the pylons and bursting into flames.

Ditching the bike, they jumped on to a moving cattle train, only to find themselves reunited with the hippies, who gave Shockley a terrible beating, using him as they might have used a punchbag. Mally saved him the only way she knew how: by being willing to be raped. (It seemed just the other day that Locke was being raped in the Nevada desert in *The Outlaw Josey Wales*.) Shockley, somehow, managed to recover in time to save her.

Clint Eastwood and
Sondra Locke in
The Gauntlet

Clint Eastwood and
Sondra Locke in
The Gauntlet

The happy pair then hijacked a country bus.
('Good luck!' said a dear little old lady, who
had just been chucked off it.) Once the bus had
been armoured with sheet metal, they ran the
gauntlet of armed police on streets and roofs.
Round upon round of ammunition hit the bus.
Shockley kept driving. When he got a token
wound in the leg, Mally gamely took over. Why
on earth didn't the police shoot the tyres? It
was all so deliberately ludicrous that it was
never exciting. The peppered bus did not
expire until it had climbed the steps of Phoenix
City Hall. It deserved a *Croix de Guerre*
(posthumous). The Commissioner then tried to
kill Shockley, but Mally killed him first.
Shockley lay on the ground, seemingly
mortally wounded. 'I love you! Ben Shockley,
don't you die on me!' she screamed; and, of
course, he didn't

The Gauntlet was outrageous; yet it had a
serious side, when Mally was explaining that
there was no difference between cops and
whores, except that whores were able to wash
away their filth at the end of the day. The
screenplay also had something to say about the
mindless use of guns. 'Cops are bastards paid
to shoot, not think,' explained the
Commissioner, putting an army of policemen
on the streets; nobody questioned his order.
Again, in a lighter vein, when Shockley
threatened a large group of hippies, Eastwood
had given a parody of how cops are perceived
to behave and talk.

The supporting cast included William Prince
as the blue-eyed, grey-haired, stony-faced
Commissioner, with a voice like the bottom of
a tomb, and Michael Cavanaugh as his corrupt
Assistant District Attorney, who was so bad at

The bus on the steps of Phoenix Town Hall in *The Gauntlet*

His best films, *Josey Wales* and *The Gauntlet* contain sophisticated character interplay within spectacles pitched low to mass audience. He is a cinema, designed more for big box office than for prestige, and in its compromised state is as exciting as it is frustrating.

Tom Allen, Voice

his job that his colleagues said 'He couldn't convict Hitler.' Pat Hingle (who had played the Judge in *Hang 'Em High*) was cast as Shockley's old, retired partner, who was used as a decoy and killed by the Attorney's snipers.

One of the key action scenes was the spectacular and comic demolition of the house where Shockley and Mally were hiding out. It was a siege out of *Bonnie and Clyde*. The building was so bullet-ridden that it was absurd they were not killed. When the house finally collapsed, it looked as if it had been eaten away by a gigantic mass of termites. The joke was underlined by the camera cutting to a road sign which read GOD MAKES HOUSE CALLS.

Bill McKinney, one of Eastwood's most regular actors, was cast as a lecherous, sexist cop who taunted Mally. She taunted him back: 'Does your wife know you masturbate?' she enquired. The cop gave a yell of rage, such as Edvard Munch and Francis Bacon would have appreciated. Not long after, mistaken for Shockley, he was ambushed and killed by the Mafia, his car riddled with bullets. So much for masturbators. This time the camera cut to a road sign which read GOD GIVES ETERNAL LIFE.

The struggle of Clint Eastwood, the director, to escape, subvert or simply have some fun at the expense of Eastwood, the star persona, now amounts to a curious and not unlikeable body of work . . . His personality as a director, however, continues to develop and *The Gauntlet* shows the first signs that he has assimilated the lessons of Don Siegel for the succint, often quasi-humorous delivery of setpieces . . . But what it confirms is that Eastwood hovers on the edge of being one of the most interesting of American directors, if only he could convincingly put down his alter, acting, ego.

Richard Combs, Monthly Film Bulletin

As an actor Eastwood is a product of his image rather than the other way round. His success is based on recognizing that fact and ensuring that every performance utilizes it in some way.

Andrew Tudor, New Society

Mr Eastwood's talent is his style, unhurried and self-assured.

Vincent Canby, New York Times

The only talent involved in this movie belongs to the agent who sold the script (by Michael Butler and Dennis Shryack); the sale price of $500,000 suggests genius.

Pauline Kael, New Yorker

EVERY WHICH WAY BUT LOOSE

Directed by James Fargo   1978

I've got a feeling Clyde may end up as the star of the film.

Clint Eastwood

Clint Eastwood and Sondra Locke in *Every Which Way But Loose*

Every Which Way But Loose was crude knockout, a silly romp, as broad as it was rowdy. The script was a shambles, the acting was coarse and the direction lumpen.

Clint Eastwood was cast as Philo Beddoe, a good-natured, easy-going, brainless trucker with a working man's taste for cold beer and country music. He gave one woman, who was rash enough to describe the country and western mentality as 'somewhere between moron and dull normal', a set of false teeth in her soup. The humour was at this crude level.

Philo was the best bar-room brawler in town and there was nobody who could hit so fast and so hard. He made money backing himself to beat local fighters. These illegal bare-fisted bouts took place in backyards and workplaces, the dirtiest being in the cold room of a meat factory among the hanging carcasses. The role was a parody of Eastwood's macho prowess.

Philo fell in love with a country and western singer (Sondra Locke) and chased after her from California to Colorado, while he himself was being chased by a motorcycle gang and two Los Angeles cops, whom he had beaten up in one of his many brawls. He was accompanied by his best friend (Geoffrey Lewis) and a girl they had picked up on the highway, plus Clyde, an affectionate, rangy, hairy, floppy-armed, full-grown, 12-stone, male orang-utan from Sumatra that he had won in a fight. Philo looked after his welfare; he not only gave him beers, he also took him to porn shows and to the zoo so that he could get laid. The best

visual joke in the whole movie was Eastwood pretending to shoot him and Clyde pretending to fall down dead. The ape, a seasoned performer from Bobby Borosini's Performing Orang-utan Show, stole most of the notices.

Philo was gauche with women. Confiding in the ape, he said: 'I suppose you think I'm crazy tramping across the country after a girl I hardly even knew. It takes me a long time to get to know a girl; even longer to let her know me. Hell, I'm not afraid of any man, but come to sharing my feelings with a woman, my stomach just turns to royal jelly.' Philo was so dumb, it took him the whole movie to realize that the singer wasn't interested in him at all. She turned out to be a hooker.

All the characters were pretty dumb. Ruth Gordon, rasping away as a tough old lady, was straight out of a cartoon strip. But nobody was

Clint Eastwood and The
Black Widows in *Every
Which Way But Loose*

Clint Eastwood and
Clyde in *Every Which
Way But Loose*

quite as moronic as the middle-aged cycle
gang, who had spider tattoos on their arms and
their stomachs and called themselves The
Black Widows. The gang, who were into leather
and Nazi emblems, regularly got beaten up and
their bikes were always left in a tangled mess.
The actors looked as if they, at least, had had a
lot of fun.

For his admirers - of whom I am one - this does
nothing to further his reputation at all. In fact it
mars it. And, for those who don't know about that
reputation, it tells them nothing at all.

Tom Hutchinson, *Sunday Telegraph*

Far from showing off Mr Eastwood to flattering
advantage, this kind of format virtually eclipses his
talent.

Janet Maslin, *New York Times*

Eastwood thinks that his screen personality is so
unshakeable that any amount of self-parody and
ridicule cannot tarnish it. He is under a
misapprehension.

Nicholas Wapshott, *Scotsman*

Clint comes a cropper.

Philip French, *Observer;* headline

ESCAPE FROM ALCATRAZ

Directed by Don Siegel   1979

Alcatraz, a solid rock island a mile from San Francisco, surrounded by treacherous and icy currents, operated as a maximum security prison between 1934 and 1963. In those 29 years, nobody escaped: 39 men tried to get away, 26 were recaptured, seven were shot, three were drowned and three were unaccounted for.

Escape from Alcatraz concerned itself with the three who were unaccounted for, concentrating on Frank Morris (Clint Eastwood). The two brothers, John and Clarence Anglin, were mere ciphers. It was presumed all three had drowned, but their bodies were never found,

Frank Morris arrived at Alcatraz on 18 January 1960, having been transferred from Atlanta. The screenplay told nothing about his background or his crimes. All that was known was that he had escaped from a number of prisons. (Asked what sort of childhood he had had, his answer was 'short'.) He was not scared of anyone, neither inmates, warders nor Warden. His intelligence, patience, nerve and inner strength gave him the edge.

The chilling opening sequence, describing his arrival on the island, was superbly handled by Don Siegel in a series of atmospheric images: the rain lashing down, the impenetrable darkness, the transfer from launch to van, the playing searchlight, the signing in, the medical check, the stripping down, the naked walk down a long corridor of cells. (New arrivals walked naked to their cells; it was designed to humiliate them.) The sequence, photographed by Bruce Surtees and edited by Ferris Webster, is a classic of its kind and got the film off to an excellent start. The cold, impersonal, almost documentary approach

Clint Eastwood in Escape from Alcatraz

continued, the action punctuated by a recurring image of the bleak island prison glowering in a red sunset.

Escape from Alcatraz was a good box-office title. Siegel, however, was not really that interested in the actual escape; he was much more concerned with the soul-destroying daily routine of the inmates and the effects of imprisonment on them and their warders. The grim conditions were austerely depicted; the convicts' incarceration was a spiritual trial, not a physical one. Every prisoner was confined alone to an individual cell. 'Inmates have no say,' said the megalomaniac Warden. 'They do what they are told. We do not make citizens, but we make good prisoners.' The Warden was not bothered about the men's dignity and rehabilitation; he was unashamedly non-reformative.

The aspects of the escape which did interest Siegel were the physical preparations: the use of nail scissors and stolen spoons; the way false grilles were moulded from stationery and lavatory paper; the way the base of the men's raft was made from raincoats stiffened with contact cement. It was incredible that the escapers' handiwork went undetected. There was only one moment of tension, when it seemed that a warder was going to discover a dummy in the bed and it turned out to be Morris all the time.

Concessions were made to Eastwood's fans: a punch-up in the showers, a near-knifing in the courtyard, some finger-chopping in the carpentry class and a heart attack in the mess. A big brutal homosexual (Bruce M. Fischer, physically gross) propositioned Morris in the showers, which allowed Morris to behave in a

Bruce M. Fischer, Roberts Blossom
and Clint Eastwood in *Escape
from Alcatraz*

way audiences would expect a Clint Eastwood
movie hero to behave. First, there was a come-
on smile, followed by a gesture implying that
he was going to give the man a hug and then
came the expected lethal blow to the groin and
balls and a bar of soap stuck in his mouth.

Eastwood, leaner and more lined, was at his
most agile in the fights and the final stretches,
creeping around in the darkness, crawling
along the ventilation shaft, clambering over
wire fences, scampering over roofs and sliding
down drainpipes.

There was a performance of great dignity by
Paul Benjamin, who played the proud black
librarian, convicted for the death of two
rednecks he had killed in self-defence. He was
serving two 99-year sentences back to back.
'Sometimes,' he said, 'I think that's all this shit-
hole is, one long count. We count the hours,
the bulls count us and the king bulls count the
counts.'

A major weakness of the movie was the way
the Warden was written and the way he was
acted by Patrick McGoohan. He came across as
a theatrical sadist, given to making smug
remarks: 'Alcatraz was built to keep all the
rotten eggs in one basket. I was specially
chosen to make sure the stink from the basket
doesn't escape.' He was there, primarily, to
read out the prison prospectus and to be
obnoxious to inmates and subordinates alike, a
supercilious figure of authority.

The ending was ambiguous. The Warden
would have preferred to believe the men had
drowned. The cinemagoing public would have
preferred to believe they had escaped. Siegel
pandered to the box office and hinted they
might have got away with a shot of a

chrysanthemum on stony ground. (The flower had been used earlier in the film as a symbol of freedom.) The final image, under the credits, was of a *papier mâché* head, the dummy's grinning face cocking a snook at all those who had believed that nobody could escape from Alcatraz.

A quiet jangling electronic score was used effectively throughout; the only wrong note was the cheap clap of thunder on the line 'Welcome to Alcatraz!' Today the prison is a number one tourist attraction and tourists are just as likely to ask which cell Eastwood occupied as they are to ask about Al Capone.

Clint Eastwood looks every inch a prisoner: in a sense, it is a role he has been playing all his life. His bleakness shines like armour; his face resembles striated granite; his mouth is so thin that only stray monosyllables can squeeze through; he has the wary expression of a man to whom the world is a trap which might suddenly be sprung. He is the professional outsider.

Peter Ackroyd, Spectator

He is such a still actor that no one else can get more effect out of a brief, reluctant smile, a sidelong glance or a one-word speech.

David Robinson, The Times

Clint Eastwood's flinty and obdurate charisma makes one feel he would be better cast as the prison itself rather than as the convict trying to escape therefrom . . . Eastwood walks through it all tall, cool and monolithic, looking more and more with each film as if it can only he a matter of time before he joins the geological immortals on Mount Rushmore.

Nigel Andrews, Financial Times

At the time when Hollywood entertainments are more overblown than ever, Eastwood proves that less really can be more.

Frank Rich, Time

Mr Eastwood fulfils the demands of the role and of the film as probably no other actor could. Is it acting? I don't know, but he's a towering figure in its landscape.

Vincent Canby, New York Times

Clint Eastwood and Larry Hankin in *Escape from Alcatraz*

The 1980s

Clint Eastwood in
Pale Rider

BRONCO BILLY

Directed by Clint Eastwood   1980

Bronco Billy, good-natured and likeable, funny and touching, was an American fable about the American dream. 'You can be anything you want,' said a member of the Bronco Billy Wild West Show. 'All you have to do is to go out and become it.'

'Everybody loves cowboys and clowns, you're everybody's hero for a while,' sang Ronnie Milsap during the opening credits; and nobody wanted to be a cowboy more than Billy McCoy, a former shoe salesman who had been raised in a one-room tenement building in New Jersey and had never seen a horse till he was 31 years old. The only cowboy he had seen had been in the movies.

Billy lived a life of fantasy as a sharp-shooting, knife-throwing, stunt-riding cowboy in a tacky travelling show. Billed as the greatest hip-shooter, the fastest draw in the West, the only time he behaved like a real, live cowboy was when he managed to foil a bank robbery; and nobody was more surprised than he was. The screenplay was an affectionate lampoon at the expense of the clichés of the Wild West, while Billy himself was a caricature of Eastwood's macho persona.

Billy had picked up his troupe while he was in prison, serving a sentence for attempting to murder his wife, whom he had discovered in bed with his best friend. The troupe, a team of losers and no-hopers, all down on their luck, included: a doctor (Scatman Crothers) who had practised without a licence and was now the MC; a former bank teller (Bill McKinney) who had robbed the bank and was a one-armed, hook-handed roustabout; a Vietnam war deserter (Sam Bottoms) who twirled a rope; a Red Indian (Dan Vadis) who kept getting bitten

Bill McKinney and
Clint Eastwood in
Bronco Billy

126

by his rattlesnake; and his squaw (Sierra Pecheur). They played to sparse audiences.

Billy, gentle, genial, kind-hearted, loyal to his team, was the best friend man ever had. He was charity itself, putting on free shows in orphanages, hospitals and mental institutions, and was loved by children, nuns, doctors and inmates alike. He had an old-fashioned, family-values morality ('You should never kill a man unless it's absolutely necessary') and he was liable, at the drop of a stetson, to mouth homely platitudes and preach against hard liquor and cigarettes. He was a kid at heart, a big kid in a man's body. His troupe loved him and they hadn't been paid in six months. When he addressed them, he sounded like he was addressing the nation.

Far and away the most dramatic exchange, partly because it was so unexpected and so uncharacteristic of an Eastwood hero, was when the local sheriff (Walter Barnes, excellent casting), a nasty bit of work, taunted Billy, forcing him to admit that he was no good and Billy, instead of beating him to pulp, allowed himself to be humiliated (and paid a bribe he could ill-afford) in order to get the Vietnam deserter out of prison.

Sondra Locke was cast as an arrogant, spoiled, headstrong New York heiress, described by her husband as a 'cold-blooded viper' and ditched by him on their honeymoon. It was a marriage of convenience; she needed to marry somebody, *anybody*, before she was 30 in order to inherit her father's fortune. The heiress was a typical Capraesque heroine, running away from herself.

There was a funny performance by Geoffrey Lewis as the frustrated groom, a wimpish termite who had married the heiress for her money and was sorely tried on his wedding night. 'Sometimes she makes me so mad I could kill her!' Denied his conjugal rights, he ran off the next morning with her car, money, clothes and jewellery.

Stranded without a cent to her name, the heiress found herself, most unwillingly, spread-eagled on a death-defying, revolving wheel of fortune and popped at with bullets and knives by a blindfolded Billy. Their romantic battle was stormy. (Locke brought a sharp, sarcastic edge to the banter.) Finally, of course, everything came up roses and she and Billy were rolling about together. 'Take it easy,' he said - and here Eastwood and Locke shared a private joke – 'we've got the rest of our lives to enjoy each other.'

There was a punch-up in a bar which seemed to be just there for the sake of a punch-up and was clearly aimed at the redneck audience who had enjoyed the brawls in *Every Which Way But Loose*. There was also a near-rape in a car park for no other reason, it would seem, than Sondra Locke always got nearly raped in a Clint Eastwood movie.

A much more original scene, and more relevant to the movie's theme, was a botched train robbery. Billy had decided to rob the train after their big tent had burnt down and they hadn't the money to buy a new one. As they rode alongside, absurdly firing their guns and shooting their arrows, the train whizzed past, totally ignoring them. 'You're living in a dream world,' observed the heiress. 'There are no more cowboys and Indians. That's in the past.'

When the heiress disappeared, and was presumed murdered by the groom, a crooked

lawyer persuaded the groom to plead temporary insanity, confess to the murder and go to a mental institution. A bribe of half a million dollars was very persuasive, and since he looked like an idiot anyway, he had no difficulty in convincing the nutty-looking principal of the asylum that he was insane. The principal had a nice line when welcoming visitors: 'You can take your meals with the staff, or the patients, whichever you feel more comfortable with.' The inmates sewed Billy a big tent made entirely from Stars and Stripes flags. This ironically patriotic finish to the movie was followed by Billy's folksy message to all the 'little pardners': 'I want you to finish your oatmeal at breakfast. Do as your ma and pa tell you, because they know best. Don't ever tell a lie and say your prayers at night before you go to bed.'

Clint Eastwood is one of the most vital forces in contemporary American cinema and only the foolish continue to ignore, patronize or dismiss him. As actor, producer and director, he rarely fails to astonish.

Philip French, *Observer*

Only the autocracy and independence conferred by such supreme stardom and command of the box office could permit him to make such an odd, unfashionable, self-deprecating and wholly attractive film as *Bronco Billy*.

David Robinson, *The Times*

There are few enough stars around who can so mock their own image, as he does here, and yet keep it intact by the fervency of an approach that shows that beneath those satirized values are others that are just as worthwhile.

Tom Hutchinson, *Now*

Clint Eastwood in
Bronco Billy

ANY WHICH WAY YOU CAN

Directed by Buddy Van Horn   1980

Clint Eastwood in *Any Which Way You Can*

Sondra Locke and Clint Eastwood in *Any Which Way You Can*

The sequel to *Every Which Way But Loose*, *Any Which Way You Can* was the same mixture as before, only rougher: a coarse, mindless entertainment, aimed at the redneck box office and appealing to the lowest common denominator. It was worse than *Every Which Way But Loose*.

Cast once more as Philo Beddoe, the toughest bare-knuckle fighter in the country, Clint Eastwood stripped to the waist and knuckled down to it. He was in good shape and no jaw was left unsocked. The movie was one long punch-up, ending with an epic brawl in the John Ford manner: a bruising, illegal, bare-knuckle fight, fought out by two rivals who had become friends and watched by a hysterical and drooling crowd of men and women. Described as the fight of the century, it went on for ever. Philo won, despite a broken arm.

'I can take pain,' he said, 'but not love pains.' Sondra Locke was again on hand in her role of country and western singer, but her character had been softened out of all recognition. She was no longer a hooker ('I didn't mean to hurt you. I was mixed-up') and was totally unfazed when she discovered Philo in bed with an ape. 'I think I love you,' she said. 'I think that's a piece of luck for me,' said Philo.

Clyde, the orang-utan, looked different. He was different; the original ape was no longer available. Jokers said he had seen the script and turned it down. (Actually, he had died.) The new Clyde dismantled Cadillacs (even while people were still in them) and had a nasty habit of defecating in police cars.

The supporting cast remained unchanged. Geoffrey Lewis was Philo's best friend and Ruth Gordon, still over-acting, was irascible, rasping, dotty Ma. The moronic, bungling, middle-aged bikers were now bald and wearing wigs. The slapstick was as crude as ever, but just to show how nice they really were, underneath all the neo-Nazism, they saved Beddoe from getting shot by the Mob, a scene which was no more convincing than the one where Clyde saved Philo from a burning car. The only remotely funny incident was when, having been drenched in oil, the gang stiffened up and keeled over one by one.

Any Which Way You Can was chiefly notable for its vulgarity, especially in the motel, with four couples making love at the same time. There was Eastwood and Locke in one room. There was an elderly couple, who hadn't had sex in years, in another room. There were two apes in a third room. (Both Clyde and Philo were discovered hanging from the light

Clyde and Clint
Eastwood in *Any Which
Way You Can*

fittings.) And if this were not enough, there was octogenarian Ruth Gordon seducing a Peeping Tom.

The most enjoyable moment came right at the beginning, listening to Eastwood singing a song he had written over the credit titles.

Eastwood, who can be a compelling, charming screen actor, seems content here to watch the other performers pamper their eccentricities while he stands off to one side, as glum and immobile as a Teamster's ashtray.

Richard Curliss, *Time*

As tribute to the virtues of beer-swilling, fist-clenching, isolationist Middle America, they may cheer Reagan voters, but, by God, they frighten me.

Alan Brien, *Sunday Times*

It's a knockabout comedy directed by Buddy Van Horn, who would appear to have the sense of humour of a hippopotamus and the sensitivity of a jackboot.

Ian Christie, *Daily Express*

They say actors should never work with animals or children. In this case, it's apes who shouldn't work with Clint Eastwood. He dominates the film with his personality and the easy comic touch of a true star.

Alan Frank, *Daily Star*

I hope I never meet anyone who actually likes such a trashy experience.

Alexander Walker, *Evening Standard*

HONKYTONK MAN

Directed by Clint Eastwood   1982

Honkytonk Man, part romantic weepie, part rite of passage, was a picaresque odyssey from Oklahoma to Tennessee. The story was set in the 1930s and came out of Clint Eastwood's own experience of the Depression years, the opening dust-storm sequence recalling John Ford's film of John Steinbeck's *The Grapes of Wrath.*

Eastwood has described the hero, Red Stovall, an untalented country and western singer, as somebody who never believed in himself and seemed actively to seek out his failure. Red made his entrance in a battered limousine; he was dead drunk, broke and all he had was a guitar, a bottle of whiskey and the clothes he was wearing. He was terminally ill with tuberculosis and should have been in a sanatorium. He covered his fear with improvised bravado and good-humoured self-mockery, always the first to admit he was a no-good bastard.

Intent on living his life on his own terms, Red was still in pursuit of his dream to be somebody before he died and was heading south for the Grand Ole Opry audition in Nashville. His sister (a fine performance by Verna Bloom, who looked as if she had stepped out of a photograph of the period) asked her 14-year-old son, Whit, to accompany him, not wanting him to go alone. Whit, a freckled farmboy who idolized his uncle and became his protector, was played by Eastwood's own son, Kyle.

The action was set mainly on the road and there were stopovers in honkytonks, flop-houses, cheap hotels, jails, dives and, finally, a recording studio. The journey was a series of comic encounters, punctuated by songs, such

Kyle Eastwood and
Clint Eastwood in
Honkytonk Man

as the very appealing 'Honkytonk Man' ('Throw your arms round the honkytonk man/We'll get through the night the best way we can') and 'One fiddle, two fiddle, three fiddle'.

Many of the interludes were included for Eastwood's regular fans. The first was when uncle and nephew stole chickens and got caught. Red was body-searched in the street by two unpleasant cops and then arrested after he had asked them if it gave them a thrill to grope a man's crotch. Whit (inspired by a poster for a Western called *When a Man Sees Red*) effected his rescue by attaching a rope to the car and the bars of a cell window and driving off, pulling the wall down. Shortly afterwards, a raging bull attacked Red. The bull did not take kindly to Red having a bath in his drinking water.

There was a delightful incident when Whit was driving the car and they were stopped by a

Bob Ferrera, John McIntire,
Verna Bloom, Tracey Shults,
Kyle Eastwood, Clint Eastwood
and Matt Clark in *Honkytonk
Man*

highway patrolman (Tim Thomerson). Whit,
being underage, naturally didn't have a licence.
The patrolman, pocketing a bribe, insisted man
and boy should change places; but as he
watched Red driving down the road, veering
from left to right, he drove after them and
suggested it would be better if the boy drove
the car after all.

There was also a very amusing scene when a
robbery went wrong. The idea was that Red
would pretend to stick up an old lady who ran
a diner. He would get the cash in the till and
she would claim the money from the insurance. The only trouble was that the old lady
hadn't been warned Red was coming and got
completely hysterical, screaming her head off.

When they finally reached Nashville, Red
collapsed in the middle of his audition. The
promoters turned him down, not wanting him
coughing up his lungs on a national radio
show. The doctor said he shouldn't even be
singing in a shower. When he was offered a
record deal ($20 a song), he took it, knowing it
was his last chance. He collapsed again during
the recording session, while singing 'Honkytonk Man', and was unable to finish. Eastwood,
coughing blood, his face completely ravaged,
was very convincing.

Honkytonk Man was an opportunity for
Eastwood to work with his son and, of course,
their special relationship, understated and
touching, was to the advantage of Clancy
Carlile's screenplay; but Kyle's limited acting
ability was obvious. The face was blank too
often and his scenes lacked spontaneity.

John McIntire, cast as the genial grandpa,
gave a vivid account of a bit of American
history, remembering how, as an 18-year-old,

Clint Eastwood and
Alexa Kenin in
Honkytonk Man

he and hundreds of other white settlers had taken part, on 16 September 1893, in the greatest horserace for the greatest prize, The Cherokee Strip. 'It wasn't just the land, just the dirt itself, I was racing for. It wasn't just the land, it was the dream. It wasn't just land-chasers, it was dream-chasers. Look at it. All turned to dust. We ruined it.'

Alexa Kenin played a crazy girl who wanted to be a singer. There was a tiny problem. She couldn't sing. There was a whole gallery of cameo roles, all nicely acted: Barry Corbin as a lying, cheating promoter, a fat porky son of a bitch who owed Red $100; Susan Peretz as a brothel madam; Steve Autry as a moronic mechanic; Jerry Hardin and Gary Grubbs as the arresting cops; and Joe Regalbuto as the talent scout who gave Red his final job.

This is a lovingly tempered, discreetly eloquent piece of moviemaking that is very close to the masterpiece that Eastwood must one day make ... *Honkytonk Man* is arcane, classic Americana, and, so help me, it's not far short of magnificent.

Richard Cook, *New Musical Express*

It is a solid, well-crafted piece of folksy Americana that might have succeeded even better had it stayed even truer to its melancholic instincts.

Philip Bergson, *What's On*

Eastwood tries to sustain the music with his voice which is charming and whispery, but just too thin to flesh out this film.

Carrie Rickey, *Voice*

The film comes across sympathetically but unconvincingly as an attempt by a well-established movie guy to reveal his tender side.

Janet Maslin. *New York Times*

The sentiment is so laid-back that it ensconces you in an uncritical coma, perhaps because the movie feels very much at home with its aims - or with the narcissistic self-mockery that is the spirit of Clint Eastwood's direction of himself. Yet it's a straight-up, four-square, honest, old-style production that disarms us all.

David Hughes, *Sunday Times*

FIREFOX

Directed by Clint Eastwood   1982

'I don't believe it!' said one of the characters. He was not alone. *Firefox*, a mixture of science fiction and propaganda, based on Craig Thomas's best-selling novel, was immensely long and immensely dull. Clumsily scripted, lacking continuity and coherence, it told an implausible and politically naïve story without suspense and thrills. There was so much exposition at the beginning that the editors clearly got worried; their fidgety editing, however, only made things worse.

Clint Eastwood was cast at Mitchell Gant, a Vietnam veteran, a retired ace flyer, reluctantly pressed back into service to carry out a suicide mission. His superiors tried a bit of flattery ('They still talk about you . . . we need you, major, you're the best we got') and a bit of blackmail, threatening to take away his land if he didn't agree. However, given his mental history it was very odd that American Intelligence should even have considered him for the job. Gant was still shell-shocked, haunted by memories of burning children in Vietnam and liable to become a twitching neurotic at the most inconvenient of moments.

Firefox was the codename for the greatest war plane ever built. The Russians had invented a deadly supersonic fighter which couldn't be detected by radar. It was operated by thought waves and could fly at six times the speed of sound. Gant's job was to steal it. Could he bring it off? He could speak Russian, But the big question was, could he *think* in Russian? He was smuggled into the USSR and once there he kept changing his identity, donning numerous disguises (businessman, tourist, driver's mate) for no good dramatic reason. There was only one genuine moment of

Clint Eastwood in *Firefox*

anxiety and that was when he was trying to avoid the KGB on Moscow's underground and murdered one of their number in a public lavatory.

His task, which had begun by being ridiculously difficult, suddenly became ridiculously easy the moment he got to the aerodrome and he was able to fly the fighter out of the hangar before anybody could say 'Biggles!' His transformation to *Boy's Own* hero was instant. The US Defense Secretary Caspar Weinberger was quoted as saying that he thought *Firefox* was exciting and good for morale because the Americans won.

The grand finale (accompanied by Maurice Jarre's patriotic music) took place over the Arctic. Gant was pursued by a Russian pilot whose plane he had pinched. The dogfight was not thrilling, mainly because, with a visor over his head, it could have been anybody in the cockpit and it didn't seem to make a scrap of difference whether Gant could think in Russian or not. The special effects by John Dykstra were disappointing, too. There were some pretty

Clint Eastwood and
Eugene Lipinski in
Firefox

pictures of snow and water shooting up, but
much of the action, especially when he was
flying through ravines, was a straight crib from
Dykstra's work in *Star Wars*.

There was so much bad writing, so much bad
acting and so many bad accents that the
Russians emerged as cartoon caricatures,
incompetent stereotypes, squabbling like a lot
of children. The use of Russian first names
only added to the general phoniness. Stefan
Schnabel, cast as the First Secretary of the
Communist Party, was made up to look like
Brezhnev. One minute he was making sensible
criticisms of American foreign policy ('They
are simply paying the price for years of
softness') and being philosophical ('If the roles
were reversed we would have acted similarly').
The next minute he was blowing his top.

Kenneth Colley, hollow-cheeked and sunken-
eyed, cast as a nasty Russian officer, behaved
in the way nasty German officers used to
behave in World War II movies. As for Freddie
Jones, let loose as an eccentric British
Intelligence officer, he rolled his eyeballs in a
manner which even Robert Newton might have
found excessive. Everybody, Russians,
Americans and Brits, spoke in clichés. The
dialogue was, unintentionally, very funny.
There were crass references to Vietnam and
Jewish dissidents who went willingly to their
deaths for Gant. 'Why are you prepared to die?'
he asked. 'It's a small thing compared to my
resentment of the KGB,' replied one scientist
(Nigel Hawthorne) before being mown down by
a hail of bullets.

Eastwood, ice-cold, displayed none of his
usual charisma. He looked worried and
careworn throughout, as if his mind were

139

Clint Eastwood in *Firefox*

elsewhere, more preoccupied with the production than the direction, the acting and his own performance. The best part was the opening sequence, before the story proper began, when Gant was being tracked by a helicopter as he jogged in his country retreat.

For simple-mindedness of attitudes, bungling confusion of narrative, and solid-from-the-neck-up actors, Clint Eastwood's *Firefox*, featuring himself as producer, director and star, can have few rivals.

Alan Brien, *Sunday Times*

As a study of a man hollowed out to a shell of instinctive responses, Eastwood sometimes looks too good for his own film.

Richard Conk, *New Musical Express*

It's a James Bond movie without girls, a Superman movie without a sense of humour.

Vincent Canby, *New York Times*

Gant, I fear, is a symbolic figure. He is meant to he America itself, traumatized by Nam, and the movie appears to be Clint's shot in the arm for a country that (as the jargon goes) 'has lost its will' to fight Communism.

David Denby, *New York Magazine*

As a cynical piece of political subversion, it's a classic. The sort of thing we've always been warned about.

Mike Parker, *The Leveller*

SUDDEN IMPACT

Directed by Clint Eastwood   1983

People are a bit edgy about the rights of the criminal taking precedence over the rights of the victims. They are more impatient with courtroom procedures and legal delays. I think the public is interested in justice and that's what Harry stands for. He is unique because he stood for the same principles from the beginning, when it wasn't terribly fashionable.

Clint Eastwood

Clint Eastwood previews
a shot in *Sudden Impact*

It was in *Sudden Impact* that Harry Callahan, famously, invited a robber to draw his gun on him. 'Go ahead,' he said, make my day.' The line immediately passed into common currency.

Seven years on, Callahan was still up against hoodlums, lily-livered liberals and his superiors. The film began with a female judge dismissing a case and the villains being set free because the evidence was inadmissible. The lads left the courtroom, laughing. San Francisco was crumbling under shootings, knifings and beatings. Old ladies were being bashed over their heads for their social security cheques. Teachers were being thrown out of fourth-floor windows because they didn't give As.

Callahan waded through the scum of a city being swept away by bigger and bigger waves of corruption, apathy and red tape. Seven years on, not surprisingly, he looked older, greyer, worn, tired. The face was tight as a mask. The brow was creased. There were new, deeper lines. The blood vessels throbbed. He still did what he had to do, though his successes were often more costly to the city and the department in terms of bad publicity and physical destruction than other people's failures. 'Harry is a real class act,' said his admirers. 'You're a dinosaur,' said his denigrators. 'Your ideas don't fit any more.'

Invading a wedding party, Callahan harassed the bride's grandfather, one of the city's biggest crime lords (the man sounded like a relation of Marlon Brando's Godfather) and caused him to have a heart attack. His bosses decided to dispatch him to San Paulo, a seaside resort, to help solve a local murder case. He had barely arrived when he spotted a bank robber and gave chase. The man jumped on a bike. Callahan jumped into the driver's seat of a senior citizens' bus. The pensioners egged him on: 'Chase his arse! Nail the son of a bitch!' they cried. 'The best day trip I had since they dumped me into that home,' said one old man.

Asked by Callahan why he was dragging his feet on the case, the San Paulo chief of police (Pat Hingle) replied he was dealing with mugging, shoplifting, burglaries, drunken

Clint Eastwood in
Sudden Impact

driving (the crimes which didn't grab the headlines), and that he was doing the best he could. 'Perhaps, it's not good enough,' said Harry, whose search for the murderer was complicated by the Mob's attempts on his life.

There was nobody Callahan could trust, except for his black partner (who, naturally, went the way of all his partners) and a young local cop (Mark Keyloun) who, contrary to all expectations, was still alive at the end of the movie. The casting of Albert Popwell as the Partner may have succeeded in tricking some cinemagoers, who had seen him play the minder in *Coogan's Bluff*, the robber in *Dirty Harry*, the pimp in *Magnum Force* and the militant in *The Enforcer*, into thinking, on his first entrance, as he crept up on a target-practising Harry, that he was a hired killer.

Sudden Impact had opened with a love scene in a car in a deserted spot. The woman (Sondra Locke) undid the man's flies and then shot him in the balls. (This is what you would call a .38 vasectomy and it is not to be recommended.) She then shot him in the head. Ten years previously she and her younger sister had been raped. Her sister had ended up in an institution. She had come back to kill all those who had been responsible. The murders were punctuated by lingering, graphic flashbacks of the two women's ordeal. Her vendetta recalled François Truffaut's *La Mariée était en noir* (*The Bride Wore Black*). There was a particularly good scene when she refused to listen to one pleading victim (well played by Wendell Wellman) who was now a respectable local businessman. Sondra Locke, sharp of feature, wan of complexion, her hair cascading down, looked as if she were understudying Veronica Lake in a 1940s *film noir*.

Callahan, as always, believed in the law of the gun and that crime should be punished. The murderess was of the same opinion. 'This

is the age of lax responsibilities and defeated justice,' she argued. 'What happens now? What exactly are my rights? And where was all the concern when I was being beaten and mauled? What about my sister's rights when she was brutalized? There is a thing called justice and was it justice that they all should walk away?' Cop and murderess (though at the time he did not know she was the murderess) shared the same beliefs and the same bed and, at the end of the film, he did not arrest her.

Clint Eastwood's production had a dark, sinister quality; much of the movie was shot at night. The final nine minutes were staged in an empty fairground. (Fairgrounds are always good value.) Callahan was discovered on the boardwalk, looking for all the world like a lawman in a Western, ready for the final shoot-out. 'Holy shit!' said one of the gang, as well he might, for there, unmistakably, was The Man With No Name reincarnated, an avenging angel in silhouette, his gun by his side and so dramatically lit that the lights had given him a halo. The darkness, the close-ups, the music and the editing were all first-rate.

Paul Drake played the raucous, cackling, crazy, impotent gang leader, attempting to out-Cagney Cagney, before he fell to his death, impaled (phallic justice, this) on an outsize horn of a carousel unicorn. Audrie J. Neenan was memorably cast as a foul-mouthed lesbian. There was also, regrettably, a farting bulldog, strayed in from another picture by mistake.

What Harry Callahan represents is not only ruthlessness but a sinister form of impatience and you don't have to be a fascist to be guilty of that.

Michael Wood, *New Society*

Albert Popwell and Clint Eastwood in *Sudden Impact*

No amount of skilful crafting can disguise the fact that this is a glib, meretricious movie, and, particularly from a film-maker of Eastwood's proven ability, a reprehensible one.

David Castell, *Sunday Telegraph*

And it is the contemptuous assumption that this blood-soaked bully is to be regarded as a fit hero for our times and box office that makes this such an ugly movie.

Tom Hutchinson, *Mail on Sunday*

By any standard Eastwood is a Hollywood great and in this film he is on firm ground. Doing what his fans want him to do - killing people. Liberals will cringe - Harry Callahan is anathema to them - but morally reprehensible or not, *Sudden Impact* is terrific entertainment.

William Russell, *Glasgow Herald*

One of the most unpleasant, reactionary and cruel pictures it has been my misfortune to see.

Ian Bell, *Scotsman*

I like Eastwood, always have. But then I have a soft spot in my heart for law and order.

Andrew Sarris, *Voice*

TIGHTROPE

Directed by Richard Tuggle   1984

*There is a darkness inside all of us. You, me
and the man down the street. Some have it
under control. Others act it out. The rest of us
try to walk a tightrope between the two.*

A psychiatrist in the film

Tightrope, a disturbing psychological drama,
was sometimes described as the thinking man's
Dirty Harry. The real subject matter this time
was not law and order but sex and violence;
and the subject was a risky one for a major star,
because it soon became apparent that the
violence was part of the turn-on.

Clint Eastwood was cast as Wes Block, a big
city cop investigating a series of sadistic
killings. There were, he pointed out, a possible
120,000 suspects. What made the movie so
absorbing was that in searching for the
murderer the cop found himself. The killer
forced him to confront his own impulses.
Sexually hungry, Wes sought relief with
prostitutes and had developed a taste for
bondage. (Since he was a cop he used handcuffs.) One by one, the prostitutes he visited
were murdered. The man he was stalking was
stalking him, acting out his desires, even
tricking him into dating a male prostitute:

  Man: He said you would like it.
  Wes: Well, he's wrong.
  Man: Why don't you try it?
  Wes: Maybe I have.

The killer and the cop could so easily have
been the same person; it was the uncertainty
which gave the film its tension. *Tightrope*, in
this respect, was not unlike *This Story of
Yours*, a play by John Hopkins, which had been
seen briefly at the Royal Court Theatre,

London, and which was later filmed by Sidney
Lumet and starred Sean Connery.

Wes was a single parent, with two young
daughters. His wife had left him because he
had treated her too tenderly; she, it seemed,
had also wanted the rough stuff. 'What's a
hard-on, daddy?' asked his youngest child. The
older (played by Eastwood's own daughter,
Alison) sniggered at her father's discomfort.

Richard Tuggle's screenplay explored Wes's
relationship not only with the prostitutes and
his children but also with a counsellor (the
admirable Geneviève Bujold) who ran the New
Orleans Rape Crisis Centre. He made a pass
over the oysters. ('I was wondering what it
would be like to lick the sweat off your body.')
They shared a work-out at the gymnasium
which *sounded* like they were having sex.
Later he had a wet dream about her, which was
cleverly photographed from her point of view
so that cinemagoers were fooled into thinking
she really was being attacked by the killer.

Eastwood, haunted and hunted, deadbeat
and ravaged, looked his age: a vulnerable,
lonely man, struggling to cope with the darker
side of his personality. His encounters drew
him deeper and deeper into a sordid world and
Tuggle, not averse to using the occasional
blatant sexual imagery (such as bottles ejac-
ulating all over the place in a bottle factory),
made excellent use of New Orleans's Red Light
district, with its dives, bars, brothels, massage
parlours and topless dancers, go-go boys,
women wrestlers and hookers. Lennie Niehaus
provided a nice jazz score accompaniment.

There was a typical Hitchcockian scene
when Wes was in a deserted warehouse full of
huge carnival heads, looking for the murderer,

Clint Eastwood and
Geneviève Bujold in
Tightrope

144

Jennifer Beck, Clint
Eastwood and Alison
Eastwood in *Tightrope*

and found the male prostitute hanging from the rafters. There was a foreseeable assault on his home. His 12-year-old daughter was tied up and nearly raped, the family pets were killed and, for an extra bit of horror, the housekeeper was murdered and stuffed into the washing machine.

There was enough lightning in the final night-chase sequence for a Gothic melodrama, A police helicopter's harsh spotlight picked out the killer as he fled through a graveyard, past the mausoleums and into the railyard, pursued by Wes. The two men fought it out on the tracks. The scene ended with the killer's arm being severed by an on-coming train, an unnecessary bit of *grand guignol*.

If only Mr Eastwood could be persuaded to stay away from lucrative junk and stick to films of this quality the cinematic world would be a better place.

Ian Bell, *Scotsman*

Tightrope offers more intricacy, suspense and atmospheric color than most of Eastwood's gumshoe safaris through the urban jungle. More important, it represents a provocative advance in the consciousness, self and social, of Eastwood's one-man genre.

Richard Schickel, *Time*

More and more he's beginning to look like the last serious man in Hollywood.

David Denby, *New York Magazine*

He's never completely convincing in his quest for the heart of sexual darkness. It's the penalty he pays for the moral strength he projects on the surface. Whatever lies underneath it is very unlikely to be sneaky or perverted.

Andrew Sarria, *Voice*

He seems to want to be fiery, but he doesn't have it in him - there's no charge in his self-disgust.

Pauline Kael, *New Yorker*

CITY HEAT

Directed by Richard Benjamin   1984

City Heat was a send-up of a typical Warner
Brothers gangster movie, set in 1932, during
the Prohibition era, the date pinpointed by a
scene taking place in the crowded foyer of a
cinema showing the Marx Brothers' *Horse
Feathers*.

The period was lovingly re-created by
designer Edward Carfango. The characters met
in speakeasies, boxing rings, bordellos and
studio-bound rainy streets. (It never stopped
raining.) The thugs wore flat caps, the prostitutes wore cloche hats and the table lamps
wore art-deco shades. There were those who
thought the director, Richard Benjamin, had
paid more attention to period detail than he
had to the drama.

The film was originally called *Kansas City
Jazz* and was intended to be directed by Blake
Edwards and have songs. It should have been a
good-humoured lark, tongue-in-cheek and
zany; and it was, but the script, broad, mechanical and facetious, was never good enough. The
repartee was weak, rarely rising above banality
('Next time, I'm going to knock you so hard,
back into the Stone Age, where you came
from') and mere vulgarity ('You're supposed to
slush that, not smoke it'). The pace constantly
sagged. The were too many unpleasant killings.
Songs would have been a good idea.

Clint Eastwood and Burt Reynolds played
rival detectives, two former buddies, now
bosom enemies, constantly at loggerheads, their
amiable, aggressive banter tempered by mutual
respect. Lieutenant Speer (Eastwood) had
remained in the force. Mike Murphy (Reynolds)
had resigned and was running a non-profitable
detective agency. Speer, grim-faced, hard-
boiled, tight-lipped, ignored any mayhem that

Burt Reynolds and
Clint Eastwood in
City Heat

might be going on around him, until it affected
him personally, when he would develop a
manic facial tic and go berserk. Reynolds
looked like a typical 1930s gigolo. Everything
about him was in period: his face, his moustache, his toupee, his teeth, his buttonhole, his
cigarette dangling from his mouth, his soft
chamois-coloured hat, his tailored suits, his
macintosh. Murphy was the dapperest of
dapper ladies' men, a narcissistic, wisecracking, cowardly rogue, oozing charm.
Reynolds played him with self-mocking vanity
and cocky cuteness. *City Heat* was his movie.

The film opened with a comic fight in a
luncheonette with Speer sitting by while his
former buddy was being beaten to a pulp and
doing nothing about it, until his coffee was
spilt. Later, there was some quasi-serious
fighting on the landing of a tenement building.

'Everything all right?' asked a tenant, coming out of his room after minutes of gunfire. 'All right for me, not so good for him,' replied Speer, who had just shot a man dead.

The major set piece was an extended street battle with everybody blasting away with a never-ending supply of ammunition. Vintage cars had their windscreens, headlights and petrol tanks riddled with bullets. Speer sat in his car and did nothing until a bullet hit his windscreen and then, suddenly, there he was - beautifully framed within the arc of shooting water from a burst street pump - walking down the centre of the street, indestructible, firing his gun, as if he were Clint (The Man With No Name) Eastwood back in the Old West of Sergio Leone. The sequence ended with Speer punching Murphy on the jaw when Murphy, who had been cowering all the while, tried to share in his success with a cry of 'We did all right!'

Another shoot-out immediately followed in a garage. This time the two ex-buddies fought side by side and the duel was even sillier, with the gangsters groaning away and Hollywood's two leading macho men upstaging each other by producing larger and larger barrelled pistols, a phallic joke at their expense.

The climax took place in a brothel. Murphy, interrupting one senator's fantasy session, pinched his costume and dressed up as the Wolf in *Red Riding Hood*. Sadly, once Reynolds was in drag, nothing was made of it. Murphy had come to save his kidnapped girlfriend, an heiress, who was playing cards with the gangsters and winning. Are you all right? he had enquired over the phone. 'Hell, no,' she had replied. 'My hair is a mess. I broke two of

my fingernails. I don't have my make-up and I'm stuck here with these two ugly, smelly garbage cans.' (She was referring to the gangsters.) The production should have made much more use of Madeline Kahn, who was perfect casting for this dizzy blonde who wore only a fur coat and undies.

Jane Alexander had the Eve Arden role of the wisecracking, unpaid secretary, but without the wisecracks. Richard Roundtree was Murphy's corrupt partner who was playing one big-shot off against another. Roundtree, bowler-hatted, waistcoated, gloved, spatted, was very stylish and looked as if he were about to start tap-dancing at any minute. He met a horrific end, when he was hurled from a fourth-floor window and landed on top of a car. The incident belonged in a different movie. So, too, did that shot of a man, drenched in gasoline, catching light and burning to death.

They succeed all too well in providing an almost offensively clownish waste of time and talent.

Philip Strick. *Observer*

Too often it's like watching a couple of cash-registers upstaging each other.

Alexander Walker, *Standard*

It is hard to know whether this is meant to be a romp or a serious thriller; perhaps because it fails to be either.

Francis Wheen. *New Statesman*

City Heat - need I say it - is a two-fisted, red-blooded, all-American macho movie with huge hairy balls and plenty good fire-power.

Mat Snow, *New Musical Exprees*

Clint Eastwood in
City Heat

PALE RIDER

Directed by Clint Eastwood   1985

And I looked and behold a pale horse: and his name that sat on him was Death, and hell followed him.

Revelations 6.8

A small community of poor, independent, hard-working gold prospectors were constantly being harassed by a big mine company that wanted to drive them off their land. The screenplay, a classic confrontation between Good and Evil, paid a nostalgic debt to the Western genre in general and to *Shane* in particular.

Pale Rider had a tremendous opening, the camera alternating between a hard-riding posse and the peaceful mining community, the menace of the riders under-scored on the soundtrack by the thundering hooves of their horses. The riders destroyed everything in their path.

A young girl prayed at the grave of her dog for a miracle and immediately Clint Eastwood appeared out of nowhere, the answer to any maiden's prayer. Since he wore a dog collar, the community presumed he was a man of God and called him Preacher. His Christianity was of the muscular sort and he was as adept at breaking boulders as he was at breaking a man's balls. Mouthing platitudes, he stressed traditional values and delivered a sermon on the need to stand tall against oppression and wanton destruction. Gradually he pulled the community together.

There was a fine performance by Michael Moriarty as the mild-mannered, decent Hull, who lived with his girlfriend, Sarah (Carrie Snodgrass), a widow, and her 15-year-old daughter, Megan (Sydney Penny). Both women

Clint Eastwood in
Pale Rider

Clint Eastwood in
Pale Rider

The bad guys were not slow to recognize his qualities: 'You're a trouble-maker, Preacher, you spell bad cess in letters that stretch from here to Seattle.' The mining company hired Marshal Stockburn (John Russell) to kill him. The Marshal brought along six deputies, professional killers every one of them. In their long raincoats, they looked as if they were modelling clothes for Calvin Klein. (The producers were at pains to point out that the raincoats were actual copies of the 'dusters' men used to wear in the 1870s.) The deputies had no individuality; they were dummies in a shop window and Preacher, in the final shoot-out, dispatched them one by one with ease.

Eastwood had felt the story needed a prior relationship between Stockburn and Preacher. What the relationship had been was never divulged. It was enough to know there was an old score to be settled. Listening to a description, Stockburn felt he knew the man but the man was dead (and the implication was that he had shot him). Face to face, he recognized him instantly: 'You! You! You!' Preacher shot him down and the bullet wounds in the Marshal's back matched the wounds in Preacher's back (which had been seen earlier while he was washing) and they matched them exactly.

Pale Rider, ecologically opportune, had a love for the land the big corporation was blasting away with their hydraulic machinery. The film was shot on location, predominantly in Sun Valley, Idaho, with additional footage in Sonora, California. The scenery, with its russet autumnal plains and snow-capped mountains, was ravishing. The striking photography was by Bruce Surtees, whose dark, sombre interiors caught what it must have been like to live with

were attracted to Preacher. He reminded Sarah of the husband who had deserted her. 'Who are you really?' she asked. 'Well, it really doesn't matter, does it?' he replied. Megan wanted to have sex and when he refused, she rode off so that she could be raped and he could come and rescue her in the nick of time.

Hull's character grew as the story progressed. It was he who persuaded the other prospectors to stay in a key speech: 'Gold ain't what we're about. I came here to raise family. This is my home. This is my dream... If we sell out now, what price do we put on our dignity next time?'

Eastwood, bringing his subtle command to bear, made the story more mystical, more biblical, more supernatural. Preacher wasn't a preacher; the dog collar was a disguise and he was liable to disappear out of the frame without warning. He was more like a Fourth Horseman of the Apocalypse, resurrected from the dead to save the poor from the rich and to exact his own personal revenge. His gift to the community was to blast the company's mine, buildings and installations.

only two or three little lamps lighting the whole house.

Mr Eastwood has continued to refine the identity of his Western hero by eliminating virtually every superfluous gesture. He's a master of minimalism. The camera does not reflect vanity. It discovers the mythical character within,

Vincent Canby, *New York Times*

It is difficult to admire Clint Eastwood: the strong, silent manner seems only to camouflage a ham actor, and that wrinkled visage only obscures the essential paucity of his imagination (when he is writer or director).

Peter Ackroyd, *Spectator*

Eastwood acts with his usual half-serious, half-mocking sense of his own flintlike authority and he holds the movie together.

David Denby, *New York Magazine*

The movie is full of recycled mythmaking, but Eastwood goes through the motions like someone exhumed, and as a director he numbs what he borrows.

Pauline Kael, *New Yorker*

Clint Eastwood, Sydney Penny and Michael Moriarty in *Pale Rider*

HEARTBREAK RIDGE

Directed by Clint Eastwood   1986

Every effort was made to ensure *Heartbreak Ridge* was as accurate and as representative of the United States Marine Corps as possible. The production was made with their technical assistance. However, when the powers-that-be saw the finished product, they withdrew their support, finding the brutality, violence and foul language non-productive.

The film began with black and white newsreel footage from Korea. Pictures of wounded and dead soldiers were not quite what the Marine Corps had had in mind as a recruiting advertisement. They would have preferred something along the lines of *Top Guns* (though, presumably, not if they had learned of Quentin Tarantino's discovery of a gay subtext). They objected to the sergeant's habit of addressing the recruits as 'ladies', 'missies', 'queer-bait', and telling them that he 'didn't want to take long, lingering showers with them'.

The movie was an elegy for a Marine lifer, an old-timer with an excellent military record and a chestful of medals to confirm it. Tough, honest and gung-ho, he had fought with valour in Vietnam and won a Congressional Medal of Honour at Heartbreak Ridge, Korea. The film's title referred not only to the battle but also to the contemporary turning point in his life when his career was nearing its mandatory end.

Sergeant Tom Highway, bull-necked, square-headed, hair close-cropped, had a will of iron and he could out-drink, out-brawl and out-swear anybody. He knew how to deal quickly and efficiently with a hulking prison lout. (The scene recalled a similar exchange in *Escape from Alcatraz*.) He was not amused when a gay

Clint Eastwood and platoon train in *Heartbreak Ridge*

ling as an NCO. The strength of the performance was the sense of failure beneath the aggressive macho posturing.

Highway went back to his old combat unit to transform raw recruits into 'lifetakers and heartbreakers'. His training was rigorous ('I understand a lot of body bags get filled if I don't do my job') and his discipline was relentless ('We may have lost the wars, but we won the battles, I'm not going to lose the next one because my men are not ready').

The platoon was a rebellious, insubordinate and recalcitrant lot and they did not hide their contempt for authority. Used to a lazy life, they resented and hated Highway until he had knocked them into shape. Then, of course, he won their loyalty. Mario Van Peebles had the most showy role of all the recruits, playing a cocky, backchatting rapper and rock singer, a self-proclaimed Ayatollah of Rock 'n' Roll. The exuberant Van Peebles sang his own songs, wore a T-shirt with the legend 'I'm sexy' on it and provided the humour.

Highway (as you would expect in a Clint Eastwood movie) was in conflict with his inefficient superiors. His lieutenant was a naïve wimp straight out of college. His major (Everett McGill, well cast) was a bureaucratic martinet with no experience of combat. 'I asked for marines,' the major observed. 'The Division sent me relics. You're an anachronism. Characters like you ought to be in a case that reads "break glass only in the event of war".' Highway, constantly usurping the major's authority, deviated from his training programme and, as is the way in American war movies, the two men, eventually, had a hand-to-hand fight, egged on by the other ranks.

Clint Eastwood in
Heartbreak Ridge

soldier on a bus gave him the eye; but then, he had only himself to blame, since he was reading a woman's magazine at the time.

Highway didn't know where he was going. He had nowhere to go: the army was his life. Unable to face the future, he decided to make it up with his ex-wife (Marsha Mason) and read women's magazines to try to find out why their marriage had failed. (Did we mutually nurture each other? he asked himself. Did we communicate in a meaningful way in our relationship? he wondered. The screenplay parodied the language of such magazines.) The marriage had failed because of his thoughtlessness, his machismo and the job itself. Marines and marriage, as far as his ex-wife was concerned, were incompatible.

The psychological traumas had warped his character. The scars run deep, said the poster. The outer wounds were visible on his neck and forehead. The leather skin was stretched like scar tissue and the voice was gravel-hoarse from drinking and barking. Eastwood, not afraid to look old and ugly, was very convinc-

Clint Eastwood and
Mario Van Peebles in
Heartbreak Ridge

Heartbreak Ridge stayed in the camp right until the very end, when the men were flown out to Grenada for a bit of jingoistic action, and Highway, inevitably going against the major's orders, led his platoon to victory, rescuing American citizens from their Cuban captors. The fact that he shot the enemy in the back and then smoked his cigar didn't go down too well with the Marines.

As director, Eastwood revitalizes old clichés, and as an actor he gives Highway considerable depth and complexity. He is the oldest character Eastwood has played, and he makes him a wonderfully tough, amusing, humane and vulnerable man.

Philip French, *Observer*

As the gritty, raspy-voiced sergeant, Mr Eastwood's performance is one of the richest he's ever given. It's funny, laid-back, seemingly effortless, the sort that separates actors who are run-of-the-mill from those who have earned the right to be identified as stars.

Vincent Canby, *Time*

It would take a board of inquiry made up of gods to determine whether this picture is more offensive aesthetically, psychologically, morally or politically.

Pauline Kael, *New Yorker*

The incessant pornographic talk, its obsessional fear of male femininity, is so homophobic as to be, in spite of itself, extremely camp. Eastwood may find his film has an admiring audience that he never intended to impress.

William Green, *Today Sunday*

Charmless advertisement for testosterone imperialism.

Adam Mars-Jones, *Independent*

BIRD

Directed by Clint Eastwood   1988

*The picture is kind of constructed like o jazz
tune. It asks the audience to listen carefully.
Otherwise they may miss elements of it, much
like a Charles Parker solo.*

Clint Eastwood,
quoted by Derek Malcolm, *Guardian*

'Bird' was the nickname of Charlie Parker, the
great bebop saxophone player who revolu-
tionized the way everyone played the
saxophone. The movie, dedicated to musicians
everywhere, was both a lament for the man and
a homage to his music.

Clint Eastwood, who had been a jazz
aficionado nearly all his life, had seen Parker
in 1945 in Oakland, California, when he was a
teenager. In attempting to create a narrative and
visual equivalent to Parker's complicated
music, he shuffled time, jumping back and
forth in time. The multiple flashbacks made it
difficult for the average audience to follow. The
soundtrack paralleled the neurotic speed of
uptake in bebop itself, blending the original
solos with fresh back-ups. The combination of
the new, the old and the refurbished material
worried the purists. The technical skill with
which it was done won an award for sound
recording at the Cannes Film Festival.

Jack N. Green's lighting was atmospheric.
Bird had the feel of a downbeat *film noir*. It
was always night-time and it seemed to be
always raining; but in creating the dark, smoky
world of the nightclubs, it was often difficult to
see what was going on, so swallowed up were
the black actors in the darkness and shadow.
As for the pretty studio street, with its period
cars, it looked like a setting more appropriate
for a period musical.

Clint Eastwood directs
Samuel E. Wright and
Forest Whitaker in *Bird*

159

Forest Whitaker and
Diane Venora in *Bird*

'There are no second acts in American lives,'
wrote F. Scott Fitzgerald. Bird (Forest Whitaker,
very impressive), musical genius, womanizer,
heroin addict, had a messy, complicated life
and an infinite capacity for causing havoc.
Dizzy Gillespie (Samuel E. Wright), unlike
Parker, always made a point of arriving on time
and he did so because he didn't want to give
white people the pleasure of having their
beliefs that 'the nigger was unreliable'
confirmed.

Joel Oliansky's often harrowing screenplay
ignored Parker's childhood, formative years
and marriages to concentrate, in a collage of
scenes and impressions, on his declining career
and his love for the protective and stoical Chan
Richardson (Diane Venora, also very
impressive), whom he constantly let down.
Perhaps the most moving moment was his
reaction to the death of his daughter when,
tearfully and drunkenly, he sent telegram after
telegram to her. There was a rare moment of joy
in the seemingly never-ending misery, when he
arrived on horseback to woo Chan. Bird ended
up in an asylum, when what he really needed
was medical treatment, not psychology. He
died of drugs and alcohol at the age of 34. The
doctor, examining the dead body, thought he
was about 65.

There were two recurring images: a doctor
showing him a corpse and a flying cymbal, a
memory of the occasion, when in mid-solo at
Kansas City Jazz Club, he had been humiliated
by drummer J. Jones untying his cymbal and
throwing it on to the floor.

Parker's relationship with the white trumpet
player, Red Rodney (Michael Zelniker), was
historically interesting and there was a fascinating sequence where, in order to be able to
play in the Deep South, Rodney had to be
passed off as an albino.

Bird won the Golden Globe award and Forest
Whitaker won the best actor award at the
Cannes Film festival.

At last American cinema has done black music
proud. Unforgettable.

Brian Case, *Time Out*

This is a hugely ambitious piece of film-making and
further proof that Eastwood stands alongside Woody
Allen in the vanguard of those pushing the
American cinema ahead.

Philip French. *Observer*

It invites us to experience the redeeming grace of his
music. And with its passionate craft it proclaims
that Eastwood is a major American director.

Richard Schickel, *Time*

It's an honourable and skilful piece of work, the
most complicated of all Eastwood's ventures as
director and the most mature.

Derek Malcolm. *Guardian*

THE DEAD POOL

Directed by Buddy Van Horn   1988

The Dead Pool raised questions about what audiences should be allowed to see on their screens and who was to decide what was harmful. Harry Callahan, strongly critical of the media, didn't like the way television intruded into people's grief and berated a film crew: 'You're only interested in death and mayhem.' It was ironic that Callahan of all people should criticize the media for doing what the 'Dirty Harry' films had been doing for years. He smashed a camera. The television company brought a law suit. His superior wanted to take him off the streets. He threatened to resign. Nothing new.

The reporter (Patricia Clarkson, who looked a bit like Sondra Locke) admitted later that she had made an error of judgement and they became good friends. Easily the most interesting scene they shared was the one in which they failed to talk a man out of suicide. Wanting his 15 minutes of fame, he decided to get on the 6 o'clock news by setting himself on fire in front of a television camera.

The Dead Pool was a hit list, a ghoulish game instigated by a paranoid film director, a cinepseud, who made cheap, schlock horror movies at the back of a meat factory. His crew took bets on who they thought was the next person most likely to die. They fixed on celebrities who weren't going to make it because they were either old or sick or in a high-risk profession, Somebody had got hold of the list and was working their way through it. A rock star was murdered. A talk-show host was murdered. A production assistant was murdered. A female film critic was murdered. (It wasn't very difficult to guess which critics the movie had in mind.) Callahan was also on the list. He had

just put a major crime figure in prison and was the hero of the hour, the target of the media, hired guns and lunatics.

The film director (Liam Neeson) was a prime suspect; but it was obvious somebody was impersonating him and trying to frame him. The director thought it could be anybody: his agent, the producers of his last film, the crew, the public, the critics. 'It's jealousy,' he whined. 'They envy my talent. They want to destroy it.' Neeson, wearing a ponytail and an earring, was not good and his accent a camp caricature. 'Let me tell you something,' he said. 'People are fascinated by death and violence. That is why my films make money. They are an escape, a vicarious release of fear. Nobody takes my film or the game seriously.'

The murderer was mentally ill and the game had become an obsession. The psychiatrist (who had let him out of an institution) said that he was someone whose sense of self-hatred was so extreme that he no longer had a self but substituted the identity of a celebrity for his own. He had stolen the director's identity.

There were occasional jokes at the expense of the crime genre and the audience, too. The first was when two guys asked Callahan for his autograph and he mistook them for hit men. The second was when he was out jogging and was being followed by two men in a car, who turned out to be bodyguards sent by the imprisoned crime lord to protect him.

The streets of San Francisco are always good for a car chase. The high spot, though not nearly exciting enough, or funny enough, and far too long, was a parody of *Bullitt*. Callahan was chased by a remote-controlled dinky toy car which was wired with explosives.

Clint Eastwood and
Patricia Clarkson in
The Dead Pool

The psychopath kidnapped the reporter; no
psychopath worthy of the name ever fails to
kidnap the hero's girlfriend in the last reel. The
final shoot-out took place in the docks, where
Callahan, finally, managed to nail the villain
with a harpoon, pinning him to the wall. The
pay-off line was very James Bond: 'He's
hanging out back there,' he said to the police,
who, as usual, only arrived when it was all
over.

Clint Eastwood's shoot-first cop, in the fifth of the
series, is so shop-soiled with cliché that it would
need a whole laundry of new ideas to freshen
him up.

Tom Hutchinson, *Mail on Sunday*

One suspects that Eastwood, aware of passing time,
has taken to quiet mockery of role and genre, to
save anyone else the trouble.

Shaun Usher, *Daily Mail*

The word 'dead' in the title is brutally appropriate.

Derek Malcolm, *Guardian*

Perhaps Dirty Harry should retire and go into local
politics.

Douglas Young, *Scotsman Weekend*

Clint Eastwood in
The Dead Pool

PINK CADILLAC

Directed by Buddy Van Horn   1989

Tommy Nowak: Have you seen a blonde in a
     pink Cadillac?
Garage Attendant: Only in my dreams.

Clint Eastwood was cast as Tommy Nowak, a
skip tracer, hired by bail bondsmen. ('That's
my job,' he said. 'Track 'em and snatch 'em.')
The role afforded him opportunities for funny
disguises while making comic arrests. He
played a disc jockey, a chauffeur, a red-nosed
clown at a rodeo and a moustached guy in a
gold lamé jacket. His most amusing disguise
was his dumbo redneck, chewing and spitting
baccy. 'Pretty thin line between what you do
and some outlaws do,' remarked one lawyer.
'Maybe a thin line, but it isn't invisible,'
Nowak retorted.

Clint Eastwood and
Bernadette Peters in
Pink Cadillac

Bernadette Peters was cast as Lou Ann
McGuinn, a young mother with an eight-
month-old baby and married to a dim-witted
and weak-willed member of The Birthright
Organization, which was run by pony-tailed
Alex (Michael Des Barres), a vicious neo-
fascist. His followers were small-time thieves,
junkies, wife-beaters, drifters and psychos, and
they spent their days shooting targets with
automatic weapons at their arsenal in the
forest. They were so moronic, they could have
joined The Black Widows bike gang in *Every
Which Way But Loose* and few people would
have noticed the difference.

Lou Ann, fed up with her husband (Timothy
Gerhart), went off with his Cadillac, his prize
possession, and, inadvertently, a quarter of a
million dollars, the prize possession of The
Birthright Organization which they had just
stolen from a bank and had told her was
counterfeit money. She was the palest thing,

with cupid-bowed lips, and at one point she
was driving down the road with the notes
flying out of the back of the car, just like any
heroine in a Frank Capra comedy. 'I'm through
taking shit from men,' she confided to Nowak.
'That's one thing we have in common,' he
replied, 'I'm through taking shit from men.'
They shared a room in a hotel and, a bit later,
they shared a bed in a motel. 'I've got a firm
policy on gun control,' he said. 'If there's a gun
around, I went to be the person controlling it.'

The innuendo wasn't bad ('I don't mean to
interfere with your marriage, but it's dangerous
messing around with a man's vehicles') and
just in case audiences missed the innuendo
first time round, it was repeated throughout the
movie. There was also a gratuitous and not
original exchange between a flasher and Lou
Ann. 'What do you think?' asked the flasher. 'It
looks like a penis,' she replied, 'only smaller.'
The screenplay should have been tighter, and
more could have made of the bungled arrest in
a crowded casino and the sequence where the
couple were trapped in a car-wash and nearly
blown up by a bomb in a baby doll.

John Dennis Johnston,
Timothy Carhart,
Bernadette Peters
and Clint Eastwood in
Pink Cadillac

The trouble with Eastwood's role was that it was totally impossible to believe that Nowak would ever have been a pushover for such a silly woman as Lou Ann and that he would have thrown in his job for her. The trouble with Peters's role was that the development of her character was equally unconvincing. The two were meant to have been brought closer by having been shooting together, but they remained a charmless, unlikely partnership and the sexual ding-dong was nil.

There was an over-the-top comic turn by Geoffrey Lewis as a zany, mangy, spaced-out guy who forged identification papers, which led to an unpleasant scene when The Birthright Organization beat him up and trashed his property, setting the place alight and leaving him to burn inside.

The climax took place in the forest. 'I am going to have to ask you, are you an organ donor, Alex?' asked Nowak, with a gun to Alex's head, giving a very good imitation of Dirty Harry. In the final chase, he and Lou Ann were so outnumbered and so out-gunned that the whole thing became farcical. Cars were

being driven off the road, cars were being driven into shacks, cars were nosediving into rivers, cars were overturning and cars were falling to bits. Bullets were flying, Eastwood was driving, Peters was screaming, the baby was crying and nobody was wearing seat-belts. The stunt men had a great time.

The soundtrack, top-heavy with country tunes, was aimed at a young audience. 'We can't see round the bend,' sang one group, 'we never know where the road might end, we just go anywhere.' Just like *Pink Cadillac*. Understandably, Eastwood's heart didn't seem to be in it.

The film gives us no reason to think these two people are even slightly attracted to each other. Mr Eastwood and Ms Peters might as well have been filmed separately and spliced together.

Caryn James, *New York Times*

I just wish this vehicle had some juice.

Georgia Brown, *Village Voice*

The 1990s

Clint Eastwood in
A Perfect World

WHITE HUNTER, BLACK HEART

Directed by Clint Eastwood   1990

It is not about the making of The African Queen. *It is not about Bogart and Hepburn and Bacall. It's about a film director with a powerful obsession that brushed everyone and everything else aside - and the deadly cost of that obsession.*

Peter Viertel

White Hunter, Black Heart was a portrait of the legendary film director John Huston, based on Peter Viertel's *roman à clef*, published in 1953, which gave a fictional account of his experiences while working on the script of *The African Queen* on location in Uganda and the Belgian Congo in 1950. The screenplay had been kicking around for 30 years and there had been any number of options taken on it before Clint Eastwood decided to do it.

John Wilson (as Huston was called in the film) was an ogre, a pain in the arse, an unreasonable, bloody-minded, unprofessional, selfish bastard, who continually violated the unwritten laws of the motion-picture business, yet had the magic, almost divine ability to land on his feet. His creative talent was never in any doubt. A professional smile always at the ready, he remained a mass of contradictions. On the one hand, he had a charismatic charm, wit and intelligence; on the other, a boorish, reckless, swaggering megalomania. 'We are gods,' he said, 'lousy little gods, who control the lives of the people we create, deciding whether they have the right to live', and he wasn't just talking about the characters in the screenplay.

Wilson was very clear about his priorities. He had got a fever; it was like a passion, a demon, and he wouldn't be all right until he had killed an elephant. He saw the film as an all-expenses-paid safari. Broke himself (he owed $300,000), he was quite willing to let the whole movie go down the drain and bankrupt the company. He didn't give a damn. 'You're either crazy or the most egocentric, irresponsible son of a bitch that I've ever met,' said Peter Verrill (the Peter Viertel role, played by Jeff Fahey).

Wilson was as much an endangered species as the bull elephant he wanted to kill. When the producer insisted the rapids sequence was too dangerous and ordered it to be cut from the film, his immediate response was to get into a tacky boat and shoot the rapids. 'Do you know why I agreed to work with him?' he asked Verrill rhetorically. 'Because it was the wrong thing to do.'

In England, dressed in jodhpurs, he adopted a patronizing English accent and rode with the hounds, a caricature of an English lord. In Africa, he followed in the footsteps of Ernest Hemingway and acted the great white hunter. His producer longed for him to drop both roles and become a film director again.

There were two set-pieces. The first, very contrived and theatrical, was with a woman (Mel Martin) Wilson had hoped to bed, but she proved so anti-Semitic that he changed his mind. 'You, my dear, are the ugliest, goddamn bitch I've ever dined with.' The second, immediately following, was with the racist hotel manager (Clive Mantle) and ended in fisticuffs, with him (contrary to the audience's expectations) rather than the manager getting beaten up. It might have been more of a moral victory had he not been drunk at the time.

Wilson would come to the aid of the under-dog, yet he could be high-handed, condescend-

George Dzundza and Clint Eastwood in *White Hunter, Black Heart*

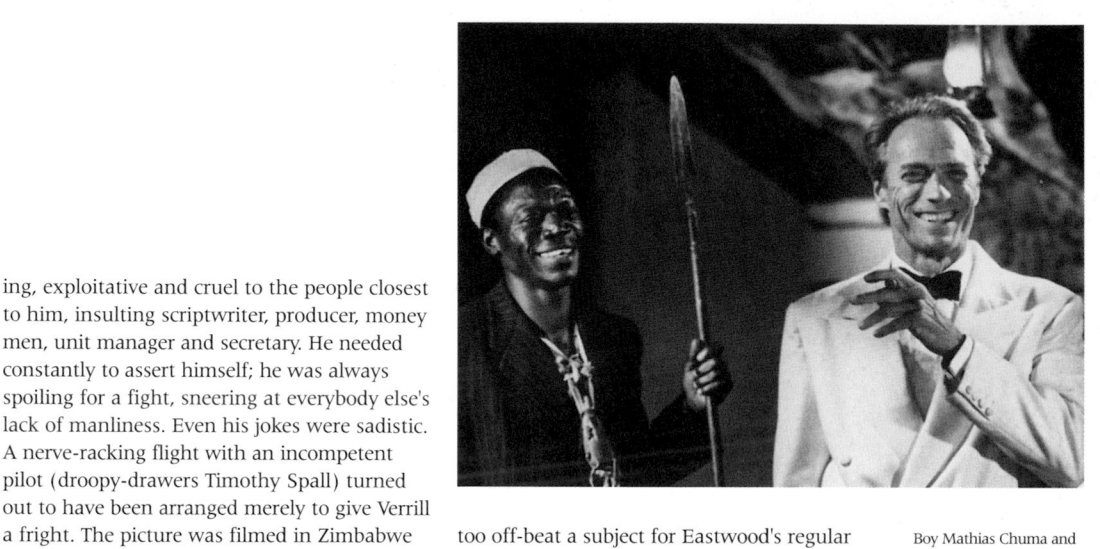

Boy Mathias Chuma and Clint Eastwood in *White Hunter, Black Heart*

ing, exploitative and cruel to the people closest to him, insulting scriptwriter, producer, money men, unit manager and secretary. He needed constantly to assert himself; he was always spoiling for a fight, sneering at everybody else's lack of manliness. Even his jokes were sadistic. A nerve-racking flight with an incompetent pilot (droopy-drawers Timothy Spall) turned out to have been arranged merely to give Verrill a fright. The picture was filmed in Zimbabwe and the flight was really an excuse for a gratuitous aerial shot of the Victoria Falls, yet little was made of the local footage elsewhere.

When the stars, Humphrey Bogart and Katharine Hepburn (played by lookalikes Richard Vanstone and Marisa Berenson) finally arrived in Africa, Wilson laid on a slap-up dinner and then proceeded to humiliate the producer in front of everybody. His humiliation was abetted by a scurrying monkey tearing up the one and only script. (George Dzundza was well cast as the exasperated butt for Wilson's contempt.) There were also major conflicts between director and scriptwriter over the screenplay. Wilson wanted to blow up the ship and kill everybody. Verrill preferred a happy ending. 'Why are you so concerned about the damn audience?' demanded Wilson. 'Because we're in show business!' replied Verrill.

Right at the very end, Wilson admitted, 'You were right, Pete, the ending's all wrong.' It was an ironic and deliberately ambiguous line, referring both to the end of the film they were about to shoot and to the end of *White Hunter, Black Heart* itself. *The African Queen*, one of Huston's most popular films, had ended happily on a silly coda and had been a huge success; *White Hunter, Black Heart*, already far

too off-beat a subject for Eastwood's regular fans, ended on a downbeat note and was a box-office failure.

The 60-year-old Clint Eastwood, playing the 45-year-old John Huston, did not resort to glib impersonation. His incarnation was rather an evocation of the man, his speech, mannerisms, clothes, cigars. There were those who found the performance a bit too laid-back, too light, vocally and physically, to be convincing; yet Wilson's comments on screenwriting could easily have been Eastwood's own credo: 'Things are always good if they are left simple. Don't complicate, you'll be wasting your time.' (Eastwood's films never get bogged down in a subplot.) 'You can't let 85 million popcorn-eaters pull you this way and that. To write a movie you have to forget anyone is going to see it.' (Maybe he was thinking of two of his favourite pictures, *Bronco Billy* and *Honkytonk Man*?)

Wilson had a key scene with the unit manager (Alun Armstrong), who was in charge of the budget. The manager was an odious, sour little man, a spy for head office, on the bottle and invariably rude to the natives. Wilson turned on him for using 'Hollywood' as a pejorative term: 'People say "Hollywood" when they want to insult you. They are not talking about the people who work and try to

Clint Eastwood in *White Hunter, Black Heart*

do something worthwhile. They are talking about the whores - whores who sell words and ideas and melodies. I know what I'm talking about because I have done a lot of hustling in my time - a hell of a lot more than I'd like to admit.' (Was he, perhaps, thinking of *The Dead Pool* and *Pink Cadillac*?)

There were intellectual debates between Wilson and Verrill about the elephant. Verrill thought it a crime to kill one of the rarest and most noble creatures to roam the earth. Wilson tried, unsuccessfully, to explain himself: 'It's not a crime to kill an elephant. It's bigger than that. It's a sin to kill an elephant. You understand that. It's the only sin you can buy a licence for and go out and commit. That's why I want to do it before I do anything else in the world. Do you understand me? Of course, you do not. I don't understand myself.'

The climax was brilliantly handled and deeply moving. Wilson, finally, came face to face with the elephant. (The casting people had more difficulty casting the elephant than any other role; in the event, the elephant was superb.) Man and beast were seen in enormous close-ups, a confrontation which some likened to Captain Ahab's with Moby Dick. (Huston had filmed the Herman Melville classic in 1956.) Wilson faltered, unable to pull the trigger. In the novel he killed the elephant. Here the elephant backed off, only immediately to turn round and charge, seemingly to protect a baby elephant. The native guide (Boy Mathias Chuma) tried to intervene and was thrown, mauled and killed, the swirling camera emphasizing the horror.

The final scene of all, back on the set, was equally well-handled, intercutting between the grief-stricken villagers and the film company. Wilson asked what the native drumbeats meant and was told that they meant bad news and that they always began with the same words: white hunter, black heart. He sat there, slumped in his director's chair, deeply shaken, a gaunt, silent, numbed, sick figure. The tragic outcome of his folly and arrogance had finally cut him down to size. He was filled with shame, self-hatred and remorse. The actors, the producer and the crew waited for him to give the signal to start. It was a long, long wait before he said, very softly, 'Action!' Eastwood was excellent.

White Hunter, Black Heart is an honourable piece of work because it refuses to remain the sort of film that audiences will expect.

Anthony Lane, *Independent on Sunday*

Eastwood can't decide whether to impersonate the great man or play it light and easy. He loses himself somewhere between the two, appearing both ludicrous and wooden.

Angus Wolfe Murray, *Scotsman Weekend*

Eastwood's portrait of the egotistical Huston is by far his best performance to date.

Adrian Turner, *Sunday Correspondent*

Eastwood's menopausal machismo nightmare is strained - lacking the tension, rigorous thought and visceral power of his best work.

Gavin Martin, *New Musical Express*

After this movie, not even Clint Eastwood's harshest judge could deny him his rightful place in the top echelons of actors and directors.

Richard Blaine, *Today*

THE ROOKIE

Directed by Clint Eastwood   1990

The Rookie, a story of a veteran cop and his wet-behind-the-ears partner, was a 'Dirty Harry' film in all but name. They were members of the Grand Theft Auto Division of the Los Angeles Police Department looking into a $2 million raid.

Clint Eastwood may have got top billing but, as the title suggested, he was playing a supporting role to the rookie. He was cast as Nick Pulovski, a sour, cynical, caustic cop who smoked cigars. (The running gag was that he never had a light.) Obsessed with avenging the murder of his partner, he patronized the rookie. Eastwood was his usual confrontational, aggressive self. The dialogue, full of cliché-ridden banalities, was often unintentionally funny.

Charlie Sheen played the rookie, David Ackerman, a poor-little-rich-boy who had joined the force two years previously to spite his parents. ('Where were you when I was in pain? You were never there for me, Dad.'). He had also joined to try to expiate guilty feelings about the death of his brother in an accident for which he had been partly to blame. His father said he needed to forgive himself. The rookie needed to forgive himself even more when, unable to kill the villainess, he dithered and Pulovski was kidnapped. 'Amateur!' she screamed, shooting him. He smashed his head against a mirror until the mirror cracked, because that is what some movie actors do when they want to signal their frustration.

Ackerman became determined to prove his manhood to his colleagues and his girlfriend. 'I'm through making mistakes,' he declared. 'It's time for me to stop being scared and other people to start.' He took off his suit, put on a

Charlie Sheen and Clint Eastwood in *The Rookie*

denim jacket and went back to the bikers' bar (where earlier he had been beaten up) and smashed up the joint, single-handedly, and then set it alight. He walked out of the burning building, no longer 'a damned yellow rookie', no longer 'a fresh-faced punk', but a man, and just in case cinemagoers hadn't noticed what a man the rookie had become, he threw away his motorcycle helmet, got on his bike and drove through his front door to save his girlfriend from being murdered. He then drove off to rescue his partner. Sheen, who managed to be both chubby and wooden, was an unlikely tough guy.

The villains were a way-over-the-top couple. 'There was Strom, a ruthless, big-time German thief, played by South American actor Raul Julia who sported a dreadful accent and a

Sonia Brage and
Clint Eastwood in
The Rookie

There was a good moment when he took a small-time crook and his car for a ride in a wrecking yard and there was also a good joke, badly handled, when he and Ackerman made a surprise entrance, stepping out of a gambling casino's safe. The highlights were two action sequences. The first, excellently edited by Joel Cox, came right at the beginning, providing the fans with what they had come to see. Pulovski was in full pursuit of Strom, who was making his escape in a double-decker transporter loaded with Porsches, Jaguars and Mercedes. A member of the gang (Marco Rodriguez, with a good pockmarked villain's face) released three automobiles on to the motorway, causing mayhem. He dodged the crashing cars and drove on to the carrier. The gang member then released the whole trailer, spewing cars all over the place in a tremendous pile-up. Bill Young's precision-driving team stole all the notices.

comic moustache. His partner and lover (Sonia Braga), a scantily clad *femme fatale*, was equally absurd. She behaved as if she were in a James Bond movie and gave Pulovski a good licking. 'Are you man? Are you any different?' she asked, ripping open his shirt and playing with a razor blade. 'You better be, because I hate anything useless. When something is no good to me, I cut it off and throw it away.' The armchair bondage and fellatio were recorded on banks of television screens. Rape was not unusual in an Eastwood movie, but this was the first time that he was the one being raped. While he was being abused, the TV networks were showing an old monster movie and a very large black spider was briefly observed on the screen. This was a private joke, which may have been missed. The movie was *Tarantula*, one of the very first movies Eastwood had made. He was the pilot who had bombed the tarantula.

The stunt work was equally impressive when Pulovski and Ackerman were making their escape from the top floor of a warehouse by driving through a floor-to-ceiling window as the building detonated. They landed on the roof of another building, fell through the skylight into a warehouse and drove straight to San Jose International Airport, where a private jet tried to run them down as they raced across the fields. Hands up all those who have seen Alfred Hitchcock's *North by Northwest*. The homage to Hitchcock had been much better expressed earlier, in a dry-cleaning shop, when a garrotted corpse was discovered hanging among the laundry on a spinning carousel.

Pulovski and Ackerman entered the main building via the luggage hold - a nice idea which would have been even better had it been

more imaginatively and wittily stage-managed. While chasing round the crowded airport, full of screaming, ducking extras pretending to be passengers, Ackerman managed to save his partner from being killed by shooting both villains dead. 'Amateur!' he screamed. The two wounded men sat together, sporting their bloody gashes, and they would have smoked a post-coital cigar had they had a light.

In an unlikely and glib coda, the veteran cop had been kicked upstairs and was doing a desk job and the rookie had stepped into his shoes. *The Rookie* was for diehard fans only.

While learning how to please arthouse audiences, Clint Eastwood has forgotten how to make popular entertainment.

Philip French, *Observer*

This is a shameless exercise in quickie production money-making that relies on the idea that audiences won't notice the joins if there is enough crash, bang, wallop.

Sue Heal, *Today*

It's sad to watch a superstar going through the motions.

Shaun Usher, *Daily Mail*

I enjoyed every minute. There is no star like an old star.

Nigel Andrews, *Financial Times*

Clint Eastwood and Raul Julia in *The Rookie*

UNFORGIVEN

Directed by Clint Eastwood   1992

I thought it was very timely to do a film where violence not only can be painful, but has consequences for the perpetrators as well as the victims. Usually in Westerns violence is glorified and romanticized. We demythicize it.

Clint Eastwood,
quoted by John Hiscock, *Daily Telegraph*

Unforgiven (dedicated to Eastwood's mentors, Sergio Leone and Don Siegel) was an elegiac Western set in 1880, the year of President Garfield's assassination. The film (originally called *The Cot Whore Killings*) opened with violence in the local brothel in the ramshackle town of Big Whiskey in Wyoming. One of the girls (Anna Thomson), new to the job, dared to laugh at her customer's little pecker and had her face slashed. The brothel owner, who treated the girls as his property, demanded compensation, not for them but for himself. The sheriff fined the cowboys seven ponies. The whores, who had expected a whipping at the very least, were outraged and, led by Strawberry Alice (Frances Fisher), the whorehouse madam, offered $1,000 reward to anybody who killed the men.

William Munny (Clint Eastwood), 'a known thief and murderer, a man of notoriously vicious and intemperate disposition', had been cured of his wickedness by his wife. Totally reformed, he was a sensitive, single parent, looking after two young children and trying, unsuccessfully, to eke out a living on a broken-down pig farm. His wife had died at 29 of smallpox, three years before the story began, but her presence was felt throughout the film. Ever faithful to her memory, the last thing he wanted to do was resume his former trade, so

Clint Eastwood and
Morgan Freeman in
Unforgiven

Previous page:
Clint Eastwood, Shane
Meier and Aline
Levasseur in *Unforgiven*

when a young bounty hunter (Jaimz Woolvett) asked him to be his partner, he turned him down. However, his destitution, and the need to feed his children, forced him to change his mind and he invited his former partner, Ned Logan (Morgan Freeman), also an old man and retired, to join him.

The bounty hunter, who called himself the Schofield Kid, was disappointed to find that Munny wasn't the mean, cold, crazy, no-good-son-of-a-bitch killer of legend that he had expected to see. The Kid was, literally and symbolically, a short-sighted youth. (His naïvety and hero-worshipping brought back memories of the role Timothy Bottoms had played in *The Outlaw Josey Wales*.)

The Sheriff (Gene Hackman) was a smiling fascist who wanted law and order and did what he thought best for the community; and what he did best was punch and kick a man when he was down. When English Bob (Richard Harris),

a veteran gunfighter, arrived in town, he immediately disarmed him and then, as a warning to all other bounty hunters, he beat the living daylights out of him and put him and his accompanying biographer in jail.

The sheriff gave the biographer, a dime novelist (a comic character played by Saul Rubinek), a true account of Bob's manly exploits and the scene afforded opportunities for satire at the expense of the heroes and legends of the West. The sheriff also enjoyed a little game, giving the Duke (or The Duck, as he preferred to call him) a chance to kill him, which the Duke made the mistake of not taking. The cowardly biographer quickly changed his allegiance.

There was an excellent scene when Munny, sick and feverish, was sitting all by himself in the saloon while his partners were upstairs humping the whores. Surrounded by the sheriff and his deputies, he was asked for his weapons

and, when he declined to give them up, he, too, was given a vicious beating. He ended up crawling out on all fours. Eastwood, unshaven, deeply scarred, didn't just look old; he looked as if he were at death's door.

The killing of the first cowboy (a nice lad, not guilty, except by association with his partner) was played for full horror. Ned couldn't bring himself to kill him. The Schofield Kid couldn't see him to kill him. So, it was left to Munny to shoot him. The boy bled to death in a gully. Ned no longer had the stomach and returned home, only to be captured by a posse and whipped to death by the Sheriff. His body was placed in an open coffin outside the saloon with a placard: 'This is what happens to assassins around here.'

The killing of the second cowboy (the fat slob who had actually done the slashing) was carried out by the Schofield Kid while the man was sitting in the privy. The Kid, who had pretended to have killed five men (not that anybody had believed him), found out what it was really like to kill. 'I guess he had it comin',' he said in a pathetic attempt at bravado. 'We all have it comin',' said Munny. The Kid was shattered: 'It don't seem real. How he can never breathe again, how he's dead, all on account of pulling a trigger. I'm going to kill nobody no more. I ain't like you, Will.'

Eastwood, who had hung on to the script, waiting some seven or eight years until he felt he was old enough to play Munny, liked the morality of the story: 'This is the first story I have ever come across where the outlaw had a conscience about what he was doing.'

The horror of the past and its killings continued to haunt Munny to the very end: 'It's a

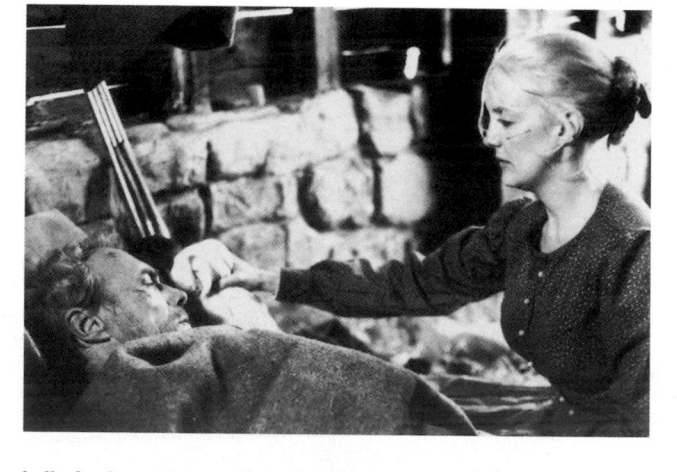

Clint Eastwood and Anna Thomson in *Unforgiven*

hell of a thing killing a man, taking away all he got and all he's ever going to have.' But goaded by Ned's murder, he yielded to that past and came back to avenge his death. Making his entrance to a clap of thunder, he was transformed into a High Plains Drifter, a Pale Rider, a Man With No Name. He killed the unarmed saloon owner ('He should have armed himself!'), the sheriff and his three deputies, the latter all decent men. 'I have always been lucky when it comes to killing folks,' he said.

The scene may have been good for Eastwood's fans, but it was tragic for Munny, a moral defeat. When the sheriff (the last man to die) said he would see him in hell, it was as if Munny had already been there and was on his way back. He rode out, threatening to return and kill every one of them. He never did come back, though. He moved on to San Francisco and - this was an unexpected, ironic touch - prospered in dry goods.

Clint Eastwood and
Jaimz Woolvett in
Unforgiven

Unforgiven, hard-bitten, hard-edged and highly dramatic, was a brooding and sombre work, its dark tones complemented by photographer Jack Green's sombre and bleak images. (It rained practically all the time.) There was superb location work in Alberta and California.

Unforgiven is Clint Eastwood's masterpiece.

It's Eastwood's best movie and the best Western by anybody in over twenty years.

USA Today

It is a grim picture, lightened by fine acting, beautiful photography, and, most of all, subversively mordant irony.

Stephen Amedon, *Financial Times*

He inhabits the genre like no other contemporary actor.

Hugo Davenport, *Daily Telegraph*

With his new film, *Unforgiven*, Eastwood comes close to pulling a wholly successful modern Western out of the hat. Only the last reel stands in the way of it attaining classic status.

Adam Mars-Jones, *Independent*

Eastwood stands alone in his commitment to directing and starring in Westerns. *Unforgiven* won't revive the genre, but it will keep the flame alive until the next talent keen to use the country's mythology can put the Western to his uses.

Chris Peachment, *Sunday Times*

If there is anything I learned from Don Siegel, it's to know what you want to shoot and to know what you're seeing when you see it.

Clint Eastwood

IN THE LINE OF FIRE

Directed by Wolfgang Petersen   1993

In the Line of Fire was a first-rate thriller about a bid to assassinate the President of the United States. The President gets 14,000 such threats a year. Clint Eastwood was cast as Frank Horrigan, an elderly undercover agent who volunteered to be attached to the White House to protect him. The big question was, had he got the guts to take the bullet? He was still haunted by his failure 30 years previously to halt the fatal bullets that had killed President Kennedy in Dallas. Had it been cowardice? Or slow reflexes due to a hangover? Could he, this time, save the present incumbent, who was in the middle of a campaign seeking re-election and trailing badly in the polls?

There were already 229 people protecting the President. Was he worth dying for? The answer was almost certainly not, but Horrigan was protecting the office rather than the man. Certainly, he did not feel the allegiance he had felt for JFK. Horrigan, a man of integrity and a patriot, was there to uphold the moral code and, indeed, in order to protect JFK's dignity he had once (very patriotically) pretended that Kennedy's girlfriend, caught in the White House, had been his girlfriend and taken the rap.

Horrigan, who worked by intuition and psychological insight rather than by tech-nology, was described by the backbiters as 'a borderline burnt-out with questionable sociable skills', and, more simply, as a 'dinosaur' and 'too old for this shit'. At 63, it was true he was no longer a young man. The face, worn and overwrought, was deeply fissured and the husky voice was huskier than ever. During a motorcade, he was seen running by the side of the President's car, puffing and coughing away. There were constant references to his age and

lots of self-deprecating jokes, as if the actor wanted to get in there first before anybody else did. When Horrigan said, not without irony, 'You're looking at a living legend', Eastwood could well have been talking about himself.

Though Horrigan was not Dirty Harry, his Dirty Harry credentials were immediately established by his abrasive and confrontational manner with colleagues, and especially in the opening sequence, when he was busting a gang of counterfeiters and put the life of his partner (Dylan McDermott) horribly at risk; and, sure enough, his partner went the way of all Harry's partners. McDermott (in a much more developed part than usual) was very good.

Mitch Leary, the assassin, called himself Booth after the famous actor-assassin who had murdered Abraham Lincoln. He was a master of disguise, constantly changing his appearance and character while dogging Horrigan's footsteps. It was a very long time before his face was seen.

John Malkovich had a sinister calmness which was liable to give way to sudden, frightening outbursts. His psychotic was not without a creepy, camp charm and he played his telephone conversations with Horrigan for malevolent black comedy, seeing them as an act of gamesmanship, a battle of wits between equals, flirting, taunting and humiliating him in front of his colleagues. Leary knew everything about the man: his private life, his drink problem, his divorce, his pain, his guilt. The telephone calls were among the screenplay's best moments.

Leary was a chilling murderer, dispatching two women bank clerks and then two men who were out fishing without a thought. He turned

Clint Eastwood in
In the Line of Fire

183

Rene Russo and
Clint Eastwood in
In the Line of Fire

The assassination attempt at a fund-raising dinner was sharply edited, cutting from the bodyguards bundling the President out of the building through the kitchens to Leary taking Horrigan hostage. The film ended with a melodramatic duel in a hotel's glass lift and Leary's all too expected fall to his death.

Horrigan flirted with a Secret Service agent (a very cool Rene Russo) three decades his junior. Their barbed dialogue was very much in a wisecracking tradition which stretched back to the gangster movies of the 1940s and 1930s. The best joke was a visual one, when they were approaching a bed and the camera stayed at floor level, observing what they were discarding: not just clothes, but handcuffs, guns and blackjacks.

out to be a disillusioned CIA assassin. He and Horrigan were two halves of the same person, mutually dependent, both feeling that the United States had once been very special and neither believing in her any more. Malkovich's quietly dangerous performance was an excellent foil for Eastwood.

Horrigan, tough yet vulnerable, was the prototype (so he said) of the heterosexual, white, over-50 American male. The assassin, by implication, was homosexual. There was an exciting chase on the rooftops which ended with Horrigan dangling over the edge, hanging on to Leary's hand. It was a scene which paid direct homage to Alfred Hitchcock's *Vertigo*, though Hitchcock would not have gone so far as to have his villain perform mock fellatio on the hero's revolver, daring him to shoot his load in his mouth and kill them both.

Eastwood is an actor who has always given more than you might suspect he's capable of, and here he does a little reprise of his *Unforgiven* portrait that is wonderfully strong on the kind of detail that doesn't draw attention to itself but makes or breaks a leading part.

Derek Malcolm, *Guardian*

What makes Eastwood so powerful in the part is the way he imbues the action of the present with the presence of the past. . . no other American star has a comparable artillery that he brings to bear. Eastwood knows his own limitations as an actor: he cannot become somebody else; he has to play an aspect of himself.

Iain Johnstone, *Sunday Times*

The two greatest landscapes in American cinema are Monument Valley and Clint Eastwood's face.

Nigel Andrews, *Financial Times*

A PERFECT WORLD

Directed by Clint Eastwood   1993

Butch Haynes, a hardened criminal serving 40 years for armed robbery, escaped from prison, taking Phillip Perry, a seven-year-old boy, hostage. The escaping convict was pursued by a Texan Ranger travelling in a high-tech mobile trailer. The story was set in 1963, two weeks before President Kennedy's fatal visit to Dallas. There were, in fact, two separate stories: the hunted, who was in total control of the situation, and the hunter, who was not. The action was absorbing so long as it stuck with the convict and the boy on the long, lonesome roads of rural Texas.

Kevin Costner, cast against type, was basically too nice to be convincing as a hardened criminal. The little boy was never in any danger. Obsessed with his own childhood, Butch identified with Phillip and became his surrogate father. 'The best thing a man can hope to be,' he said, 'is a fine family man,' He was more paternal than criminal; yet he was capable of brutality and had killed two men. The first had killed his mum; the second was his fellow fugitive, who had molested Phillip.

Butch was an implacable enemy of child abusers. The most electrifying, the most frightening scene in the whole film was when he threatened a black farmer (Wayne Dehart, excellent), forcing him at gunpoint to say he loved his child. The change in his character was so sharp as to be unbelievable and was there only so that Phillip could have a dramatic reason to shoot and wound him. His death, a sentimental, tear-jerking, elegiac finale, took place in a lovely meadow. The film had opened with the same lyrical shot, when it had seemed to be a picture of a man asleep in the windswept grass.

Clint Eastwood in
A Perfect World

Butch, the lifelong loser ('I ain't a good man. I ain't the worst neither, just a breed apart') was a role Clint Eastwood might have played when he was younger. Costner acted with intelligence, charm and dry humour; the performance could have done with more anger, more nihilism.

Eastwood was cast as Red Garnett, the Texan Ranger, a role so perfunctory there was not much he could do with it. Garnett had been the

Clint Eastwood in
A Perfect World

arresting officer who had recommended that the teenage Butch should be sent to prison. He had hoped he would reform once he was away from the home influence; instead prison had turned him into an hardened criminal, just like his dad.

Eastwood acted with rugged authority, but the scenes in the mobile were never interesting enough and the attempts to introduce some sparring between him and an accompanying criminologist (Laura Dern) didn't work as well as the scenes between him and Rene Russo had

done in *In the Line of Fire*. The criminologist, a feminist, merely came across as an anachronism in 1963. There was also a feeble attempt to introduce some comedy when the governor's prize mobile became separated from its driver and they all ended up in the trees.

Eight-year-old T. J. Crowther played the hostage: a shy, sad little boy from a broken home, denied the simplest pleasures because his mother was a Jehovah's Witness. Phillip looked cute in his Hallowe'en mask and got on just fine with Butch, especially after Butch had

reassured him about the size of his penis. ('It's a good size for a boy of your age.') The bonding of man and child was all the more touching for being saccharine-free. Crowther had been extremely well-directed and edited.

Bradley Whitford was cast as the odious, arrogant sharp-shooter who finished off the wounded Butch and was rewarded for his too eager marksmanship with a sock to the jaw by the Texan Ranger and a kick in the balls by the criminologist.

A Perfect World was a small-scale movie, inflated by the presence of its two famous stars. The film should have been shorter, sharper, tougher, smaller; at 138 minutes, it was overlong and the pace was far too leisurely. There was too much narrative and not nearly enough suspense.

Eastwood is canny enough to hold on to at least one basic rule of American movies: if you get a big star and put him in a big landscape - Texas will do - you can't go far wrong.

Terence Rafferty, *New Yorker*

His tough-cop role resembles many others he's played before, but this time remains a strictly one-dimensional supporting figure who doesn't really do much.

Todd McCarthy, *Variety*

As the decent, grizzled Ranger, the self-abnegatory Eastwood never uses his power as director to upstage other actors.

Philip French, *Observer*

A Perfect World evinces the perfect integrity, the unstinting modesty of Eastwood's work all along. (The reticent directorial style meshes absolutely with the persona.)

Georgina Brown, *Village Voice*

Its tone is pretty much unique, but then why would anyone set out to make a film that is sentimental without being sweet, that manages to be bleak and mawkish at the same time? The film is a mustard sandwich on white bread, bland in texture but still leaving a harsh taste in the mouth.

Adam Mars-Jones, *Independent*

THE BRIDGES OF MADISON COUNTY

Directed by Clint Eastwood. 1995

Meryl Streep and
Clint Eastwood in
*The Bridges of
Madison County*

Robert James Walker's romantic novel was in the best seller list for 15 weeks. 'The worst book in living memory,' said *The New Yorker*. 10 million copies sold worldwide. The film, intelligent, charming, subtle, sensitive, restrained, was so much better than the pretentious novel. 'I wanted,' said Clint Eastwood, 'to concentrate on story telling and trying to give as much scope to the simplicity of the picture as I could.'

The Bridges of Madison County, with its moral dilemma and painful choice, was the perfect movie for late middle-aged audiences, who didn't go to the cinema that often and could identify with the poignancy of an opportunity not taken and regretted for the rest of life.

Walker described a four day affair in 1965 between an Ohio housewife and photographer who was on an assignment to shoot bridges

for *National Geographic*. The Italian born housewife had met her husband when he was a soldier in World War 2. They had two children: a girl of 17, a boy of 16. He was a hardworking farmer, a good, caring father and life was nice; but it was not the life she had dreamed of when she was a girl.

The photographer was a chivalrous guy who didn't want to compromise her, living, as she did, in a small community where gossip and ostracism were rife. 'We're not doing anything wrong,' he pretended, 'nothing you couldn't tell your children about.' They ate, danced and kissed in the kitchen and then shared a bath and a bed.

The photographer, a divorced man without any commitments, wanted to seize the moment. 'A certainty of this kind comes but once in a lifetime,' he pleaded, not wanting to

cram a whole lifetime into four days. But she put duty to her husband and her children before love. 'The love you give up,' she argued, 'is the only one you truly possess.'

The story was framed by her grown-up children reading her will in which she expressed a wish for her ashes to be thrown from a bridge. The children, married with families of their own, found it difficult at first to accept their mother had had an affair, but the knowledge helped them with their own marital problems. The framing device was the least satisfactory part of the script.

The production, filmed in virtually the exact locations of the book, was shot in sequence so that the relationship between actor and actress on screen could develop as naturally as the relationship between housewife and photographer. The studio, initially, had wanted a much younger actress to play the housewife, but when Eastwood came on board he had insisted on an older actress. Meryl Streep, matronly and dowdy, gentle and sad, was excellent casting. Eastwood had never been so tender and loving.

The outstanding scene was the farewell at the traffic lights. He was in his truck. She was in her car with her husband. Would she get out and join him. He got out of the truck. The tension was palpable, despite knowing she wouldn't. The most striking single shot was of his face in close-up, standing in the rain, drenched and bedraggled, silently pleading with her to come with him. Eastwood had no vanity. He looked his age and made no attempt to hide it.

Streep and Eastwood are like champion skaters, twirling beautifully on the thinnest of ice.
Geoff Brown *The Times*

In short top-quality, tear-jerking, lachrymose but literate.
Alexander Walker *Evening Standard*

Meryl Streep and Clint Eastwood in *The Bridges of Madison County*

ABSOLUTE POWER

Directed by Clint Eastwood 1997

Power tends to corrupt and absolute power corrupts absolutely.

Sir J.E.E.Dalberg, *First Baron Acton*

One of the great thieves of the world was in the middle of a routine burglary when he was interrupted. He hid in a strong room, which had a two-way mirror, and witnessed a drunken couple having rough sex which got so rough that they started to try and murder each other. The man called out for help. Two men entered and shot the woman dead. The man

was the President of the United States and the murderers were secret servicemen. A cover-up followed. The thief became the prime suspect but instead of absconding with the loot he decided to take on Eastwood's familiar role of lone avenger.

Gene Hackman, as the President, reprised the performance he had given in *No Way Out* and was a very obvious smarmy villain. Judy Davis, cast as the President's chief-of-staff, who always had to clean up the President's sexual messes, was clearly at a loss how to

Ed Harris and
Clint Eastwood in
Absolute Power

Clint Eastwood
and Laura Linney in
Absolute Power

play her role seriously and acted in a number of different comic styles. She was at her most ludicrous on the dance floor with the President.

The murdered woman was the wife of a billionaire power broker who was also the President's benefactor. The 88-year-old cuckold turned murderer, giving the film its final *coup de grâce*. The scene was so unbelievable that E G Marshall (always good value) had to play it off-screen. Scott Glenn and Dennis Haysbert were the secret servicemen. Glenn was the one with a guilty conscience. Haysbert was the one who believed 'My President, right or wrong.' He tried to murder the thief's daughter not once, but twice. The thief, gaunt and grim-faced, showed him no mercy.

Everything that could be done to make the thief Mr Nice Guy was done. Not only was he a former Korean War hero, but he also secretly filled his estranged daughter's fridge with health food. Eastwood looked his age and was willing to make jokes about it. 'I've got to get my pacemaker checked,' he told the detective. 'It's been so exciting talking to you.' The detective was played by Ed Harris. The rapport between him and Eastwood had such charm and wit, that it was a pity they didn't have more scenes together.

The long opening sequence followed by a chase through a forest at night got the film off to an excellent start. There was a reasonably well-staged ambush scene in an outdoor café, but the ending was far too rushed and abrupt. The script was by William Goldman, who wrote the screenplay for *All the President's Men*, and *Absolute Power* would have benefited from more politics.

MIDNIGHT IN THE GARDEN OF GOOD AND EVIL

Directed by Clint Eastwood 1997

John Cusack and Kevin Spacey in *Midnight in the Garden of Good and Evil.*

John Berendt's best-selling book was based on a real life murder trial, though cinemagoers would never have guessed it from the film's courtroom exchanges, which were, as an on-screen attorney was the first to admit, straight out of the *Perry Mason* television series.

A famous socialite (Kevin Spacey), a closet homosexual who lived in Savannah, was tried four times for first degree murder. He claimed he killed his lover (Jude Law), a volatile street hustler, in self-defence. He was acquitted, but had already confessed to a journalist (John Cusack) that he had murdered. Shortly after the trial, he had a fatal heart attack. As he crashed to the floor, he saw his dead lover lying on the carpet beside him, smiling happily.

Spacey's languid and very *nouveau riche* Southerner looked very smug and quite capable of murder. John Cusack dropped his jaw so often it became his trademark. Both actors were completely upstaged by Lady

Chablis, a black transsexual, who played herself and a fictionalised version of herself. 'I have a man's toolbox,' she said, 'but everything else about me is pure lady.' Camp, outrageous, self-mocking, Chablis gatecrashed a black debutante's ball and used the courtroom as a coming-out party.

Just in case anybody might be thinking the journalist was gay and might be having a fling with the socialite he was provided with an unconvincing girl friend. The film did, however, suggest in a jokey aside that he was going to have a one-night stand with the transvestite.

There were some very strange people in Savannah. A man covered in horseflies threatened to poison the water supply. Another man walked an imaginary dog. A cackling voodoo priestess communed with the dead. 'It's like *Gone with the Wind* on mescaline,' said the journalist.

TRUE CRIME

Directed by Clint Eastwood 1999

'I don't give a rat's arse about Jesus Christ
and I don't care about justice in this world or
the next. I don't even care about right and
wrong. So I'm going to ask you, did you kill
that woman or not?' Thus spoke an
investigative reporter (Clint Eastwood), giving
a very good imitation of Dirty Harry in make-
my-day mode.

A black mechanic (Isaiah Washington),
convicted of a murder committed six years
before the film began, was about to be
executed. A born-again Christian he believed
he was going to heaven. A proud and noble
man he refused to say sorry for something he
hadn't done.

A local newspaper wanted a human story
about the man's last hours. The reporter was
convinced the man was innocent. He had only
eight hours to prove it. 'Dear God,' said the
condemned man's wife, 'where were you all
this time?'

The reporter looked haggard. He was in
deep trouble. He neglected his wife and child.
He was a womaniser. He was chatting up
women old enough to be his grandchildren
and sleeping with the wife of his immediate
boss. He also smoked. Self-destructive, yet
tenacious, he chased salvation. But whose arse
was he trying to save? The prisoner's? Or his
own?

The race against time was so unbelievable
that it was robbed of any tension and
especially in the silly car chase at the end. The
real climax should have been the condemned
man's death and it looked like it was going to
be just that. The state governor's call to cancel
the execution came after the lethal injection
had been administered. But the film lost its

Clint Eastwood and
James Woods in
True Crime

nerve and there was a coda to show the man
was still alive, walking the streets at
Christmas time with his family, and giving
Eastwood a friendly wave.

True Crime clearly wanted to say something
about capital punishment, racial prejudice,
humane prison staff and no-good prison
chaplains. But the script only really came to
life in the sexual banter between the reporter
and his editor-in-chief. Eastwood and James
Woods had a great time. The fast-talking,
wisecracking sparring had the machinegun
ratatat tempo of the 1930's stage and film
newspaper classic, *The Front Page*.

An Eastwood pause is more expressive than another
actor's aria. An Eastwood look can silence or
incinerate at will.

Nigel Andrews *Financial Times*

A great performance, shame about the film

Derek Malcolm *Guardian*

The 2000s

SPACE COWBOYS

Directed by Clint Eastwood 2000

Clint Eastwood, Tommy Lee Jones, James Garner and Donald Sutherland in *Space Cowboys*.

Four crack pilots in the 1950s, destined to be the first men to fly in space, discovered at a press conference that they were to be replaced by a chimpanzee and retired. Forty years on an obsolete Russian communications satellite's guidance system had broken down and was heading to earth with six nuclear missiles attached to it. The superannuated quartet carried out a rescue operation.

Their former commander was not keen to fill up a space shuttle with geriatrics. But if Senator John Glenn could return to space at 77, why couldn't these guys? Clint Eastwood was 70. James Garner was 72, Donald Sutherland was 65. Tommy Lee Jones was only 53.

Eastwood's cowboy was having sex with his wife in the garage. Lee Jones's cowboy was chatting up a NASA scientist. Sutherland's cowboy was proudly showing off his private parts to anybody who wanted to see them. Garner was playing a clergyman so he didn't get to have sex. He just said a prayer.

The first part of *Space Cowboys* was devoted to the men's physical and technical training. The only scene anybody remembers is the medical with the four actors standing stark naked. Saggy bottoms are not a pretty sight. 'They look like the rear view of Mount Rushmore or four pictures of Dorian Gray's arse by Francis Bacon,' said John Paterson in *The Guardian*. The second part of the film was the mission and meant to be serious, but its schoolboy heroics would have been more appropriate in *Airplane!* The final shot had Lee Jones (in his role of the navigator who was dying of cancer) sitting all alone on the moon, while Frank Sinatra sang *Fly Me to the Moon* on the soundtrack.

NASA meets Peter Pan.
Alexander Walker
Evening Standard

Oldies are still a blast.
Christopher Tookey
Daily Mail

BLOOD WORK

Directed by Clint Eastwood 2002

Clint Eastwood was cast as a celebrity FBI profiler who had a near fatal heart attack whilst chasing a suspect. He received a heart transplant and learned later that the donor was a murder victim. He felt he owed it to her to track down her killer. His cardiologist nearly had a heart attack when he said he was back on the job.

Eastwood said he was attracted to the role because of the character's physical and psychological vulnerability and because it provided him with 'a different slant on a familiar role, one which was more appropriate to a man of my maturity'. The script said he looked like crap, Eastwood looked like crap. His voice was hoarse, his face was gnarled, his brow was knitted, his neck was scrawny and his torso had a very nasty zip-like scar. There was also an unflattering shot of his agonised face when he was having the heart attack.

The twist to the story was that the killer so enjoyed playing cat-and-mouse with the FBI profiler that when he realised the man needed a new heart, he went out and murdered a person with the same blood type so that he wouldn't die and that 'their great partnership' could continue. 'I gave you life. I saved you,' he boasted. But the partnership was never in the same league as the one Eastwood had had with John Malkovich in *In the Line of Fire*.

There was absolutely no chemistry between Eastwood and Wanda de Jesus, who was playing the sister of the murdered woman and meant to be providing the love interest. There was much more chemistry going on between Eastwood and Angelica Huston (as the cardiologist) and Eastwood and Tina Lifford (as sheriff, a former lover and colleague).

There was a short, sharp classic *Dirty Harry* sequence when Eastwood went to the boot of his car, took out a gun and started 'shooting up the valley', spraying bullets as the murderer made a getaway. The final sequence, on board a rusted cargo boat with everybody creeping around in the dark, was a big anti-climax.

Eastwood (despite the profiler's dickey heart) looked trim, relaxed and good-humoured. Jeff Daniels, star of *Dumb and Dumber*, was cast as the funny sidekick, a dumb marina bum, who became the cop's driver and turned out – no surprise – to be the killer.

It's always nice to see Clint and especially nice to see him play someone whose humanity – no, whose mortality – is all too apparent.

Michael O'Sullivan *Washington Post.*

Clint Eastwood and Angelica Huston in *Blood Work*

Clint Eastwood in *Blood Work*

MYSTIC RIVER

Directed by Clint Eastwood 2003

Dennis Lehane's best-selling novel described the traumatic effects on three eleven-year-olds (Jimmy, Dave and Sean) when one of them (Dave) was abducted and repeatedly raped over a four day period until he managed to escape. The sins of the neighbourhood were revisited on the children 25 years later when Jimmy's 19-year-old daughter was murdered. Sean was the detective in charge of the murder hunt. Dave became the prime suspect.

Dave (Tim Robbins), married with a child of his own, was still haunted by the past. Cowed, shambling and visibly damaged, Robbins looked like a werewolf on a bad day; yet under interrogation he showed unexpected steel.

Jimmy (Sean Penn) a shopkeeper, a former criminal, who still had associates to do his dirty work, became convinced that Dave had killed his daughter and took the law into his own hands. The climax, excellently handled, had a frightened Dave confessing to a crime he hadn't committed in a desperate effort to save his life.

There was a powerful scene when the police were holding Jimmy back from the scene of the crime. 'Is that my daughter?' he howled as the camera rose high above him. Penn's pain and anguish were histrionic enough for Greek tragedy. There was also a deeply effecting scene when he was on a porch, absolutely distraut, telling Dave he couldn't cry whilst he was actually crying. Jimmy wept because he knew his actions in the past had been responsible for his daughter's death.

Marcia Hayden was very moving as Dave's wife who feared Dave was a murderer and fatally could not hide her fears from Jimmy. Laura Linney, as Jimmy's wife, had an extraordinary over-the-top scene when she turned into Lady Macbeth willing her husband to return to crime and become king of the neighbourhood. Kevin Bacon, leaving the more showy performances to the rest of the cast, was his usual effective, understated self.

Eastwood gave subtle weight to the shocking coda, played out, with superb irony, against a patriotic parade.

Solemnity rides roughshod over subtlety, making
Mystic River muddy and sluggish indeed.
                    Jonathan Romney *Independent*

This movie is a historic achievement: Clint Eastwood,
an icon of violence, has made us loathe violence as an
obscenity.

                    David Denby *New Yorker*

Kevin Bacon,
Laurence Fishburne
and Clint Eastwood
on the set of
Mystic River

MILLION DOLLAR BABY

Directed by Clint Eastwood 2005

Clint Eastwood, Hilary Swank and Morgan Freeman accepting their awards for *Million Dollar Baby*.

Boxing is about respect – getting it yourself and taking it away from the other guy. *Million Dollar Baby* was one of the best films about boxing, fit to stand alongside Robert Rossen's *Body and Soul* (1947), Robert Wise's *The Set Up* (1949) John Huston's *Fat City* (1972) and Martin Scorsese's *Raging Bull* (1980). It had a 1930s/1940s film noir feel about it.

Clint Eastwood, weathered, hoarse, no longer young, but still lean, was cast as a professional boxing trainer and manager, who ran a run-down backstreet gym in downtown Los Angeles. In his heyday he had trained and managed the best fighters in the business. One boxer lost his eye. This disaster had led him to be over-cautious about setting up fights, and this had led to boxers, who were impatient to

be getting on with their careers, to leave him.

His special skill was as a cut man. He could patch up wounds and stop the blood flowing so that a fight could continue, even when it should have been stopped. Paul Haggis's screenplay was based on F X Toole's *Rope Burns*. Toole had been a professional cut man.

A 31-year-old woman was convinced she could become the champion of the world if he trained and managed her. He refused because he didn't train girls and because she was far too old to be starting a career in boxing. Against his better judgement he took her on and found a surrogate daughter. He was estranged from his own daughter. (What had caused the estrangement remained a mystery but he had been going to Mass every day for

the last 23 years to atone.) In him the boxer found a surrogate father. Her family were trailer trash. Their behaviour was so disgusting their scenes verged on caricature.

Hilary Swank, totally focused, had her best role since *Boys Don't Cry*. Resilient and gutsy, she was very convincing in the ring. In the big fight with 'the dirtiest fighter in the world' she ended up completely paralysed, a major shock, catching cinemagoers completely unawares and leaving the critics with the difficulty of doing the film justice without giving the story away. Swank won an Oscar for best actress.

There was no happy ending. She asked him to switch off the life-support machine. His priest warned him that if he did he would never find himself again. The manager argued it was committing a sin to be keeping her alive. Given the objection by many to euthanasia in America, it was, perhaps, surprising that the film came away with Oscars for best film and best director.

Morgan Freeman was cast as the one-eyed ex-boxer, who worked as janitor and lived on the premises. A good friend to his boss and the young boxers, he also acted as the off-screen narrator and the manager's conscience. Morgan, laidback, subtle, had all his familiar gravitas and he, too, won an Oscar for best supporting actor. The laconic backchat between him and Eastwood was perfectly timed. Jay Baruchell had a showy cameo as a pathetic, brainless boxer, a fantasising no-hoper and Brian O'Byrne registered in the small role of the priest.

Eastwood has never done anything better as an actor and director. *Derek Malcolm* Evening Standard.

Borderline trite but has the sweet melancholy of a great jazz piece. *New Yorker*

Knockout. More like washout. *Daily Telegraph* headline.

Film Chronology

DATE	TITLE	ROLE	SCREENPLAY	DIRECTOR
1955	Revenge of the Creature	Lab assistant	Martin Berkeley	Jack Arnold
1955	Tarantula	Pilot	Robert M. Fresco and Martin Berkeley	Jack Arnold
1955	Lady Godiva of Coventry	First Saxon	Oscar Brodney and Harry Ruskin	Arthur Lubin
1955	Francis in the Navy	Jonesby	Devery Freeman, based on the character Francis created by David Stern	Arthur Lubin
1955	Never Say Goodbye	Will	Charles Hoffman	Jerry Hopper
1956	Away All Boats	Marine medic	Kenneth M. Dodson and Ted Sherdeman	Joseph Pevney
1956	The First Traveling Saleslady	Jack Rice	Devery Freeman and Stephen Longstreet	Arthur Lubin
1956	Star in the Dust	Tom ranch hand	Oscar Brodney, based on the novel *Lawman* by Lee Leighton	Charles F. Haas
1957	Escapade in Japan	Pilot	Winston Miller	Arthur Lubin
1957	Lafayette Escadrille	George Moseley	A. S. Fleischman, from a story by William A. Wellman	William A. Wellman
1957	Ambush at Cimarron Pass (a.k.a. Hell Bent for Glory)	Keith Williams	Richard G. Taylor and John K. Butler, Story by Paul Sawtell and Bert Shefter	Jodie Copelan
1959–66	Rawhide (television series)	Rowdy Yates	various	various
1964	A Fistful of Dollars (Italian title: Per un pugno di dollari)	Joe	no acknowledgment on screen	Sergio Leone
1965	For a Few Dollars More (Italian title: Per qualche dollari in più)	Manco	Luciano Vincenzoni	Sergio Leone
1966	The Good, the Bad and the Ugly (Italian title: Il buono, il brutto, il cattivo)	Blondy	Age-Scarpelli, Luciano Vincenzoni and Sergio Leone	Sergio Leone
1966	The Witches (Italian title: Le Streghe)	Mario	Cesare Zavattini, Fabio Carpi and Enzo Muzii	Vittorio de Sica
1968	Hang 'Em High	Jed Cooper	Leonard Freeman and Mel Goldberg	Ted Post
1968	Coogan's Bluff	Coogan	Herman Miller, Dean Reisner and Howard Rodman. Story by Herman Miller	Don Siegel
1968	Where Eagles Dare	Schaffer	Alistair MacLean	Brian G. Hutton
1969	Paint Your Wagon	'Pardner'	screenplay and lyrics: Alan Jay Lerner; adaptation: Paddy Chayefsky; music: Frederick Loewe; music for additional songs: André Previn	Joshua Logan
1969	Two Mules for Sister Sara	Hogan	Albert Maltz. Story by Budd Boetticher	Don Siegel
1970	Kelly's Heroes	Kelly	Troy Kennedy Martin	Brian G. Hutton
1970	The Beguiled	John McBurney	John B. Sherry and Grimes Grice, from the novel by Thomas Cullinan	Don Siegel
1971	Play Misty for Me	Dave	Jo Heims and Dean Reisner. Story by Jo Heims	Clint Eastwood
1971	Dirty Harry	Harry Callahan	Harry Julian Fink and R. M. Fink and Dean Reisner. Story by Harry Julian Fink and R. M. Fink	Don Siegel
1972	Joe Kidd	Joe Kidd	Elmore Leonard	John Sturges
1972	High Plains Drifter	The Stranger	Ernest Tidyman	Clint Eastwood
1973	Breezy*	—	Jo Heims	Clint Eastwood
1973	Magnum Force	Harry Callahan	John Milius and Michael Cimino. Story by John Milius, based on characters created by Harry Julian Fink and R. M. Fink	Ted Post
1974	Thunderbolt and Lightfoot	Thunderbolt	Michael Cimino	Michael Cimino
1975	The Eiger Sanction	Jonathan Hemlock	Hal Dresner, Warren B. Murphy and Rod Whitaker, based on the novel by Trevanian	Clint Eastwood
1976	The Outlaw Josey Wales	Josey Wales	Phil Kaufman and Sonia Chernus, from the novel *Gone to Texas* by Forrest Carter	Clint Eastwood
1976	The Enforcer	Harry Callahan	Stirling Silliphant and Dean Reisner. Story by Gail Morgan Hickman and S. W. Schurr, based on characters created by Harry Julian Fink and R. M. Fink	James Fargo

DATE	TITLE	ROLE	SCREENPLAY	DIRECTOR
1977	The Gauntlet	Ben Shockley	Michael Butler and Dennis Shryack	Clint Eastwood
1978	Every Which Way But Loose	Philo Beddoe	Jeremy Joe Kronsberg	James Fargo
1979	Escape from Alcatraz	Frank Morris	Richard Tuggle, based on the book by J. Campbell Bruce	Don Siegel
1980	Bronco Billy+	Billy McCoy	Dennis Hackin	Clint Eastwood
1980	Any Which Way You Can	Philo Beddoe	Stanford Sherman, based on characters created by Jeremy Joe Kronsberg	Buddy Van Horn
1982	Honkytonk Man*	Red Stovall	Clancy Carlile, based on his novel	Clint Eastwood
1982	Firefox*	Mitchell Gant	Alex Lasker and Wendell Wellmano, based on the novel by Craig Thomas	Clint Eastwood
1983	Sudden Impact*	Harry Callahan	Joseph C. Stinson. Story by Earl E. Smith and Charles. B. Pierce, based on characters created by Harry Julian Fink and R. M. Fink	Clint Eastwood
1984	Tightrope*	Wes Block	Richard Tuggle	Richard Tuggle
1984	City Heat +	Lieutenant Speer	Sam O. Brown and Joseph C. Stinson from a story by Sam O. Brown	Richard Benjamin
1985	Pale Rider*	Preacher	Michael Butler and Dennis Shryack	Clint Eastwood
1986	Heartbreak Ridge*+	Sergeant Tom Highway	James Carabatsos	Clint Eastwood
1986	Round Midnight*	–	Bertrand Tavernier	Bertrand Tavernier
1986	Ratboy*	–	Rob Thompson	Sondra Locke
1988	Bird*	–	Joel Oliansky	Clint Eastwood
1988	The Dead Pool	Harry Callahan	Steve Sharon, Story by Steve Sharon, Durk Pearson and Sandy Shaw, based on characters by Harry Julian Fink and R. M. Fink	Buddy Van Horn
1988	Thelonious Monk: Straight No Chaser**	–	documentary	Charlotte Zwerin
1989	Pink Cadillac	Tommy Nowak	John Eskow	Buddy Van Horn
1990	White Hunter, Black Heart*	John Wilson	Peter Viertel, James Bridges and Burt Kennedy, based on the novel by Peter Viertel	Clint Eastwood
1990	The Rookie	Nick Pulovski	Boaz Yakin and Scott Spiegel	Clint Eastwood
1992	Unforgiven*+	William Munny	David Webb Peoples	Clint Eastwood
1993	In the Line of Fire	Frank Horrigan	Jeff Maguire	Wolfang Petersen
1993	The Man from Malpaso	Himself	documentary	Gene Feldman
1993	A Perfect World	Red Garnet	John Lee Hancock	Clint Eastwood
1995	The Bridges of Madison County	James Kincaid	Richard La Gravese and Ronald Bass, from the novel by Robert James Waller	Clint Eastwood
1995	The Bridges of Madison County**	Robert Kincaid	Richard LaGravenese based on the novel by Robert James Waller	Clint Eastwood
1997	Absolute Power*+	Luther Whitney	William Goldman	Clint Eastwood
1997	Midnight in the Garden of Good and Evil*	–	John Lee Hancock based on the book by John Berendt	Clint Eastwood
1999	True Crime*+	Steve Everett	Larry Gross, Paul Brickman and Stephen Schiff based on the novel by Andrew Klavan	Clint Eastwood
2000	Space Cowboys*+	Frank D Corvin	Ken Kaufman & Howard Klausner	Clint Eastwood
2002	Blood Work*	Terry McCaleb	Brian Helgeland based on the novel by Michael Connelly	Clint Eastwood
2003	Mystic River*+	–	Brian Helgeland based on the novel by Dennis Lehane	Clint Eastwood
2004	Million Dollar Baby**+	Frankie Dunn	Paul Haggis based on stories from Rope Burns by F X Toole	Clint Eastwood
2006	Flags of Our Fathers (pre production)		Paul Haggis. Based on the book by James Bradley	Clint Eastwood

* Clint Eastwood also producer.
** Clint Eastwood producer only.
+ Clint Eastwood composer.
– Eastwood did not appear in Breezy, Bird, Midnight in the Garden of Good and Evil and Mystic River.

Television Chronology

DATE	TITLE

ACTOR

1956	Highway Patrol episode: Motorcycle A
	TV Reader's Digest episode: Cochise, Greatest of the Apaches
	Death Valley Days episode: The Last Letter
1957	Men of Annapolis
	Wagon Train episode: The Charles Avery Story
1958	Navy Log episode: The Lonely Watch
	West Point episode: White Fury
1959	Maverick episode: Duel at Sundown
1959-66	Rawhide
1962	Mr Ed episode: Clint Eastwood meets Mr Ed

DIRECTOR

1985	Vanessa in the Garden

SELECTED APPEARANCES

1971	Dirty Harry's Way
1973	The Hero Cop: Yesterday and Today
1976	Harry Callahan/Clint Eastwood: Something Special in Films
1977	The Man with No Name
1980	Don Siegel: Last of the Independents
1987	The Ultimate Stuntman: A Tribute to Dar Robinson
1991	Thank Ya, Thank Ya Kindly
1991-93	"Harvey Shine Presents"
1992	Clint Eastwood on Westerns
1992	Eastwood & Co: Making Unforgiven
1992	Eastwood...A Star
1993	In the Line of Fire: Behind the Scenes with the Secret Service
1993	Clint Eastwood: The Man From Malpaso
1996	Wild Bill: Hollywood Maverick
1997	Eastwood After Hours: Live at Carnegie Hall
1997	The American Film Institute Salute to Martin Scorsese
1997	Big Guns Talk: The Story of the Western
1997	Eastwood on Eastwood
1998	Monterey Jazz Festival: 40 Legendary Years
1999	AFI's 100 Years...100 Stars/American Masters: Clint Eastwood
2000	Clint Eastwood: Out of the Shadows
2001	Kurosawa
2003	Piano Blues
2004	Mystic River: From Page to Screen
2004	Épreuves d'artist aka words in progress

AWARDS AND HONOURS

1971
Appointed by President Richard Nixon to the National Council of Arts

Golden Globe Awards
  World Film Favourite – Male

1980
New York Museum of Modern Art
  Retrospective of his films

1985
Cinémathèque Française
  Retrospective of his films
Chevalier des Arts et Lettres

1986-8
Mayor of Carmel, California

1987
Golden Globe Awards
  Cecil B. de Mille Prize

1988
Golden Globe
  Best Director: *Bird*

1992
Los Angeles Film Critics Association
  Best Director: *Unforgiven*

The American Academy of Motion Picture Arts and Sciences
  Best Director: *Unforgiven*
  Nomination for Best Actor: *Unforgiven*

Golden Globe Awards
  Best Director: *Unforgiven*

1993
British Film Institute Fellowship
  NATO/Showest Director of the Year

1994
President of Cannes Film Festival Jury

1995
American Academy of Motion Pictures
and Sciences
   Irving G Thalberg Memorial Award

FilmFest Hamburg
   Douglas Sirk Award

1996
American Film Institute
   Lifetime Achievement Award

1998
PGA Golden Laurel Awards
   Lifetime Achievement Award

Academie des Arts Techniques
   César: Honorary Award

1999
National Board of Review
   Career Achievement Award

2000
Venice Film Festival
   Golden Lion: Career Award

Kennedy Centre Honors
   Award for lifetime contribution to arts and
   American culture

Wesleyan University
   Honorary Doctorate in Fine Arts

2001
Tokyo International Film Festival
   Kurosawa Award

Art Directors Guild Awards
   Cinematic Imagery Award

2003
Venice Film Festival
   Future Film Festival
   Digital award: *Blood Work*

2003
Cannes Film Festival
   Golden Coach: *Mystic River*
   Nomination for the Golden Palm

The American Academy of Motion Picture
Arts and Sciences
   Nomination for Best Director: *Mystic River*

Golden Globe Awards
   Nomination for Best Director: *Mystic River*

Screen Actors Guild Awards
   Lifetime Award

2004
Academie des Arts Techniques
   César: Best Foreign Film: *Mystic River*r

National Society of Film Critics Awards
   Top Director: *Mystic River*

ASCAP Opus Award
   Singular contribution of music to film

2005
The American Academy of Motion Picture
Arts and Sciences
   Best Picture: *Million Dollar Baby*
   Best Director: Clint Eastwood

Golden Globe Awards
   Best Picture: *Million Dollar Baby*

Nomination for best original score:
Million Dollar Baby

Directors Guild of America Awards
   Best Director: *Million Dollar Baby*

National Board of Review Awards
   Special Film Making Achievement:
Million Dollar Baby

Index

158535

The kitten approached

　　and he pawed Ava's toe,

Then (silently) miaowed

　　a warm-hearted 'hello!'

Oh! How delightful!

　　Ava grinned and she giggled

As he rolled on his back

　　and playfully wriggled.

10

His invisible fur

was all silvery white,

His invisible whiskers

shone in the light.

His invisible nose

twitched as he sniffed

At something he smelled

in the air through the mist.

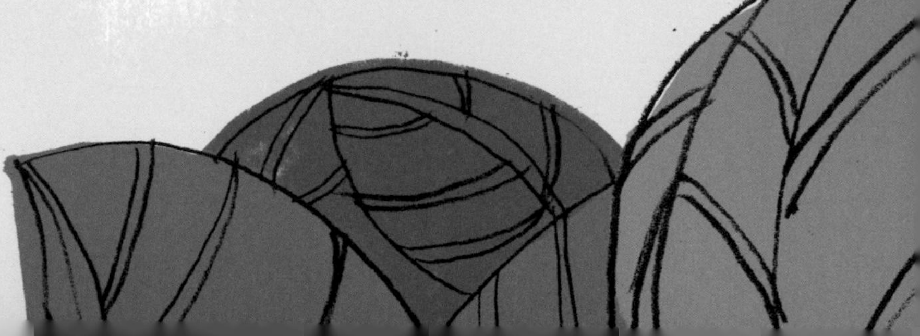

KT-547-884

EASTWOOD

Contents

v

CONTENTS

The View From the Front
interview with Geoffrey Bailey, Crime in Store 86

Crime-Writing Quotations *93*

Top Fifteen Crime Fiction Authors *95*

LISTINGS

UK Publishers with Crime Fiction/Thriller Lists *99*

UK Literary Agents *111*

Professional Associations *123*

Literary Societies *127*

Arts Councils and Regional Arts Boards *130*

Editorial, Research Services and Courses *138*

Prizes *140*

Crime Museums *143*

Libraries and Specialist Bookshops *145*

Further Reading *147*

Useful Websites at a Glance *148*

Introduction

Every successful book must have a built-in page-turner. Somehow the reader has to be persuaded that her mind will not rest easy until the big question is answered: what happens next? Many who are classed as serious novelists ignore this basic rule, choosing instead to believe that when they are pontificating, their readers should have the good manners to pay attention. Crime fiction is not at all like that. Tension is at the core of the entire genre, ranging all the way from the cosy country murder mystery to the mean street thriller, which is why crime fiction is so popular. According to the Nielsen BookScan survey, sales of crime fiction totalled over £40 million for 2001. At the time of going to press, 200 new crime titles are set for publication in the next six months. This is big business by any standards.

But competition is tough. Never underestimate how many clever writers are struggling to get into the market. What this book seeks to do is to call on the experience of those who have broken the barrier to discover the secrets of success. Writing talent is 90 per cent God-given, but turning it into a profitable career is something that has to be learned from others or acquired by the hard knocks of trial and error. Clearly, the first option is more appealing. *The Writer's Handbook Guide to Crime Writing* cannot promise success but it can help to make the way easier.

GUIDE TO CRIME WRITING

Why Crime Fiction is Good for You

Ian Rankin

Why is crime fiction good for you? Well, it is about tragedy, and emotional responses to tragedy, and moral choices and questions. It can be very serious in intent, but also entertaining. It is often dismissed by the literary establishment (book reviewers and critics) as mere genre fiction ('genre' meaning a kind of literature, usually used in a pejorative sense about a kind of literature you don't think worthwhile). These critics would say that crime fiction is fine if you want something to pass the time, but not important enough to merit serious study – yet ironically, many literary novels have crime and the basics of the crime novel at their centre.

In the widest sense, of course, all *fiction* is good for you. It relaxes and entertains; it takes you out of your own consciousness and into that of other people in very different situations. In doing so, it broadens your appreciation of human nature and of the world around you. However, at some point in history – at least in Great Britain – crime fiction (and other genre fiction such as the historical novel or science fiction) became separated from literary or main-stream fiction, which is supposedly more serious in its ambitions. Yet one could argue that early pulp fiction, to give one example – 'pulp fiction' being short stories published in cheap magazines, and meant for a popular audience; the early stories of Dashiell Hammett and Raymond Chandler are good examples – is the child of the serials and stories written by Charles Dickens, Sir Arthur Conan Doyle and others. These are stories which in their day were regarded as mass entertainment, even sensationalist, like modern television soap operas, but are now regarded as *literature*. Dickens, in his own day, was not regarded as a particularly great or worthy writer. He was rather, a forerunner of the modern-day 'best-seller'. This gives me hope that many of today's crime writers and thriller writers will one day, sometime in the future, come to be regarded as great moralists and stylists as well as tellers of fascinating tales.

If one looks at the canon of Western literature (by which I mean those works that are widely accepted as being worth reading, works that will endure down the centuries), and especially at the novel, one finds that the main ingredients of crime fiction – violence, sudden reversals, mystery, deception, moral dilemmas, and so on – can be found everywhere, from the Greek epics to the present day. They are important to the novel form because a novel takes a long time to read, and therefore the novel must have suspense and pose questions throughout. It is this that keeps us reading – the very basic need to know what happens next. If the author makes us curious, then he will have no trouble keeping us reading. And so, in a very real sense, all readers are detectives, trying to solve the message coded in the plot, trying to work out symbols and layers of meaning.

The great crime writer and critic Julian Symons described the folk tale *Little Red Riding Hood* – a tale for children in which a young girl's grandmother is eaten by a wolf which then pretends to be the grandmother in an attempt to trap and eat the girl – as an interesting case of disguise and attempted murder. He would, I'm sure, agree with me that murder, suspense and betrayal can be found as easily in *The Odyssey* or *Hamlet* as in the work of Ruth Rendell or P. D. James. The poet and detective writer C. Day-Lewis thought that the detective story *was* a twentieth-century folk tale, while the poet W. H. Auden said that the classical detective story was an allegory of the 'death' of happiness. In real life, we never know what killed off our happiness; whereas in the crime novel the senseless acts of existence are given explanation. In crime novels, death never happens without a reason and the causes of death never go unpunished.

4

It is important to stress that Auden was talking about the *classical* detective story. It is also time to discuss the genre's elasticity before talking about more recent developments. The crime genre is an extremely broad category, as can be seen when one looks at the various names it employs. We can talk of the crime novel, the detective novel, the whodunnit, the suspense novel, the cosy, the hard-boiled, the *roman noir*, pulp fiction, the police procedural, the mystery novel . . . And so on and so on. There's a reason for this. People are confused about the basic identity of the crime novel. (This applies to authors as well as to critics and readers.) This is a genre that would seek to include everything from the most basic puzzle-style mystery to Dostoyevsky's *Crime and Punishment*. The esteemed crime novelist P. D. James tries to have it both ways when she says that a good crime novel combines 'the old traditions of an exciting story and the satisfying exercise of rational deduction with the psychological subtleties and moral ambiguities of a good novel.' Certainly, crime novels are designed to entertain. They are the products of popular culture. As such, they must make a profit, for no one will subsidize them. Crime fiction may have literary aspirations, but its emphasis on entertainment ensures that these do not frighten away potential readers. In other words, crime fiction is democratic, in that it is accessible to the general reader.

Before the Second World War, the crime novel reassured the middle classes that all would be well; that in the long run they and their possessions had nothing to fear from criminals, communists, anarchists, and of course from the lower classes. It was a comforting sort of genre, made more comfortable by its country village settings and a cast of upper-middle-class characters. The eruption of murder into an orderly bourgeois society did not attack the basis of that society, but rather confirmed the goodness of everyday life, and celebrated the return of happiness once the murderer had been apprehended. In this sense, the classical British whodunnit owed much to the pastoral, a type of literature concerned with the countryside and how much better the simple life enjoyed in the countryside was compared to life in the towns and cities. Even now crime fiction

5

functions as a literary comforter, helping us to come to terms with the increasing violence of the modern world. The modern crime novel, however, has become much less reassuring. In Britain there has been a shift away from the comfortable worlds of Agatha Christie, Dorothy L. Sayers and Margery Allingham – three British crime writers who can be said to stand for the 'old order'. When crime readers around the world think of Britain, they think of this *traditional* whodunnit, of Sherlock Holmes or Miss Marple, of sedate country villages suddenly interrupted by a violent (but usually bloodless) murder, and of the detective – usually an amateur – who, by process of rational deduction, brings the culprit to light.

This tradition is one very large reason why crime fiction is not taken seriously as literature in Great Britain. The crime novel, it is said, provides too neat a plot, too tidy a solution or series of solutions to its central mystery. Since life isn't like that, the crime novel must be escapist literature which does little more than play a game with the reader. In other words, by the end of the crime novel the reader should know who the murderer was, why they committed the crime, and how this was achieved. Many fans of the traditional crime novel would feel cheated without this, since the crime novel has always consisted of the same basic elements and has always delivered the same sorts of storyline. A few threads may be left hanging, but the central complexities should have been made clear. The sense of fun – of achievement – for the reader lies in trying to work everything out before the revelation of the culprit – the reader as detective again – and the author tries his or her damnedest to trick the reader by introducing false clues and a battery of suspects (the famous 'red herrings' of the traditional crime novel).

Agatha Christie had a lot of fun with these conventions. There are Christie books where the narrator is revealed as the murderer, and even where all the suspects are revealed to be involved in the killing. As Christie herself found, once you have explored the form to this extent, you've done just about everything that can be done with it. However, across the Atlantic, and writing at much the same time as Christie, Dashiell Hammett and Raymond Chandler were espousing a new kind of detective story, one which would take the form out of the sleepy English villages and baronial halls and on to the 'mean streets' – Chandler's phrase – of contemporary urban life.

Chandler summed up the traditional British mystery story while writing his 'Ten Commandments' for the detective novel. Numbers six and seven read: 'The detective novel must baffle a reasonably intelligent reader; and the solution must seem inevitable once revealed.' Chandler saw one of the attractions of the mystery novel; that readers like to have the world explained to them. To feel that everything has its place and meaning makes them feel at ease with the world. Crime fiction fulfils – or used to fulfil – this expectation. Traditional British whodunnits concentrated almost exclusively on the *game* aspect of the narrative. These were pure stories of deception and detection. They gave all the clues to the reader, and at the end, as in a crossword puzzle, all the squares in the grid were complete. This sense of completion, of no loose endings, gave readers a sense of comfort – all is well in the world, order will come out of chaos, reason and logic can and will defeat the darker powers and man's bloodlust. And at the end of the puzzle novel, the reader must feel that the game was there to be won, by having guessed the identity of the murderer from the clues provided.

But this won't do. It wouldn't do for Chandler and Hammett – especially Chandler, whose 'Ten Commandments' seem at times a direct challenge to the unwritten Christie rules. Chandler argued against the amateur detective – the shrewd old lady or titled gentleman – and against the many flukes and lucky coincidences that one finds in Christie. I too find the 'game' or 'puzzle' element of the crime novel its least satisfactory aspect, especially that last-but-one chapter where the suspects are lined up, clues and red herrings explained, and the finger pointed by the power of deductive reasoning at the true culprit. It is too artificial, too removed from the real world, and with it crime fiction is reduced to the level of a board game or an intelligence test.

7

What crime fiction needs is a sense of the *incomplete*, of life's messy complexity. The reader should go to crime fiction to learn about the real world, not to retreat from it with comfortable reassurances and assumptions. Crime writers in Great Britain – my contemporaries – are beginning to realize this. Good does not always triumph in today's crime fiction; evil cannot always be rationalized. Sometimes the villains escape justice altogether, and in many cases the reader is invited to take sides with the assassin or criminal against the powers of law and order. There are even novels with no detectives and no mysteries, showing a world in which criminality, especially organized crime, operates openly and without hindrances.

I feel this is good news, because the crime genre is capable of so much more than simply telling a good story or playing an elaborate game with the reader. Crime writers throughout the world – notably in South America and mainland Europe – have known for years that the crime novel can be a perfect tool for the dissection of society. In spite of all its exaggerations and heightened effects, crime fiction often tells us more about the world around us than does 'realistic', 'mainstream' or 'literary' fiction. Crime fiction is capable of tackling the bigger contemporary issues in Great Britain – corruption, exploitation, child abuse, and violence and the fear of violence – and in using these for its plots and themes, crime fiction offers commentary on them. It makes the reader *think*. Because crime fiction is capable of tackling big issues, it need never fear boring its audience. Crime fiction has always been 'a good read' – and for the more conventional writers this was enough of a reason to write the books – but for the new school of British crime writers, entertainment is a means to an end rather than an end in itself, and that end is the heightening or altering of the reader's sensibilities.

I'm thinking here of writers such as Frances Fyfield, Liza Cody, Val McDermid, Sarah Dunant, John Harvey, Julian Rathbone and Michael Dibdin, who are, whether they realize it or not, political writers. They see the roots of petty crime in poverty, in the present-day social problems of Britain. They also see how petty crime can escalate, and they have a view to the larger, never publicized crimes: crimes of conspiracy and corruption committed by 'the Establishment' and by the big corporations. I like to class myself among these practitioners, and would term us a more 'realistic' school than that of the traditional whodunnit author. As writers we are committed to an engagement with the real world. We deal with urban Britain, with its cities, youth problems, drug culture, with the alienation felt by a growing under-class.

My own novels are set in contemporary Edinburgh and my desire to write them came from my time spent living there, and the wish to show a side of the city the tourist never sees. To the outside world, Edinburgh was, and is, one gigantic historical monument or theme park, with almost no contemporary life of its own. The film of the novel *Trainspotting* may have blown that notion to pieces. It's a task I embarked upon as early as 1985. I did not write from the tradition of the classical English whodunnit (I'd never read any), but from a dark gothic tradition of Scottish writers such as Robert Louis Stevenson and James Hogg, filtered through a love of American cinema and fiction. Stevenson was important because his novel *Dr Jekyll and Mr Hyde*, while ostensibly set in London, seemed to me – *still* seems to me – the archetype of an Edinburgh novel. Scotland, you see, has a very different character to its neighbour. Our language is different, our education system is different, and our system of law is very different. And though *Dr Jekyll and Mr Hyde* is located in London, it is essentially Scottish in character. (It is also a brilliant whodunnit, howdunnit and whydunnit – a gem of a detective novel.) Stevenson took as his source the true story of an eighteenth-century Edinburgh citizen, Deacon Brodie, who by day was a respectable man about town but who at night led a gang of housebreakers. Brodie was eventually caught and hanged on a scaffold that he himself, as Deacon of Wrights, had helped repair and improve. Brodie has come to be seen as a symbol of Edinburgh, a city which hides its private vices behind a face of public respectability. It was this aspect of the city's character that I wished to explore.

In my first 'Inspector Rebus' novel I created an evil alter ego – a dark side to the detective – in the shape of someone who had been very close to him, and who now hated him. This man sets out to destroy the hero in a way not dissimilar to the baffle between Dr Jekyll and Mr Hyde. In my second 'Inspector Rebus' novel, *Hide & Seek*, I went further. The very name Hyde appears as a pun in the novel's title, and in the book a section of Edinburgh's great and good are exposed as members of a bizarre and evil club, called Hyde's. Later books have ventured to other Scottish cities, most notably Glasgow and Aberdeen, as Inspector Rebus confronts hidden facets of his native country, as well as confronting his own fears, shortcomings, darker desires and capabilities. Along with other contemporary Scottish novelists such as Iain Banks, William McIllvanney, Janice Galloway, A. L. Kennedy and Irvine Welsh, I hope to show the wider world that there's more to Scotland than tartan, golf and whisky.

The mechanics of the whodunnit – its narrative conventions – do not really interest me as a writer. What interests me is the soul of the crime novel – what it tells us about humanity, what it is capable of discussing. Good crime fiction tackles big issues. My own crime novels have discussed the morality of big business, political corruption, child abduction, the drug scene, the ramifications of the oil industry, and so on. But always, I hope, with reference to the effects of any investigation upon those doing the investigating. We are all inquisitive and curious animals, learning through questioning, and crime fiction touches this deep need both to ask questions and to get answers.

Crime fiction also enters dangerous territory – murder, jealousy, revenge – and so stirs up emotional responses we might otherwise not feel. Reading is not a passive experience in the way that sitting through a film is. In film, we watch violence on the screen, but seldom feel it in our hearts. A well-executed narrative description can make us feel the pain of the sufferer. In a world which is safe, crime fiction provides a sense that we are on the edge of danger. It heightens our basic survival instincts, gives us a primal reminder of the cave and the predator. And yet – here is the irony – we read these books in our safe middle-class world. There is little demand for crime fiction in a war zone. This explains the dearth of crime fiction from that potentially most fruitful region of Great Britain, Northern Ireland. Where there is conflict and the real daily fear of sudden violent death, there is no need to read fictional accounts of the same. Only recently has the author Colin Bateman emerged from Northern Ireland, and he, tellingly, is a humorous writer, a writer of great satirical intent.

Which is, in fact, only fitting, since it seems to me that the true spirit of the crime novel, be it cosy or hard-boiled, is anarchic, whether its practitioners realize it or not. We are absurdist writers; we write in the realm of satire and irony, from the light of the 'cosy' (owing much to Jane Austen, as realized most recently by Reginald Hill in his novel *Pictures of Perfection*) to the harsh, derisive ironies and dark exaggerations of a James Ellroy, or, in England, a Derek Raymond or a Mark Timlin. A dictionary definition of 'satire' would be: a poem or prose composition in which prevailing vices or follies are held up to ridicule. From its earliest days, the novel was found to be an ideal vehicle for satire, and one can draw a line from Swift through the social satire of Dickens and Thackeray to the likes of Evelyn Waugh and, more recently, Martin Amis, Alasdair Gray and Jonathan Coe.

The crime novel, dealing as it does with exaggerated characters, prevailing vices and habits, and a society ill at ease with itself, seems to fit the dictionary definition of satire, something few of its practitioners realize. Of course, as a form, the crime novel is itself open to satirizing. Michael Dibdin, in his short novel *The Dying of the Light*, has a lot of fun with the conventions of the whodunnit, as does playwright Tom Stoppard in *The Real Inspector Hound*. Serious literary novelists have also either plundered or paid homage to the whodunnit – for example Umberto Eco with *The Name of the Rose*, Muriel Spark with *The Driver's Seat* (a whydunnit rather than a whodunnit) and Alain Robbe-Grillet with nearly all his early novels. Walk into the crime section of a British bookshop, however, and you won't find books by Eco or Spark or Robbe-Grillet. These works are said to have 'transcended' the genre, and in doing so they cease, in the critics' eyes, to be whodunnits or crime novels. The same can be said of more recent successes, such as *Miss Smilla's Feeling for Snow* by Peter Høeg, or *Snow Falling on Cedars* by David Guterson. So it is that while crime specialists are keen to include works such as *Crime and Punishment* and *Bleak House* in the 'canon' of the crime or mystery novel, literary critics are just as keen to pluck them out again. But there is something worthwhile to be learnt from any crime novel.

These days, when a fictional act of extreme violence occurs in a country town or village, it is harder to imagine everything settling back to 'normal' once the culprit has been identified or arrested. British crime writers now live in a post-Hungerford, post-Dunblane world. We have seen real-life towns in England and Scotland explode into violence, and we have experienced the aftershock of such events. The traditional English whodunnit, if it continues as though nothing has altered, is distorting the world even more than before.

As the Scottish novelist Muriel Spark has said, 'The rhetoric of our times should persuade us to contemplate the ridiculous nature of the reality before us, and teach us to mock it. We should know ourselves better by now than to be under the illusion that we are all essentially aspiring, affectionate and loving creatures. We do have these qualities, but we are aggressive too.'

In dealing with these aggressive qualities in the human animal, crime fiction provides both a salutary warning and the cathartic effect of all good drama. The tight, sometimes mechanistic, structure of the crime novel pays tribute to the fact that the human race hungers for form, if only as a temporary container for the dangerous chaos of existence. Crime fiction provides not only the dangerous chaos but also something to put it in. It seems likely that the crime novel is merely the last vehicle for themes that have been fascinating people for thousands of years. It fascinates so many people partly because it entertains, partly because it offers the rewards of any good quality fiction, and partly because it deals with some of the uglier aspects of human nature. The human race has always been obsessed with death. It is something that will happen to us all. The crime novel gives us a way of exploring a few of the implications – and of enjoying ourselves while we do it.*

Ian Rankin's Ten Best Thrillers

The Murder of Roger Ackroyd by Agatha Christie
The Big Sleep by Raymond Chandler
Cop Hater by Ed McBain
Fifty Two Pick Up by Elmore Leonard
The Moonstone by Wilkie Collins
The Nine Tailors by Dorothy L. Sayers
A Taste for Death by P. D. James
The Mermaids Singing by Val McDermid
A Demon In My View by Ruth Rendell
The Black Dahlia by James Ellroy

The Independent 13 May 2002

Ian Rankin Quotes

'There's this pathologist in Edinburgh I wanted to meet because I had a few questions about drowning and how could you tell a body had drowned or whether it was dead when it went in the water. I went for the meeting and his secretary said, "Oh, just go in his office, he'll be there in a minute or two." So I went in and he comes back and says, "Look I'm sorry to keep you." He's got a folder in his hand, starts opening it up and he chucks all these glossy colour photographs at me. "Now look, as you can see here, the head has been separated almost completely from the body, by what I take it is a large knife, like a kitchen knife and it's just hanging on by this thread here." And he could see the blood draining from my face and he said, "Detective

* This article first appeared in Issue 102 of the *Edinburgh Review*.

Sergeant Brown?" I said, "No." and he said, "Oh shit, sorry" and started collecting all the photos up.'

studentUK 2001

'I find deadlines are a great cure for [writer's] block. So far, I've had few problems finding themes and stories. For me, the block comes of fear – the fear that the writing won't be as good as previously, the fear of failure. When up against a deadline, you throw such fears aside and just get on with it.'

The Independent, 18 July 2002

'I was an obsessive kid with a very active fantasy and very active imagination. By the time I got to Edinburgh university I had a poem published, joined the poetry society and used to go and hassle the writer in residence. It changed every year so it could be a poet and the next year it might be a playwright. Eventually the writer in residence also happened to be the judge in a short story competition that was run by a national newspaper in Scotland and he awarded me second prize, and that's how it all started. I thought, I'm making money from this and people seem to like it.'

studentUK 2001

From the Editor's Desk

Maria Reijt, head of Macmillan crime publishing,
explains what it takes to be a successful crime writer.

BARRY TURNER: What are you looking for in a crime novel? What is
it in a manuscript or synopsis that makes you think it could become
a popular book?

MARIA REIJT: It is easier to say what I am not looking for: I don't
look for fashions. I don't wake up in the morning and immediately
start thinking in terms of the gothic historical novel or the psychological thriller or whatever happens to be the current rage. I always
start and end with the writing. The power of writing, the originality
of the writing and the characterization, that is what attracts me. You
can write about any situation in any setting and make it interesting
as long as you can get the reader to believe in your characters. And
the best way to learn how to do this is to go away and study the
masters. Analyse why their books work. How do they portray their
characters; how do they make them distinctive and memorable? The
next thing is to work on the dialogue. Editors can do a lot of things.
We can affect the pace of a book, we can cut a book down to the
right size, we can tell a writer how to structure, we can say when
a character is losing interest. We can then say a character isn't
believable in a particular context. But the one thing we cannot do is
to write dialogue. I don't know of any editor who can write better
dialogue than an author.

BT: When you talk about studying the masters, are you thinking
about contemporary writers or those who have long since gone?

MR: Both. It depends on the sort of writer you want to be. If, say, you are the Peter Robinson or Ian Rankin school of police procedure, very much dialogue driven, your masters are probably going to be Chandler, Hammett and somebody who is less well known these days but I think is one of the great writers in American crime fiction, and that is Charles Willeford. He wrote a series of novels about a detective called Hoke Moseley out of Florida in the sixties. In one of the novels, Hoke Moseley doesn't say anything for the first 75 pages because he's had a nervous breakdown. And yet Willeford succeeds in making it all so intriguing, you're completely hooked. One of his best novels is called *The Pick-up*, which keeps you guessing right up until the last line. It's an absolutely brilliant novel.

BT: What about Dorothy L. Sayers, Margery Allingham, Agatha Christie or, even further back, Conan Doyle?

MR: I would start with Wilkie Collins – *Woman in White*, the first detective novel. But whatever the author, you've got to enjoy what you read. It's no use studying the masters and thinking, 'I'm going to do better.' I know writers do this sometimes, and you can always tell when somebody has studied a book without engaging with it. The result is writing by numbers. It never works. You must have an interest in people, in humanity. Margery Allingham, Dorothy Sayers, Agatha Christie – they wrote some fantastic plots, Christie in particular. But she did some daring things in her career. *Ten Little Niggers* could also be called *Big Fat Cheat*. What a way to finish a novel! She was daring enough to do that. But I must come back to the point. You've got to enjoy those books to get something out of them. Some people do and some people don't. I think there was a big divide between what we used to call the English 'cosy' writers and the American 'hard-boiled' writers.

BT: Where would you put Ian Rankin?

MR: Well, you wouldn't call him a cosy writer. And some of the toughest writers are women, don't forget. Think of Val McDermid, her books are very hard-hitting. Several women writers are now taking on this mantle of the hard-boiled, so called. Actually I've always hated those two definitions, 'hard-boiled' and 'cosy', because I think every author is unique, every book is unique and if the voice of that book engages the reader, then it will be published and find a market.

BT: So it's the power of the writing you are looking for. But you've also mentioned characterization.

MR: Characters are key. It's often said of cosy English crime that plots are more important than the characters. So you get people saying of Christie, 'I enjoy her stories but I can't believe in the characters.' Up to a point there is some truth in that, but nowadays the characters are more important than the plot. Of course there has to be a plot and a structure, but that's only the start. Read Lionel Davidson who has written some of my favourite ever crime novels. *The Chelsea Murders* is just brilliant, so is *The Rose of Tibet*, in fact everything he's written is great. Lionel has got it because you'd follow his characters to the ends of the earth and in fact you do, you follow one of them to Tibet, you follow one of them to Wenceslas Square in Czechoslovakia, and you follow one to Israel. They're all flawed human beings, but so believable. Then he gives you an awesome plot. I don't know why he's not more popular than he is.

BT: Yes, he faded a bit after *Kolymsky Heights*. I'm not quite sure why.

MR: I remember I had lunch with him about six years ago and said, 'Lionel, how's the new book coming along?' And he said to me, 'I'm on the last chapter.' I'm still waiting. I don't think that book has been published. But you can't hurry genius. This was what I felt when I bought Minette Walters' first novel, *The Ice House*. It was 1990 and every publisher was looking for a television series to rank with Colin Dexter's Morse. I was lucky enough to be Colin's publisher and had seen how his sales graph, since television, had gone through the roof. And I was reading this novel called *The Ice House* and I thought, 'This won't make a series. But so what.' I love the characters in this book, they are flawed, they've all got baggage.

Some of them have rather sinister secrets. But they are totally believable. And the policemen are real policemen. These are not your ivory-towered policemen with a love of jazz or something. These are how you imagine cops to be. I just had to publish that book. But it was going against what we were all trying to do which was to find another Morse. A lot of publishers turned it down for that very reason.

BT: *The Ice House* is a marvellous book.

MR: I think Minette is one of the most outstanding crime writers ever. She makes you believe certain assumptions about a character and then halfway through you think, 'That's not it at all.' Think of Jack Blakeney in *The Scold's Bridle*. First off, you say, 'What a shit.' And halfway through, he's not that at all. Her characters always come up with a surprise. But also she has the pace and she has the plots.

BT: Wasn't it some time before she decided she wanted to be a writer? She's not one of these people who made up her mind at the age of twelve.

MR: That's right. She did many things. Her husband was working, they were living in Richmond, she was bringing up two small children and she was editing weekly novelettes. When she ran short of stories she decided to write a few herself. So that's how she started. And then her husband said, 'Look, you've always wanted to write a full-length novel, so do it.' So that's how *The Ice House* came about. That's when the pressure increased. You can spend twenty-five years writing a first novel because nobody has any expectations. But the second novel is critical. With Minette, I knew that if the second novel was as good, she would be a best-seller without question. *The Sculptress* was a hit. Now she's doing a book a year.

BT: That's quite a pace to keep up. Is it realistic?

MR: It depends. It's easier if you have a series going. I don't know what Patsy Cornwell's sales are, but she's probably the biggest-selling crime writer in the UK, male or female. She writes at least a book a year but she has all her main characters in place. With Minette, it's like going back to the drawing board every single time. Her achievement is awesome.

BT: May we go back for a moment to dialogue? One of the great things about Ian Rankin is his ear for dialogue, it's quite extraordinary. It's something I realized when I was re-reading Rankin that his characters are not closely drawn, I mean they are not closely described, it's just the dialogue that actually makes them visible.

MR: I think we get this from television, particularly American TV which is so pacey. But it's also the way we live our lives. We're all intercutting, emails bouncing every way, always doing something different, our minds on many different things. And the best writers, the very best writers know that. They know how our minds are stimulated by dialogue. It's how we link into other people's lives. Rankin doesn't patronize his readers. He puts them into police canteen politics and they grab into it. And that is something that has come from the States. It can go too far. I remember reading a novel by George V. Higgins, who was one of the greats at dialogue. In this novel, set in the Boston underworld, there was only one paragraph of narrative in the whole book, the rest of it was dialogue. I got hopelessly confused because it was about two brothers, both called by their surname, so you really didn't know who was talking at any particular time. But it is still a truism that if you can do dialogue, if your ear is attuned so that you can transform what you hear to the page and make it read like you're listening to a real conversation, you're nearly there. That's something that no editor can teach a writer.

BT: How important is research?
MR: I would much rather have the author's imagination. You know when you're going to have a row with an author because he's not going to want to give up what has taken two years in some archive to learn. And you think, 'But it's so obvious to me.' Colin Dexter said to me, 'I know nothing about the workings of Thames Valley

Police. I've been in there a couple of times for a cup of tea. But I don't go in and hang around with a microphone and see what they're up to. I make it all up. If I don't know something, I don't put it in.' And that is so much better than doing years of research which may, or may not, lead to something interesting.

BT: When, as a publisher, you know you are on to a winner, do you immediately start thinking about the television potential?

MR: No. TV is the jam on the bread. Books can sell without TV support. And if the TV is bad, you're not going to get one extra single sale out it, in fact it might be detrimental to the books because people who see the screen version think, 'Oh, that was pretty ghastly, I'm not even going to bother to try the books now.' And of course it's all out of your hands when you sign over to a studio.

BT: We were talking earlier about writers from the golden age of crime fiction. Authors like Sayers, Allingham and Christie are still selling in large numbers but we don't seem to get any new writers who are interested in what might be called the cosy crime novel.

MR: I think you're right. Publishers sometimes say, 'This is good but it's old-fashioned.' Old-fashioned sounds like a death knell. Why this is I don't know, perhaps we are always wanting to attract younger readers and they would be put off by old-fashioned crime. But for me old-fashioned also suggests a lack of credibility. Christie, Allingham and Sayers wrote about a gilded world, private income and servants, the posh world that no longer exists outside the big country houses. What we are looking for today is realism. But that doesn't mean that a book has to have a modern setting. I have just bought a new writer who has produced a beautifully structured, very traditional, commercial crime novel set in 1537 during the time of the dissolution of the monasteries. It's called *Dissolution* and it's by Christopher Sansom. We met the author and we met his agent and I think he chose us because we were the most passionate of the publishers he met. But I think everyone could recognize his potential, I could not believe it was his first novel.

BT: I wonder who it was among crime writers who inspired Christopher Sansom?

MR: I asked him that. Just out of interest. And I wasn't at all surprised to hear it was P. D. James.

BT: And of course, P. D. James is the modern version of the cosy crime writer. There aren't many like her. Ruth Rendell up to a point, but I think really P. D. James dominates that market. She's the modern Dorothy L. Sayers.

MR: I think one calls her a modern Dorothy L. Sayers just because she is a woman of a certain age who happens to write crime fiction. I love P. D. James for her morality. The plots are fantastic, absolutely brilliant. You know that every time you read a P. D. James you are going to be completely entranced. She is one of life's optimists and I would say Ruth Rendell is one of life's pessimists. Some of her books take you really down among the dead men. I think one of the best crime novels ever written is *A Dark-Adapted Eye*. It's not actually a crime novel, it's a novel about the consequences of crime, an absolutely brilliant book. But back to P. D. James. I read her most recent novel, *Death in Holy Orders*, last year and it's as fresh as the stuff she was writing in the late 1960s. It's not real life but it is wonderfully escapist. I think there's quite a difference between people who like reading P. D. James or my new author, Christopher Sansom, and those who favour Ian Rankin who is more gritty and real. I love reading a Rankin story but I'm glad not to be part of it.

BT: Is a crime novel something that grabs you very early on?

MR: I'd hate to say yes, because I'm sure I'll get no end of manuscripts with a horrible murder in the first sentence. You don't have to have a crime on the first page. But there does have to be something interesting, a character or an event. If the first line of dialogue grabs you, if a description of the person grabs you then you'll read on. But don't try to be too clever. No tricks. The best advice I can give to the newcomer to crime fiction is to enjoy what you're writing and believe in who you're writing about. Give them motivation. And please don't do the divorced policeman with a rumpled suit who likes a single malt. We've got him, and he's the best, so we don't need any more. What about a happy policeman? That could be fun.

Character

Minette Walters

The question I am asked more than any other is: 'Are your characters based on real people?' The assumption seems to be that you can't create believable men and women unless you have first dissected your friends, acquaintances and relations and then reconstructed them on the written page under different names and thin disguises. Well, this may be true of some authors (although I have yet to meet one who's brave enough to admit to it), but it certainly isn't true of me. Every character I create is born out of my own imagination. And my imagination is stimulated through reading fiction and non-fiction, through watching films, stage dramas and television, and through a constant diet of newspapers and current affairs broadcasts.

Of course I watch people – we all do – but I would never seek to reproduce anyone in their entirety in a story. Ultimately, my characters are a synthesis of a thousand experiences, a useful eclectic memory and a lifetime of running the gamut of emotions from A (the abyss) to Z (the zenith). It is how an author uses this wealth of accumulated knowledge that makes him or her a successful writer of character. The freer your imagination, the more lifelike your characters. Take Dracula, who is one of the most fantastic of all fictional creations, and yet whose legend lives on because Bram Stoker breathed life into the living dead. Constrain your imagination and you and your characters will die of sheer boredom, because the process is a dynamic one and requires a constant dialogue between you and them as their story advances.

Nothing in the world fascinates me quite so much as human nature, our good deeds and our bad deeds, our individual ambitions which conflict all too regularly with the ambitions of our tribes, and our often vain attempts to prove to ourselves that mankind is intrinsically superior to the rest of the animal kingdom. We are in every respect a quite extraordinary evolutionary product, with traditions based on wonderful but different cultures, with a diversity of religions and philosophies that strive to bring us close to ideals of perfection, and with thousands of different languages and dialects. But against these structured backdrops, six billion of us across the planet have six billion individual personalities, six billion physical characteristics and six billion sets of private thoughts.

It would be a very unimaginative author who could not embroider on to this amazing tapestry some realistic fictional people. Even the most phlegmatic among us must recognize that the permutations for character profiling are infinite.

Finding characters' voices
(not to be confused with writing dialogue)

Creating characters means finding voices. In the end, it is not how people dress that differentiates them, but how they think and speak. Identical twins may look alike but they don't have identical thoughts; just as ten soldiers wearing the same uniform will have ten different reasons for wearing it. It is not enough to imagine what your characters look like, what houses they live in or what jobs they do, you must talk to them and delve inside their heads to discover what is going on in there. Otherwise, they will be puppets on a stage with no independence of thought or action, and no reality beyond the purely visual.

There is, of course, an inherent paradox in that last sentence. You, the author, have invented these people. Their very existence depends on you; they have no freedom to do anything unless you allow it. However, in just the same way that good parents encourage their children to make lives of their own, so a good author must give his characters enough integrity to predict their own behaviour. Partially developed people have only partially developed aims and emotions, both in real life and in fiction, and they will behave unpredictably because they don't know who they are, why they are there, or what they are supposed to be doing. Nothing is less satisfying for a reader than to be presented with a muddled picture of unlikely people performing unlikely actions simply to push a plot forward.

Contrast Agatha Christie's two most famous creations: Miss Marple and Hercule Poirot. Miss Marple always seems to me to be a credible character: the inquisitive old lady living in a village, applying her knowledge of human nature in St Mary Mead to the greater world beyond because she understands that human motivation is much the same everywhere. She has a clear identity and a clear voice. She is the wise woman of folk literature, who derives her skills from a lifetime of watching the comings and goings of her neighbours. This is well demonstrated at the end of a short story published in 1932, near the beginning of Miss Marple's career.

In the story, her nephew, Raymond West, wonders how she made the leap between a Mr Hargraves, late of St Mary Mead, who, despite being respectably married left all his money to a housemaid by whom he'd had five children, and a murderous travelling salesman, Mr Jones, who did away with his wife with the help of a servant girl.

> 'Well, Aunt Jane, this is one up to you,' [said Raymond]. 'I can't think how on earth you managed to hit upon the truth. I should never have thought of the little maid in the kitchen being connected with the case.'
>
> 'No, dear,' said Miss Marple, 'but you don't know as much of life as I do. A man of that Jones's type – coarse and jovial. As soon as I heard there was a pretty young girl in the house I felt sure that he would have not left her alone. It is all very distressing and painful,

and not a very nice thing to talk about. I can't tell you the shock it was to Mrs Hargraves, and a nine days' wonder in the village.'

'The Tuesday Night Club' (in *The Thirteen Problems*,
first published by William Collins, 1932)

Hercule Poirot, by contrast is quite *in*credible. He is a buffoon whom we are told repeatedly is intelligent. He is depicted as a man of absurd affectations, who speaks smatterings of French interspersed with poor English and who is vain about his moustache and his 'little grey cells'. He is neither very funny nor very convincing. For a long time I avoided reading the Poirot stories because, for me, they were just an exercise in plot construction with a variety of wooden characters – Poirot himself, the idiotic Hastings and the even more idiotic Inspector Japp, all of whom were just pale imitations of Sir Arthur Conan Doyle's Sherlock Holmes, Dr Watson and Inspector Lestrade.

'*Mon ami*, Hastings!' [Poirot] cried. '*Mon ami*, Hastings!'

And, rushing forward, he enveloped me in a capacious embrace. Our conversation was incoherent and inconsequent. Ejaculations, eager questions, incomplete answers, messages from my wife, explanations as to my journey, were all jumbled up together.

'I suppose there's someone in my old rooms?' I asked at last, when he had calmed down somewhat. 'I'd love to put up here again with you.'

Poirot's face changed with startling suddenness. '*Mon Dieu!* But what a *chance épouvantable*. Regard around you, my friend.'

The Big Four (first published by William Collins, 1927)

Although both characters have been interpreted widely for film and television, Miss Marple in her various guises usually retains her dignity and wisdom, while Poirot, despite being clever enough to think his way through problems (in the manner of Holmes), invariably becomes a figure of fun. Not until David Suchet's inspired portrayal of the character for television did Poirot achieve any sort of serious substance, for Suchet translates Poirot into a caring man, who is less concerned about voicing his own brilliance and more concerned for others' pain, and who has enough wry humour to poke fun at his own vanities. I would argue that this is *not* the character Agatha Christie invented, but a logical extension of it, and has resulted in the little Belgian finally receiving an authentic voice.

So how do you set about finding these voices? Well, as in everything else, there are probably a hundred ways of doing it and you have to choose a method that suits you. Your aim is to establish within your head people of such clear identities and personalities that when you put them on the page they virtually write themselves. This may take time, but it's time well spent. I tend to play with ideas on character for several weeks before I begin a story. This may involve writing them down and trying them out, or letting them lie in my subconscious while I work on something else. But, as I said, this is a dynamic process. Your characters will react with each other as they come together in the story; they will evolve and develop through their relationships with each other, just as we do in real life. The trick is to try to understand them well enough to know which way they are likely to jump.

(This doesn't always work. I've had to alter plots in the past when it's become clear to me that characters *would* not or *could* not do what I wanted.)

John, Michael, Mary and Hannah: A case in point

You will usually begin with your principal characters. Let's say you are looking for four of them – two men and two women. You don't know yet what their names are going to be but we will call them John and Michael, Mary and Hannah. Depending on the plot you have chosen, be it fully fledged or still in embryo, you will know roughly what, if any, relationships exist between these four protagonists. For the sake of argument, let's say that John and Mary are married, Michael is Hannah's brother, and Hannah, whose husband has been murdered, is having an affair with John.

It is irrelevant at this stage to know how Hannah's husband was killed, who the killer is or how you intend to work through to the eventual denouement. What is important is to establish clear reasons why any one of these four might have been driven to see murder as a solution, and to do that you must examine the pain/anger/ jealousy they have suffered as a result of Hannah's marriage to the dead man and Mary's marriage to John.

This is the beginning of your own dialogue with these imaginary people. Does Hannah feel any regret for her dead husband? Why has she been having an affair with John? Because she's promiscuous? Because she hated her husband? Because she felt unloved? Why was John having an affair? Because his marriage to Mary has broken down? Because Hannah is just another trophy? What was going on between Michael and his dead brother-in-law before the murder? Were they partners in a business venture? How long has Mary known Hannah? Does she know about the affair? Are she and Hannah friends?

If I were writing this story, the characters would begin to take shape along these lines.

Hannah projects herself as a victim. She has been used by two men, her husband and John, and the net result of both relationships is a growing despair. Like anyone who is searching for love, she appears to be deeply confused about how love demonstrates itself. Is it through sex with John? Or through the tearful love that her husband offered her between his drunken bouts of jealous rage? Her despair is exacerbated because she and Mary are friends, and, when her initial infatuation for John dies, she seeks to extricate herself without Mary ever finding out what she's done. But she learned shortly before her husband's death that he already knew and was threatening to make the fact public. How far does the image she projects reflect the real Hannah?

John has long since lost any affection for his wife but remains with her because it suits him to do so. (Perhaps she owns the house, or earns more money, or he doesn't want her to have control over his children.) He plays the field with any women who are interested, but has few feelings for them until he becomes involved with

Hannah and falls for the despair and the vulnerability that are her trademark. He is more accustomed to forceful women (mother, wife), and the appeal that Hannah makes to his dormant protectiveness is powerful, particularly when she comes to him, bruised and battered after a row with her husband. But how long would this sort of defenceless woman hold his attention? Does he really like clinging women?

Michael understands his sister better than anyone else because he grew up with her. He believes that the image she projects is very different from the reality because he knows Hannah to be more manipulative than anyone recognizes. (*Why? What happened in the past to persuade him of this?*) However, he knows that her husband is a pathologically jealous man, who knew about the affair and who is capable of extreme violence. Michael's position is complicated by a financial bond with the dead man (business? debt?) so his brother-in-law's death would be convenient. How far does the family talent for manipulation extend? Is the image that Michael projects as false as his sister's? And does he dislike her enough to push the guilt on to her?

Mary will always be the most tantalizing of the four characters. She appears, after all, to have the least reason for wishing Hannah's husband dead. She doesn't like her own husband but she does nothing to get rid of him. She undoubtedly knows about the affair because the dead man will have told her, if only to revenge himself to John. So what motivates her? It *must* be self-interest, because that is the most basic of all human instincts. My own suspicion is that she has two teenage children towards whom she is extremely protective (perhaps they've given a point to her life that was never there before – *NB Some interesting resonances here in terms of John's protectiveness towards Hannah*). I think Mary has already consulted a solicitor with a view to divorce, has learned the unpalatable truth that divorce will result in her children having the right to choose which parent they would prefer to live with, and is afraid that one of them, at least, won't choose her. (*Which one? An area of conflict – adolescent turmoil, made worse by John's waywardness and Mary's over-*

protectiveness. More resonances with what happened between Michael and Hannah during their childhood.) Only prolonged and proven drink or drug addiction or a criminal conviction would lead a judge to award sole custody to Mary. In view of the fact that Hannah's husband, before his death, was threatening to expose the scandal of all their double lives to the respectable community they live in, does Mary hate John enough to set him up as the fall guy for the murder and so get him off her back for good?

Anyone who has read my stories will know that these preliminary sketches are bare bones only. After all, these four people haven't even met each other yet. So, like Jack Blakeney, my artist in *The Scold's Bridle* who paints character in colour-coded abstract, I will 'go on now for weeks, working layer on layer, attempting . . . to build and depict the complexity of the human personality'. But my point is, the voices have begun.

As yet, they are muted because there's still far too much that we don't know. How old are they? How do they speak to each other? What sort of backgrounds do they come from? Are their names really John, Mary, Michael and Hannah? How much of themselves is hidden?

Off the top of my head, I'd say Mary has the potential to hide more of her real self than the others, but she may still emerge as the only honest character in this story. Hannah's hidden self may be a double bluff. I'm tempted to think she really *is* a vulnerable woman who, in this modern age, can't admit it and complicates everything by persuading her brother she has far more control than she actually does. And who's to say Michael's telling the truth about Hannah? He claims she's manipulative. But does anyone else? Surely this is a case of the pot calling the kettle black. And what of John? He must be an attractive man because he persuades women into bed with remarkable ease, yet he cares nothing for them. This is a dangerously egocentric personality, and all the more intriguing because of it. Barbara Peters, the highly respected owner of The Poisoned Pen Bookshop in Scottsdale, Arizona, argues that egocentricity (i.e. seeing the world with yourself at its centre) may be a character trait common to murderers. It's a very selfish mentality that takes the life of another in order to make things better for itself.

However, if I explore these people any further, I shall end up writing their story and, sadly for them, they *were* just examples plucked from the air.

Secondary characters and their function

Like the extras on a stage or in a film, your secondary characters are there to give the story life and body. Of course you could write about four people only. Jean-Paul Sartre's play *Huis Clos* portrays three people shut in a room together. As the play unfolds, they come to recognize that they have died and gone to hell, and that for the rest of eternity they are destined to be closeted together in this one small room, repeating the same boring conversations over and over again. But most of us lack Sartre's genius, and secondary characters are useful.

In terms of a crime story, they serve to point the finger of suspicion at the various protagonists and, as in any novel, help in the dynamic process of character evolution through what they can reveal. Because I try to give all my characters weight, though clearly some will have more weight than others, I find it important to see where and how my secondary characters fit into the scheme of things.

If we revert briefly to our embryonic story, then we know that there are already three extras in this plot: John and Mary's two children and the solicitor she consulted about her divorce. In addition, there may be a lover from John's past; and his mother, the strong-minded woman who brought him up – does she have a role in this? As a living presence or a dead one? There are also Michael and Hannah's parents, who must carry some responsibility for the fact that one or both of their children feel it necessary to hide their true self behind a façade. For example, how have they contributed to their daughter's disastrous marriage?

If the story is set in a village or a small community, then neighbours become important; if it is centred on a place of work, then colleagues become important. In the end, it is what the secondary characters reveal about the protagonists that keeps the suspense going, for they, being less directly affected by the murder, will probably be the most objective. I am interested in the fact that truth is always relative (i.e. each of us is highly selective about what we choose to see and believe), so I try to give my secondary characters strongly defined backgrounds with some sort of indication of the values they hold. Then the reader has a chance of deciding how valid their opinions are.

A good example of this is Sister Bridget in *The Sculptress*. Her credentials are impeccable. She is a nun, a convent school headmistress, she was one of Olive Martin's teachers, and she visits Olive regularly in prison. We should be able to have faith in what she says both about Olive and about the murders of Olive's sister and mother. Certainly, we feel that she is *trying* to be as honest as she can. However, she admits that she has never liked Olive, and this may or may not colour her perceptions of what Olive might have done.

Or, as Anne Cattrell reflects in *The Ice House*: 'Could reality be quantified,' Anne wondered, 'any more than truth? To say yes to such a question from such a man would be a betrayal. His capacity for understanding was confined by his prejudices.'

The investigating character

This is most commonly a policeman or a detective and is often a series character. But it can, of course, be anyone you like. In *The Sculptress*, the investigator is an author. In *The Scold's Bridle*, the job is shared between a detective sergeant, approaching retirement and hoping for promotion, and a female doctor who seeks to fend off her own arrest after her patient is murdered.

In many ways, the investigating character is the least constrained of all the characters. He or she can go anywhere, talk to anyone, ask anything. He can also try to interpret what is going on as it's happening. Whether or not the interpretation is correct is immaterial: it's one way of heightening suspense. If you choose to write in the first person, as many crime authors do, then you can bring to this investigating character all the terrible uncertainties, fears and weaknesses that any normal person experiences when faced with things they don't understand. You do, however, limit yourself in terms or action to what can be relayed through one person's eyes.

For all sorts of reasons, I have deliberately avoided writing a series, largely because I relish my freedom to write about who I want, when I want, but for those who choose series characters, there is a different kind of freedom. You already have a protagonist who is sharply defined and well-rooted in place and time. You know how he or she thinks before you even begin your story, and you know how he or she will react in any given situation. This is a bonus. Where I am feeling my way, the series-character writer marches forward with confidence because they are hand-in-hand with someone who already exists.

I offer a small caveat on the creation of series characters. Do not encumber your first novel with minute details about the character's life because you will be stuck with them for ever, and you may well wonder what on earth you can say about your character in the future that will be as interesting as their first appearance. Be vaguer than you feel you should because, as the series progresses, you may not want his or her birthday to be June 27, or his or her dog to be called Fido, or his or her mother to be an alcoholic. It's a tragedy for readers when authors become so bored with their over-defined characters that they send them hurtling over the Reichenbach Falls just to get rid of them.

The murder victim

If, as I do, you murder your victim in the first few pages, then that character can only be depicted through what other people say. The dead are always silent. This area fascinates me, simply because I doubt anyone's ability to 'know' another person when much of the time we don't even 'know' ourselves. There is a visual parallel of this in the reversed reflection of the mirror. Unless we appear regularly on television or in the cinema, the only picture we have of our faces is an inverted one.

However, the victim is in many ways the central character in a crime story. Without his or her death there can be no action, so it is very important to bring that person back to life through the eyes of those who knew him or her. Unless you are writing about a stranger murder – one where the victim is unknown to the killer – then the motive for the victim's death must lie somewhere in the victim's personality and/or history and/or relationships. If we return to John, Mary, Michael and Hannah, clearly it is the dead man and how he affected all their lives that will be the driving force of the story. Why did one of them hate him and fear him enough to kill him?

You may choose to depict your victim alive before his or her death, as Ngaio Marsh did in most of her books. Then the emphasis of the story shifts because the victim can speak for him or herself and you are setting up clear reasons in advance why various people might want to do away with this often-unpleasant person. I use diary extracts in *The Scold's Bridle* as a way of giving the victim (Mathilda Gillespie) a chance to speak for herself. This means she can explain in her own words why she was a victim, and her explanation is very different from the largely simplistic motives that the police uncover.

The murderer

Unless, like Patricia Highsmith in her Tom Ripley books, you make the murderer/psychopath your lead character, your murderer will simply be one of the many people featured in the story. Only at the end will he or she become in any way extraordinary, and then it's up to you how the person chooses to deal with the shock of exposure. There are some excellent non-fiction books on the market which contain interviews with convicted murderers, and they give insights into the kind of thought processes that go on at the time of the murder, the arrest and the trial. They are worth reading if for no other reason than that they show how like the rest of us most murderers are!

Character and dialogue

How your characters speak is of such fundamental importance to the development of their personas that a few hints on dialogue may be appropiate here. You can, of course, develop your plot through speech just as successfully as you can develop your characterization, so dialogue must be tight and to the point. The mistake that some authors make is to take it down to a bare minimum, with the result that full stops are the only punctuation and sentences are lucky to reach five words in length. But this kind of dialogue is the preserve of film and television, where paragraphs of speech mean the camera must focus too long on one person, and where the pace slows when an actor or actress cannot produce enough facial expressions to keep the watcher's interest.

To a certain extent, the same is true of a novel – waffle and spoken padding become tiresome – but to attempt to read a book where every character is allowed to deliver only one sentence at a time is a breathtaking experience. The pace becomes so rapid, and the characters so shallow, that you might as well be on the receiving end of machine-gun fire. As in everything else, writing a dialogue is a balancing act. You don't want to underdo it and you don't want to overdo it. Page-long paragraphs of speech are probably overdoing it. One-liners all the way through are probably underdoing it. The more natural you can make it, bearing in mind that you must impose some stylistic discipline – you should not allow a character to repeat the same word five times in a piece of dialogue any more than you would repeat it in a paragraph of descriptive prose – the better it will be.

Naming your characters

My only advice on this is to be comfortable with the names you choose. If you're happy with exotic names, then use exotic names, but don't rely on a name to give your character anything extra. In the end, it is your portrayal of the people you write about that matters, and if your hero or heroine is sympathetic then it doesn't matter whether you call them Maxmilian de Winter and Mrs de Winter, Sydney Carton and Miss Manette, Robin Hood and Marian, Mr Darcy and Elizabeth Bennet, or Rhett Butler and Scarlett O'Hara. (My own favourites among that little lot are Sydney Carton, from *A Tale of Two Cities*, by Charles Dickens; Mr Darcy and Elizabeth Bennet, from *Pride and Prejudice*, by Jane Austen; and the first Mrs de Winter in *Rebecca*, who sprang from Daphne du Maurier's amazing genius. And they all have such ordinary names.)

Memorable characters

Many successful books have been written on plot alone, with only the barest nod towards character creation and development. The most obvious examples are the various types of formula thriller, where action is everything and the characters fall into two or three stereotypical categories – the gung-ho, brave hero; his shadowy, some-times sadistic, always rich, evil counterpart; and the pale heroine who clings to the hero when he rescues her. They sell and make money, so it's certainly not a prerequisite of success to take the trouble to build and explore the people you write about.

However, the books that endure and continue to sell long after the authors are dead are the ones whose characters take such a powerful hold on readers' imaginations that they seem to exist in their own right, simply because everybody knows them: Philip Marlowe (created by Raymond Chandler); Emma Bovary (created by Gustave Flaubert); Ebenezer Scrooge (created by Charles Dickens); Lady Macbeth (created by William Shakespeare); Dr Jekyll and Mr Hyde (created by Robert Louis Stevenson). These people were portrayed so perfectly that we know them as well as we know Winston Churchill or Marilyn Monroe. We can even cite them in conversation because they've become known points of reference, as in 'He's a real Jekyll and Hyde.'

Certainly, for me, a large part of the thrill of being an author lies in the relationship I develop with the people I write about. After a while, they can become very real and, like the actor who is playing Hamlet, I have to school myself to 'drop out of character'. One day a poor friend of mine telephoned to give me the latest tearful account of her ongoing break-up with a man in her life, and I was so caught up in a confrontational scene I was writing between two women in *The Scold's Bridle* that I told her to pull herself together and be glad she'd got rid of him so easily. In the circumstances, this was hardly the most tactful response, and it was six months before she spoke to me again. I expect Flaubert had similar problems when he created Emma Bovary. When asked who the character was based on, he always said: 'Madam Bovary is myself.'

The aim of any author must surely be to draw his readers into the fantasy world he has created and then invite them to participate. So I want my readers to feel involved, I want them to love, I want them to fear, I want them to experience anguish. Ultimately, I want them to turn the last page and regret that the story has finished.

And they won't do that unless they have heard the voices, too.

FOX EVIL

Bringing crime uncomfortably close to home . . .

The new best-seller from award-winning Minette Walters.

Minette Walters is a writer who consistently tackles subject matters in gripping psychological fiction before they hit the news headlines. Her most recent number one bestseller, ACID ROW, took us to the world of sink estates, where mob rule whipped up a frenzy of hatred against suspected paedophiles. Her new thriller, FOX EVIL, is set in an isolated Dorset village where lives are shattered by

relentless victimization. The community feels threatened by travell-
ers – but who are the real outsiders? A world away from the urban
depravity of ACID ROW – the foxhunting country setting of FOX
EVIL once again proves Minette Walters to be one of our sharpest
political voices and disturbing and prescient novelists.

When elderly Ailsa Lockyer-Fox is found dead in her garden,
dressed only in nightclothes and with bloodstains on the ground
near her body, the finger of suspicion points at her wealthy, land-
owning husband, Colonel James Lockyer-Fox. A Coroner's inquest
gives a verdict of 'natural causes' but the gossip surrounding James
refuses to go away.

Why? Because he's guilty? Or because resentful women in the
isolated Dorest village where he lives rule the roost? Shenstead is a
place of too few people and too many secrets. What happened in
the past to create such animosity within the family? And why is
James so desperate to find the illegitmate child – his only grandchild
– who was put up for adoption when she was born?

Friendless and alone, his reclusive behaviour begins to alarm his
London-based solicitor, Mark Ankerton, whose concern deepens
when he discovers that James has become the victim of a relentless
campaign which accuses him of far worse than the death of his
wife. Allegations which he refuses to challenge ... Why? Because
they're a motive for murder?

*Minette Walters won the Crime Writers' Association John Creasey Award for the
best first crime novel of 1992, with her debut novel,* The Ice House. *Rapidly
establishing her reputation as one of the most exciting crime novelists writing
today, her second novel,* The Sculptress, *was acclaimed by critics as one of the
most compelling and powerful novels of the year and won the Edgar Allan Poe
Award for the best crime novel published in America in 1993. In 1994 Minette
Walters achieved a unique triple when* The Scold's Bridle *was awarded the CWA
Gold Dagger for best crime novel of the year. Her following novels,* The Dark
Room, The Echo, The Shape of Snakes, *and* Acid Row, *were published to*

further critical accclaim throughout the world. Acid Row *has also been shortlisted for the 2002 CWA Macallan Gold Dagger for Fiction and was a number one bestseller for Pan in 2002.*

Her first five novels have been adapted for BBC Television with huge success. The first, The Sculptress, *which was shown in 1996 and starred Pauline Quirke, proved the most successful television drama of recent years.*

Fox Evil *will also be published in Macmillan audio, read by Sean Barrett. (Two cassettes price £9.99 inc. VAT.)*

Minette Walters *lives in Dorset with her husband and two children. She has worked as a magazine editor but is now a full-time writer. For further information, please contact Philippa McEwan on 020 7014 6179, or email* p.mcewan@ macmillan.co.uk

Success Story

Val McDermid heads the crime bestseller lists here and in the US. Samantha Wyndham finds out how she does it.

SAMANTHA WYNDHAM: Your books are wonderfully varied. Readers are never quite sure what to expect when the next one comes along. Where do the ideas come from?

VAL MCDERMID: Usually from small details, from tangents. Something catches my interest – a detail in a news story, an item on radio, even a throwaway line in a conversation.

SW: Your biggest success so far, *A Place of Execution*, is about an investigation into a child murder, set in the 1960s. Presumably, it was the Moors Murder case that set this going?

VM: Actually, no. The starting point was the setting. I lived in Buxton in the heart of the Peak District for twelve years, and I did – and still do – a lot of walking around there. I love the White Peak, which has amazing beauty in all seasons and which seems possessed of an almost unearthly quality of light. There is something utterly magical about a limestone landscape. Although Scardale itself does not exist, the features of the village and its surroundings do all occur in the White Peak area, and it is an incredibly atmospheric place to spend time. I didn't specifically research the area for the book, though I did have dozens of photographs stuck around my desk while I was writing the book, just to remind myself of what I should be seeing in my mind's eye.

SW: So you matched the story to the setting.

VM: Not immediately. It took me quite a long time to come up with a story that was somehow right for the place and time. Setting is important. It's almost an extension of character, like Manchester is in the Kate Brannigan novels. The books are as much a chronicle of the city as a story about the character, Kate Brannigan. And if readers believe the setting, if it's real to them, they will believe anything else you say.

sw: To go back to *A Place of Execution* for a moment, the Moors murderers must have come into this early on as a big influence.

vm: In fact, I'd already started on the story when I realized that I couldn't write about the abduction of children in Manchester in the early '60s without mentioning Myra Hindley and Ian Brady. But I've never been drawn to the idea of writing about real crime. The problem with real life is that it's messy and untidy and the dramatic climaxes never work themselves out neatly enough to be entirely satisfying. Call me a control freak, but I like to be in charge of what happens when I'm writing! As to the Moors Murders – I am very aware of the sensitivities around that case, because as a journalist working out of Manchester, I was involved in elements of the story many times and interviewed several of those directly concerned, including families of the victims, the mother of Ian Brady and a former lover of Myra Hindley. So I was very careful not to use the real-life material in an exploitative way.

sw: How do you make your characters live; how do you make them real for your readers?

vm: I talk to them. The story is the starting point. Once I have that clear in my head and I know who the characters are going to be, I start up a conversation with them. I do this when I'm out for a walk, or driving the car, or doing some shopping. I get some funny looks from people in the street, but I find it's the only way of getting to know my characters. I must hear their voices in my head. I end up knowing more about them than I ever need to use, but that doesn't matter. Hearing their voices is important because the reader can learn a lot about a character from dialogue. You don't always need physical description. We know that Lindsay Gordon is Scottish, a former journalist and gay, but after that the reader has to build up their own image of the character. Beyond a few passing hints about her appearance, I never describe Lindsay; she was intended to be everywoman. Or rather whatever the reader wanted to make of her.

sw: You've described how you give life to your characters. Does this apply to the villains as much as to the good guys?

vm: Every bit as much. The writer has to know how the villain's mind works. You've got to have an understanding of the reasons behind a crime, otherwise you end up with two-dimensional characters.

sw: Is there a set of rules for story construction that would help a newcomer?

vm: There are the fundamentals of a good novel, any novel, not just crime fiction. I call it the three-legged-stool principle of good writing – character development, a well-told story and an atmospheric setting. After that it's hopeless to talk about rules because the story dictates the structure. Some stories start at the beginning, some in the middle and some at the end. For some stories, the first-person narrative is best because it allows you a more intimate relationship with the reader. But you're restricted in what you can show because nothing can happen that the narrator isn't witness or party to. So, for example, in a Brannigan novel, there's no possibility of revealing the inner life of the criminal. In other novels, particularly those that involve an ongoing police investigation, it's important to be able to show various strands unravelling at the same time.

sw: Clearly, you enjoy trying out different ways of putting across a story.

vm: That is what novel writing is all about. A novelist should be creative. I do like to try different kinds of books, partly to keep myself interested and partly to push myself harder as a writer. I want each book I write to be better in some way than the last, and that is a challenge that gets tougher every time! I thought it would get easier the more I did, but I was wrong. When you're starting out, you don't know much about craft and technique, so you can make great leaps and bounds forward quite easily. But the more technical skill you acquire, the harder it is to make that next tiny step up to the next level.

sw: When you talk about craft and technique, you're surely implying that there are rules to be followed?

vm: No rules. Every writer has to find her own voice, otherwise where is the creativity? It would be ridiculous if we all ended up writing the same way.

sw: So it is a case of improving by trial and error? Were you helped by anybody or anything to avoid mistakes?

vm: I learned from my mistakes. I came to recognize my weaknesses and, in particular, my early inability to plot carefully in advance. This lack of preparation meant that I wasted a great deal of time trying to sort out problems. I think what I managed to do was to identify my weaknesses, the things I found difficult, and then I concentrated on making sure that I attended to those aspects. I made sure I didn't make the same mistakes again.

sw: But surely there are guidelines that may help new writers; on how to create tension, for example?

vm: Suspense and tension should come from the story and there are many ways you can make this happen. I found my own instinct for what is most effective by reading other crime writers and watching movies. One of the easiest techniques for building up surprise is to put your characters in jeopardy, but this should not be allowed to dictate the story. I find it helpful to go over the story in my head. In this way I can see where the tension is rising or where it needs to be increased.

sw: What about research; is it a big part of crime fiction?

vm: Well, obviously, you've got to get your basic facts right. I tend to do backwards research, in other words I look up the details of a subject when I need them. It's very useful talking to people who know a lot about the subject you're interested in. They tell you things you wouldn't necessarily think to ask about. For example, when I was working on *A Place of Execution*, I spent some time with a friend who had been a policeman in the 1960s. He not only told me about the hierarchical structure of the police at that time but also gave me fascinating sociological details, such as the fact that policemen's wives were expected to socialize only with other policemen's wives – something I would never have expected. Newspaper archives are invaluable for period detail like the price of household goods, how people lived, what was considered news. I also find it helpful to read novels published at that time.

sw: Can there be too much detail?
vm: Oh, yes. There are writers who love showing off their nuggets of research. But facts are only important in so far as they move on the plot or characterization. Another thing, I wouldn't try to write in too much detail about police investigations because the deeper you get, the more inside knowledge you need. It's amazing how little you can get by with!

sw: What about describing places?
vm: The thing to watch here is that you don't get caught up in boring geographical details. You can talk about streets and buildings that are part of a real city like Manchester, but the Manchester of my novels also has to be a sort of universal city, one that is recognized by overseas readers who may never have been to Manchester or have even heard of it before picking up one of my books.

If you invent places make sure they come over as real. For example, if you introduce a nightclub where they sell drugs, obviously you can't use one that actually exists, but you have to make sure it's in a part of town where there might be a nightclub, not in some leafy suburb.

sw: Crime goes with sex and violence. But how do you decide how much and how often?

VM: I'd better deal with those two separately. On the first, I have to say it's much easier to do good sex than to write about it. I only use sex when it moves the plot forward or tells the reader something about a particular character in a way that would otherwise be impossible. In my own work, I sometimes suggest that sex has taken place when it serves a function but I rarely go into details about precisely what has happened.

SW: And violence?
VM: The use of violence is conditioned by the type of book I am writing. In the Kate Brannigan novels it would not be appropriate, but if I am writing about serial killers, then obviously it becomes necessary. But any reference to violence must be made with a sense of responsibility. Violence is not cool or glamorous and you should show what it does to people. It's immoral to make it glamorous and glitzy and groovy – I find it quite insulting to the reality of human pain. Violence is nasty and degrading; it degrades the perpetrators, the victims and the lives of the people who touch it. Thoughtful crime fiction must reflect the pain of the victims and the perpetrators. Writing about violence is a tightrope between what is necessary and what is gratuitous.

SW: How difficult is it for a woman to write as a man and vice versa? Would you advise aspiring writers to stick to the gender they know?
VM: Most novice writers don't have much confidence and when they start they generally lack skills of technique, narrative sophistication, characterization and so on, so yes, it's easier to write from what you know. You have enough challenges and problems to contend with, so don't make life even more difficult for yourself. But the more you exercise the muscle, the stronger it gets. Therefore, the more you write, the more you learn and develop skills, so you can move into different shoes. I started out with Lindsay Gordon (a Scottish journalist lesbian) because that was what I was and therefore that was what I knew. Then I began to push myself on. As my confidence grew, I moved on to writing about Kate Brannigan, a

very different type of woman from me, and then on to Dr Tony Hill, a man.

sw: Do you think of yourself as a perfectionist?
vm: If I did I'd never get to the point of handing over a book to the publisher. I always feel slightly dissatisfied when I've finished a book; but you have to acknowledge that there comes a point when you can't do anything more with it. Anyway, a feeling of failure is not a bad thing; it drives me on to write the next book. I do believe it's important to read certain critics and take note of what they say. Nobody gets it right first time. Always remember that agents and editors want to produce a successful book as much as you do, so listen and take note of their suggestions and advice.

sw: Do you have a daily routine or do you wait for inspiration to strike?
vm: I have an office and I work from about 9 in the morning to 4.30. Writing is my job and I treat it as such. As a crime writer, I don't have to feel precious about my books. In literary terms, I and other crime writers are seen as second-class citizens, which is very liberating.

sw: But you don't accept that judgement?
vm: Not at all. In *Killing the Shadows*, I explore the whole notion of writers having a responsibility to the wider world. Books have to be entertaining, otherwise why would people read them? But I like to think that my writing has a life beyond a good read, that it makes readers think about issues in the real world. Crime writing has become increasingly concerned with the society we live in. It may be because crime writers have become younger; we know we're in this for the long haul, we want to write books that spark our interest. We are not only telling a story but are also commenting on our world and, at best, shining a sharp light on our lives.

sw: Why do you think it is that so many writers and readers of crime fiction are women?
vm: It must have something to do with the fact that women were

programmed from birth to be non-confrontational. Traditionally, they have had no respectable outlets for feelings of rage and frustration. They therefore project these suppressed feelings into books connected to violent crime or deviant behaviour. This is a story told to me by a librarian: she had a female customer who, for about ten years, came in every week and borrowed every crime novel she could get her hands on – from Agatha Christie to Thomas Harris. Nothing was too gruesome or unpleasant for her, she just lapped it up. One day, she came in and asked about women's fiction. She wanted to read something slushy, non-violent and romantic. The librarian asked her if something in a crime novel had upset her. No, she replied, it was simply that her husband had died the week before, so she didn't need to read crime any more. She had been directing all her rage and hatred into the books she read. Who knows? Maybe they had stopped her from murdering her husband.

sw: What is the essential advice you would give to a crime writer in the making?
vm: Crime writing allows you to write about anyone, anywhere, in any context. As I said earlier, you must have character development, a well-told story, and an atmospheric setting. But don't be hidebound by what has gone before, let your own voice be heard. Just because crime fiction is a genre doesn't mean you have to write like everybody else.

Val McDermid was born in Kirkcaldy in Fife and worked as a journalist for fourteen years on national newspapers in Glasgow and Manchester. Her first novel, Report for Murder, *was published in 1987 by The Women's Press. She also writes occasional journalistic pieces and broadcasts regularly on BBC Radio 4 and BBC Radio Scotland. She has written the following books:*
    Common Murder *(The Women's Press, 1989);* Final Edition *(The Women's Press, 1991);* Dead Beat *(Gollancz, 1992);* Union Jack *(The Women's Press, 1993);* Kick Back *(Gollancz, 1993);* Crackdown *(HarperCollins, 1994);* A

Suitable Job For a Woman *(HarperCollins, 1994)*; Clean Break *(HarperCollins, 1995)*; The Mermaids Singing *(HarperCollins, 1995; winner of the Crime Writers' Association Macallan Gold Dagger)*; Blue Genes *(HarperCollins, 1996)*; Booked For Murder *(The Women's Press, 1996)*; The Wire In the Blood *(HarperCollins, 1997)*; The Writing on the Wall and other stories *(Revolver, 1997)*; Star Struck *(HarperCollins, 1998; winner of the French Grand Prix des Romans d'Adventure)*; A Place of Execution *(HarperCollins, 1999; winner of the Anthony Award for best novel; the Macavity Award for best crime novel; the Los Angeles Times Books of the Year Award for best mystery/thriller; the Independent Mystery Booksellers' Association Dilys Award; the Barry Award for Best British Mystery; and a New York Times Notable Book of the Year)*; Killing the Shadows *(HarperCollins, 2000); and* The Last Temptation *(HarperCollins, 2002). Her plays are:* Like a Happy Ending *(1981)*; Clean Break *(1998); and* The Right Chemistry *(1999)*.

> 'The dominant modern category of crime fiction is the "police profiler vs serial killer" novel, and its dominant British author is Val Mc-Dermid. The profiler is the new Sherlock Holmes, making amazing deductions from pure observation. Striking a balance between bloody horror and scientific method isn't easy. McDermid walks the walk and talks the talk with consummate ease.'
>
> Reginald Hill on Val McDermid, whom he chose as one of his
five top crime writers. (Financial Times, 29 June 2002)

The others are Conan Doyle, Dorothy L. Sayers, Dashiell Hammett and Ed McBain. Reginald Hill created the detective duo Dalziel and Pascoe, which successfully transferred to television.

On the Way to the Bank

How to get published and make a living from writing

Barry Turner

Where to start? Crime fiction is like any other category of writing; success is not by literary effort alone. It is important to realize this from the beginning. Behind every best-selling author is a support team that may well include an agent, editor, marketing manager, publicist and honest, straight-talking critic, who could be one of the preceding but is just as likely to be a partner in life who is not afraid to tell you when you get it wrong. This is not to belittle the creative effort, but simply to point out that the biggest mistake made by aspiring authors is to assume that the act of writing a book is, of itself, sufficient justification for everyone to sit up and take notice. It can happen. A work of genius may be recognized instantly, propelling the author to boundless fame and fortune. But the rarity of this makes the national lottery seem like a safe bet.

So, to repeat the question, where does one start? First comes the idea. You may be able to recall when the idea took hold; maybe on a walk, soaking in the bath, waiting for the next 77 bus to turn the corner, whenever. The fact is that at some point along the way the germ of a story came to mind. Hold on to this central idea and don't allow it to be lost in the twists and turns of a convoluted plot. The reason has less to do with literary excellence than with practical salesmanship, something many prospective authors prefer to ignore, but do so at their peril. To catch the interest of a commissioning editor, it must be possible to put across the essential concept of the book in just a few words. Be sure that if it is a rigmarole to explain what you are about, no one, except your nearest and dearest, will have the patience to find out if you really do have the talent to succeed.

Now you have the idea, is it a good one? And if it is good, is it also relevant? Will it appeal to popular taste? Before taking the plunge into serious writing, study the market, not in order to copy slavishly what is already there but to be able to think ahead to what will interest readers a year or two from here when your book will be stacked on the front counter of Waterstone's. In a companion volume to this one, on writing for the screen, Mal Young, the controller of BBC drama series, complains that he is forever getting scripts about wisecracking private detectives who do good out of dingy, back-street offices. 'Boring,' he says. This is not to belittle Dashiell Hammett or Raymond Chandler or to deny their enduring appeal. It is simply to make the point that studying the masters – always a good thing – is not an invitation to ape them. A few years ago, spy stories were all the rage; then, with the end of the Cold War, the thrill went out of MI5 and the rest. Writers of this genre had to find new inspiration which some, like John le Carré, did with conspicuous success. Others fell by the way, while yet others, the latest talents, are revisiting the spy story in the context of inter-national terrorism. The lesson is obvious and yet there is still a queue of hopefuls with their retreads of *The Ipcress File* or *The Spy Who Came in From the Cold*.

The idea is beginning to take shape. You have the essence of a plot and one or more central characters who will give life to the story. It is time to start writing. There is mixed advice on the opening. The first page of a crime novel – or any novel for that matter – is critical. Somehow you have to pull in the reader with a beginning that is strong enough to hold them until there is no possibility of escape. But it is a mistake to spend too long, at least initially, on dreaming up the perfect opening. Many a writer has been so obsessed with capturing the magic in the first sentence that his hands stay poised above the keyboard until depression or paralysis set in. Better to get going on a chapter that comes more easily. There is nothing like a few sequential words on the page to inspire confidence that all things are possible. Time to get back to the opening a bit later when the plot has advanced sufficiently to suggest a choice of compelling entrées. Just don't forget the opening altogether. And don't fall for the common temptation of using the first chapter as a sort of introduction, explaining what is going to happen long before we need to know. I heard recently from a writer who had what I thought was an ingenious idea for a novel about a massive financial swindle that owed something to the crooked genius of the late Robert Maxwell. Though not in the business of touting manuscripts, I responded with encouraging words only to get by return an opening chapter, which explained in some detail how a corporate pension scheme works. Even as a feature in a financial journal it would have scored low marks for interest.

Nor is the answer to make a dash for the other extreme of literary pretension, to sock them in the eye with a first-line murder or an explosion of violence so horrendous as to make the rest of the book anticlimactic. The opening has to intrigue, to draw in the reader, and this can be done by introducing a character, a place or an event or all three. There is no clear-cut formula. The best advice is to look at how other crime writers meet the challenge.

Talking with authors who have made the breakthrough can help, not only with the opening but with all aspects of story telling. As with any craft, there is at the heart of writing an essential gift, usually made evident by an irrepressible desire to write, no matter how many reject slips line the walls. But a talent needs the stimulant to grow, which may come from a sympathetic critic or teacher, one who, to paraphrase Bagehot, is there to be consulted, to encourage and to warn. This is not an invitation to sign up for one of the writing schools promoted in the small ads of the Sunday press. A few may give value for money but the volume of complaints that comes to *The Writer's Handbook* suggests that many more are in for the fast buck, which means signing you up for a year, cash in advance, in the hope that you'll get bored after a couple of dismal lessons but won't press for the money to be returned. University courses usually have more to offer, but even here, care comes before commitment. If a course takes your fancy, check it out with those who have gone before. The ambition to write a crime novel may not be assisted by lengthy seminars on the meaning of life, a form of self discovery that some academics seem to think is the sole purpose of literary endeavours. Writers' groups, on the other hand, do come highly recommended if only for the opportunity to talk out problems with those of like mind. This, if any place, is where the honest and constructive critic is likely to be found.

Books on writing by writers can also help, though their failing is to discourage inventiveness and originality by suggesting a set of golden rules, which may work for them but not necessarily for others. On matters of style, George Orwell has handed down a set of guidelines that has proved its worth:

- Never use a metaphor, simile or other figure of speech which you are used to seeing in print.
- Never use a long word when a short one will do.
- If it is possible to cut a word out, always cut it out.
- Never use the passive where you can use the active.
- Never use a foreign phrase, a scientific word or a jargon word if you can think of an everyday English equivalent.
- Break any of these rules sooner than say anything outright barbarous.

As you launch off into the serious business of writing a crime novel, make sure you know what you are talking about. Check the facts. There are those who argue that to turn out a successful story you should write from experience. In crime this is rarely practical or even desirable. But it is wise to carry out basic research. Readers can be unforgiving when careless errors throw the whole plot into doubt.

The work is moving on. You may yet be some way short of a complete novel. There are all those rewrites to come, not to mention the correction of silly mistakes, invariably brought to mind in the middle of a restless night. How could A be discussing the case with

B when B is supposed to be fifty miles away investigating C? Don't worry. Failure of continuity is one of the besetting problems of crime fiction. To his dying day, Raymond Chandler was unable to explain convincingly the ending of *The Big Sleep*. But however imperfect the product, maybe now is the time for it to be given the treatment by a professional, one who is able to assess its bookshop value. That means an agent or a publisher.

It used to be that the publisher invariably came first. The agent was pulled in only when the author had scored a hit or had established a track record that called out for bigger and more frequent royalty cheques. But in recent years the agent has assumed more of the function of a talent spotter, ready to take on and promote newcomers who show promise. Some publishers like it this way because someone else does the hard work. Talent spotting is a labour-intensive task and is never easy, particularly in the current climate when the market is subject to abrupt changes of fashion. Other publishers remain fiercely independent, ready to back their own judgement against the opinion of any outsider. For the first-time author, the balance has to be in favour of getting an agent at the earliest possible moment, one who can shop around for the best possible deal (something few authors are capable of doing), with a publisher who is best placed to advance the writer's career. Because, incidentally, it is a career we are talking about. Nobody is much interested in the one-book author, particularly in fiction, where the heavy costs of marketing a newcomer have to be spread over several titles.

A good agent is interested in money, but not exclusively so. He, or, increasingly nowadays, she, will negotiate a contract that illuminates the small print. This is more important than it sounds. The simple agreement to publish, a two- or three-page document much favoured by publishers of the old school, has typically grown to fifteen pages or more. This is in order to encompass book club deals, promotion budgets, cover design, the timing of publication, print number and subsidiary rights – the latter capable to attracting earnings long after the book is out of print. The sheer range of potential subsidiary rights is mind-boggling. It includes overseas publication (the publisher will try for world rights but when an agent is acting, US and translation rights are nearly always held back), film and television adaptations, audio cassettes and video – to mention only the most obvious. A book does not have to be a best-seller to earn advances and royalties in several countries, languages and formats, sums which in themselves may be quite small but which can add up to a healthy income. A writer acting on his own behalf is unlikely to realize all the possibilities.

But back to basics. If an agent is required, where best to find one? The list on page 111 gives the names of most of those who handle crime fiction. But there is no sure way of matching a writer and agent merely by glancing through the list of names and addresses. The famous names exercise the heaviest clout, of course, but the most powerful agencies are not necessarily suitable for a beginner who may feel the need for the close personal contact offered by a smaller agency. On the other hand, a smaller agency may already have taken on its full quota of newcomers. Those who are struggling for a toehold in publishing are by definition low-earners who must, for a time, be subsidized by the more profitable sector of a client list. The agent who gets the balance wrong is heading for the bankruptcy court.

Advice frequently given by the happily agented to the agentless is to seek out the opinion of authors who have been through the mill and to learn from their experiences. Writers' circles and seminars organized by the Society of Authors and the Writers' Guild (see pages 124 and 125) are fruitful sources of gossip.

Once the prime choice is identified, there remains the formidable problem of persuading the agent that you are next in line for stardom. Start with the knowledge that unsolicited manuscripts clog the agent's post. An average intake is thirty to fifty packages a month but two are in the eighty to one hundred category and one agent tops 150. Of these submissions, less than five per cent show real promise. An agent who receives twenty to thirty unsolicited manuscripts a month reports 'five strong leads in fourteen years'.

Of course, they are keen to find the next Ian Rankin or Minette Walters but experience tells them that this morning's post is unlikely to be the place to find them. They need to be persuaded otherwise. To achieve this, it is essential to put some effort into your presentation. What follows applies to publishers just as much as to agents. If you decide to make a direct approach to a publisher, and there may be very good reasons for doing so such as knowing someone who works on the crime list or, having failed to come up with an agent who suits your requirements, choosing to conduct your own business, the challenge is still to make your pitch as strong as possible. A grimy manuscript, frayed at the edges, typed single spaced with loads of corrections, tied up in a bundle that comes apart on delivery, will not – surprise, surprise – get a fulsome welcome. Obvious? Maybe, but it happens all the time.

To seek a professional opinion, you too must be professional. In writing to an agent or publisher set out your wares in the most attractive way possible. Start with a few lines of justification. What is the book about? Why does it cry out to be written? This is where you recall the central idea that started you on your way. Having settled on a snappy justification, the synopsis can be used to describe the book in some detail. It is impossible to specify length but two or three pages should do it. What is essential is for the synopsis to be a clear and logical description of the book. It should be typewritten or word processed with double spacing.

Along with all this goes some sample chapters. Even if you have a finished novel in manuscript, it is unwise at this stage to send off the whole thing. A sample is easier to digest and if it is tasty enough, the agent or publisher will soon come back for more. The covering letter of introduction should say who you are, what you do and whether you have been published before in whatever form. Never e-mail. Have you seen what a manuscript can do to gum up the technological works?

More advice on the related matters comes from a *Writer's Handbook* survey of agents (not all specializing in crime fiction, it must be stressed), most of which applies every bit as firmly when corresponding with publishers.

1 Write – don't telephone – to one agent at a time, sending a brief covering letter to the agent concerned. Too often authors send photocopies addressed 'Dear Sir/Madam' so it is obvious all the agents in this book are being approached at the same time. These go straight into the agent's bin.

2 Do not try to submit to publishers first and then decide to use an agent without admitting to rejections. Either write direct to publishers or use an agent from the outset.

3 Always send return postage – preferably a stamped addressed envelope – and a stamped card if you want an acknowledgement.

4 *Always* keep a copy of any material submitted – don't use registered post or recorded delivery as this can entail collection from a distant post office – and allow at least a month for a response.

Do not be disappointed if an agent, or even several agents give the thumbs down. They may be overloaded with clients. But even if this is not so, remember that all writing is in the realm of value judgement. And where one agent fails to see talent, another may be more perceptive. The only advice is to keep trying.

In the event of a rejection, do not expect as of right a detailed analysis of where you may be going wrong. If you want constructive criticism go to those who specialize in editorial advice such as The Literary Consultancy (see page 138).

Agents do not come free. Ten per cent is standard but an increasing number take 15 per cent of your earnings and a few pitch as high as 17.5 or 20 per cent – plus VAT. A VAT-able author can reclaim the tax. Others must add 17.5 per cent of the commission to calculate the agent's deduction from their earnings. Some agents invoice you certain administrative costs such as photocopying but no reputable agent charges a reading fee. There are too many scandals attached to reading fees, which are one of the easiest ways

for the unscrupulous to make money from the gullible. It is sometimes argued that if an agent is paid to assess the value of a
manuscript, he's bound to give it full attention. Maybe. But if there
are responsible agents who justify a reading fee, they are most
certainly outnumbered by the charlatans who take the money and
run.

When the day comes (perhaps this should read, *if* the day comes,
but we are taking a positive line) that an agent or publisher shows
an interest in your crime novel, discussion must inevitably turn to
the financial deal that will secure the best possible return on your
labour and talent. If an agent is acting as the front man, he will
eventually come back with an offer contained within a publisher's
contract which may or may not be acceptable. That's up to you and
your bank manager. If you are dealing direct with a publisher and
have no experience of contracts, the Minimum Terms Agreement
(MTA) formulated by the Society of Authors and the Writers' Guild
and accepted by most leading publishers, is a useful benchmark. A
copy can be got from either the Society or Writers' Guild (free of
charge to members who send a stamped, addressed envelope). One
of the great virtues of the MTA is that it guarantees an author's
involvement in every stage of publication from jacket design through
to catalogue copy.

Where the MTA is less assertive is on the question of royalties.
Old hands remember the days where it was standard for a publisher
to offer 10 per cent on hardback and 15 per cent on paperback with
built-in increases tied to volume of sales. No longer. High-pressure
marketing now requires a more flexible approach. Concessions to
powerful booksellers by way of increased discounts have to be paid
for and it can well be that the writer is asked to take a lower royalty
so that his book may be sold more aggressively. Fair or unfair? Who
is to say until the cheque arrives in the post and the author jumps
for joy or rings the Samaritans.

And now to the most critical questions of all, the size of the
advance on royalties. Any author who wants to make a living by
writing must establish early on that his publisher is prepared to

make a down payment on account of royalties. The bigger the advance, the more likely the publisher will be to put his back into the marketing effort. Even if he winds up hating the book, he will want to earn his money back by pushing sales.

But don't be misled by the highly publicized mega-deals. They are not typical. An established writer may celebrate with £20,000-plus, but a first-time novelist is lucky to get more than £1,000. A reasonable advance for all but the top names is a sum equivalent to 60 per cent of the estimated royalties payable on the first edition. The advance should be non-returnable, except when the author fails to deliver a manuscript by the due date, or if it is not in line with what was agreed with the publisher. Usually, it is split three ways, part on signature of contract, part on delivery of the manuscript and part on publication. What proportion of the advance will be due on signature? Ideally one-third (or more if you can present a good case) with the remaining two-thirds due on delivery and publication respectively. As a spot check on the acceptability of a contract, confirm four essential points before signature.

First, there should be an unconditional commitment to publish the book within a specified time, say, twelve months from delivery of the typescript, or, if the typescript is already with the publisher, from signature of the agreement.

The obligation to publish should not be subject to approval or acceptance of the manuscript. Otherwise what looks like a firm contract may be little more than an unenforceable declaration of intent to publish. It is equally important to watch that the words 'approval' or 'acceptance' do not appear in the clause relating to the advance payment. This point about the publisher's commitment to publishing a book is of vital importance, particularly since publishers' editors change jobs with increasing frequency. An author who has started a book with enthusiastic support from his editor may, when he delivers it, find he is in the hands of someone with quite different tastes and ideas.

Secondly, there should be a proper termination clause. This should operate when the publishers fail to comply with any of the provisions of the contract or if, after all editions of the work are out of print or off the market, they have not, within six months of a written request, issued a new edition or impression of at least 1,500 copies.

Thirdly, there should not be an option clause that imposes unreasonable restrictions on future works. The best advice is to strike out the option clause but if this proves impossible, an option should be limited to one book on terms to be mutually agreed (not 'on the same terms').

Next, get it in writing. A recent article in *The Author* says it all: 'Your editor may be wonderful. Your faith in human nature may be undented. It may seem pedantic, pushy, bossy. But if you ever agree something important with a publisher which is not in your contract – be it regarding deadlines, amendments, publicity or, especially, money – follow up the meeting or conversation with a friendly letter, confirming the salient points. If things go wrong and all you have is the memory of an airy promise on the telephone that the publisher has since "forgotten", you will be in a much stronger position if you can produce a copy of a letter as evidence of that promise.'

Success begets success. An author who makes a hit can usually rely on his publisher's marketing team to help him repeat the trick. While it is only the super earners who qualify for an advertising campaign, there will be bookshop promotions with eye-catching displays conveniently close to the till. Then there are the literary editors to be solicited for reviews and the feature pages to fill with author interviews. In the week of publication you may be taken off round the country to talk about your 'number one best-seller' on radio and television. Outrageous hype is part of the game and has been with us for a long time. Go with it. It may not be your idea of fun but it is all part of a carefully orchestrated campaign to put your name before the public, to make it easily recognizable and, eventually, to have it equate with a good read.

No crime fiction writer can ask for more.

Talent Spotted

Tony Strong's first crime novel, *The Poison Tree*, was greeted by *The Times* as 'a debut to die for'. Since then he has written three more novels. Barry Turner seeks his advice on starting out on a life of crime writing.

BARRY TURNER: How did you get into writing?

TONY STRONG: Like most people I started writing the kind of stuff I like to read. Because I could never find enough of it, I sensed there was a market for it. I used to write short stories and gradually two of them kind of joined to make a full-length story. But it was still only thirty pages long so it wasn't very successful. Then one summer when I had nothing to do at work I revised my thirty-page story and realized that it was actually a synopsis. Working in advertising, I was used to writing short, sharp scenes and this is what I had done with the novel. So all I had to do was go through the relatively easy process of unpadding it and turning it into a book. This was *The Poison Tree*.

BT: But how did it get published?

TS: I had a friend who was working in publicity at Transworld and I asked her for the names of some agents who might be interested in this sort of book. She put me on to Ursula Mackenzie (Transworld Editorial Director) who said that Transworld was actually looking for someone in my area, so why not send the manuscript to her and she'd have a look at it and advise which agent to go for. The next day I was invited to meet Ursula to chat about the book. She told me she really liked it and that I didn't need an agent as she would publish it. So Transworld started publishing me. It was a bit of an experiment for them as at the time they didn't have much in the way of crime thrillers. They had American thrillers and a few home-grown storyteller, Robert Goddard-type books, but not any crime.

BT: You came in on a new fashion – really quite gritty stuff, a move away from both cosy detective fiction and from the police procedural.

TS: It wasn't careful planning on my part. The sort of stuff I really liked had come about in the early '90s – there was Ian McEwan who had gradually moved from his brand of very gritty, gory, slightly grotesque realism in the psycho-sexual area with books like *The Cement Garden* and *The Innocent* into areas that were more psychological and more criminal. So that was an influence. Also a few writers were doing interesting things with the crime format – Peter Høeg's *Miss Smilla's Feeling for Snow*, Donna Tartt's *The Secret History* and *Snow Falling on Cedars* by David Guterson. Often their heroes were quite ordinary people rather than private eyes or the stock figures and that was what seemed to me to be new – to take ordinary, reasonable people, and drop them into some criminal event.

BT: On the practicalities of writing. Do you have a regular routine? Are you disciplined?

TS: I have to be because I'm quite a slapdash person. I have a day job which is quite pressurized and I want to do it properly. So I work four days a week for an advertising agency and write on one day. I don't write at weekends at all. That's family time. On the days I am at the agency, I go to work at around 10am and I hope to have done a couple or even three hours' writing before then.

BT: And how many words in a day?

TS: I treat the week more as planning time. The day I write, I try to work from 8.30 in the morning until 8.30 at night. I use my son's bedroom as my office so I can't leave papers out or be messy and I can't go downstairs because the nanny is there with the youngest child.

BT: That's a hard day.

TS: Yes, my head is often spinning by the evening but it is the only day I get to write.

BT: How many thousand words do you have at the end of that?

TS: It varies enormously. On a really good day I may write a chapter; maybe around 8,000 words but more usually around 4 to 5,000 words.

BT: Do you do rewrites?

TS: Yes. And I do rewrites as I go along. I can only rewrite on something that's been printed out, on the physical page. Every writer I've ever spoken to always says don't edit until you've finished otherwise you'll get bogged down. I find if I do get stuck I haven't got the time to wait for it to work itself out. I have to be doing something as it's my one day of writing so I start to rewrite. As well as rewriting, I'm looking for a grasp of the character or a little event or something in what I've already done that will give me a clue to get on to the next bit.

BT: Does that mean when you start on a novel you don't have the complete plot in mind?

TS: Apart from my first book, I've always had the complete plot in mind but always changed it as I went along.

BT: How do the ideas flow? What inspires you?

TS: Advertising is all about ideas. Having that background, as well as making me able to write short scenes, means all my books have started with a very defined idea. In the first book there were two ideas – the predicament and the character. It boils down to the idea of an academic who is lecturing on detective fiction but is involved in an American-type, modern psycho-killing. Everything else is how the character works it out. In *The Death Pit* it is modern-day witchcraft and my academic (the same person) is studying a seventeenth-century witch. Again, very simple: two things collide and after that comes the whole plot. In *The Decoy* it is an actress who is involved, tangentially, in the death of a woman – she's asked to act the part of someone who's the next potential victim. The latest, *Tell Me Lies*, is actually based on a true story I was told (although it turned out to have been distorted in the telling) where a woman has been raped and her best friend murdered. The police think they know who did it but can't get the guy to court – they've got evidence but it's not admissible – and she agrees to lie in court to get a conviction and then there are the consequences of all that. In my books, there are usually two elements – a person and a predicament – which come together and that's it. I'm not saying that's the only way to write a book but that's the kind of thing I like because it's very simple. I know where I'm going with it and you're instantly in to a 'so what might happen next' situation.

BT: Do you think visually with your books?
TS: Well, I like visual writing. But, funnily enough, I surprised myself with some of the un-visual bits in my first book. Then, my third book, *The Decoy*, I saw very much as a movie partly because the heroine was an actress and I wanted it to play out like a movie; you never know what she's thinking because that would destroy the plot. So I wrote it in the present and didn't describe what anyone is thinking or feeling. I simply told the reader, who becomes the viewer, what they see. That made for an easy write, once I'd set myself that rule. Every time I started to think what shall I say, I thought, don't say it, just write the next thing that happens. And I guess that's why it's more of a thriller. And then with my last book I wanted to do the complete opposite, so I wrote it from the first-person perspective – there's much better action with that, it's more psychological. But at the moment I have no idea if that will work or not. The manuscript is with my editor. Also, since the main character is a twenty-five-year-old girl and it's written in her voice, I sent it to a whole bunch of twenty-five-year-old girls. The title is *Tell Me Lies* and it will be published next year.

BT: Is *The Decoy* likely to become a movie?
TS: Yes, it's been optioned by a very good Hollywood producer, the man who made *The Fugitive*, *Seven* and *The Perfect Murder* so, in

the sense that it's got to a Hollywood studio, it's achieved all that a writer could hope for. Whether it gets made into a movie or not is in the lap of the gods or whatever one calls Hollywood producers.

BT: One of the points made about your books is that (like Minette Walters) every time you produce a new book it is *really* a new book; there's no running character. The character is not so vital as to override the plot. Is this serendipity?

TS: No. I had an American publisher who was very keen I should write a series (they didn't like my idea for a second book, which I thought was a great one) and they said I must write a follow-up to my first book, which I did. They published it and then dropped me as they said nobody was buying it. They'd been insistent that I should write a series and also persuaded my UK publisher that I should. I feel that series books are never going to be quite as ambitious as concept books. But equally I don't like the fact that I left my original character after two books.

BT: Does your mind stray to thinking, 'What couldn't I do with a Rebus-type character?' Are you, in the back of your mind, thinking of creating a long-running character?

TS: I'd take my first character, the academic. I really liked her and I liked what happened to her in the course of the first two books. Because she got involved in the witchcraft thing she became a wiccan – despite the fact that she doesn't believe in it – because she saved the life of a small child who was the daughter of a wiccan and became a godmother to that child in the religious cult of witchcraft. I imagine she's living in London and she's probably lecturing (at something that's called a university but only recently became one) on detective fiction. She's probably got a bunch of people living at her house and they probably have wiccan rituals, and although she doesn't really believe she still finds it quite comforting. A bit like the way parents of my generation still go to church even when they don't believe in it. So I know what she's doing now, but it's just that she hasn't come across any crimes that are worth writing about. I might write a prequel to the *Poison Tree* because I know what the crime might have been there.

BT: I suppose my own psychological block against thinking of her as your character is because you're writing about a woman. And that's a tricky thing to do. Aren't you making life unnecessarily hard for yourself?

TS: Life would have been much easier if I'd used a female pseudonym because female readers in particular assume that you've got it wrong and therefore read your book in a more critical way, particularly any sex scenes. If there was any way of removing that critical distance I would, but there doesn't seem to be. I've no idea why I prefer to write about women, except that the women I write about are women I like so I have an almost romantic relationship with them. If you're going to create a character it seems to be easier to create one you're going to have a romantic interest in. My characters are white, middle class, usually in their thirties or thereabouts, in the arts or media or are academics. The only real difference between them and me is that they're female. And yet, if I'd written about a Scottish male tramp, people would say that's fine. But I'd find that so much harder. There's this assumption that the sexual divide is the biggest one.

BT: So you're writing from your own experience but switching sexes. And that's easier for you than staying with your own sex and writing about something about which you know nothing at all. Do you do research?

TS: Yes, quite a lot but mainly through the Internet rather than books. In *Tell Me Lies* the first chapter is a woman being examined in a rape suite. You gradually realize that not only has she been raped but she's been drugged with the date-rape drug, and she has discovered her best friend's body in the flat they lived in after the attack. On the Internet you can look up 'rape suite protocols' and 'medical protocols', so you know exactly the process a woman goes through in a rape suite even down to the kind of detail such as colour coding on the tubes for the blood samples. On another level you can go to rape survivors' websites where people talk about their experiences so you can know what your subject is thinking. Maybe it's voyeuristic of me to go trawling through these sites to research but it seems to me if you're going to write about that kind of thing you have to get it right. So I do try to get both the facts and the human reactions right.

BT: You can research necrophilia on the Internet?

TS: Yes. When I started off with *The Decoy* I typed 'necrophilia' into a search engine and discovered there were over 20,000 web-sites. Again, I started off with the idea that this character should be a necrophiliac for all sorts of structural reasons. At that point he was just a kind of cartoon villain in my mind in the same way that Hannibal Lecter was a cannibal. And as I started to read more about necrophilia and accounts by necrophiliacs of what they see as their misunderstood psychology, the character gradually acquired a bit more depth. He's still a cartoon villain because that is his role, but he's more of a rounded cartoon villain than if I'd not done the research.

BT: And the funeral business?

TS: In America they have a big tradition of what they call 'cosmo-tology'. They embalm the body and they have open caskets. So undertaking is a much bigger business there than here. And I found an undertaker in the middle of America who was offering training courses for mortuary science attendants on the Internet and, as a sweetener, as I guess he wasn't getting much custom, he was offering a free module as a sample. So I did Module One, took my test and got a distinction.

BT: But you didn't go on with it?

TS: No. I covered the only bit I needed, which was the preparation of a dead body.

BT: Have you always had a strong stomach?

TS: I think so or maybe the opposite. I've always been very interested by gross, gruesome stuff, but I've always been very squeamish in real life. For example, I faint when anyone ever takes my blood. I always say to them, 'Look, I'm not nervous at all but I will faint when you take that blood,' and they say, 'No, you'll be fine. I can always tell those who are nervous and you're not.' And they take the blood and I faint; just like that. I don't know why.

BT: One or two other writers I know who write about grisly subjects are excessively sensitive in real life. I've only come across one other person like me who picks up worms in the street and puts them back on the soil and that's Brian Masters, who has written several books about mass killers. Are you like that?
TS: No. Not to that extent. But I think perhaps writing about crime has made me more secretive, as you spend a lot of your time thinking about really dark things, and maybe going a bit further into them than you might otherwise have done.

BT: Has it changed your life in any way? Does it affect your life, psychologically?
TS: I think I'm a less aggressive person than I was five years ago but that may be because my children are getting older and winding me up less. But I do find that when I'm writing something, particularly if I'm writing in the evenings as well as mornings, it completely takes over my life and I don't bother to clean the flat for months. It's a complete tip but I quite like the idea that, like a sculpture studio, it's a complete mess and something pristine comes out of it. That's how I like to write. To be focused on the one thing and forget everything else. I so look forward to the day I finish a book but now, today, I find myself for the first time in nine months without a book to write, and I feel completely bereft. You lose this huge thing that takes over your life and you can't wait to get back into another one. It's addictive.

BT: How old are you?
TS: Thirty-nine.

BT: If a young writer came to you now and said I want to be Tony Strong, would you have any advice to pass on? Is there anything that you feel you've done right or done wrong that you would pass on to others?

TS: I would say that once you write your first book it will set the template for all your future books. If you start writing things which are in the crime area, you will always have to write in this area because your editors and publishers will expect it. I'm lucky that in my day job I tend to write comedy. I might just as easily have started writing humour books but I'm quite glad I didn't. So I'd say, don't rush into print. I think it's good to spend a few years writing short stories, whatever, so that when you do commit yourself to a book you don't find you've gone down a path that you will regret later.

BT: Is that the book shaping an author or the publisher shaping an author? Is there a danger of becoming typecast?

TS: Yes. I have had agents and publishers, particularly publishers, saying, 'That's a nice idea, Tony, but it's not really a Tony Strong idea.' So you become two people. You're the person who wants to write a book about X and you're also the person who, like it or not, is also called Tony Strong and is a brand. In a sense, it's better if you're not successful because if I say to my publishers that the last book didn't sell that well and perhaps if I write something different it might be a best-seller, they'd say OK. Whereas if I write a real best-seller and said I wanted to do something different they'd say, no. That's the paradox.

Tony Strong was born in Uganda in 1962, though his parents came back to the UK when he was six weeks old. He was educated at Winchester and Oxford, where he read English and graduated with a First. For twelve years he worked as a copywriter for the advertising agency Ogilvy and Mather, where writers Salman Rushdie and Fay Weldon also started their careers. He now works for Abbott Mead Vickers and divides his time between his family home in Oxfordshire and his flat in London. He is married with three children. He has written the following books: The Poison Tree (Bantam Books, 1998); The Death Pit (Bantam Books, 2000); and The Decoy (Bantam Books, 2002).

Making Crime Pay

Bob Ritchie tracks down the legendary heroes of crime fiction

In common with many early writers of crime fiction, Arthur Conan Doyle was somewhat embarrassed by the popularity of his most famous creation. In an interview he once claimed that his 'lower work' obscured his 'higher', that *The White Company*, for example, 'was worth a hundred Sherlock Holmes stories'. Given that Conan Doyle's higher works are now largely unread, while his famous detective lives on in almost undiminished popularity, we can conclude that an author is rarely the best judge of his own work. It is true that the Sherlock Holmes stories are not read as avidly as before, but the character of Sherlock Holmes thrives in TV series, movies, pastiches and sequels. It is, perhaps, the true test of a legendary character, that he should outgrow the form in which he was first introduced to the world, just as Frankenstein has so spectacularly outgrown Mary Shelley's novel.

This chapter introduces detectives in roughly chronological order, but though it starts with Sherlock Holmes that does not mean he was the first. Holmes did not spring from nowhere. Before him came C. Auguste Dupin of Edgar Allan Poe's *The Murders in the Rue Morgue*, the (largely fictional) *Memoires* of Eugène-François Vidocq, the first head of the Paris Sûreté, Inspector Bucket in Charles Dickens' *Bleak House*, Sergeant Cuff in Wilkie Collins' *The Moonstone*, Emile Gaboriau's Inspecteur Lecoq, William Russell's 'Waters'. Yet it is only in the rounded character of Sherlock Holmes that we see the familiar elements of the fictional detective come together for the first time.

From Poe, Doyle borrowed the central narrative device: a brilliant solver of crimes who modestly allows his admiring friend to tell the story of his cases. (Though 'crime' may not always be the right word: Doyle once confessed that around half his stories didn't involve the actual commitment of any crime at all.) In his somewhat antisocial and dysfunctional character, Holmes anticipates the contemporary fictional detective: his cocaine habit, his frequent desire for solitude, the music motif. Yet, whereas these elements are now used to demonstrate a specifically modern – almost politically correct – vulnerability in characters like Ian Rankin's Rebus and James Lee Burke's Robicheaux, both recovering alcoholics, in Holmes they are no barrier to his brilliance. They aren't weaknesses; they are simply part of the picture.

Piercing intellect and acute observation are his hallmarks, characteristics adopted by many later detectives, though less common now. Stories frequently start with some clever deduction about a person after only a few seconds' acquaintance. Scientific rationalism is at the heart of his method, aided by encyclopaedic knowledge and the ability to spot things that are out of the ordinary, a skill parodied by his friend J. M. Barrie, who has Watson writing up *The Adventure of the Man without a Cork Leg*.

Holmes is, of course, contemptuous of the police, a luxury few modern detectives allow themselves, unless, as in James Ellroy's novels, for example, the failings of the police are the main theme. Initially, Holmes is also fairly contemptuous of Watson, though that changes to something like affection as time passes. Their marriage of opposites is another legacy exploited by some modern writers, most notably Reginald Hill with Dalziel and Pascoe. Watson is everything Holmes is not: solid, predictable, straightforward, conventional, unimaginative – indeed, perhaps it is this last trait that enables him not only to put up with a colleague who any normal person would have quickly found impossibly arrogant, but to remain a loyal and true friend. Could Holmes have lasted as long as a character without Watson?

For all the inevitable emphasis on his remarkable powers of

deduction, Holmes is a complex and contradictory character. He is a scientist who loves art, an athlete who spends a lot of time lying down, a confirmed bachelor who can charm women, a calm man who can become as restless as a cat on a hot tin roof. A Sidney Paget illustration for *The Naval Treaty* in *The Strand Magazine* portrays him as a slim, languid aesthete, almost an Aubrey Beardsley, yet he is also a man of action, 'one of the finest boxers of his weight'. Contradiction is also shown, symbolically, in his penchant for disguise. We see him as a late Victorian, moving in a shadowy world of mist-shrouded moors and fog-laden London alleyways; yet 221b Baker Street is large and airy, 'cheerfully furnished, and illuminated by two broad windows'.

These contradictions mirror the conflict within all crime stories; the conflict between reason and unreason, between the rational and the irrational, between civilization and chaos. (It is no coincidence that in Poe's *The Murders in the Rue Morgue* the crime Dupin investigates turns out to have been committed by an enraged ape.) The detective's job is to restore order to the world, which is why to a certain extent, like Holmes, he must live above it, motivated by a superior moral code. Detection may be a game for Holmes, but it is a game that has to be played fairly. The endangered and the falsely accused are his clients, people Doyle himself came to champion when in later life he became an active campaigner against racism and injustice – in the cases of George Edalji, a half-Indian solicitor victimized by racist neighbours, and Oscar Slater, a German Jew wrongly convicted of murder. These were brave and uncommon activities for an Edwardian gentleman, activities Holmes himself would have been proud of.

G. K. Chesterton's Father Brown is the start of a tradition of clerical detectives, at first glance not a promising profession, since men of the cloth are assumed to be somewhat unworldly. In fact, they are likely to come into almost daily contact with the sins of the world and those who commit them. Despite his appearance in more than sixty stories, very little can be learned about the cleric. He was by all accounts modelled on Father O'Connor, the friend and priest who took Chesterton into the Roman Catholic Church, and the stories can be viewed as a disguised chronicle of Chesterton's own spiritual progress. It is also difficult not to conclude from them that O'Connor must have been rather dull. Father Brown is meek and almost entirely without charisma, a colourless figure in a black clerical outfit and hat, without home life, childhood or youth.

While Sherlock Holmes became more like his creator as time passed, Brown resolutely remained the opposite of Chesterton, who was bluff, larger than life. He is almost an anti-detective, even to the extent that the stories are sometimes thought of as a spoof of the genre. Like Doyle, Chesterton also became slightly embarrassed by his creation's popularity. In later life he made no secret of the fact that he was continuing to write the stories mainly to finance his weekly socialist journal. It is a clue to their main thrust. Like the work of his contemporaries H. G. Wells and George Bernard Shaw, Chesterton's stories contain an implicit socialist bias, often taking as their starting point the murder of an unpleasant millionaire. And once Brown has unmasked the wrongdoer, revealing him to be who he really is, the cleric is more concerned with giving him a chance at forgiveness than with bringing him to justice. Father Brown does not merely solve puzzles, he gives us lessons in morality.

The 1920s saw the beginning of what is referred to as 'the golden age' of detective writing. Agatha Christie's Hercule Poirot made his first appearance in 1920 in *The Mysterious Affair at Styles*, A. A. Milne's *The Red House Mystery* (savaged so comprehensively by Raymond Chandler in his essay *The Simple Art of Murder*) was published in 1922, Freeman Wills Croft's *Inspector French's Greatest Case* introduced French in 1924, Margery Allingham's Albert Campion appeared in 1929, and so on. In 1923 Dorothy L. Sayers introduced arguably the most rounded hero of this age: Lord Peter Wimsey, connoisseur and gentleman of leisure.

Despite his name ('whimsy' is defined in the *Concise Oxford Dictionary* as 'playfully quaint or fanciful behaviour or humour'), Sayers had grand aspirations for her creation. Perhaps as befits an honours graduate in medieval studies from Oxford, she thought of the detective as 'the latest of the popular heroes, the true successor of Roland and Lancelot'. Be that as it may, the most obvious comparison that springs to mind is with Fred Astaire. Yes, Lord Peter may be a gentleman-scholar, a bibliophile and as upper class as they come, but in looks and in his appeal to women he is Astaire: well-groomed, slimly athletic, graceful, romantic – he even wears a top hat. He is sexy yet sexless, an exemplar of that golden age of nonchalant expertise and high style. He drives a Daimler, changes his jacket two or three times a day and can talk, as Melodie Johnson Howe put it, 'about love, music and murder all in the same sentence'.

The golden age preferred their detectives to be gentlemen rather than players and they didn't come much more gentlemanly than Lord Peter, so much so that with his monocle and aristocratic slang, he was constantly at risk of becoming like many of his contemporaries: a twit. Aware of the danger, Sayers attempted to transform him from a clichéd aristocrat into a rounded human being by providing him with a love interest in the form of Harriet Vane. It seems to be generally agreed that Sayers was in love with Wimsey and invented Harriet Vane so that she could vicariously enjoy an affair with him. However, the number of novels over which this eventually came about suggests she felt somewhat guilty about it. After seventeen years of life with her upper-crust hero, like Doyle with Holmes and Chesterton with Brown, she evidently fell out of love. She turned her back on Lord Peter and devoted herself to religious writing.

Philip Marlowe

It is sometimes assumed that the American 'hard-boiled' school of crime writing was a reaction to the golden age, but this theory doesn't fit the facts. Dashiell Hammett's story 'Arson Plus' appeared in *Black Mask* in 1923, and *The Maltese Falcon* was published in 1930, the year that also saw the first appearance of Agatha Christie's Miss Marple. The fiction that gave rise to Raymond Chandler's Philip Marlowe and Ross Macdonald's Lew Archer was born in the pages of magazines like *Black Mask* and was a purely American form of writing within a purely American culture.

That said, there is no doubt that the writing of the hard-boiled school is almost diametrically opposed to that of the golden age, and Chandler, for one, spent a lot of time extolling the virtues of the former and attacking what he saw as the weaknesses of the latter. '. . . whether it is possible to write a strictly honest mystery of the classic type. It isn't. To get the complication you fake the clues, the timing, the play of coincidence, assume certainties . . .' Although Philip Marlowe didn't appear until 1939, he is the private investigator who set the standard for the hard-boiled hero and is as unlike the detectives of the golden age as it is possible to imagine.

Chandler once wrote that he did not care much about Marlowe's private life, but in a letter to an English fan in 1951 he confirmed many biographical details, despite admitting that the fan seemed to know more about Marlowe than he did and that in future he might have to do the asking. Marlowe is about thirty-eight years old. He never speaks of his parents and has no living relatives, though 'this could be remedied if necessary'. He spent a couple of years at college in Oregon, but no one knows why he came to southern California, except that 'eventually most people do'. He had some experience as an insurance investigator, then as an investigator for the Los Angeles District Attorney, a job from which he was sacked because 'he got a little too efficient at a time and in a place where efficiency was the last thing desired by the persons in charge'.

Marlowe is just over six feet tall, about 13st 8lbs, with dark-brown hair and brown eyes. Though he can be tough, he doesn't look it. For those of us brought up on the various tough-guy movie versions, it may come as a surprise to learn that Chandler thought the rather gentlemanly Cary Grant the most suitable-looking actor to play him. He often wears horn-rimmed sunglasses (again, unlike most movie versions, but as Chandler pointed out, 'most people in southern California wear sunglasses at some time or other'). He doesn't have much money to spend on clothes – or on anything else. A hat – yes, but a trenchcoat only when it's raining.

He smokes, drinks (practically anything that isn't sweet), and takes his coffee with cream and sugar. He cooks his own breakfast but no other meal. Unlike Holmes with his Watson, Wimsey with his Bunter, Poirot with his Hastings, Marlowe is a loner. He never had even a secretary, despite his two-room office. 'When last heard' he carries a Smith & Wesson .38, 'probably with a four-inch barrel', its most important feature being that it is 'effective'. For a character like Marlowe, his gun is as much a part of him as the laconic wisecrack. Though he rarely uses it, he needs people to know that he can.

The most well-known description of Marlowe comes from *The Simple Art of Murder*: '... down these mean streets a man must go who is not himself mean, who is neither tarnished nor afraid ...' But towards the end of his life Chandler emphasized the less enviable aspects of the private investigator's life. '... he is a lonely man, a poor man, a dangerous man ... he will always have a fairly shabby office, a lonely house, a number of affairs, but no permanent connection ... he will always be awakened at some inconvenient hour by some inconvenient person, to do some inconvenient job ... No one will ever beat him, because by his nature he is unbeatable. No one will ever make him rich, because he is destined to be poor. But somehow I think he would not have it otherwise ... I see him always in a lonely street, in lonely rooms, puzzled but never quite defeated.'

Miss Marple

While it may be unwise to delve too deeply into Marlowe's past for fear of what one might find, the same cannot be said of Agatha Christie's Miss Marple. With her, there is nothing to hide. She comes from a respectable upper-middle-class family with strong ecclesiastical connections, and though when we first meet her she is already the single, elderly, rather frail and somewhat poor woman she remains throughout her astonishing forty-six years of literary life, she is wealthy enough to be regularly concerned with the problem of servants. After the Second World War she has a live-in companion, whose annoying lower-middle-class gentility is eventually swapped for a daily help. She has a sister and a ne'er do well brother, and is a dedicated and expert gardener, whose suspicions can be aroused merely by the offer of unsuitable rocks for her rock garden.

Miss Marple brought detection down from Wimsey's giddy social heights into a milieu more people could recognize: St Mary Mead, a deceptively quiet English village – rather bizarrely, still a hugely popular setting for acts of multiple murder, witness the current popularity of TV's *Midsomer Murders*. Like the country house favoured by many golden age writers, it is an ideal setting: a closed environment, subject to unwritten social rules and conventions and with a limited number of suspects. Although a real English village has many types and classes of people, the Miss Marple stories move largely among the respectable and middle class. In forty-six years St Mary Mead may change outwardly a little, but in all significant respects it would still be recognizable to Jane Austen's Emma Woodhouse, with its population of squire, vicar, doctor, solicitor, retired military man, shopkeeper, domestic servants and genteel but impoverished spinsters.

Our perception of Miss Marple has been inevitably coloured by the various screen representations. Christie didn't approve of Margaret Rutherford's interpretation but she would probably have liked Joan Hickson's. Tiring of Poirot, she apparently based the character partly on her 'auntie-grannie', of whom she once wrote, 'though a cheerful person, she always expected the worst of everything and everyone and was, with almost frightening accuracy, usually proved right'. Miss Marple similarly knows every single thing that happens within her admittedly rather confined world and draws the worst inferences from it.

Unlike Marlowe she is rarely alone. She relies on a large cast of contacts and relatives: Sir Henry Clithering (one time of Scotland Yard), Dolly Bantry, Miss Wetherby, Reverend Clement, nephew novelist Raymond West, and so on. Indeed, she often depends on the assistance of the young, who do all the physical stuff while she provides the intuition.

It is almost a cliché of Christie's novels that the least likely person turns out to be the perpetrator, so much so that some readers accuse her of cheating, i.e. not giving all the clues. In fact, sexual passion and financial greed are the motivations behind many of the crimes and the success of the mystery depends not so much on the manipulation of clues, but more on the concealment of the true relationships between the cast of suspects. Miss Marple eventually knows what is going on because she listens to gossip and because people and events always remind her of people and events she has come across in the past: 'I've known one or two like him.'

Christie believed it was the ordinariness of the world in which murder was committed, and the ordinariness of the people who committed it that gave her Miss Marple stories one of their main strengths, but it is more likely that the extraordinary longevity of the character's popularity rests on the ever-increasing ingeniousness of the plots and the cleverness with which Miss Marple unravels them. Ian Ousby has explained the demise of the classic 'puzzle' detective story by their readers' growing sophistication: 'They knew the victim had not really been killed where the corpse was found, and had probably died at a different time from the time everybody supposed. They knew the first suspect was likely to become the second victim. They knew the character with an unshakable alibi was probably lying and the character with no alibi was probably innocent.'

Miss Marple is the exception that proves the rule.

Inspector Maigret

For many Britons, Georges Simenon's Inspector Maigret stories provided not only their first images of Paris but also their most lasting, especially those of us who can recall the cobbled streets and the beautiful, low-slung Citroëns of the TV series starring Rupert Davies, a screen-Maigret Simenon himself respected highly. From the pipe smoke in cafés to the quai des Orfèvres we feel we are experiencing the very sights and sounds of the city, conveniently forgetting that many of the novels – particularly the early ones – are set outside Paris, amid the rain, canals and harbours of northern France.

Simenon's slow-moving, slightly grumpy police inspector is in many ways the forerunner of the familiar, modern fictional police detective: Morse, Wexford, Frost, Dalziel. As formerly with Morse, his forename is uncertain: Simenon usually used Jules, but also Amédée, Anthèlme, Joseph and François. Maigret has an apartment on the non-existent fourth floor of a real building, a wife, Madame Maigret, and loves beer and white wine. His office has a unique old-fashioned stove, of which he is very proud, and he has never learned to drive. A commissaire working from the Paris head-quarters of the Police Judiciaire, he is a big man, forty-five years old, with a bowler hat, heavy overcoat and pipe. His face, however, is indistinct – Simenon himself insisted he had never seen it – a convenience for the numerous screen representations. Essentially he is ordinary, almost anonymous. His main characteristic is that of an observer, a 'connoisseur of souls' as Thomas Narcejac put it.

At the heart of a Maigret story is often a psychological mystery; Maigret's role is to fathom the motivation behind it. His method is to soak up the atmosphere of a place and immerse himself in the complex of relationships presented by the suspects until the solution becomes clear. His actual detective work may be minimal; he doesn't unravel the mystery by logic or analysis, his most useful quality is his insatiable curiosity. He has empathy with the people he meets and is interested in them beyond his need for information. He hasn't a very high opinion of individual men, but he believes in man. He understands but does not judge. When he finds men's weak points he is not triumphant. C. Day-Lewis called him the 'bloodhound of heaven'.

Maigret spelled the end of the infallible detective; he is a human being, like the rest of us. In the course of his investigations he is often affected, even changed, by what he discovers. Every case extends the range of his compassion. At the end of *Maigret and the Hundred Gibbets*, having discovered the terrible truth, he downs six Pernods in the Brasserie Dauphine then mutters to Sergeant Lucas, 'Ten more cases like this and I'll pack it in.'

Inspector Ghote

H. R. F. Keating had been writing about Inspector Ghote of the Bombay CID for ten years before he actually visited the city. It is a luxury of omission no current writer – or reader, come to that – with his insistence on solid research and authentic background detail would permit himself. Nevertheless, Ghote moves in a convincing landscape, with its diverse cultural layers – caste, class, racial, religious and regional – and its sympathetically portrayed population.

Yet for all this attention to an altogether foreign environment, Keating's main aim was to 'put a recognizable human being into broad general situations likely to happen to any one of us'. Like Maigret, Ghote is far from infallible. He is a very human web of contradiction: shrewd and bumbling, pompous and self-effacing, determined and uncertain, clumsy and charming.

As a rather insignificant cog in the creaking machine of an impoverished bureaucracy, he is no conventional hero. Particularly prone to being pushed around by the rich and powerful, he often has to decide between the right course of action and the sensible, to decide where his loyalties lie. Being neither a genius nor a revolutionary, Ghote invariably simply perseveres, does his duty and refuses to be deflected from it. He is one of the first detectives as underdog, the classic Chaplin hero, the little man who triumphs.

Ghote knows the peculiarities of his country and in solving the crime he exposes these to our curious gaze, revealing a far more alien and fascinating place than Maigret's Paris or Marlowe's southern California. In *Filmi, Filmi, Inspector Ghote* he even explores the Bollywood phenomenon. Indeed, one of Keating's main themes is the meeting of sub-cultures within larger national cultures, with his slightly tongue-in-cheek – but sympathetic and admiring – use of Indian character and language. And the traffic is not all one way. When Keating has Ghote travel to London to deliver a paper on drug smuggling, it is the opportunity to toy not only with the Indian's rather literary preconceptions of England but also with our own.

Two other, more recent examples of using the detective genre as a way of examining the mores of a foreign country are Michael Dibdin's Italian commissioner Aurelio Zen and Martin Cruz Smith's Russian detective, Renko. Like Ghote, Zen and Renko are no super-heroes, they make their way by skirting round, accepting the corruption of their establishments by bowing halfway. They are outsiders, occasionally enjoying the praise of their superiors but more often not. More significantly perhaps, while these foreign detectives have every reason to be cynics, they remain, like Ghote, good men who haven't yet abandoned hope.

Dalziel and Pascoe

Superintendent Dalziel (pronounced Dee-ell) and Sergeant (later Inspector) Pascoe are, like Holmes and Watson before them, a partnership of opposites. Dalziel, the archetypal blunt Yorkshire-man, is fat, gross, vulgar and rude. He takes great gulps of whisky and greedily shovels plateloads of unhealthy food down his gullet. Pascoe, meanwhile, the archetypal liberal, university-educated late-twentieth-century new man, is introspective, intellectual, hard-working, balanced, decent, honest, sympathetic, steady and tolerant.

Yet each has respect, albeit grudging, for the other. Dalziel's coarseness conceals considerable experience, cunning and intuition; he is plainly no blind bigot. While Pascoe understands the system and works it, even if he doesn't like it, his liberal tolerance slips into dark waters as he becomes embroiled in ever more brutal and confusing crimes.

A third character gains more flesh in the later novels: Pascoe's wife Ellie – feminist, social worker, committed class warrior – and a fourth, Sergeant Wield, turns out to be a closet homosexual. The message is clear: Pascoe, though liberal, is conventionally male and married and therefore can no longer be the authentic voice of contemporary society. The recent TV series contains reasonable representations of the characters but Reginald Hill is reportedly unhappy with them, to the extent that he now writes each successive novel with the deliberate aim of making it as difficult to adapt for the screen as possible. Somewhat ironically, television, in the form of Lynda La Plante's *Prime Suspect*, has probably gone furthest in modernizing the detective-plus-assistant format – with a female DCI and a resentful male subordinate.

We have come a long way from Sherlock Holmes and Dr Watson.

Inspector Morse

A product of the CAMRA generation, Colin Dexter's Chief Inspector Morse is a policeman with a serious taste for real ale, crossword puzzles and opera. He is a detective in the grumpy tradition, not a big man, but bulky, prepared to be intimidating if necessary. He seems to have little private life, but presumably he's had relationships with the opposite sex, otherwise how would he know what makes lovers kill each other? As a confirmed bachelor, he is of course cynical about marriage, but he has occasionally been known to fall for a woman, in a rather restrained, polite, restaurant invitation sort of way. One only hopes he left the gabardine raincoat at home.

Famously Morse hid his first name, though he obviously has an implied second surname, a clue to the cryptic nature of the stories. A nonconformist, he's inclined to see complicated motives where simpler ones would serve. He is somewhat irritating to his colleagues, particularly his sidekick Sergeant Lewis, a rather faceless character who was considerably rewritten for television.

After the phenomenal success of the TV series, it is difficult to separate Dexter's Morse from John Thaw's. Maybe one shouldn't try – Dexter was reportedly very happy with Thaw's portrayal.

Though many earlier detectives found Oxford to have a gratifyingly high murder rate – colleges in particular providing the enclosed and quarrelsome communities essential to classic detective fiction – it was Morse who really put the university city on the map. There are now even Morse tours. Indeed, with Morse we are really back in the golden age, with plots like crossword puzzles and a conveniently small cast of suspects. The chief enjoyment is in searching out the clues – though in the TV plays locals like myself can overcome longueurs by playing 'spot the pub'.

The Name of the Rose

Many mystery writers have placed their detective in a convincingly imagined distant past, notably Lindsay Davis in her series about the Roman secret agent Marcus Didius Falco, and Ellis Peters in her enormously popular novels starring the twelfth-century Welsh monk and herbalist Brother Cadfael. My personal favourite is a medieval investigator who appears in only one book: Brother William Baskerville of Umberto Eco's *The Name of the Rose*.

Set in an unnamed Italian monastery in 1327 against a backdrop of political and religious turmoil, Umberto Eco's novel is more than just a historical mystery story. Perhaps most obviously, it is an affectionate pastiche of Conan Doyle's Sherlock Holmes; Eco's hero is, after all, named after one of Holmes' most famous cases and physically bears more than a passing resemblance: thin and taller than average, with sharp, hawkish features.

The story is told by Baskerville's Watson, his young assistant Adso of Melk, who admires his master at least as much as his nineteenth-century predecessor did, and laces his respect with much the same degree of superficial criticism. Baskerville is a sardonic English Franciscan who in the past escaped the attentions of the Inquisition only by the intervention of powerful patrons. Like Holmes, he is a keen observer of human nature, detached but not cynical, with a passion for logic and deduction. Though he is a middle-aged bachelor, he displays a compassionate view of human weakness and sexuality. He has, after all, his own occasional drug habit, though perhaps his use of herbs may be thought a milder addiction than Holmes' cocaine.

Negotiating much of the paraphernalia of classic detective fiction – hidden passageways, a labyrinthine building, secret manuscripts – Baskerville imposes order by methods similar to those of Holmes: long periods of reflection followed by frantic action, with plenty of sermonizing to Adso along the way about applying observation, detection and logic, the tools fortunately available to any good detective no matter what century he finds himself in.

Tough-guy tradition

While many European writers spent much of the second half of the twentieth century exploiting the legacy of Holmes, Marple and Maigret, their counterparts in America battled with the 'tough-guy' detective epitomized by Marlowe, from Ross Macdonald's angst-ridden Lew Archer and Mickey Spillane's unreconstructed Mike Hammer to Robert B. Parker's new man Spenser. Some modern writers are having more success than others in varying the basic character, though even Walter Mosley's black detective Easy Rawlins inhabits Los Angeles in the 1950s, a tacit admission that, white or black, this kind of detective doesn't belong in the modern world. Even women detectives like Sara Paretsky's V. I. Warshawski and Patricia Cornwell's forensic pathologist Kay Scarpetta, for all the female issues they bring to the form, have yet to demonstrate they are a significant departure from the tough-guy tradition.

For my money James Lee Burke's Dave Robicheaux and James Ellroy's Lloyd Hopkins are the two most convincing contemporary manifestations of the hard-boiled school. With Robicheaux we're in the heat and humidity of the Louisiana swamps, where the sweat-drenched atmosphere of rampant growth and fetid decay saps the moral will, a metaphor for the unchecked spread of corruption and evil.

In keeping with the political correctness that dictates a modern detective must be vulnerable, Robicheaux is a recovering alcoholic (unlike Marlowe, who swigs neat whiskey and still gets his man), so his drink of choice is 7-Up. He's an ex-homicide detective from the New Orleans Police Department, which, echoing Marlowe, he had to leave because he was getting into too much trouble. He doesn't go looking for it, but trouble has a habit of finding him. His nickname is Streak, he's fond of Cajun music and he owns a bait shop and boat rental business. He spent a year in Vietnam as a lieutenant and has a degree in English. He dealt with his drink problem by going to Alcoholics Anonymous, but still suffers from insomnia. He's been married twice and has an adopted child he rescued from a plane crash.

Robicheaux would really just like a quiet life, run his shop and go fishing once in a while. So when he gets involved it's usually with reluctance. But corruption and murder get to him. Despite the fact he knows he's going to be beaten up at least once, he can't let the bad guys get away with it. Because he's one of the good guys. A description it would be difficult to pin on Ellroy's Lloyd Hopkins. An anti-hero, he's a cop in 1940s Los Angeles whose demons are way beyond anyone's help. With his murderous past – and no doubt murderous future – it's sometimes difficult to tell who is the bad guy, the pursued or the pursuer. Indeed, it's sometimes difficult to tell who is pursuing whom. As with Robicheaux, Hopkins' targets are the corrupt and the powerful. But in his case the hunt for the killer is also the hunt for himself.

The following are the novels in which the detectives made their first appearance:

A Study in Scarlet, 1887, Arthur Conan Doyle
The Innocence of Father Brown, 1911, G.K. Chesterton
Whose Body?, 1923, Dorothy L. Sayers
The Murder at the Vicarage, 1930, Agatha Christie
The Strange Case of Peter the Lett, or *Maigret and the Enigmatic Lett*,
    1933, Georges Simenon

The Big Sleep, 1939, Raymond Chandler
The Perfect Murder, 1964, H. R. F. Keating
A Clubbable Woman, 1970, Reginald Hill
Last Bus to Woodstock, 1975, Colin Dexter
The Name of the Rose, 1980, Umberto Eco
Blood on the Moon, 1984, James Ellroy
The Neon Rain, 1987, James Lee Burke

The View From the Front

Geoffrey Bailey, manager of the Crime in Store bookshop in London, gives Samantha Wyndham an insight into popular taste in crime fiction

SAMANTHA WYNDHAM: Why have a bookshop selling only crime?
GEOFFREY BAILEY: Well, for one thing, what we sell in big numbers doesn't necessarily sell in general bookshops. For example, our big one last year was Jasper Fforde's *The Eyre Affair*. A general bookshop might have sold a few but we shifted 300 copies. And that was for a new writer. A little further back, we had a great success with *Greenaway* by Jane Adams, and, you know, while we couldn't get enough copies of it, it went out of print almost immediately.

SW: But her latest book, *Angel Falling*, did not do so well.
GB: It was simply not up to her best standard. But there's another reason why an author's sales vary from book to book. It's when they're not consistent, when they try something different every year. The most interesting books of last year and the year before, were by Minette Walters, who started off in the '90s with *The Ice House*, which everybody went berserk about. And then she suddenly started veering into psychological thrillers, and in 2000 she did *The Shape of Snakes*, which was brilliantly written. It's the ideas that make the book. But I thought, 'Hmmm, you know, this isn't what I expected.' And then last year, she did *Acid Row*, which was even more off-beam, again brilliantly written, but totally different from what you expected if you'd read her earlier books. And that makes it difficult for the bookseller even with heavy promotion by the publisher.

sw: Do you think psychologicals have dropped off a bit? Ruth Rendell doesn't sell as well as she used to?
GB: The mild stuff doesn't do so well. Many of the popular titles have more violence, really scary stuff.

sw: Really gruesome?
GB: Yes, and very much part of today's life, rather than the Miss Marple village.

sw: And that's a recent change, you think?
GB: Yes. Definitely. But it comes and goes. I mean, John Harvey was doing it in the '70s. And Thomas Harris, of course. The other big move has been towards historical mysteries led by Lindsey Davis, Steven Saylor, David Wishart, Alan Massie and Paul Doherty. We sell a lot of copies of their books, but nowhere in the numbers we get for contemporary crime. Except Lindsay Davis, that is. She outstrips everybody. She'll sign 300 copies of her new book, and we will sell them all within two months.

sw: Can you identify types of people who buy crime novels? Are they mainly men? Or women? Are they mainly young? Old?
GB: It depends on the genre. But if you want a generalization, the majority of customers are middle-class, middle-aged, professional women.

sw: Why do you think they are so fascinated by crime?
GB: P. D. James summed it up, though she got an absolute rollicking for saying it. She said that 'murder in the traditional detective stories is a middle-class crime.' If you look at the golden age of detective stories – Dorothy L. Sayers, Margery Allingham, Agatha Christie – they're always involved with middle-class people, and not with the working class. Donna Leon continues the line. Her books are traditional murder mysteries, all set in Venice. But she analyses her characters very closely. You need to read her books from the beginning, work through them, because the characters develop. The antagonism between the detective and his immediate

superior flares up in one book and then it calms down a little in the next, but it's always there bubbling on the surface.

SW: It's interesting that you say that her characterization is very strong. Is that what makes a book a success? Or is it setting? Or plot?
GB: I think it's a combination. If you look at P. D. James, she's consistent with the detective Dalgleish, with the London or East Anglian settings, and her characters are so well drawn. It's interesting with her last book, *Death in Holy Orders*, that it was very, very strong on location and characters, but on plot it was ... I wouldn't say shallow, but it wasn't the most important aspect of the book. Whereas in the classic Agatha Christie, it's the plot that's predominant, and apart from Hercule Poirot, the characters are rather two-dimensional. Maybe that's why she's continued to sell so well. You can't say of any of her plots, 'Oh, that was written in the '30s' or 'That was written in the '40s,' because you can read a '60s one and a '20s one, and you couldn't place them at all, possibly other than by the way the characters speak.

SW: But if you had to choose a single feature of crime books with pulling power, what would it be?
GB: If people meet characters they like, they just want to see them again, in a future series, they like following them through. Sometimes, if the plot's good, you can live with the characters, but mostly I think, if the characters are dodgy and you don't feel sympathy for anybody, and you don't like any of them, most of us will give up. By the same token, it's risky giving up a strong character. Philip Kerr wrote three extremely good books set in pre-war Berlin and one in post-war Vienna, and then he made so much money, he decided he was going to give up his character. Since then, he's written a completely different sort of book. Each time he comes up with something new, his publishers complain because they can't say it's 'as good as the last one'. He just writes what he wants to write. But his books don't sell as well as they should do, because people don't know where they are with them. It's like finding a new author each time.

sw: How many genres of crime fiction do you think there are?

GB: On our computer classification, we have well over thirty genres. They are: academic, adventure, animals, antiques, archaeology, art, bibliophile, cookery, cosy, crime, espionage, finance, foreign – that's an area where there are so many more books being translated now: Arturo Pérez-Reverte from the Spanish, Henning Mankell from Swedish – gardening, gay, hardboiled, history, humour, legal, medical, music, oriental, PI, police, politics, psychological, religious, sea, sport, supernatural, suspense, theatre, thriller – and that's not all of them.

sw: There seems to be much more emphasis now on quite detailed research into police procedures and the science of detection.

GB: That's all part of the process, and of course if they don't do the research, it's immediately picked up by reviewers or readers. 'Oh, they don't know what they're talking about!' is just about the worst thing anyone can say of a crime writer. You've got to know what you're doing. There's a whole series of books we keep in our reference section, which cover all aspects of crime, such as forensics, poisoning and gunshot wounds. A popular buy is *The Police Investigators' Handbook*.

sw: And presumably you're selling these books to writers, or aspiring writers?

GB: Yes. We get lots of them coming in with lots of notes from their writing courses on what they should be reading and looking for.

sw: I can imagine if you're a historical crime writer, then it's even worse, because then you've got to know your period as well?

GB: And they always get picked up on it when they get it wrong. David Dickinson, in his first book, *Goodnight Sweet Prince*, proved he knew nothing at all about the peerage. All the knights' wives were called Lady Kitty or Lady Ursula, and whether they were a marquess or a baron, they were referred to as 'Lord'. And then he shoved in the Christian name for good measure. And, you know, it ruined the book because it made a nonsense of the period.

sw: Picking up mistakes like that is partly an editor's job, surely?

GB: Oh, it is. But, you know, editors are editors. I mean, coming out of Montpelier Square and crossing Knightsbridge to go to Harrods ... totally wrong, you cross Brompton Road. That's the sort of things that copy editors and editors should be picking up, but they don't because editing is slipshod now.

sw: D'you think that's true of publishing in general? Or just crime?

GB: Oh, publishing in general.

sw: If you were approached by an aspiring crime writer, what advice would you give?

GB: I might have said last week it would be a good idea to go on a writers' course, but you've got to choose your writers' course very carefully. A marketing director told me that when he went on a writers' course and asked some questions, the lecturer said, 'Well, you appear to know far more about it than I do, so why don't you tell me?' But having said that, there are good writers' courses but it is going to cost you £300 or £400 to do it properly. Also, research your subject thoroughly and know that you are comfortable with it. If you want to do a historical drama set in Elizabethan England, don't just write it and think this is what it should be like. You've got to understand the minds – and the language particularly – of the period. You can adapt it into modern English, but not so that it becomes ''ere, mate'. And if you can't afford the writers' course, there are many books. Harry Keating's done a very good one on writing crime fiction (*Writing Crime Fiction*, A&C Black). There's also *Death Investigator's Handbook: A Field Guide to Crime Scene Processing, Forensic Evaluations and Investigative Techniques* by Louis N. Eliopulos (Paladine Press) and *A Writers' Guide to Police Organisation and Crime Investigation and Detection* by D. J. Cole (Robert Hale). And then Val McDermid has written an extremely good book on PIs: *A Suitable Job for a Woman: Inside the World of Women Private Eyes* (Poisoned Pen Press). And there's *The Writers' Handbook*, which is a far more important book. And then usually, after you've written your book, make sure you get a good agent. Oh yes, and all crime writers should join the CWA (see page 123).

sw: Who are your favourite authors?
GB: Well, I'd say Donna Leon, because of her characterization and consistently good writing. Hazel Holt, because of her characters and settings, and ingenious plotting. And then, almost at the other extreme, there is Lawrence Shames, who sets his books in Florida and goes for black humour. Lawrence Block does so many brilliant PI books. He's got the funny burglar ones, and the darker ones, and then there is this hit man who is a new character, who is brilliant. And his books are humorous as well. Then there are the darker hard-boiled authors such as Dennis Lehane and even Andrew Vachss, who have mean streaks.

sw: What about your younger readers?
GB: Up to twenty-five, thirty, the girls love the Martina Cole books, which are more suspense than crime, but they involve crime.

sw: And then, as readers get older, they move on?
GB: Yes. But I think they're tending now, as they get older, not to go on to the traditional. Although the police procedurals are in between, they're for both ages. Somebody like Gwendoline Butler, who invented the police procedural really ... well, she's been writing for how long ... thirty years? And she's been consistently good. By modern standards, she's considered old-fashioned, but her detective, Inspector Coffin, still sells. But that brings us to another important point. Many of the traditional writers who used to be published by Macmillan, HarperCollins and the Collins Crime Club, Hodder Headline and the other big houses are now being given the push.

sw: Why?
GB: Because the sales figures don't justify the amount of work that goes into selling the books. And so it's smaller publishers like Constable and Allison Busby who are picking up these second-league sellers. The bigger publishers are more interested in new

writers who could become mega-sellers, like Stephen Booth and Mark Billingham.

sw: Any warnings for new writers?

gb: Any writer who wants to go it alone without an agent, the worst thing they can ever do is go to a vanity publisher. Many have been tempted. They say to themselves, 'Oh, I long to see myself in print and I don't care if it costs me £5,000.' But we've just seen Minerva Press, the biggest of the vanity publishers, go down the tube. Vanity publishers fool writers into thinking that they're getting all sorts of wonderful things, and when you look at what they're offering, it's nothing that any writer couldn't get from a conventional publisher. And, of course, vanity guys never actually sell the book. They print it and they take the author's money, but they don't send a rep off on the road to sell the book. It's better to stick to the conventional route to publication. It may take longer but it will be worth it in the end.

Crime in Store

32 Store Street, London WC1E 7BS
Tel 020 7436 7736 Fax 020 7436 7636
E-mail: CrimeBks@aol.com
Website: www.crimeinstore.co.uk
Monthly catalogue, available on application

Crime-Writing Quotations

'At the risk of generalizing, plotting is essential in a crime novel. There might be a crime novel which didn't follow some basic rules to do with narrative structure, to do with the pacing of the plot and the unfolding of the story towards some kind of resolution – but how would it be? Someone gets killed, everyone mills around for a while musing on the nature of death, maybe the murderer is amongst them, maybe he or she got away long ago – maybe no one really cares. Hey, it's the nineties. By the end of the book everyone has wandered off to some party or other, and we're all none the wiser. A great idea for a novel, but I'm not sure it counts as crime fiction.

'All of which is to say, you need a structure. This means serious work, in storyline, character development, weaving clues through the narrative that are sufficiently clear so that your reader doesn't feel cheated by you pulling out loads of information at the end that you've previously hidden, but that aren't so obvious that everyone guesses by chapter three who dunnit. Although, if your story and your characters are strong enough, people will read as much to find out Why as Who.'

Alison Joseph, author of the Sister Agnes series of novels,
published by Headline

'If it sounds like writing, I rewrite it.'

Elmore Leonard's most important rule, quoted in
the *Daily Telegraph*

' "There are a lot of crime writers who say that at the beginning of a novel there's a murder that sets the world off balance," said George P. Pelecanos, who bases his stories in the murkier regions of Washington. "And that when you put that world back in order at the end of the book, you're doing a service to the reader. But I don't believe you can ever solve a murder." He added: "When somebody's dead, they're dead forever, and it ripples out into the community and into people's lives. The world is forever off balance. And I don't want to make people feel comfortable with it. I want them to be entertained but also uncomfortable by the time they finish a book." '

George P. Pelecanos, author of Shame the Devil, Hell to Pay and
Soul Circus, quoted in the International Herald Tribune

'Chandler's appeal is across the brow: low, middle and high. His major creation, Marlowe, was the traditional American hero: a loner, an avenger, an idealist and, finally, incorruptible. The cowboy transplanted to the city. The ultimate cool man. Chandler's novels – like *The Big Sleep, The Long Goodbye* and *The Lady in the Lake* – were morality plays, and his prose was crisp, original and funny.'

Martin Arnold, New York Times

'A rapid glance at either the British or the US best-seller lists on any given week during the past decade bears evidence to the robust health of the crime and mystery genre. It is unusual if at least half of the best-seller lists are not occupied by titles featuring a sturdy mix of death, deduction and suspense.'

Maxim Jakubowski of Murder One bookshop

Top Fifteen Crime Fiction Authors

52 weeks ending 6 July 2002*

		Volume	No. of titles	Value
1	Ian Rankin	898,756	41	£5,335,024
2	Patricia Cornwell	494,455	48	£3,330,241
3	Kathy Reichs	293,376	13	£1,943,188
4	Minette Walters	246,772	23	£1,627,495
5	John Grisham	203,728	14	£1,393,119
6	Martina Cole	188,023	6	£1,375,119
7	Dick Francis	215,362	85	£1,248,463
8	Michael Connelly	213,368	27	£1,183,205
9	James Patterson	173,945	20	£1,094,979
10	Agatha Christie	168,897	205	£969,940
11	Jeff Deaver	148,614	20	£893,984
12	Harlan Coben	188,620	22	£891,809
13	P. D. James	95,541	25	£888,028
14	Robert Goddard	129,436	18	£880,520
15	Ruth Rendell	122,188	63	£854,129

* *The Bookseller*, 16 August 2002

LISTINGS

UK Publishers with Crime Fiction/Thriller Lists

Allison & Busby

Suite 111, Bon Marche Centre, 241–51 Ferndale Road,
London SW9 8BJ

☎ 020 7738 7888   Fax 020 7733 4244

Email all@allisonbusby.co.uk

Website www.allisonandbusby.ltd.uk

Publishing Director *David Shelley*

FOUNDED 1967. Publishes literary fiction, crime fiction, biography and writers' guides. About 40 titles a year. Send synopses with two sample chapters, not full mss. No replies without sae.

Crime authors: David Armstrong, Jo Bannister, Brian Battison, Lawrence Block, Janie Bolitho, Michael Bond, Rhys Bowen, Ann Cleeves, Clare Curzon, John Dickson Carr, Stephen Dobyns, Martin Edwards, James Ellroy, Penelope Evans, John Gano, Jonathan Gash, Bartholomew Gill, Ed Gorman, Patricia Hall, Jane Jakeman, Anita Janda, J. J. Robert Janes, Roderic Jeffries, Susan Kelly, Bill Knox, Deryn Lake, Roy Lewis, Ted Lewis, Joan Lingard, Gillian Linscott, Peter Lovesey, Ed McBain, Ross MacDonald, John Malcolm, Jessica Mann, Jennie Melville, Frank Palmer, Stuart Pawson, Julian Rathbone, Barrie Roberts, Lynda Robinson, Sax Rohmer, Mary Scott, Frank Smith, Charles Spencer, Sally Spencer, Mickey Spillane, Cath Staincliffe, Richard Stark, June Thomson, Rebecca Tope, M. J. Trow, Martin Waites, Christopher West, Donald E. Westlake.

Canongate Books Ltd
14 High Street, Edinburgh EH1 1TE
☎ 0131 557 5111   Fax 0131 557 5211
Email info@canongate.co.uk
Website www.canongate.net

Publisher *Jamie Byng*
Managing Director *David Graham*
FOUNDED 1973. The Canongate Crime Paperback series features writers from all around the world and includes Canongate Crime Classics, dedicated to reprinting lost classics of the genre.

Crime authors: John Franklin Bardin, Anthony Bourdain, Hugh Collins, Bobby Gold, Alex Gray, Chester Himes, Dorothy Hughes, Jon A. Jackson, Ross Macdonald, Shane Maloney, Maurice Power, Bill Pronzini, Chad Taylor, Andrew Vachss, Boris Vian, Charles Willeford, Douglas E. Winter.

Chivers Press Ltd
Windsor Bridge Road, Bath BA2 3AX
☎ 01225 335336   Fax 01225 310771
Email sales@chivers.co.uk
Website www.chivers.co.uk

Managing Director *Julian R. Batson*
Publishes reprints for libraries mainly, in large-print editions, including biography and autobiography, children's, crime, fiction and spoken word cassettes. No unsolicited material.

Crime authors: Margery Allingham, David Baldacci, Lawrence Block, Simon Brett, Lee Child, Agatha Christie, John Cleary, Michael Connelly, Patricia Cornwell, Robert Crais, John Creasey, Colin Dexter, Michael Dibdin, Ruth Dudley Edwards, Linda Fairstein, Jessica Fletcher, Dick Francis, John Francome, Alan Furst, Frances Fyfield, Erle Stanley Gardner, Jonathan Gash, Elizabeth George, Caroline Graham, Ann Granger, John Grisham, Dashiell Hammett, Carl Hiaasen, Mary Higgins Clark, Reginald Hill, Graham Hurley, Greg Iles, P. D. James, Alison Joseph, Jonathan Kellerman, Dean Koontz, Lynda La Plante, James Lee Burke, Donna Leon, John

Lescroart, Peter Lovesey, Ed McBain, Ross Macdonald, Ngaio Marsh, Robert B. Parker, James Patterson, Anne Perry, Ellis Peters, Bill Pronzini, Ellery Queen, Ian Rankin, Kathy Reichs, Ruth Rendell/Barbara Vine, Jonathan Ross, John Sandford, Dorothy L. Sayers, Josephine Tey, Jill Paton Walsh, Minette Walters, Gillian White.

Constable & Robinson Ltd

3 The Lanchester, 162 Fulham Palace Road, London w6 9ER
☎ 020 8741 3663   Fax 020 8748 7562
Email enquiries@constablerobinson.com
Website www.constablerobinson.com

Non-Executive Chairman *Benjamin Glazebrook*
Managing Director *Nick Robinson*
Directors *Jan Chamier, Nova Jayne Heath, Adrian Andrews*
Constable & Co FOUNDED in 1890 by Archibald Constable, a grandson of Walter Scott's publisher. Robinson Publishing Ltd founded in 1983 by Nick Robinson. In December 1999 Constable and Robinson combined their individual shareholdings into a single company, Constable & Robinson Ltd. Crime titles are published under the Constable (Editorial Director *Carol O'Brien*) and Robinson (Senior Commissioning Editor *Krystyna Green*) imprints. Unsolicited sample chapters, synopses and ideas for books welcome. No mss; no e-mail submissions. Enclose return postage.

Crime authors: Martin Babson, M. C. Beaton, Pauline Bell, Janie Bolitho, Stephen Burgen, Barbara Cleverly, Anthea Cohen, Brian Cooper, Freda Davies, David Dickinson, Paul Doherty, Marjorie Eccles, Philip Gooden, Juliet Hebden, Mick Herron, Bill James, Alanna Knight, Bill Knox, Thomas Laird, Roy Lewis, Keith McCarthy, Pat McIntosh, Michael Malone, Jessica Mann, Anthony Masters, Gwen Moffat, Ed O'Connor, Michael Pearce, Elizabeth Peters, Peter Rawlinson, Nicholas Rhea, Mike Ripley, David Roberts, Steven Saylor, Gerard Williams, Derek Wilson.

The Do-Not Press

16 The Woodlands, London se13 6ty
☎ 020 8698 7833   Fax 020 8698 7834
Website www.thedonotpress.co.uk

Publisher *Jim Driver*
FOUNDED 1994. Imprints: Bloodlines; Frontlines. Submissions through recognized agents only. 'Have you ever bought a book published by The Do-Not Press? No, thought not. You've got a bit of a cheek expecting us to gamble thousands on your stuff when you can't be bothered to invest less than a tenner on quality merchandise. Out of sixty-odd books, there must be something you'd like and if not, what's the point of sending us anything? . . . In the real world our entry would read: "Don't bother" . . . If you insist on submitting a manuscript or sample chapters, a synopsis is useful, a stamped-addressed return envelope essential. Hand-written manuscripts are too difficult to read, so don't bother. And it really is best not to telephone to enquire on progress. Due to the virus situation with Microsoft files, we are unable to access such files sent over the Internet . . . Yes, we know how hard it is for fledgling writers. We wish we could help and be more positive, but we really don't have time.'

Crime authors: Ken Bruen, Paul Charles, Carole Anne Davis, Maxim Jakubowski, Bill James, Russell James, Gary Lovisi, Jerry Raine, Mike Ripley, John B. Spencer.

Faber & Faber Ltd
3 Queen Square, London WC1N 3AU
☎ 020 7465 0045   Fax 020 7465 0034
Website www.faber.co.uk

Chief Executive *Stephen Page*
Editor-in-Chief: Fiction *Jon Riley*
FOUNDED in the 1920s, with T. S. Eliot as an early recruit to the board.

Crime authors: Salar Abdoh, John Creed, Michael Dibdin, Kinky Friedman, Reg Gadney, P. D. James, Andrew Martin, Reggie Nadelson, Lucy Wadham, Paul Watkins.

HarperCollins Publishers Ltd
77–85 Fulham Palace Road, London W6 8JB
☎ 020 8741 7070   Fax 020 8307 4440
Website www.fireandwater.com

Also at: Westerhill Road, Bishopbriggs, Glasgow G64 2QT
☎ 0141 772 3200   Fax 0141 306 3119

CEO/Publisher *Victoria Barnsley*
HarperCollins is the second largest book publisher in the UK, with titles ranging from cutting-edge contemporary fiction to block-busting thrillers, from fantasy literature and children's stories to enduring classics. The wholly-owned division of News Corporation also publishes a selection of non-fiction including history, celebrity memoirs, biographies, popular science, mind, body and spirit, dictionaries, maps and reference books and is also the third largest education publisher in the UK. About 1500 titles a year.

Collins Crime: Publishing Director *Julia Wisdom.*

Crime authors: Campbell Armstrong, Michael Asher, Giles Blunt, Stephen Booth, Dale Brown, Mark Burnell, Agatha Christie, Michael Crichton, James Crumley, Len Deighton, Frank Delaney, Michael Dobbs, Tim Dorsey, Ruth Dudley Edwards, Gregory Hall, James Hall, Stuart Harrison, Jack Higgins, Reginald Hill, Maggie Hudson, Gordon Kent, Laurie King, Dean Kootz, José Latour, Gay Longworth, Phil Lovesey, Robert Ludlum, Val McDermid, Michael Marshall, Fidelis Morgan, Jefferson Parker, Iain Pears, Danuta Reah, Lisa Scottoline, Simon Shaw, Boris Starling, Andrew Taylor, Penn Williamson, Robert Wilson, Elizabeth Woodcraft.

The Harvill Press Ltd
20 Vauxhall Bridge Road, London SW1V 2SA
☎ 020 7840 8400   Fax 020 7233 8791
Website www.harvill.com

Publisher *Christopher MacLehose*
Editorial Director *Margaret Stead*
FOUNDED in 1946. Purchased by the Random House Group in March 2002.

Crime/thriller authors: Leif Davidsen, Jean-Christophe Grangé, Peter Høeg, Sébastien Japrisot, Pierre Magnan, Henning Mankell, Daniel Pennac, Arturo Pérez-Reverte.

Macmillan Publishers Ltd

Pan Macmillan, 20 New Wharf Road, London N1 9RR
☎ 020 7014 6000   Fax 020 7014 6001
Website www.panmacmillan.com

Chief Executive *Richard Charkin*
FOUNDED 1843. Macmillan is one of the largest publishing houses in Britain, publishing approximately 1400 titles a year. Pan was founded in 1947 and became a wholly owned subsidiary of Macmillan in 1987. The Macmillan group was bought in 1999 by Verlagsgruppe Georg von Holtzbrink.

Pan Macmillan: Managing Director *David North*. Adult fiction and non-fiction is published in hardback under Macmillan, Picador, Sidgwick & Jackson, Boxtree and Channel 4 Books. Paperbacks are published by Pan, Picador, Boxtree and Channel 4 Books. Imprints Macmillan/Pan/Picador/Sidgwick & Jackson/Boxtree/Channel 4 Books. Publishing Director *Jeremy Trevathan*; Macmillan/Pan/Picador Publishing Director *Maria Rejt*; Macmillan/Pan Fiction Editorial Directors *Imogen Taylor* and *Peter Lavery*. No unsolicited mss.

Crime/mystery authors: Jane Adams, Catherine Aird, Eric Ambler, Andrea Badenoch, Jo Bannister, Adam Baron, C. C. Benison, John Bingham, John Binias, Nicholas Blake, Stephen Bogart, Jay R. Bonansinga, Christianna Brand, Simon Brett, John Burns, Pat Cadigan, Ann Cleeves, Edmund Crispin, Deborah Crombie, Colin Dexter, Michael Dibdin, Anabel Donald, Janet Evanovich, Clare Francis, Dick Francis, John Gano, Jonathan Gash, Nancy Geary, Joseph Glass, Sue Grafton, Laurence Halochte, Dashiell Hammett, Gerald Hammond, Cyril Hare, Victor Headley, Daniel Hecht, Carl Hiaasen, Hazel Holt, Carl Huberman, James Humphreys, Bill Hutchinson, Francis Iles, Bill James, H. R. F. Keating, Alana Knight, Jean Hanff Korelitz, Andy Lane, B. Montalbano, Lynda La Plante, Janet Laurence, Hilda Lawrence, Margaret Lawrence, Donna Leon, Jill McGown, Elizabeth McGregor, Max Marquis, Priscilla Masters, Jennie Melville, Walter Mosley, Margaret Murphy, John J. Nance, Chris Niles, Julie Parsons, Thomas Perry, Chris Petit, David Ramus, Peter Robinson, Kerri Sakamoto, Alan Scholefield, Sally Spedding, Julian Symons, Boston Teran, Donald Thomas, Jim Thompson, Marilyn Todd, Minette Walters.

Oldcastle Books Ltd

18 Coleswood Road, Harpenden, Hertfordshire AL5 1EQ
☎ 01582 761264   Fax 01582 761244
Email info@noexit.co.uk
Website www.noexit.co.uk *or* www.pocketessentials.com

Managing Director *Ion S. Mills*
FOUNDED 1985. Publishes crime/noir fiction, gambling non-fiction and 96pp mini-reference titles on film, ideas, history, music, etc. *No unsolicited mss.* Send synopses and ideas.

Crime authors: David Aitken, Jakob Arjouni, Mark Behm, Lawrence Block, D. W. Buffa, Edward Bunker, John Gregory Dunne, Anthony Frewin, Ira Genberg, Joseph Hansen, Sparkle Hayter, Kem Nunn, Robert B. Parker, William D. Pease, James Sallis, Jason Starr, Mark Timlin, Daniel Woodrell.

The Orion Publishing Group Limited

Orion House, 5 Upper St Martin's Lane, London WC2H 9EA
☎ 020 7240 3444   Fax 020 7240 4822
www.orionbooks.co.uk/pub/index.htm

Chairman *Jean-Louis Lisimachio*
Chief Executive *Anthony Cheetham*
Group Managing Director *Peter Roche*
Orion Fiction Publishing Director *Jane Wood*
Crime/mystery authors: Kenneth Abel, Tom Ackland, Edgar Allan Poe, Harry Asher, John Baker, Francis Bennett, Lawrence Block, David Bowker, John Brady, Simon Brett, Mark Bryant, Fiona Buckley, W. J. Burley, James Cain, Caroline Carver, Harlan Coben, Arthur Conan Doyle, Michael Connelly, Thomas H. Cook, Stephen Coonts, Catherine Coulter, Robert Crais, David Cray, Denise Danks, Linda Davies, Sarah Diamond, John Dickson Carr, Stanley Ellin, James Elliott, Liz Evans, Kenneth Fearing, Philip Finch, Joseph Finder, Duane Franklett, Lisa Gardner, Joe Gores, Jeff Gulvin, Steve Hamilton, Dashiell Hammett, Lynn E. Harris, Tony Hillerman, Tami Hoag, Lesley Horton, Geoffrey Household, Graham Hurley, Robert J. Janes, Jenny Jones, Melissa Jones, Stuart M. Kaminsky, Thomas Kelly, Jonathon King, Joe R. Lansdale, Emma Lathen, John Lawton, Christopher Lee, James Lee

Burke, Laura Lippman, Adam Lloyd Baker, Robert Ludlum, Jim Lusby, Ed McBain, John D. Macdonald, Ron McKay, Alastair MacNeill, Barry Maitland, D. M. Martin, Margaret Millar, Viviane Moore, Richard Morgan, Ian Morson, Barry Norman, Joyce Carol Oates, Charles Palliser, Ridley Pearson, George P. Pelecanos, Keith Peterson, Anthony Price, Michael Pye, A. J. Quinnell, Ian Rankin, Robert Richardson, Laurence Shames, John Shannon, Jenny Siler, Georges Simenon, Charles Spencer, Michelle Spring, John Straley, Peter Straub, Andrew Taylor, Nancy Taylor Rosenberg, Gordon Thomas, Ross Thomas, Jim Thompson, John Tilsley, Mark Timlin, Joseph Wambaugh, Laura Wilson, Cornell Woolrich.

Penguin UK

80 Strand, London WC2R ORL
☎ 020 7010 3000   Fax 020 7010 6060
Website www.penguin.co.uk

Group Chairman & Chief Exective *John Makinson*
CEO: Penguin UK, Dorling Kindersley Ltd *Anthony Forbes Watson*
Managing Director: **Penguin** *Helen Fraser*
Owned by Pearson plc. The world's best-known book brand and for more than 60 years a leading publisher whose adult and children's lists include fiction, non-fiction, poetry, drama, classics, reference and special interest areas.
Penguin General Books: Managing Director *Tom Weldon* Adult fiction and non-fiction is published in hardback under Michael Joseph, Viking and Hamish Hamilton imprints. Paperbacks come under the Penguin imprint. Imprints Viking/Penguin Publisher *Juliet Annan* Publishing Director *Tony Lacey*; Hamish Hamilton Publishing Director *Simon Prosser*; Michael Joseph/Penguin Publishing Director *Louise Moore*. No unsolicited mss.

Crime/thriller authors: Peter Abrahams, Margery Allingham, Suzanne Berne, T. R. Bowen, Raymond Chandler, G. K. Chesterton, Tom Clancy, Wilkie Collins, Edmund Crispin, Charles Cumming, Clive Cussler, Arthur Conan Doyle, Barry Eisler, Janet Evanovich, Ian Fleming, Dick Francis, Nicci French, John Gilstrap, Dashiell Hammett, P. D. James, Jim Kelly, David Lawrence, Elmore Leonard, Hector Macdonald, John Matthews, Sara

Paretsky, John Rickards, Michael Ridpath, Liz Rigbey, Simon Tolkien, P. J. Tracey, Scott Turow, Barbara Vine, Francesca Weisman.

The Random House Group Ltd

Random House, 20 Vauxhall Bridge Road, London SW1V 2SA
☎ 020 7840 8400 Fax 020 7233 6058
Email enquiries@randomhouse.co.uk
Website www.randomhouse.co.uk

Chief Executive/Chairman *Gail Rebuck*
Deputy Chairman *Simon Master*
Managing Director *Ian Hudson*
Random's increasing focus on trade publishing, both here and in the US, has been well rewarded, with sales continuing to grow over the last year.

Crime authors include: Hilary Bonner, Paul Carson, Michel Crespy, Leif Davidson, Lindsey Davis, William Diehl, Margaret Doody, Kerstin Ekman, James Ellroy, John Farrow, Robert Ferrigno, Karin Fossum, Jean-Christophe Grangé, John Grisham, Thomas Harris, John Harvey, Lauren Henderson, Mary Higgins Clarke, Patricia Highsmith, Stephen Hunter, Donald James, Sebastian Japrisot, Brian Johnston, Philip Kerr, Frank Lean, James Lee Burke, Donna Leon, Henning Mankell, David Ralph Martin, Adrian Mathews, Peter Moore Smith, Richard North Patterson, Carol O'Connell, Michael Palmer, Eliot Pattison, David Pirie, Mario Puzo, Kathy Reichs, Rob Reuland, Ruth Rendell, Candace Robb, Pernille Rygg, Lisa See, Karin Slaughter, Sarah Smith, Lyndon Stacey, Alison Taylor, Josephine Tey, Don Winslow.

Serpent's Tail

4 Blackstock Mews, London N4 2BT
☎ 020 7354 1949 Fax 020 7704 6467
Email info@serpentstail.com
Website www.serpentstail.com

Contact *Ben Cooper*
FOUNDED 1986. Serpent's Tail has introduced to British audiences a number of major internationally known writers. Noted for its strong emphasis

on design and an eye for the unusual. Send preliminary letter outlining proposal with a sample chapter and sae. No unsolicited mss. Prospective authors unfamiliar with Serpent's Tail are advised to study the list before submitting anything.

Crime authors: Alex Abella, Gopal Baratham, Antoine Bello, Pieke Biermann, Nicholas Blincoe, Ken Bruen, Agnes Bushell, Charlotte Carter, John Dale, Didier Daeninckx, Stella Duffy, David Goodis, Graeme Gordon, Gar Anthony Haywood, Vicki Henricks, Chester Himes, Maxim Jakubowski, Danny King, Diane Langford, Elsa Lewin, Martin Limón, Horace McCoy, Dacia Maraini, Stewart Meyer, Vasquez Montalbán, Walter Mosley, David Peace, George P. Pelecanos, Dorothy Porter, Mark Ramsden, Julian Rathbone, Derek Raymond, Sam Reaves, Juan Jose Saer, Louis Sanders, Caroline Shaw, Jon Stock, Newton Thornburg, John Williams, Oscar Zarate.

Severn House Publishers

9–15 High Street, Sutton, Surrey SM1 1DF
☎ 020 8770 3930   Fax 020 8770 3850
Email info@severnhouse.com
Website www.severnhouse.com

Chairman *Edwin Buckhalter*
Editorial *Amanda Stewart*
FOUNDED 1974. A leader in library fiction publishing. No unsolicited material. Synopses/proposals preferred through *bona fide* literary agents only.

Crime authors: Vivien Armstrong, Jeffrey Ashford, Tessa Barclay, John Gardner, Christine Green, J. M. Gregson, Gerald Hammond, Judith Kelman, Peter Lovesey, Amy Myers, Anne Perry, Ann Purser, Kate Sedley, Sally Spencer, Stella Whitelaw.

Time Warner Books UK

Brettenham House, Lancaster Place, London WC2E 7EN
☎ 020 7911 8000   Fax 020 7911 8100
Email uk@TimeWarnerBooks.co.uk
Website www.TimeWarnerBooks.co.uk

Chief Executive *David Young*
Publisher *Ursula Mackenzie*
FOUNDED 1988 as Little, Brown & Co. (UK). Part of Time-Warner Inc. Imprints: Little, Brown *Ursula Mackenzie, Alan Samson, Barbara Boote, Hilary Hale, Tara Lawrence* Hardback fiction and general non-fiction; Abacus *Richard Beswick* Literary fiction and non-fiction paperbacks; Orbit *Tim Holman* Science fiction and fantasy; Time Warner *Alan Samson, Barbara Boote, Hilary Hale* Mass-market fiction and non-fiction paperbacks; X Libris *Sarah Shrubb* Women's erotica; Illustrated *Julia Charles* Hardbacks; Virago *Lennie Goodings* Fiction and non-fiction by women. Approach in writing in the first instance. No unsolicited mss. Royalties paid twice-yearly.

Crime authors: Bruce Alexander, Bernard Bastable, Paul Bennett, Mark Billingham, Christopher Brookmyre, Caleb Carr, Kate Charles, Patricia Cornwell, Clare Curzon, Nelson Demille, Jonathan Davies, Sarah Dunant, Linda Fairstein, Nicolas Freeling, Frances Fyfield, Paula Gosling, Susanna Gregory, Cynthia Harrod-Eagles, Carol Higgins Clark, George V. Higgins, Jonathan Kellerman, Mary Kelly, Michael Ledwidge, Gillian Linscott, Peter Lovesey, Jenny Maxwell, Maureen O'Brien, Sara Paretsky, Ellis Peters, Dorothy Simpson, Carol Smith, Martin Stephen, Ross Thomas, Stephen White, Margaret Yorke.

Transworld Publishers Ltd

61–63 Uxbridge Road, London W5 5SA
☎ 020 8579 2652   Fax 020 8579 5479
Email info@transworld-publishers.co.uk
Website www.booksattransworld.co.uk

Chairman *Mark Barty-King*
Joint Managing Directors *Larry Finlay, Patrick Janson-Smith*
FOUNDED 1950. A subsidiary of Random House, Inc., New York. Publishes general fiction and non-fiction, gardening, sports and leisure. Divisions: Adult Trade *Patrick Janson-Smith*. Imprints: Bantam *Francesca Liversidge*; Bantam Press *Sally Gaminara*; Corgi; Black Swan *Bill Scott-Kerr*; Doubleday *Marianne Velmans*; Eden *Katrina Whone*; Expert Books *Gareth Pottle*.

Crime authors: Lisa Appignanesi, Alice Blanchard, W. J. Burley, George Dawes Green, Frances Fyfield, Susan Elizabeth George, Tess Gerritsen, Janet Gleeson, Robert Goddard, Andrea Hart, Mo Hayder, Dylan Jones, Simon Kernick, Will Kingdom, Dennis Lehane, Adam Lury and Simon Gibson, Denise Mina, Gemma O'Connor, Tony Strong, Paul Sussman, Gillian White, R. D. Wingfield.

UK Literary Agents

* = members of the Association of Authors' Agents

Darley Anderson Literary, TV & Film Agency*
Estelle House, 11 Eustace Road, London sw6 1JB
☎ 020 7385 6652   Fax 020 7386 9689/5571
Email darley.anderson@virgin.net

Contacts *Darley Anderson* (thrillers), *Kerith Biggs* (crime/foreign rights), *Elizabeth Wright* (women's fiction/love stories/'tear-jerkers'), *Carrie Neilson* (TV/film, children's books), *Hayley Wood* (non-fiction)
Run by an ex-publisher who has a knack for spotting talent and is a tough negotiator. Handles commercial fiction and non-fiction; children's fiction; also selected scripts for film and TV. No academic books or poetry. *Special interests*: Fiction: all types of thrillers and young male fiction. All types of American and Irish novels. All types of women's fiction. Also crime/mystery and humour. Non-fiction: celebrity autobiographies, biographies, sports books, 'true life' women in jeopardy, revelatory history and science, popular psychology, self-improvement, diet, health, beauty, fashion, animals, humour/cartoons, gardening, cookery, inspirational and religious. Send letter and outline with first three chapters; return postage/sae essential.

Clients: Richard Asplin, Anne Baker, Catherine Barry, Paul Carson, Caroline Carver, Lee Child, Martina Cole, John Connolly, Joseph Corvo, Margaret Dickinson, Rose Doyle, Joan Jonker, Rani Manicka, Carole Matthews,

Lesley Pearse, Lynda Page, Allan Pease, Adrian Plass, Carmen Ryan, Mary Ryan, Fred Secombe, Rebecca Shaw, Peter Sheridan, Kwong Kuen Shan, Linda Taylor, Elizabeth Waite, David Wishart.

Commission: home 15%; US 20%; translation 20–25%; TV/film/radio 20%.

Overseas associates: APA Talent and Literary Agency (LA/Hollywood); Liza Dawson Associates (New York); and leading foreign agents throughout the world.

Anubis Literary Agency
79 Charles Gardner Road, Leamington Spa, Warwickshire CV31 3BG
☎ 01926 832644   Fax 01926 311607

Contacts *Steve Calcutt, Maggie Heavey*
FOUNDED 1994. Handles mainstream adult fiction, especially science fiction, fantasy, horror, crime and women's. Also literary fiction. Scripts for film and TV. No children's books, poetry, short stories, journalism, academic or non-fiction. No unsolicited mss; send a covering letter and brief (one-page) synopsis (sae essential). No telephone calls. No reading fee.

Clients: Lesley Asquith, Georgie Hale, Tim Lebbon, Adam Roberts, Elon Salmon, Steve Savile, Zoe Sharp.

Commission: home 15%; US & translation 20%.

Works with the Marsh Agency on translation rights.

Artellus Limited
30 Dorset House, Gloucester Place, London NW1 5AD
☎ 020 7935 6972   Fax 020 7487 5957

Chairman *Gabriele Pantucci*
Director *Leslie Gardner*
FOUNDED 1986. Full-length and short mss; scripts for films. Handles crime, science fiction, historical, contemporary and literary fiction; non-fiction: art history, current affairs, biography, general history, science. No reading fee. Will suggest revision. Works directly in the USA and with agencies in Europe, Japan and Russia.

Commission: home 10%; overseas 12.5–20%.

Brie Burkeman*

14 Neville Court, Abbey Road, London NW8 9DD
☎ 0709 223 9113   Fax 0709 223 9111
Email brie.burkeman@mail.com

Contact *Brie Burkeman*
FOUNDED 2000. *Handles* commercial and literary full-length fiction and
non-fiction. Film, TV, theatre scripts. No academic, text, poetry, short
stories, musicals or short films. No reading fee but return postage essential.
Unsolicited email attachments will be deleted without opening. Also independent film and TV consultant to literary agents.

Commission: home 15%; overseas 20%.

Juliet Burton Literary Agency

2 Clifton Avenue, London W12 9DR
☎ 020 8762 0148   Fax 020 8743 8765

Contact *Juliet Burton*
FOUNDED 1999. Handles fiction and non-fiction. Special interests: crime
and women's fiction. No plays, film scripts, articles, poetry or academic
material. No reading fee. Approach in writing in the first instance; send
synopsis and two sample chapters with sae. No unsolicited mss.

Commission: home 10%; US & translation 20%.

Mic Cheetham Literary Agency

11–12 Dover Street, London W1S 4LJ
☎ 020 7495 2002   Fax 020 7495 5777
Website www.miccheetham.com

Contact *Mic Cheetham*
ESTABLISHED 1994. Handles general and literary fiction, crime and science
fiction, and some specific non-fiction. No film/TV scripts apart from
existing clients. No children's, illustrated books or poetry. No unsolicited

mss. Approach in writing with publishing history, first two chapters and return postage. No reading fee.

Clients include Iain Banks, Carol Birch, Anita Burgh, Laurie Graham, Toby Litt, Ken MacLeod, China Miéville, Antony Sher.

Commission: home 10%; US & translation 20%.

Works with The Marsh Agency for all translation rights.

Teresa Chris Literary Agency
43 Musard Road, London W6 8NR
☎ 020 7386 0633

Contact *Teresa Chris*
FOUNDED 1989. Handles crime, general, women's, commercial and literary fiction, and non-fiction: history, biography, health, cookery, lifestyle, sport and fitness, gardening, etc. Specializes in crime fiction and commercial women's fiction. No scripts. Film and TV rights handled by co-agent. No poetry, short stories, fantasy, science fiction or horror. Unsolicited mss welcome. Send query letter with first two chapters plus two-page synopsis (*sae essential*) in first instance. No reading fee.

Clients include Stephen Booth, Susan Clark, Tamara McKinley, Marguerite Patten, Danuta Reah, Kate Tremayne.

Commission: home 10%; US 15%; translation 20%.

Overseas associates: Thompson & Chris Literary Agency, USA; representatives in most other countries.

Curtis Brown Group Ltd*
Haymarket House, 28–29 Haymarket, London SW1Y 4SP
☎ 020 7396 6600   Fax 020 7396 0110
Email cb@curtisbrown.co.uk
Also at: 37 Queensferry Street, Edinburgh EH2 4QS
☎ 0131 225 1286/1288   Fax 0131 225 1290

Chairman *Paul Scherer*
Group Managing Director *Jonathan Lloyd*

Directors *Mark Collingbourne* (Finance), *Fiona Inglis* (MD, Australia)
Books, London *Jonathan Lloyd, Anna Davis, Jonny Geller, Hannah Griffiths, Ali Gunn, Camilla Hornby, Anthea Morton-Saner, Peter Robinson, Vivienne Schuster, Mike Shaw, Elizabeth Stevens*
Books, Edinburgh *Giles Gordon*
Long-established literary agency, whose first sales were made in 1899. Merged with John Farquharson, forming the Curtis Brown Group Ltd in 1989. Also represents directors, designers and presenters. Handles a wide range of subjects including fiction, general non-fiction, children's books and associated rights (including multimedia) as well as film, theatre, TV and radio scripts. Outline for non-fiction and short synopsis for fiction with two or three sample chapters and autobiographical note. No reading fee. Return postage essential.

Commission: home 10%; US & translation 20%.

Overseas associates in Australia, Canada and the US.

Mark Dawson Literary Agency
30 Valentine Road, London E9 7AD
☎ 020 8986 3252   Fax 020 8986 3346
Email markj.dawson@virgin.net

Contacts *Mark Dawson, Mette Olsen*
FOUNDED in 2001 by author and media lawyer Mark Dawson. Handles thrillers, crime, science fiction, literary fiction. No TV, film, theatre, radio scripts or poetry. Send preliminary letter, synopsis and first two chapters in the first instance. No reading fee.

Clients: Sean Doolittle, Christopher Kenworthy, Ray Nayler.

Commission: home 10%; US & translation 15%.

Dorian Literary Agency (DLA)*
Upper Thornehill, 27 Church Road, St Marychurch, Torquay, Devon TQ1 4QY
☎ 01803 312095   Fax 01803 312095

Contact *Dorothy Lumley*
FOUNDED 1986. Handles general fiction, specializing in popular fiction: women's (from romance and historical to contemporary); crime (from historical to *noir* and thrillers); science fiction, fantasy (but cautious about humorous/soft fantasy, i.e. unicorns), dark fantasy and horror. Adult and young adult but no children's under-ten, poetry or drama. Introductory letter with outline and 1–3 chapters (with return postage/sae) only, please. No enquiries or submissions by fax or email. No reading fee.

Clients include Gillian Bradshaw, Stephen Jones, Brian Lumley, Amy Myers, Rosemary Rowe.

Commission: home 10%; US 15%; translation 20–25%.

Works with agents in most countries for translation.

Gregory & Company, Authors' Agents*
(formerly Gregory & Radice)
3 Barb Mews, London W6 7PA
☎ 020 7610 4676   Fax 020 7610 4686
Email info@gregoryandcompany.co.uk
Website www.gregoryandcompany.co.uk

Contact *Jane Gregory*
Editorial *Broo Doherty*
Rights *Jane Barlow, Claire Morris*
FOUNDED 1987. Handles all kinds of fiction and general non-fiction. Special interest: fiction – literary, commercial, crime, suspense and thrillers. 'We are particularly interested in books which will also sell to publishers abroad.' No original plays, film or TV scripts (only published books are sold to film and TV). No science fiction, fantasy, poetry, academic or children's books. No reading fee. Editorial advice given to own authors. No unsolicited mss; send a preliminary letter with CV, synopsis, first three chapters and future writing plans (plus return postage). Short submissions by fax or email.

Commission: home 15%; US, translation, radio/TV/film 20%.

Is well represented throughout Europe, Asia and US.

Vanessa Holt Ltd*

59 Crescent Road, Leigh-on-Sea, Essex ss9 2PF
☎ 01702 473787   Fax 01702 471890
Email vanessa@holtlimited.freeserve.co.uk

Contact *Vanessa Holt*
FOUNDED 1989. Handles general fiction, non-fiction and non-illustrated children's books. No scripts, poetry, academic or technical. Specializes in crime fiction, commercial and literary fiction, and particularly interested in books with potential for sales abroad and/or to TV. No unsolicited mss. Approach by letter in first instance; sae essential. No reading fee.

Commission: home 15%; US & translation 20%; radio/TV/film 15%.

Represented in all foreign markets.

Kate Hordern Literary Agency

18 Mortimer Road, Clifton, Bristol BS8 4EY
☎ 0117 923 9368   Fax 0117 973 1941
Email katehordern@compuserve.com

Contact *Kate Hordern*
FOUNDED 1999. Handles quality literary and commercial fiction including women's, suspense and genre fiction; also general non-fiction. No children's books. Approach in writing in the first instance with details of project. New clients taken on very selectively. Synopsis required for fiction; proposal/chapter breakdown for non-fiction. Sample chapters on request only. Sae essential. No reading fee.

Clients: Richard Bassett, Jeff Dawson, James Gray, Will Randall.

Commission: home 15%; US & translation 20%.

Overseas associates: Carmen Balcells Agency, Spain; Synopsis Agency, Russia and various agencies in Asia.

Jane Judd Literary Agency*

18 Belitha Villas, London N1 1PD
☎ 020 7607 0273   Fax 020 7607 0623

Contact *Jane Judd*
FOUNDED 1986. Handles general fiction and non-fiction: women's fiction, crime, thrillers, literary fiction, humour, biography, investigative journalism, health, women's interests and travel. 'Looking for good contemporary women's fiction but not Mills & Boon-type.' No scripts, academic, gardening or DIY. Approach with letter, including synopsis, first chapter and return postage. Initial telephone call helpful in the case of non-fiction.

Clients: Patrick Anthony, the John Brunner estate, Andy Dougan, Jill Mansell, Jonathon Porritt, Rosie Rushton, Manda Scott.

Commission: home 10%; US & translation 20%.

Marjacq Scripts Ltd
34 Devonshire Place, London W1G 6JW
☎ 020 7935 9499   Fax 020 7935 9115
Email mark@marjacq.com
Website www.marjacq.com

Contact *Mark Hayward*
Handles general fiction and non-fiction, and screenplays. Special interest in crime, sagas and science fiction. No poetry, children's books or plays. Send synopsis and three chapters; will suggest revisions for promising mss. No reading fee.

Commission: home 10%; overseas 20%.

David O'Leary Literary Agents
10 Lansdowne Court, Lansdowne Rise, London W11 2NR
☎ 020 7229 1623   Fax 020 7727 9624
Email d.o'leary@virgin.net

Contact *David O'Leary*
FOUNDED 1988. Handles fiction, both popular and literary, and non-fiction. Special interest in thrillers, history, popular science, Russia and Ireland (history and fiction). No poetry or science fiction. No unsolicited mss but happy to discuss a proposal. Ring or write in the first instance. No reading fee.

Clients: David Crackanthorpe, James Kennedy, Nick Kochan, Jim Lusby, Derek Malcolm, Ken Russell.

Commission: home 10%; US 10%.

Overseas associates: Lennart Sane, Scandinavia/Spain/South America; Tuttle Mori, Japan.

John Pawsey
60 High Street, Tarring, Worthing, West Sussex BN14 7NR
☎ 01903 205167   Fax 01903 205167

Contact *John Pawsey*
FOUNDED 1981. Experience in the publishing business has helped to attract some top names here, but the door remains open for bright, new ideas. Handles non-fiction: biography, politics, current affairs, popular culture, travel, sport, business and music; also fiction: crime, thrillers, suspense or 'genuine originals' but not science fiction, fantasy and horror. Special interests sport, current affairs and biography. No children's, drama scripts, poetry, short stories, journalism or academic. Preliminary letter with sae essential. No reading fee.

Clients include Jennie Bond, Dr David Lewis, David Rayvern Allen, Patricia Hall, Elwyn Hartley Edwards, Peter Hobday, Jon Silverman.

Commission: home 10–15%; US & translation 19–25%.

Overseas associates in the US, Japan, South America and throughout Europe.

Shelley Power Literary Agency Ltd*
13 rue du Pré Saint Gervais, 75019 Paris, France
☎ 00 33 1 42 38 36 49   Fax 00 33 1 40 40 70 08
Email shelley.power@wanadoo.fr

Contact *Shelley Power*
FOUNDED 1976. Shelley Power works between London and Paris. This is an English agency with London-based administration/accounts office and the editorial office in Paris. Handles general commercial fiction, quality fiction, business books, self-help, true crime, investigative exposés, film and

entertainment. No scripts, short stories, children's or poetry. Preliminary letter with brief outline of project (plus return postage as from UK or France) essential. 'We do not consider submissions by email.' No reading fee.

Commission: home 10%; US & tanslation 19%.

The Sayle Literary Agency*
Bickerton House, 25–27 Bickerton Road, London N19 5JT
☎ 020 7263 8681   Fax 020 7561 0529

Proprietor *Rachel Calder*
Handles fiction, crime and general. Non-fiction: current affairs, social issues, travel, biographies, historical. No plays, poetry, children's, textbooks, technical, legal or medical books. No unsolicited mss. Preliminary letter essential, including a brief biographical note and a synopsis plus two or three sample chapters. Return postage essential. No reading fee.

Clients: Stephen Amidon, Pete Davies, Margaret Forster, Georgina Hammick, Phillip Knightley, Rory MacLean, Denise Mina, Malcolm Pryce, Kate Pullinger, Ronald Searle, Gitta Sereny, Stanley Stewart, William Styron, Mary Wesley.

Commission: home 10%; US & translation 20%.

Overseas associates: Elaine Markson Literary Agency; Darhansoff, Verrill and Feldman; Anne Edelstein Literary Agency, USA; translation rights handled by The Marsh Agency; film rights by Sayle Screen Ltd.

Sheil Land Associates Ltd*
(incorporating Richard Scott Simon Ltd 1971 and Christy Moore Ltd 1912)
43 Doughty Street, London WC1N 2LF
☎ 020 7405 9351   Fax 020 7831 2127
Email info@sheilland.co.uk

Agents, UK & US *Sonia Land, Luigi Bonomi, Sam Boyce, Vivien Green, Amanda Preston*

Film/Theatrical/TV *John Rush, Roland Baggot*
Foreign *Amelia Cummins, Helen Philpott*
FOUNDED 1962. Handles full-length general, commercial and literary fiction and non-fiction, including: social politics, business, history, military history, gardening, thrillers, crime, romance, fantasy, drama, biography, travel, cookery and humour, UK and foreign estates. Also theatre, film, radio and TV scripts. Welcomes approaches from new clients either to start or to develop their careers. Preliminary letter with sae essential. No reading fee.

Clients: Peter Ackroyd, John Blashford-Snell, Seve Ballesteros, Melvyn Bragg, Stephanie Calman, Catherine Cookson estate, Anna del Conte, Seamus Deane, Alan Drury, Erik Durschmied, Alan Garner, Bonnie Greer, Susan Hill, Richard Holmes, HRH The Prince of Wales, John Humphries, James Long, Richard Mabey, Colin McDowell, Van Morrison, Patrick O'Brian estate, Esther Rantzen, Pam Rhodes, Jean Rhys estate, Richard and Judy, Martin Riley, Colin Shindler, Tom Sharpe, Brian Sykes, Jeffrey Tayler, Alan Titchmarsh, Rose Tremain, John Wilsher.

Commission: home 15%; US & translation 20%.

Overseas associates: Georges Borchardt, Inc. (Richard Scott Simon). UK representatives for Farrar, Straus & Giroux, Inc. US film and TV representation: CAA, APA, and others.

Zebra Agency
Broadland House, 1 Broadland, Shevington, Lancashire WN6 8DH
☎ 0794 958 4758
Email admin@zebraagency.co.uk
Website www.zebraagency.co.uk

Contacts *Dee Jones, Cara Wooi*
FOUNDED 1997. Handles non-fiction and general fiction including crime, suspense and drama, murder, mysteries, adventure, thrillers, horror and science fiction. Also scripts for TV, radio, film and theatre. No reading fee. Editorial advice given to new authors. No unsolicited mss; send preliminary letter giving publishing history and brief CV, with synopsis and first

three chapters of novel or ten pages of script (plus return sae). No phone calls or submissions by fax or email.

Commission: home 10%; US & translation 20%.

Professional Associations

Crime Writers' Association (CWA)
PO Box 273, Borehamwood, Hertfordshire, WD6 2XA
Website www.thecwa.co.uk

Hon Secretary *Liz Evans*
Membership Secretary *Rebecca Tape* (Crossways Cottage, Walterstone,
Hertfordshire, HR2 0DX
Membership £45
Full membership is limited to professional crime writers, but publishers,
literary agents, booksellers, etc. who specialize in crime, are eligible for
Associate membership. The Association has regional chapters throughout
the country, including Scotland. Meetings are held regularly in central
London, with informative talks frequently given by police, scenes of crime
officers, lawyers, etc., and a weekend conference is held annually in
different parts of the country. Produces a monthly newsletter for members
called *Red Herrings* and presents various annual awards (*see* Prizes).

Mystery Writers of America, Inc.
17 East 47th Street, 6th Floor, New York, NY 10017, USA
☎ 001 212 888 8171   Fax 001 212 888 8107
Email mwa_org@earthlink.net
Website www.mysterywriters.org

Admin Director *Mary Beth Becker*
Subscription $80 (US); $60 (Corresponding members)
FOUNDED 1945. Aims to promote and protect the interests of writers of the mystery genre in all media; to educate and inform its membership on matters relating to their profession; to uphold a standard of excellence and raise the profile of this literary form to the world at large. Holds an annual banquet at which the 'Edgars' are awarded (named after Edgar Allan Poe).

Society of Authors

84 Drayton Gardens, London SW10 9SB
☎ 020 7373 6642   Fax 020 7373 5768
Email info@societyofauthors.org
Website www.societyofauthors.org

General Secretary *Mark Le Fanu*
Subscription £70/75 p.a.
FOUNDED 1884. The Society of Authors is an independent trade union with some 7,000 members. It advises on negotiations with publishers, broadcasting organizations, theatre managers and film companies; assists with complaints and takes action for breach of contract, copyright infringement, etc. Together with the **Writers' Guild**, the Society has played a major role in advancing the Minimum Terms Agreement for authors. Among the Society's publications are *The Author* (a quarterly journal) and the *Quick Guides* series to various aspects of writing (all free of charge to members). Other services include vetting of contracts, emergency funds for writers, and various special discounts. There are groups within the Society for scriptwriters, children's writers and illustrators, educational writers, academic writers, medical writers and translators. Authors under 35 or over 65, not earning a significant income from their writing, may apply for lower subscription rates. Contact the Society for a free booklet and a copy of *The Author*.

The Society of Authors in Scotland

Bonnyton House, Arbirlot, Angus DD11 2PY
☎ 01241 874131   Fax 01241 874131

Email: info@eileenramsay.co.uk
Website www.writersorg.co.uk

Secretary *Eileen Ramsay*
The Scottish branch of the Society of Authors, which organizes business meetings, social and bookshop events throughout Scotland.

The Writers' Guild of Great Britain

15 Britannia Street, London WC1X 9JN
☎ 020 7833 0777   Fax 020 7833 4777
Email admin@writersguild.org.uk
Website www.writersguild.org.uk

General Secretary *Bernie Corbett*
Assistant General Secretaries *Anne Hogben, Christine Paris*
Annual subscription A basic subscription of £125 and 1% of that part of the author's gross income earned over £12,500 in the areas in which the Guild operates, with a maximum of £1,250.

FOUNDED 1959. The Writers' Guild is the writers' trade union, affiliated to the TUC. It represents writers in film, radio, television, theatre and publishing. The Guild has negotiated agreements on which writers' contracts are based with the BBC, Independent Television companies, and PACT (the Producers' Alliance for Cinema and Television). Those agreements are regularly renegotiated, both in terms of finance and conditions. In 1997, the Guild membership joined with that of the Theatre Writers' Union to create a new, more powerful union.

In 1979, together with the Theatre Writers' Union, the Guild negotiated the first ever industrial agreement for theatre writers, the TNC Agreement, which covers the Royal National Theatre, the Royal Shakespeare Company, and the Royal Court. Further agreements have been negotiated with the Theatrical Management Association which covers regional theatre and the Independent Theatre Council, the organization which covers small theatres and the Fringe.

The Guild initiated a campaign over ten years ago which achieved the first ever publishing agreement for writers with the publisher W. H. Allen. Jointly with the Society of Authors, that campaign has continued and most years see new agreements with more publishers. Perhaps the most important breakthrough came with Penguin on 20 July 1990. The Guild now also has agreements covering HarperCollins, Random House Group, Transworld and others.

The Guild regularly provides individual help and advice to members on contracts, conditions of work, and matters which affect a member's life as a professional writer. Members are given the opportunity of meeting at craft meetings, which are held on a regular basis throughout the year. Writers can apply for full membership if they have one piece of written work for which payment has been received under a contract with terms not less than those negotiated by the Guild. Writers who do not qualify for full membership can apply for candidate membership. This is open to all those who wish to be involved in writing but have not yet had work published. The subscription fee for this is £75.

Literary Societies

The Baskerville Hounds
6 Braham Moor, Hill Head, Fareham, Hampshire PO14 3RU
☎ 01329 667325

Chairman *Philip Weller*
Subscription £6 p.a.
FOUNDED 1989. An international Sherlock Holmes society specializing solely in studies of *The Hound of the Baskervilles* and its Dartmoor associations. Publishes an annual journal and specialist monographs. It also organizes many social functions, usually on Dartmoor. Open membership.

Wilkie Collins Society
4 Ernest Gardens, London W4 3QU
Email paul@wilkiecollins.org
Website www.wilkiecollins.org

Chairman *Andrew Gasson*
Membership Secretary *Paul Lewis* (at address above)
Subscription £10 (UK/Europe); £16 (RoW – remittance must be made in UK sterling)
FOUNDED 1980 to provide information on and promote interest in the life and works of Wilkie Collins, one of the first English novelists to deal with the detection of crime. *The Woman in White* appeared in 1860 and *The*

Moonstone in 1868. Publishes newsletters, reprints of Collins' work and an annual academic journal.

The Arthur Conan Doyle Society (UK)

PO Box 1360, Ashcroft, British Columbia, Canada VOK 1AO
☎ 001 250 453 2045   Fax 001 250 453 2075
Email ashtree@ash-tree.bc.ca
Website www.ash-tree.bc.ca/acdosy.html

Joint Organizers *Christopher Roden, Barbara Roden*
Membership Contact *R. Dixon-Smith*, 59 Stonefield, Bar Hill, Cambridge CB3 8TE
Subscription £16 (UK); £16 (Overseas); Family rates available
FOUNDED 1989 to promote the study and discussion of the life and works of Sir Arthur Conan Doyle. Occasional meetings, functions and visits. Publishes a biannual journal together with reprints of Conan Doyle's writings.

The Franco-Midland Hardware Company

6 Braham Moor, Hill Head, Fareham, Hampshire PO14 3RU
☎ 01329 667325
Email franco.midland@btinternet.com
Website www.btinternet.com/~sherlock.fmhc

Chairman *Philip Weller*
Subscription £12 p.a. (UK); £14 (Europe); £16 (RoW)
FOUNDED 1989. 'The world's leading Sherlock Holmes correspondence study group and the most active Holmesian society in Britain.' Publishes annual journal, a biannual news magazine and an individual case study as a subscription package. Also publishes at least two specialist monographs a year. It provides certificated self-study courses and organizes monthly functions at Holmes-associated locations. Open membership.

Sherlock Holmes Society (Northern Musgraves)

Hallas Lodge, Greenside Lane, Cullingworth, Bradford, West Yorkshire BD13 5AP

☎ 01535 273468
Email hallaslodge@btinternet.com

Contacts *John Hall, Anne Jordan*
Subscription £17 p.a. (UK)
FOUNDED 1987 to promote enjoyment and study of Sir Arthur Conan Doyle's Sherlock Holmes through publications and meetings. One of the largest Sherlock Holmes societies in Great Britain. Honorary members include Bert Coules, Richard Lancelyn Green, Edward Hardwicke, Clive Merrison and Douglas Wilmer. Past honorary members: Dame Jean Conan Doyle, Peter Cushing, Jeremy Brett and Michael Williams. Open membership. Lectures, presentations and consultation on matters relating to Holmes and Conan Doyle available.

Arts Councils and Regional Arts Boards

The Arts Council of England
14 Great Peter Street, London SW1P 3NQ
☎ 020 7333 0100/Minicom: 020 7973 6564   Fax 020 7973 6590
Email enquiries@artscouncil.org.uk
Website www.artscouncil.org.uk

Chairman *Gerry Robinson*
Chief Executive *Peter Hewitt*
The Arts Council of England is the national policy body for the arts in England. It develops, sustains and champions the arts. It distributes public money from government and from the National Lottery to artists and arts organizations both directly and through the ten Regional Arts Boards. The Arts Council works independently and at arm's length from government. Information about Arts Council funding programmes are available on the website, by email or by contacting the enquiry line on 020 7973 6517. Information about funding available from the Regional Arts Boards can be found on the website (www.arts.org.uk) or by contacting your Regional Arts Board.

The Irish Arts Council/An Chomhairle Ealaíon
70 Merrion Square, Dublin 2, Republic of Ireland
☎ 00 353 1 6180200   Fax 00 353 1 6761302
Email info@artscouncil.ie
Website www.artscouncil.ie

Literature Officer *Sinéad Mac Aodha*
The Irish Arts Council has programmes under six headings to assist in the area of literature and book promotion: a) Writers; b) Literary Organizations; c) Publishers; d) Literary Magazines; e) Participation Programmes; f) Literary Events and Festivals. It also awards a number of annual bursaries.

The Arts Council of Northern Ireland
MacNeice House, 77 Malone Road, Belfast BT9 6AQ
☎ 028 9038 5200   Fax 028 9066 1715
Website www.artscouncil-ni.org

Literature Arts Officer *John Brown*
Funds book production by established publishers, programmes of readings, literary festivals, writers-in-residence schemes and literary magazines and periodicals. Occasional schools programmes and anthologies of children's writing are produced. Annual awards and bursaries for writers are available. Holds information also on various groups associated with local arts, workshops and courses.

Scottish Arts Council
12 Manor Place, Edinburgh EH3 7DD
☎ 0131 226 6051   Fax 0131 225 9833
Email administrator@scottisharts.org.uk
Website www.scottisharts.org.uk

Chairman *James Boyle*
Acting Director *Graham Berry*
Literature Director *Jenny Brown*
Literature Officers *Gavin Wallace, Jenny Attala*
Literature Secretary *Catherine Allan*
Principal channel for government funding of the arts in Scotland. The Scottish Arts Council (SAC) is funded by the Scottish Executive. It aims to develop and improve the knowledge, understanding and practice of the arts, and to increase their accessibility throughout Scotland. It offers around 1,300 grants a year to artists and arts organizations concerned with the visual arts, crafts, dance and mime, drama, literature, music, festivals and

traditional, ethnic and community arts. It is also a distributor of National Lottery funds to the arts in Scotland. SAC's support for Scottish-based writers with a track record of publication includes bursaries, writing and translation fellowships and book awards. Information offered includes lists of literary awards, literary magazines, agents and publishers.

The Arts Council of Wales

Museum Place, Cardiff CF10 3NX
☎ 029 2037 6500   Fax 029 2022 1447
Website www.artswales.org.uk/language.htm

Senior Literature Officer *Tony Bianchi*
Senior Officer: Drama *Sandra Wynne*
Funds literary magazines and book production; writers on tour and bursary schemes; Welsh Academy, Welsh Books Council, Hay-on-Wye Literature Festival and Ty Newydd Writers' Centre at Criccieth; also children's literature, annual awards and translation projects. The Council aims to develop theatrical experience among Wales-based writers through a variety of schemes – in particular, by funding writers on year-long attachments.

English Regional Arts Boards

English Regional Arts Boards are support and development agencies for the arts in the regions. Policies are developed in response to regional demand, and to assist new initiatives in areas of perceived need; they may vary from region to region. The RABs are now responsible for the distribution of Arts Council Lottery funding for capital and revenue projects under £100,000.

Support for writers: All the Regional Arts Boards offer support for professional creative writers through a range of grants, awards, advice, information and contacts. Interested writers should contact the Board in whose region they live. At the time of writing the current system of RABs is under review and anyone experiencing problems getting in touch with their RAB is advised to contact the Arts Council of England.

East England
Eden House, 48–49 Bateman Street, Cambridge CB2 1LR
☎ 01223 454400   Fax 0870 2421271
Email east@artscouncil.org.uk
Website www.artscouncil.org.uk/aboutus/contact_east.html

Literature Officer *Lucy Sheerman*
Drama Officer *Alan Orme*
Cinema & Broadcast Media Officer *Martin Ayres*
Covers Bedfordshire, Cambridgeshire, Essex, Hertfordshire, Norfolk and Suffolk and the non-metropolitan authorities of Luton, Peterborough, Southend-on-Sea and Thurrock. Policy emphasizes quality and access. Support is given to publishers and literature promoters based in the EEB region, also to projects which develop audiences for literature performances and publishing, including electronic media. Also provides advice on applying for National Lottery funds.

East Midland
St Nicholas Court, 25–27 Castle Gate, Nottingham NG1 7AR
☎ 0115 989 7520   Fax 0115 950 2467
Email eastmidlands@artcouncil.org.uk
Website www.artscouncil.org.uk/aboutus/contact_eastmidlands.html

Literature Officer *Gill Adams*
Drama Officer *Michaela Waldram*
Covers Derbyshire, Leicestershire, Lincolnshire (excluding North and North-East Lincolnshire), Northamptonshire, Nottinghamshire, and the unitary authorities of Derby, Leicester, Nottingham and Rutland. A comprehensive information service for regional writers includes an extensive *Writers' Information Pack*, with details of local groups, workshops, residential writing courses, publishers and publishing information, regional magazines, advice on approaching the media, and information on unions, courses and grants. Also available is a directory of writers, primarily to aid people wishing to organize workshops, readings or writer's residencies. Literature grants are given for work on a specific project – local history and biography are ineligible for support. Writing for the theatre can come under the aegis of

both Literature and Drama. A list of writers' groups is available, plus contact details for the East Midlands Literature Development Officer network.

London
2 Pear Tree Court, London EC1R ODS
☎ 020 7608 6100   Fax 020 7608 4100
Email london@artscouncil.org.uk
Website www.artscouncil.org.uk/aboutus/contact_london.html

Literature Administrator *Sarah Sanders*
London Arts is the Regional Arts Board for the capital, covering the thirty-two boroughs and the City of London. Grants are available to support a variety of literature projects, focusing on three main areas: live literature, including storytelling; support for small presses and literary magazines in the publishing of new or under-represented creative writing; bursaries for writers who have published one book and are working on their second work of fiction or poetry. There are two deadlines each year for applications. Please contact the Literature Unit for more information and an application form.

North West
Manchester House, 22 Bridge Street, Manchester M3 3AB
☎ 0161 834 6644   Fax 0161 834 6969
Email northwest@artscouncil.org.uk
Website www.artscouncil.org.uk/aboutus/contact_northwest.html

Arts Officer: Literature *Bronwen Williams* (Email bwilliams@nwarts.co.uk)
Arts Officer: Drama *Ian Tabbron* (Email itabbron@nwarts.co.uk)
NWAB covers Cheshire, Cumbria, Lancashire, the metropolitan districts of Bolton, Bury, Knowsley, Liverpool, Manchester, Oldham, Rochdale, St Helens, Salford, Sefton, Stockport, Tameside, Trafford, Wigan and Wirral, and the unitary authorities of Blackburn with Darwen, Blackpool, Halton and Warrington. Offers financial assistance to a great variety of organizations and individuals through a number of schemes, including Writers' Bursaries, Residencies and Placements and the Live Writing scheme. NWAB publishes a directory of local writers' groups, a directory of writers and a range of information covering topics such as performance and

publishing. For further details please contact the Literature or Drama Department.

North East

Central Square, Forth Street, Newcastle upon Tyne NE1 3PJ
☎ 0191 255 8500   Fax 0191 230 1020
Email northeast@artscouncil.co.uk
Website www.artscouncil.org.uk/aboutus/contact_northeast.html

Director Arts & Development *Mark Robinson*
Literature Officer *Kate Griffin*
Covers Durham and Northumberland, and the metropolitan districts of Gateshead, Newcastle upon Tyne, North Tyneside, South Tyneside and Sunderland, and the non-metropolitan districts of Darlington, Hartlepool, Middlesbrough, Redcar and Cleveland, and Stockton-on-Tees, and was the first regional arts association in the country to be set up by local authorities. It supports both organizations and writers and aims to stimulate public interest in artistic events. The Northern Writers' Awards scheme is operated through New Writing North. Northern Arts makes drama awards to producers. Also funds writers' residencies, and has a fund for publications. Contact list of regional groups available.

South West

Bradninch Place, Gandy Street, Exeter, Devon EX4 3LS
☎ 01392 218188   Fax 01392 229229
Email southwest@artscouncil.co.uk
Website www.artscouncil.org.uk/aboutus/contact_southwest.html

Director of Visual Arts and Media *David Drake*
Visual Arts and Media Administrators *Sara Williams, Kate Offord, Lis Spencer*
Covers Cornwall, Devon, Dorset, Gloucestershire, Somerset, Wiltshire and the unitary authorities of Bristol, Bath and North East Somerset, Bournemouth, Swindon, South Gloucestershire, North Somerset, Torbay, Poole and Plymouth. The central theme running through the Board's aims are 'promoting quality and developing audiences for new work'. Specific

policies aim to support the development and promotion of new writing and performance work in all areas of contemporary literature and published arts. There is direct investment in small presses and magazine publishers, literary festivals, writer residencies and training, and marketing bursaries for individual writers. There is also a commitment to supporting the development of new writing in the performing arts, and critical writing within the visual arts and media department.

South East

13 St Clement Street, Winchester, Hampshire SO23 9DQ
☎ 01962 855099   Fax 0870 242 1257
Email southeast@artscouncil.org.uk
Website www.artscouncil.org.uk/aboutus/contact_southeast.html

Literature Officer *Keiren Phelan*
Performing Arts Officer *Roger McCann*
Covers Buckinghamshire, East Sussex, Hampshire, Isle of Wight, Kent, Oxfordshire, Surrey, West Sussex; and the unitary authorities of Bracknell Forest, Brighton and Hove, Medway Towns, Milton Keynes, Portsmouth, Reading, Slough, Southampton, West Berkshire, Windsor and Maidenhead, and Wokingham. Grant schemes accessible to all art forms in the areas of new work, presentation of work and venue development. Awards for individuals include training bursaries and writers' awards schemes. The literature programme aims to raise the profile of contemporary literature in the region and encourage creative writing and reading development projects. Priorities include live literature, writers and readers in residence and training bursaries for writers resident in the region. A regular feature on literature appears in the *Arts News* newsletter.

West Midlands

82 Granville Street, Birmingham B1 2LH
☎ 0121 631 3121   Fax 0121 643 7239
Email westmidlands@artscouncil.org.uk
Website www.artscouncil.org.uk/aboutus/contact_westmidlands.html

Literature Officer *Adrian Johnson*
Covers Shropshire, Staffordshire, Warwickshire and Worcestershire; also

the metropolitan districts of Birmingham, Coventry, Dudley, Sandwell, Solihull, Walsall and Wolverhampton, and the non-metropolitan districts of Herefordshire, Stoke-on-Trent, Telford and Wrekin. There are special criteria across the art forms, so contact the information office for details of general support funds for the arts, especially *Creative Ambition Awards* for writers (six application dates throughout the year) and other arts lottery schemes, as well as for the *Reading (Correspondence Mss Advice) Service*. There are contact lists of writers, storytellers, writing groups, etc. WMA supports the regional publication, *Raw Edge Magazine*: contact PO Box 4867, Birmingham B3 3HD, the Virtual Literature Centre for the West Midlands (and beyond) called 'Lit-net' (www.lit-net.org) and the major storytelling and poetry festivals in Shropshire and Ledbury respectively.

Yorkshire Arts

21 Bond Street, Dewsbury, West Yorkshire WF13 1AX
☎ 01924 455555   Fax 01924 466522
Email yorkshire@artscouncil.org.uk
Website www.artscouncil.org.uk/aboutus/contact_yorkshire.html

Literature Officer *Jane Stubbs*
Theatre Development Officer *Mark Hollander*
Covers North Yorkshire, the metropolitan authorities of Barnsley, Bradford, Calderdale, Doncaster, Kirklees, Leeds, Rotherham, Sheffield and Wakefield, and the unitary authorities of East Riding of Yorkshire, Kingston upon Hull, North Lincolnshire, North East Lincolnshire and York. 'Libraries, publishing houses, local authorities and the education service all make major contributions to the support of literature. Recognizing the resources these agencies command, Yorkshire Arts actively seeks ways of acting in partnership with them, while at the same time retaining its particular responsibility for the living writer and the promotion of activities currently outside the scope of these agencies.' Funding goes to a range of independent publishers, festivals and literature development agencies. Yorkshire Arts also offers a range of development funds to support the individual and the promotion and distribution of literature. Holds lists of writers' groups throughout the region and publishes *Write Angles*, a bi-monthly newsletter. Contact *Kelly Amoss* for further information.

Editorial, Research Services and Courses

The Literary Consultancy
2nd Floor, Diorama Arts, 34 Osnaburgh Street, London NW1 3ND
☎ 020 7813 4330
Email info@literaryconsultancy.co.uk
Website www.literaryconsultancy.co.uk

Contact *Rebecca Swift*
FOUNDED in 1996 by former publishers to offer an editorial service and advice for aspiring authors. Will provide a detailed report on fiction, non-fiction, autobiography, scripts and poetry at all stages of development.

London School of Journalism
22 Upbrook Mews, London W2 3HG
☎ 020 7706 3790   Fax 020 7706 3780
Email info@lsjournalism.com
Website www.home-study.com

Contact *Student Administration Office*
Correspondence courses with an individual and personal approach. Students remain with the same tutor throughout their course. Options include: *Short Story Writing; Writing for Children; Poetry; Freelance and Features; Internet Journalism; Media Law; Improve Your English; Cartooning; Writing a Thriller; English for Business; Journalism and Newswriting.* Fees vary but range from £295 for *Enjoying English Literature* to £395 for *Journalism and*

Newswriting. NUJ-recognized Postgraduate Journalism Diploma (three- and six-month attendance).

Murder Files

81 Churchfields Drive, Bovey Tracey, Devon TQ13 9QU
☎ 01626 833487   Fax 01626 835797

Contact *Paul Williams*
FOUNDED 1994. Crime writer and researcher specializing in UK murders. Holds information on thousands of well-known and less well-known murders dating from 1400 to the present day. Copies of press cuttings available from 1920 onwards. Details of executions, particularly at Tyburn and Newgate. Information on British hangmen. CD-Rom *The Ultimate Price – The Unlawful Killing of British Police Officers*, Part 1 (1700–1899) & Part 2 (1900–2000), available £15 each or £26 for both including p&p. Specialist in British police murders since 1700. Service available to general enquirers, writers, researchers, TV, radio, video, etc.

Scribo

1/31 Hamilton Road, Boscombe, Bournemouth, Dorset BH1 4EQ
☎ 01202 302533

Contact *K. & P. Sylvester*
Scribo (established for more than 20 years) is a postal workshop for novelists. Manuscript criticism folios cover fantasy/sci-fi, crime/thrillers, mainstream, women's fiction, literary. Forums offer information, discussion on all topics relating to writing and literature. No annual subscription. £5 joining fee only. Full details from the address above; enclose sae, please.

Prizes

Crime Writers' Association (Debut Dagger)
PO Box 273, Borehamwood, Hertfordshire, WD6 2XA
Website www.thecwa.co.uk

Contact *The Secretary*
ESTABLISHED 1998. Awarded to the winner of the Association's annual new writing competition. Open to anyone whose work has not been published before. 2001 winner: Edward Wright, *Clea's Moon*.
Award: Dagger, plus cheque.

Crime Writers' Association (Cartier Diamond Dagger)
PO Box 273, Borehamwood, Hertfordshire, WD6 2XS
Website www.thecwa.co.uk

Contact *The Secretary*
An annual award for a lifetime's outstanding contribution to the genre. 2002 winner: Sara Paretsky. 2003 winner: Robert Barnard.
Award: Dagger.

Crime Writers' Association
(The CWA Ellis Peters Historical Dagger)
PO Box 273, Borehamwood, Hertfordshire, WD6 2XA
Website www.thecwa.co.uk

Contact *The Secretary*
ESTABLISHED 1999. Annual award for the best historical crime novel.
Nominations from publishers only. 2001 winner: Andrew Taylor, *The Office of the Dead*.
Award: Dagger, plus cheque.

Crime Writers' Association (The Ian Fleming Steel Dagger)
PO Box 273, Borehamwood, Hertfordshire, WD6 2XA
Website www.thecwa.co.uk

Contact *The Secretary*
FOUNDED 2002. Annual award for the best thriller, adventure or spy novel.
Sponsored by Ian Fleming (Glidrose) Publications Ltd to celebrate the best of
contemporary thriller writing. 2002 winner: John Creed, *The Sirius Crossing*.
Award: Dagger, plus cheque.

Crime Writers' Association
(The Macallan Gold Dagger for Non-Fiction)
PO Box 273, Borehamwood, Hertfordshire, WD6 2XA
Website www.thecwa.co.uk

Contact *The Secretary*
Annual award for the best non-fiction crime book published during the
year. Nominations from publishers only. 2001 winner: Philip Etienne and
Martin Maynard with Tony Thompson, *The Infiltrators*.
Award: Dagger, plus cheque (sum varies).

Crime Writers' Association
(The Macallan Gold and Silver Daggers for Fiction)
PO Box 273, Borehamwood, Hertfordshire, WD6 2XA
Website www.thecwa.co.uk

Contact *The Secretary*
Two annual awards for the best crime fiction published during the year.
Nominations for Gold Dagger from publishers only. 2001 winners: Henning

Mankell, *Sidetracked*, translated by Steven T. Murray (Gold); Giles Blunt, *Forty Words for Sorrow* (Silver).
Award: Dagger, plus cheque (sum varies).

Crime Writers' Association (The Macallan Short Story Dagger)
PO Box 273, Borehamwood, Hertfordshire, WD6 2XA
Website www.thecwa.co.uk

Contact *The Secretary*
ESTABLISHED 1995. An award for a published crime story. Publishers should submit three copies of the story by 30 September. 2001 winner: Marion Arnott, 'Prussian Snowdrops', in *Crimewave 4*.
Award: Dagger, plus cheque.

Crime Writers' Association (John Creasey Memorial Award)
PO Box 273, Borehamwood, Hertfordshire, WD6 2XA
Website www.thecwa.co.uk

Contact *The Secretary*
ESTABLISHED 1973 following the death of crime writer John Creasey, founder of the Crime Writers' Association. This award, sponsored by Chivers Press, is given annually for the best crime novel by an author who has not previously published a full-length work of fiction. Nominations from publishers only. 2001 winner: Susanna Jones, *The Earthquake Bird*.
Award: Dagger, plus cheque.

Crime Museums

The Black Museum
Little Park Street, Coventry, Warwickshire CV1 2JX

Police records and items connected with infamous crimes from the Coventry area.

Greater Manchester Police Museum
Newton Street, Manchester M1 1ES
☎ 0161 856 3287
Open on Tuesdays only. Visits by appointment.

150 years of police history.

Galleries of Justice
Shire Hall, High Pavement, Nottingham N91 1HN
☎ 01159 520 555
Website www.galleriesofjustice.org.uk

Major collection of British police equipment including a collection of evidence from famous trials.

House of Correction
St Marygate, Ripon, North Yorkshire HG4 1LX
☎ 01765 690799

Law enforcement over the centuries housed in a former Victorian prison.

House of Detention
Clerkenwell Close, Clerkenwell, London EC1R 0AS
☎ 020 7253 9494

Recreation of one of London's oldest prisons.

Scotland Yard Crime Museum
Broadway, London SW1H 0BG
☎ 020 7230 1212
Website www.met.police.uk/history/crime_museum.htm

Known as the 'Black Museum'; one of the oldest crime museums in the world. No longer open to the public.

Sherlock Holmes Museum
221b Baker Street, London NW1 6XE
☎ 020 7935 8866
Website www.sherlock-holmes.co.uk

Dedicated to the life and times of Sherlock Holmes, the fictional address of the famous detective is maintained as described in Conan Doyle's novels.

Thames Valley Police Museum
Thames Valley Police Training Centre, Sulhamstead,
Reading, RG7 4DX
☎ 0118 932 5748

History of policing plus exhibits of material connected to the Thames Valley Police including items on the Great Train Robbery.

Libraries and Specialist Bookshops

Sherlock Holmes Collection (Westminster)

Marylebone Library, Marylebone Road, London NW1 5PS
☎ 020 7641 1206   Fax 020 7641 1019
Email c.cooke@dial.pipex.com
Website www.westminster.gov.uk/el/libarch/services/special/
sherlock.html

Open 9.30 a.m. to 8.00 p.m. Monday, Tuesday, Thursday, Friday; 10.00
a.m. to 8.00 p.m. Wednesday; Closed Saturday and Sunday (unless by prior
arrangement)
Access By appointment only

Located in Westminster's Marylebone Library. An extensive collection of
material from all over the world, covering Sherlock Holmes and Sir Arthur
Conan Doyle. Books, pamphlets, journals, newspaper cuttings and photos,
much of which is otherwise unavailable in this country. Some background
material.

Crime in Store

32 Store Street, London WC1E 7BS
☎ 020 7436 7736   Fax 020 7436 7636
Email CrimeBks@aol.com
Website www.crimeinstore.co.uk

Monthly catalogue, available on application.

Murder One
71–73 Charing Cross Road, London WC2H 0AA
☎ 020 7734 3483   Fax 020 7734 3429
Email murderone.mail@virgin.net
Website www.murderone.co.uk

Catalogue, available on application.

Further Reading

Becoming a Writer by Dorothea Brande (Macmillan, 1995)

Bloody Murder – From the Detective Story to the Crime Novel: a History by Julian Symons (Faber & Faber, 1972)

Conflict, Action and Suspense by William Noble (Writer's Digest Books, 1994)

The Crime and Mystery Book by Ian Ousby (Thames & Hudson, 1997)

The Mammoth Encyclopedia of Modern Crime Fiction compiled by Mike Ashley (Constable Robinson, 2002)

One Hundred Great Detectives edited by Maxim Jakubowski (Xanadu, 1992)

Plotting and Writing Suspense Fiction by Patricia Highsmith (Poplar Press, 1983)

A Suitable Job for a Woman: Inside the World of Women Private Eyes by Val McDermid (Poisoned Pen Press, 1995)

Twentieth Century Crime and Mystery Writers edited by John M. Reilly (Macmillan 1985)

Twentieth Century Suspense edited by Clive Bloom (Palgrave Macmillan, 1990)

Writing Crime Fiction by H. R. F. Keating (A&C Black, 1994)

Writing Popular Fiction by Rona Randall (A&C Black, 1992)

Writing a Thriller by André Jute (A&C Black, 1999)

Useful Websites at a Glance

The Arts Council of England
www.artscouncil.org.uk

Includes information on funding applications, publications and the National Lottery.

Author-Network
www.author-network.com

Writers' resource site, operated by Puff Adder Books.

British Library
www.bl.uk

Reader service enquiries, access to main catalogues, information on collections, links to the various Reading Rooms and exhibitions.

Crime Time
www.crimetime.co.uk

On-line magazine of crime fiction. Reviews, interviews and features.

Crime Writers' Association (CWA)
www.thecwa.co.uk

Website of the professional crime writers' association.

Dictionary of Slang
dictionaryofslang.co.uk

A guide to slang 'from a British perspective'. Research information; search facility.

The Eclectic Writer
www.eclectics.com/writing/writing.html

US website offering a selection of articles on advice for writers on topics such as 'Proper Manuscript Format', 'Electronic Publishing', 'How to Write a Synopsis' and 'Motivation'. Also a Character Chart for fiction writers and an online discussion board.

Guide to Grammar and Style
www.andromeda.rutgers.edu/~jlynch/Writing

A guide to grammar and style which is organized alphabetically, plus articles and links to other grammatical reference sites.

Sherlock Holmes Web
www.sherlockian.net

Comprehensive resource covering all things Sherlockian.

The Literary Consultancy
www.literaryconsultancy.co.uk

Editorial service for aspiring writers established by former publishers.

Murder Squad
www.murdersquad.co.uk

A collective of seven north of England crime writers – John Baker, Ann Cleeves, Martin Edwards, Chaz Brenchley, Margaret Murphy, Cath Staincliffe and Stuart Pawson.

Mysterynet
www.mysterynet.com

US website dedicated to mystery writing; reviews, on-line mysteries to solve, 'Mystery Greats', books for sale.

Mystery Women
www.mysterywomen.freeserve.co.uk

UK group established in 1997 to raise the awareness and profile of female crime writers.

Mystery Writers Forum
www.zott.com/mysforum

Resources for mystery writers including police procedure information, industry news and links to other sites of interest.

New Writers Consultancy
www.new-writers-consultancy.com

Advice for writers and critiques, offered by Diana Hayden and Karen Scott of Puff Adder Books.

New Writing North
www.newwritingnorth.com

Essentially for writers based in the north of England but also a useful source of advice and guidelines.

Novel Advice Newsletter
www.noveladvice.com

A free US journal aimed at the fiction writer; full text of current and past issues online.

Pure Fiction
www.purefiction.com

Described as 'the website for anybody who loves to read – or aspires to write – bestselling fiction.' Contains book reviews, writing advice, a writers' showcase and an online bookshop.

Scottish Arts Council
www.sac.org.uk

Information on funding and events; 'Image of the Month' and 'Poem of the Month'.

Shots
www.shotsmag.co.uk

On-line crime and mystery magazine.

Society of Authors
www.societyofauthors.org

Includes FAQs for new writers, diary of events, membership details, links to publishers' and other societies' websites.

Tangled Web UK
www.twbooks.co.uk

'Dedicated to crime, mystery and fantastic fiction.' Book digests, reviews, author profiles, events.

Triple Hitter
www.triplehitter.net

New website dedicated to 'aiding aspiring writers in obtaining their big break' by showcasing their work free of charge. Includes various interviews, links and helpful hints.

The Arts Council of Wales

www.artswales.org.uk/language.htm

Information on publications, council meetings, the arts in Wales. Links to other arts websites.

Webster Dictionary/Thesaurus

www.m-w.com/home.htm

Merriam-Webster Online. Includes a search facility for words in the Webster Dictionary or Webster Thesaurus; word games, 'Word of the Day' and Language Info Zone.

WordCounter

www.wordcounter.com

Highlights the most frequently used words in a given text. Use as a guide to see what words are overused.

Writers' Guild of Great Britain

www.writersguild.org.uk

A wide range of information including rates of pay, articles on topics such as copyright, news, writers' resources and industry regulations.

Writers' Circles

www.writers-circles.com

Offers free pages to writers' circles. Listings and information.

WritersServices

www.WritersServices.com

Established in March 2000 by Chris Holifield, former deputy managing director and publisher at Cassell. Offers factsheets, book reviews, advice, links and other resources for writers including editorial services, contract vetting and self-publishing. (Enquiries to: info@writersservices.com)